FALL

BRIAN GUTHRIE

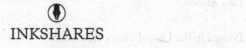
INKSHARES

Published by Inkshares, Inc., Oakland, California
www.inkshares.com

Edited by Noah Broyles & Laura Kenney
Interior design by Kevin G. Summers

Paperback: 9781950301751
Ebook: 9781950301768
LCCN: 2024945785

First edition

Printed in the United States of America

To those looking for their place in this world,
Who often feel like they don't belong,
We see you

CONTENTS

Scribe's Note: The following events occur directly after the events chronicled in *Rise*. In summation of the narrative, the Colberran fleet's surprise attack on the Expeditionary Forces' outpost on the Nomad shell sent Quentin and the entire outpost tumbling toward the core. Micaela and Suyef remained on the shell post-battle. In summation of the interviews, Micaela informed me of Quentin's demise, and Suyef and Quentin had vanished from their hidden home. That left me with no clue where to go, except for the still-closed box entrusted to me. I opened it.

CHAPTER 1

OLD

A stick.

The box lay open, Suyef's note underneath it. Inside was a stick, smooth and round on one end, fragmented on the other. A tan hue, the wood felt smooth, with only two slight bends in the otherwise straight length. The fragmented tips were very sharp. Nothing else lay inside.

"What is this?" I whispered.

A memory bubbled up, a man and his stick. I flipped through pages of memories, of a story as convoluted as my notes. It took several moments to find the Queen's list of names and a note from a session with Quentin, all quickly jotted down. A phrase next to one name.

Nidfar. Ask about Stick.

I looked at the object. Could this be the one he'd spoken to? The one Micaela and Quentin insisted he'd had with him each time they met.

I scanned my notes. Page after page, memory after memory. Theirs and my own. Images flitted to the surface as I read, of them sitting before me, of their stories, all mixed. I shook my head, eyes darting back and forth until finding what I sought.

Micaela's first encounter with the old man who once lived near a younger Quentin. The baffling old man who talked to a stick.

This isn't any ordinary stick.

I'd written those words down exactly, circling the contraction. What could that have meant? I scanned the page.

Piece of fabricated wood.

Another circle enclosed the word *fabricated.* My eyes darted to the stick. Being fabricated wasn't necessarily strange. Most wood came from matter reforgers. Still, the words showed something more about this stick.

My eyes shifted to Suyef's note, then back to the box. Yes, there was definitely more to this stick. Something powerful. Dangerous.

Something worth hiding.

I tucked the stick away, returning the box to my sack before sitting. Quentin and Suyef remained absent. Waiting seemed tenuous without knowing when they'd return. I considered going back to the Nomads, but their previous dearth of helpfulness didn't bode well.

Pondering my limited options and my notes, I heard a sound nearby. A shuffling, like feet not lifted from the ground. A sniffle. Someone was crying?

"Quentin?"

I moved toward his room, gathering up my notes and sack. No answer; just another sniffle. I stopped at his door, but it wasn't Quentin. An old man sat on the bed, hair barely clinging to his head, a cloak hanging from his bony shoulders. A gray one adorned with a good deal of colorful cloth strips. His eyes flitted from one sketch to another, and he clutched something in his fist at his side. A strip of gray cloth. The one Quentin had torn from my cloak.

"Nidfar?"

He jolted, head spinning around. Bright blue eyes locked with mine, and his fist clenched tighter.

"Who is it?" he asked, his voice cracking.

"My name is Logwyn," I said, stepping into the room.

He shifted away, and I froze, not wanting to scare him. His eyes darted over my shoulder to the door, and I realized he might feel trapped. I moved to the side, leaving the path to him if he chose it. His eyes followed me, darting once at the door.

"Do you know the Dragon Queen?"

His eyes widened.

"Do you know her, Nidfar?"

"Shh!" he hissed, shaking his clenched fist at me. "Don't say that name!"

"There's no one here but us."

His eyes, wild and roaming a moment before, locked on to mine. "In this place, he is always here," he whispered.

I pressed my lips together, nodding. He calmed, lowering his fist.

"Are you going to use that cloth?" I asked.

He looked down at the fabric. "Maybe. It's not as bright as my others."

Among the myriad of colors on his garment, the gray cloth looked horribly plain.

"Why all the colors?" I asked.

He shrugged. "Seemed a good idea. Now I like it."

His fingers toyed with the gray cloth, his eyes staring off over my shoulder. As he sat there, I thought of the box. Questions formed, questions about the object inside. Suyef's words held me back. Could I trust the old man? Did it belong

to him? Was my need to know driving me to do something I
shouldn't?

The old man shuddered, shaking his head and looking
at me.

"Well, hello, have we met?" he asked, a smile splitting his
face. "I'm afraid my memory's not what it once was."

He tapped at his forehead with his balled hand.

"Glitching and messing up," he said, then noticed his fist.
"What have we here?" He sniffed at the gray cloth. "Hmm,
lower shell fabrication, if my nose is near the mark." He licked
the cloth. His hand balled around the fabric, one finger pointing at me. "Several decades old. Inherit that cloak, did you?"

I frowned at him. "You can tell that from licking and sniff-
ing it?"

He grinned. "Nope, made it all up."

I shook my head, holding up my notes. "Do you know
what this is?"

"Paper?" he asked, favoring me with a toothy grin.

I glared at him. "Do you know what's on it?"

"What do you take me for, a saysoother?"

"You mean soothsayer," I said, smiling.

"S'what I said, witnit!"

I smothered another smile, trying to keep my face calm.
"So, what is this?"

"A waste of valuable paper, it looks like." He leveled a gaze
at me. "Hope you got the authorization to use all that. Had to
cost a fortune in reforge credits, I'd wager."

I wanted to say they hadn't come from the reforger, but
stopped. The first page hadn't; the rest had. I waved the pages
at him.

"I've got your name in here," I whispered. "Written as clear
as day."

That got his attention. He sat bolt upright, looking around. He pointed at the sketches. "It was that girl, wasn't it? Blast it, I told her not to go blabbing."

I shook my head. "Micaela didn't give it to me," I said. "The Queen did."

His eyes widened. "She mentioned me?"

"Gave me your name herself."

His face transformed, a glorious smile melting into place, dancing in his eyes, his mismatched teeth jutting out.

"She mentioned me," he whispered.

"The Queen said you were one of the only people who could help me," I went on, embellishing a bit for his sake.

He looked at the papers. "That's what all that is, isn't it? What she needs help with?"

"These are my notes. I have a padd for recording people, too."

His head moved up and down, his empty hand patting his cheek as he stared at my notes. "And you want me to talk? You said *record*, so I guess you mean my voice."

I shifted the papers and pulled out the padd, keeping the box hidden. "On this, yes."

His eyes narrowed, locking on to the device. "Is it safe?"

"The Queen assured me it was."

"Isolated? Domain blocked or masked? Connectivity of any kind? Can you detect any packet transfers? Any pings?"

I held it out to him. "Check her work. I trust the Queen when she says something's safe."

He looked at me, then the padd.

"She assured you? She's very thorough. Very capable. If she said it was safe, it must be."

We fell silent—him watching the device; me, him.

"So, you want me to talk." Nidfar pointed at my papers.
"And you want to take notes? But you haven't told me what you
want me to talk about."

I contemplated what I should say, how I should say it.

"What was necessary?"

Necessary.

A lot of things are necessary. Food, water, love. Those
things fill our lives. But there are more. Moments that make
us or break us. Lessons. Successes. Failures. The things that fill
pages, that people want to read about. The things that make
us real.

When Micaela stepped onto that platform, so much flashed
through my mind. Whereas before all was chaos, a swirling
surge of memories boiling as I struggled to stay afloat, her presence brought a moment of clarity like a light appearing in a
tunnel. A point on a map guiding me home.

And it was all summed up in one word: *necessary*.

As she dropped from sight, I cried out that word. I hoped
she would make sense of it. I couldn't say more. Not for lack of
time, but lack of knowledge. So much unknown to me. What
might happen if I said too much? What events might change?
A singular struggle I alone have faced for so long.

No, not alone. The Dragon Queen, as eternal as the water
shield. Yes, she's struggled against this with me. Rather, she's
struggled in her own way, a point of disagreement between us.
A wedge, so small at first, driven deep with the blows of time's
infinite, omnipotent hammer. A gulf as vast as the atmosphere
is empty. But I digress.

Unlike the Queen, I've spent all this time keeping my footprint through the ages small. Still, I knew this would become impossible one day. When Micaela and her companions would walk into my tower, setting in motion a series of events so powerful the world still shakes from them.

How do you tell a person she must go forward? How do you say all that while saying nothing at all?

You say it in one word: *necessary*.

And you trust the person to figure it out.

"Nidfar, are you claiming you've lived as long as the Queen?"

"And how old is your Queen?"

I frowned. "No one knows. She's been around longer than our history records."

"Yet you call her eternal, yes? Without evidence? Does she ever confirm this descriptor?"

I shook my head. "It's rude to ask such things."

He wheezed, his chest heaving with what sounded like a laugh.

"Why? Because she's your Queen?"

"No. Not just that. She's a lady. It's rude to ask."

He pointed a knobby, wrinkled finger with a jagged fingernail at me.

"You're a scribe. It's your *job* to know such things. Does this stop you from asking?"

I shook my head.

"So, why haven't you?"

I paused, contemplating his words. "I haven't needed to."

His eyebrows raised as his finger pointed up to the ceiling. "Haven't needed to. So, in all this time, no one has ever needed to know?"

"I don't know. Maybe it's protected information."

"Possibly. Or it's not there because no one knows."

"What does this have to do with *your age*?" I asked, my face warming.

"Simple. If you can't say how old she is, how can you say how old I am?"

"You claimed to be that old!"

"No, I said I'd struggled long in this fight. Just like her." He locked gazes with me, finger back pointing at my face. "You assumed. Stop doing that. You've done it most of your life, and it's done you no good."

I narrowed my eyes. "How do you know so much about me?"

He grinned. "Spoilers."

Once Micaela left, one thing remained certain. What came next was going to be rough. The battle at the outpost didn't have a good ending. It wasn't an ending at all. Just another beginning followed by a dark chapter.

You must understand the predicament I faced in knowing what was coming while being fuzzy on the details. It was like looking at a painting from a distance. You can make out major elements, but you lose the details over the distance. So much time passed to prepare for that day, but something held me in place. Something inside urged me not to look, not to fill the gaps. To stay in the dark. Maybe I was protecting myself, or maybe her and her companions.

I knew I couldn't follow. Not right away. The events at the outpost had to happen. So, I waited, pacing the tower, talking to myself and my stick. For once, the infernal thing stayed around. It's quite annoying misplacing something as simple as a stick when you need it. But let's leave Stick out of this. I've got a feeling the thing's annoyed with me, as I haven't seen it in a while.

After all the ships passed over and the computer informed me the Nomad tower stood empty, I considered going. Still, dread held me prisoner. Some of what came next I knew, and part of me dreaded witnessing it again. So, I waited, contemplating, hemming and hawing, waffling, and several other -*ing*s for good measure.

Then something compelled me to move. As my feet carried me around the chamber, I ventured out to check on the attacking ships. An empty sky to the south meant they were off to their deadly appointment. What lay to the north drew my attention. The sight of more ships massing over the citadel. Many more ships than the departed fleet that filled the sky above the mountains.

An invasion force.

The panel chime rang from inside, beckoning me nearer the network station.

"Computer, what is it?"

"Incoming message, sir."

The hair on my back stood on end. "From where?"

"Attempting to identify. Someone breached the firewall."

"Put it on screen."

A face I remembered from long ago appeared.

"Ah, there you are," the face said. "My word, time is not your friend, is it?"

"Rawyn," I whispered. "How did you find me?"

The man frowned, his still-young face wrinkling. "Honestly, I don't have a clue where you are. I've been trying to find how you and your infernal beast allies communicate without using the citadel network, and I stumbled across this connection." He leaned forward, his cold, black eyes gazing at me. "You're on this shell, probably in the Wilds." He chuckled, leaning back. "I don't really care where you are. As long as you're here and not elsewhere."

"You can't stop what happens next."

"Don't talk to me about temporal mechanics. You will not stop me this time."

"I didn't stop you before," I whispered.

"Yes!" he hissed, hand slapping down onto a surface out of my sight, his eyes flaring wide. "Yes, you did." He paused, taking deep breaths to calm himself. "The two of you did. You locked the system. She told me."

"Who told you what?" I asked. "The Queen wouldn't talk to the likes of you."

"Oh, not your precious 'Queen,'" he said. "I'll deal with her soon enough." He pointed at me. "You know who I'm talking about."

"If you've convinced Celandine to help you, then your problems should be over."

He laughed, head shaking, hair falling over his face. "No one controls that woman. She has the entire citadel network at her disposal." He leaned in, voice lowering. "Let's just say she and I have common interests, one of them being you."

He grinned, an act that turned his face truly hideous. "Well, no, not you. Rather, your stick."

I clutched the stick tight when he mentioned it. "There's no controlling that thing. She barely tolerates me."

"Yes, Celandine mentioned that little irony." He shrugged. "That's your problem. Mine is simple. I want it, so I'm going to go get it. Sometime soon, your precious little Micaela will find it. I thought she had already, but she never used it."

I held my breath, wondering what he knew.

"When she does, I'll take it from her." His face loomed large on the screen. "Then everything will change."

His voice lowered, and I struggled to hear his next words.

"And then I will kill her."

"Wait, you had the stick in your hand, yes?" I asked, interrupting the old man.

He nodded, smiling and saying nothing.

"So, if you had it, how was Micaela going to find it?"

Both eyebrows on the man's face rose. I shook my head, scanning my notes, trying to make sense of his account.

"You called him Rawyn?"

He nodded.

"Is this *the* Rawyn our history books mention?"

No answer.

"He vanished just after the world split apart."

He just sat there.

"Are you going to answer?"

"Are you ever going to learn to fly?" he asked.

"My past is not what we're talking about here."

He leaned toward me. "Our conversation topic may prove as intricate and complicated a matter as your failure."

I held his gaze, heart rate speeding up slightly. My jaw tightened.

"I tried . . . my hardest that day," I said. "On that test. Harder than anything I've ever done."

My next breath shook my torso, a shiver running from my neck to my waist.

"The blessing wasn't meant for me."

A tear rolled down his face, vanishing into the wrinkles next to his enormous nose. "My dear, the 'blessing' is meant for everyone," he whispered.

CHAPTER 2

ALONE

Wasting no time, I grabbed Stick and jumped on the platform. As I flew, the Colberran fleet lay along the edge of the shell, moving toward the outpost and the battle raging there. As the Colberran ships rained lasers down on the peninsula, I tried to spot the approaching Nomad ships. Suddenly, a deafening explosion tore through the peaks around the outpost. Just before I dropped below the ridge line, the Nomad ships raced down to attack the Colberrans.

I tried using the station's terminal to contact the outpost. Unlike the Expeditionary Forces, the Nomads never blocked my access to their network. No answer came, and a second attempt netted the same result.

I stepped to the balcony and looked down to where I knew one speeder lay left behind. A few moments later, the terrain raced by as I steered toward the battle. Deafening explosions echoed off the canyon walls despite the howling wind. My course of action remained unclear, as I lost the details shared with me to time, but I knew where it started. When the dust settled, Micaela needed to see me.

I passed through the rocks, across a wide, familiar valley, and up toward the gap between the last row of peaks. The same gap Micaela and her companions used before me. *Her companions.* My brain made better sense of them to just call them that.

I crested the gap just as a ring of explosions detonated around the outpost. The ships circling above ceased fire. Several speeders hovered near a rise halfway up the northern slope of the valley. People stood on the hill, some pointing at an outpost built on a peninsula. A familiar location from deep in my memory. A cracking sound echoed off the mountains, and the protrusion of land tipped over the edge, ripping away and taking everything and everyone still there with it.

Taking Quentin away.

Images filled my mind, and I shook my head. I needed to be here, but was this too soon? My mind spun with so much information to recall, like a painting so vast standing at one end made the other fade into a blur. *The words. I need to remember the words.* I pressed my hands to my head, willing the words to come out.

"As I sat there, staring into the abyss, that strange old man sat down next to me."

My eyes shot open. This was too early. I fled back into the gap and waited.

Watching.

Micaela, adorned in a gown of rich blue, stood waiting for me in the Queen's chamber. Her long, red hair hung straight, not a strand out of place. A gold necklace nestled against skin as white as marble. Her lips glistened a light pink, and her eyes, flecked green and blue with hints of gray, watched me.

"High One," I said, inclining my head.

Her lips pursed.

"I trust you are well today, Micaela," I said, correcting myself.

She shrugged, a slight lift of her shoulders.

"As well as expected."

I paused, my mouth opening and closing several times. Micaela remained still, eyes on me.

"Out with it, Logwyn," she said, waving a hand at me. "Say what's on your mind."

"How is he dead?"

She arched an eyebrow. "Who said he was dead?"

"You. Suyef. For frag's sake, even he said it."

"How could he say it if he's dead?" she asked, her head cocking to one side, hair shifting over her shoulder.

"Which is why I'm asking you."

"I never said he was dead." She nodded at my sack. "Check your notes."

I glared at her, but she didn't move. I pulled out my notes from the day before.

"Here. You said he died."

"And he did," she said, smiling and turning to the window.

"On that shell?" I moved next to her, nodding at the distant object.

"No, he survived that." She leaned toward me. "I'm sure he'll revel in telling you. He can be an arrogant idiot sometimes."

"So, how did he die?" I asked.

"Wrong question."

"Excuse me?"

"Wrong question," she repeated, eyes never leaving the window.

"How is it wrong?"

"Is 'how' the only thing you can ask?"

"No, there's what, where, when, wh—" I cut myself off when she arched an eyebrow. "Wait, you did that thing you do."

The other eyebrow joined the first.

"What thing?"

"With your eyebrows," I said, waving at her face. "When I stumble onto something. When I feel more like a student than a scribe."

"And?" she asked, the corners of her lips twitching.

"When," I said, snapping my fingers. "All right, when did he die?"

She dipped her head.

"Now you're getting somewhere," she said, moving to sit.

I remained standing, waiting. When she stayed quiet, I moved closer. "So, when did he die?"

"Seventeen days ago," she stated, folding her hands across her lap.

"Then how have I been talking to him?" I asked, frowning.

Again, her eyebrow twitched. "*How*, indeed."

Something about that day struck a chord in me. Something important just over two weeks ago.

"Why such a specific recollection?"

"I think a person's entitled to be specific when speaking of trauma," Micaela replied, voice quiet. "Particularly when it happens on a person's birthday."

Something itched along the edge of my memory. That day she referenced held a measure of importance to more than just her. What was it? I struggled to grasp the memory, but it vanished like water through a sieve.

"Someone revived him," I whispered. "You?"

No response.

"The Queen?"

Silence.

"Suyef?"

Still nothing.

"All right, who else?"

"The *who* is not important right now," Micaela said. "What you need to know now is that he died."

"But we weren't talking about that incident." I pointed out the window. "You just said the battle and his death were unrelated."

"Oh, they're related, just not chronologically speaking. Well, not in direct relation to each other." She shrugged. "Time connects everything."

"Why were you harping about his dying and leaving you when we weren't talking about that?" I asked.

"They didn't happen consecutively, but the two incidents share a connection. In both instances, he broke his word." She looked at the window. "He left me."

"Well, he had little control over what happened in the battle," I said, nodding at the window. "The Colberrans knocked that settlement off the shell."

"True, but he went back."

"To help people!"

Her eyes flared, and I stepped back.

"Apologies, High One," I whispered.

"Yes, he went to help people," she said after a long pause. "Yes, he meant well. When he did, he still broke his promise. He went knowing what the Colberrans intended to do."

"And when he died?" I asked. "Did he have a choice, then?"

"Very much so," she whispered, looking at her hands. "In some ways, his was the only choice."

She paused, taking in several deep breaths. Her next words were tremulous.

"And his choice took more from me than just him."

After the settlement fell, the battle ended. The Nomads chased the Colberran fleet west along the shell's edge. Survivors stood still, eyes staring toward their vanished homes. To their credit, the Nomads saved most of the populace, but that left too many refugees to transport on their mounts. So the Nomads took the injured and children and raced off to get help. That left only a few to stand with the remaining survivors.

I found my way to a nearby rock and sat alone. Suyef approached my rock once or twice, even bringing food and water, but let me be. I appreciated that and sat staring at the destruction. The night shield activated, shrouding us in gloomy darkness. Still, I sat, replaying the battle in my mind. Watching Quentin race back without a care in the world, recklessly trying to save more people. And he failed, falling with those he tried to save. Vanishing like Jyen, my mother, father. My brothers. All gone.

I sat there, angry with them all. Angry with myself. Why hadn't I tied Quentin to the Nomad or taken his belt? Why had I let my brother and me get separated at the prison? Stayed with Maryn?

Eventually, my cramped legs forced me to move. I stumbled closer, the two fallen Colberran ships still burning and casting eerie shadows that fit my mood. Moving east, I stopped near the line of missile and laser scars to find a rocky, shattered slice cutting down to the expanse. Precision work that took careful planning. Why hadn't the Nomads seen it coming; had not seen them? Could they have stopped them? Had they really tried?

My legs, still aching from the battle and prolonged sitting, lodged another protest and stopped working. I tumbled down next to a large rock. There, I stared down into the dimly lit maw. An abyss that swallowed yet another person from my life. No, an abyss into which that person jumped intentionally.

A figure moved away from the wreckage, face obscured by the poor light. A Nomad, probably Suyef. As I looked away, the flash of a tattered cloak caught my eye. One with strips of colored cloth.

I looked back into the abyss, ignoring him as he sat. The old man remained quiet for some time, listening to the crackling fires twist metal as they consumed the ships. More figures moved around the stricken vessels.

"Searching for survivors, I reckon," he muttered.

"You mean murderers," I whispered, my voice cracking from dryness.

"Soldiers will fight you on that moniker. They never think of battle deaths as murder."

"How is wiping out an entire settlement of non-combatants not murder?" I asked. "A settlement of their own people."

He shuddered, head dropping. Even in the dim light, I could see the same agony from the tower on his face.

"You know something, old man," I whispered. "About all this."

His face twisted, lips pursing. His eyes squeezed shut, one hand gripping his cloak.

"So much," he whispered, voice strained. "Too much knowledge. Don't know what to do."

For a split second, something moved deep inside me. Pity. For this strange, old hermit living alone deep in the Wilds.

"Who are you?" I asked.

His eyes shot open, and he smiled.

"Pleased to make your acquaintance, my dear." He held out a hand. "Pleasure's all mine, I'm sure."

"We've alread—" I started. "No, I'm not doing this."

"Not doing what? Talking? 'Fraid you are, dearie."

"I'm not playing these games," I said, jaw tight. "Tell me. Now."

He looked at the wreckage, then down at the chasm.

"This had to happen," he whispered.

"Why?"

He shook his head. "I'm sorry. I don't know what happens next." His voice rose in pitch as he pulled his legs in and rocked back and forth. "She would know. She always does."

"Who?"

He just went on. "She'd have a solution. Some answer." He looked at me, eyes twinkling and mouth split in a half grin. "She always takes care of everything."

"Who is she?" I asked. "Is she here?"

His shoulders sagged, head bowing, eyes closing.

"No," he whispered. "She's gone. A long time this time. Avoiding me, I think."

"Nidfar, who's avoiding you?"

His eyes glistened with tears, and I realized that I'd seen them before. Seen those eyes cry. He wiped at his face, and a small smile danced across his lips.

"No, not me." A single, knobby finger pointed at me. "Avoiding you."

"Me? Why?"

He nodded slowly.

"Yes, that makes more sense. She can't risk spoiling anything."

A conversation came to mind, one with the warden, Mortac. He had felt confused about some woman doing things no one understood.

"The Dragon Queen?" I asked.

His eyebrows rose, and he chuckled.

"Troublesome thought that," he said. "Why'd you do that?"

"Try to make sense of your words?"

"No chance of help now," he said, shaking his head. "And trouble's coming. Just had to open your mouth, you old fool."

He thumped himself on the head with his palm.

"Had to plant thoughts, get her all thinking." He looked over at me. "Foresight's twenty-twenty, you know."

"Hindsight," I corrected.

"S'what I said, wasn't it?"

A slight chuckle escaped my lips. "Why am I arguing with a senile old man?"

His nostrils flared, mouth opening with some retort, but I stopped him.

"Old man, I want to be alone."

"First time for everything," he whispered.

"What do you mean?"

"Being alone is hard," he said. "You think you want it, that it's best."

A figure approached, casting a shadow across us.

"You think it will solve all your problems," he said, squinting at the figure. "But it exacerbates them."

A tremor shook his entire body, and he turned to look at me.

"Don't be alone, my dear," he said, voice dropping. "Bad things happen when you're alone."

CHAPTER 3

HOPE

"Do you think he knew?" I asked, drawing Micaela's gaze.

"What do you mean?"

"'Bad things happen when you're alone.'"

She frowned and looked at the window.

"Nidfar's tricky. He confuses everyone with his cryptic words. Mostly, I think he just enjoys messing with people." She shrugged. "Sometimes, yes, he knew. But not every time."

"Did he this time?"

"Very much so."

Suyef stopped near me, face hidden in shadow.

"How are you doing?"

"Trying to be alone," I muttered. "Which I'm not allowed to do. Right, old man?"

The Nomad cleared his throat, head turning to look around. I pointed at Nidfar and found him gone. Standing partway up, I searched for the old man.

"The old guy in the tower. He was just here."

Suyef sat exactly where the old man had just been sitting. "I know how he is. Are you certain he was here?"

"It's hard to forget that face."

"Or that cloak." The Nomad chuckled, shifting his Seeker's robes. His dark features remained obscured beneath his hood. "Found anything?" he asked, pointing at the chasm.

"I'm just thinking."

He started to leave, but I grabbed his sleeve.

"Please stay."

A swelling filled my throat when I spoke, making my voice quiver. I shivered and pressed my eyes shut. My body trembled, my lungs clenching, then releasing, then clenching. I gripped his sleeve tighter as he settled back down, something real I could keep hold of; not taken from me.

Soon, tears dripped from the tip of my nose and onto my cheeks. A sob shook my torso. Over and over, my body shuddered, and I covered my mouth with my hand to stifle the sound. The whole time, Suyef just sat in silence, his arm steady beneath my hand. He never spoke, didn't stop me or whisper empty words of comfort. He just stayed with me. A welcome moment of stability in my tumultuous world.

With each shudder, weariness overtook me. I'm not sure how long I cried, hand clinging to his sleeve. Eventually, the tears slowed, and a cramp forced me to release his arm and flex my hand. Suyef remained silent while I dried my face with my scarf and pushed my hair back into place, surreptitiously watching him. His eyes followed the searchers near the fires.

"How is it you are so calm?" I finally asked.

"Don't assume from outward appearances," he said. "For now, I choose not to share my pain."

"Sorry if I embarrassed you," I said, working my finger through a stubborn knot in my hair. "I-I think that was necessary."

"The culmination of many events," the Nomad said. "As you said, necessary."

"Heck, I barely even knew him," I whispered. "I don't get why this would set me . . . set . . ."

My throat clenched.

"Knew?"

"You can't possibly believe he survived that. He fell into the core."

"No, he fell toward the core," he said, raising a finger. "A fine point, but still."

"The force of that fragment hitting the core will crush him and whoever fell with him."

"Fact." The Nomad nodded. "Assuming they are still on it."

I frowned at him, shaking my head, but then stopped.

"Wait, you think he used that belt and board to get off?"

"It increases his chances of survival."

"But it requires an anchor. He can't just fly off it."

"Just because we can't imagine a reality wherein he survives does not prevent it from existing."

"That's poppycock, and you know it," I retorted, shaking my head.

"Then why did your heart rate go up? Your face lighten?"

"You can sense my heart rate?"

He looked down, and I followed his gaze to find his hand wrapped around my wrist.

"Sneaky," I muttered, pulling my hand back. "It changes nothing."

"Part of you still hopes," he said. "Something I've seen very little of in you."

"So why give me false hope that he might survive?"

"Does the validity or reality of his survival depend on your faith? On your hope?"

I felt my face heat. "Don't toy with me, Nomad. I'm not stupid."

"No one is saying you are," he said, bowing his head slightly. "Part of you hopes for it. Something in there"—he pointed at my head—"is stopping something in here"—he pointed at my heart—"from daring to hope." He lowered his hand, eyes locked with mine. "Fear? Doubt?"

"Experience?" I replied. "Reality? My whole life?"

He bowed his head again, reminding me very much of Dyad.

"Your past is what it is. It has no bearing on the future," he said. "You do. Maybe not right now, or tomorrow." He held his hand just over my heart. "This holds the future," he said, raising the hand to point at my head. "And in here. They both see the larger picture. Just not together right now."

His words touched on a strong feeling of brokenness, an internal struggle, but also a sense of recognition. The words I couldn't say out loud. Taking a deep breath, I shrugged.

"Part of me wants to believe you," I said.

"That's the thing about faith. It gives assurance about what we can't see."

"I thought we were talking about hope."

"We are."

"You believe he's alive?"

He shrugged.

"I don't know. But I hope he is."

"Why?"

His dark eyes turned back to me. "Because believing otherwise gains me nothing."

"Except pain, if you're wrong," I said.

"Possibly." He smiled, white teeth splitting his dark complexion. "But not right now."

Shaking my head, I looked at the burning ships. "Wish my head would let me do that." I took in a huge breath, letting it out slowly. "But he's not coming back. He threw himself into that without thinking. Like the need to save just a few people mattered more than what we are doing. Mattered more than us."

Suyef shifted next to me. "His is a broken spirit that he hides with enthusiasm and determination. Part of him broke, so now he tries to prevent others from being broken."

"I get that," I said. "But trying to save others who might not be savable?"

"He believed he could."

"But how many more might suffer because of his choice?"

"That we cannot know," Suyef stated. "We can only focus on our choices and, if it becomes necessary, honor his choice by saving those we can."

I took a deep breath and forced it out quickly.

"Honor his choice," I said. "Sure."

"So, what now?"

"What do you mean?"

He nodded at the scene before us.

"What do we do now?"

"I don't know," I whispered.

"We still have answers to find," he said, pointing toward Colberra. "Our network is no better than theirs, but they're running out of water."

I gazed toward my home, obscured beyond the night shield. "I know this sounds petty, but I could not care less about them right now."

"Even the people of your settlement?" he asked.

"They did nothing for us when the Seekers came."

"Your father?"

That gave me pause. "Here I'm getting on Quentin for being too focused on one part, and I'm doing it, too."

Suyef touched my shoulder. "We can't go back for him."

"I know," I said. "It just hurts."

"I didn't mention him to hurt you," he said, pointing off beyond the burning wreckage. "Merely to give you a reason to continue in the lack of any other."

"What are you thinking?"

"Seek the wisdom of the elders," he said. "Inform them of what we know."

"Will they listen to a Colberran?" I asked, nodding at the wreckage. "My people did just do this."

"The Seekers differ from your people."

He pointed at the makeshift refugee camp beyond the fallen ships. "My family sent help. That is a good sign."

"Your family?"

"Yes, all you have seen, all the ships, this was my clan. Guarding this region falls to us."

"That entire fleet is yours?" I asked.

He chuckled. "No, they are merely under my clan's command."

"Are there more?" I asked.

He cocked his head to one side.

"Do the other clans have more?"

"Very much so," he said, nodding. "And we're going to need them."

"Why?"

"They conducted a quick strike on the one settlement to prevent a warning. It also could have made an excellent base of operations." He pointed north. "There aren't many Ancient outposts for leagues." He lowered his hand and looked down at the chasm. "This attack served one purpose: to cut this end off from the rest."

"But your clan came," I said. "So, they failed."

"We kept watch on this outpost. My clan clearly detected the invading ships, so they were ready to repel it. But warning the rest of the shell is more complicated."

"Why do we need to get word back?" I nodded at the crashed ships. "Do you fear another attack?"

"Maybe, but we merely repelled them. They lost only two ships." He pointed toward Nidfar's tower. "The mostly intact fleet went east," he said. "My clan is shadowing them."

I looked east and at the distant peaks to the north.

"Where are they going?"

He shrugged. "We don't know. The Seekers were racing eastward, mostly ignoring our ships."

"They're running?"

"Maybe," the Nomad muttered, turning his gaze to the dark expanse. "I don't trust Seekers. Quentin's assessment might have been right about their big ships, but not all of them were."

The old man's words came back to me.

"He said trouble's coming," I whispered.

"Excuse me?"

"The old man." I waved at Nidfar's former seat, now occupied by Suyef. "Before you came. He said trouble was coming."

"Micaela, you were alone," the Nomad said, drawing my gaze. "The whole time."

"Don't ask me to explain what that old man does," I said, shaking my head. "But he sat right there, muttering a lot of things. One thing I recall clearly is those words. 'Trouble's coming.'"

Suyef watched me for a moment. "Did he say anything else?"

It felt good for him to just believe me, to listen. The tension gripping my shoulders released.

"He said to not be alone," I said. "That bad things happen when I am."

"That, at least, I can do something about," he said, smiling and standing, hand held out to me. "Regarding the trouble, there's only one way to find out what trouble he's talking about."

Taking his proffered hand and standing, I said, "The old man's tower."

"Precisely."

I held up a hand, and Micaela stopped. She cocked her head to one side, one eyebrow raised.

"Your 'you interrupted me' look is quite amusing, High One," I muttered, smirking and glancing over my notes.

She sniffed. "Maybe if you interrupted less, I wouldn't need the look."

"I have questions."

"Yes, yes, I know," she said, waving at me. "Out with it."

"You changed when Suyef believed you about Nidfar," I said. "Something changed inside, didn't it?"

A small smile danced across her face.

"Yes. I couldn't articulate it, lost in my own feelings and all. So much had happened with my family and everyone chasing us and then the battle that I started taking pity on myself. And I had missed something very obvious."

She paused, drawing my attention. Her face expressionless, she stared over my shoulder. Turning, I found a series of images hung on the wall. I moved closer to see several faces, most of them unfamiliar. Except two. I pointed at one frame.

"Is that Suyef and Quentin?"

She stood and shifted to stand next to me, shoulders rolled back, head held high. Her bearing must have taken years to perfect. She let out a long breath, eyes locked on the photo. "Yes."

"Why does the Queen have this?"

"Because they were her friends also," she whispered.

"Who are you?"

"That's a new one," she said, looking at me.

"All three of you," I said, nodding at the picture. "I lack options without the network. All I have is the word of you three."

"Does the Queen's word count?" she asked, one eyebrow rising.

"It does, but she didn't introduce us."

"Merely told you to come in here and what?" Micaela turned, looking about the room. "Were you supposed to find this place empty?"

"She told me you would be here."

"Is that not an introduction?"

"Yes, but that's not what I meant. Who are all of you?" I asked. "The Queen clearly values you three. Why?"

Micaela smiled, eyes resting on the image.

"That's a better question. You really are the right person to help her," she said, then nodded at the image. "The best answer I can give you for now is that, without us, the Queen would not be who she is today."

She brushed a finger across the frame. Her eyes watered as she looked at the pair. "Especially them."

"They matter to you."

I watched her face. Her eyes remained on the image, particularly on one side of it. I pointed at the Nomad. "Especially him."

She laughed slightly. "He's been an invaluable friend, and always has." She nodded toward the cavern. "Her, too, else you wouldn't be here."

She looked at the Nomad a moment longer, then returned to her seat.

"In that moment, so blinded by self-pity, I didn't realize what was standing right in front of me."

"Him?"

"Family." She looked at the image from across the room. "And hope."

CHAPTER 4

INVASION

The Nomad in charge of recovery operations stood on a rock overlooking the makeshift refugee camp. He needed little persuasion from Suyef, barking orders for a padd to be brought and our speeder prepped.

"When will they take the refugees away?" I asked as we mounted the speeder.

"When more ships arrive," Suyef said. "Safer to take them all at once, considering we don't know what's coming."

As he spoke, the commander approached and handed Suyef a padd.

"Updated reports on our situation. We haven't heard from our first convoy yet." He turned his gaze from the camp to Suyef and me, looking us over. "This outpost. Could we use it as a base camp?"

"The *resident* may object to us bringing a bunch of people to his doorstep," I said. "He's a very . . . private soul."

"He can make an exception for this," Suyef said before looking at the commander. "That old man is volatile and could present a challenge. But we'll go placate him. You follow as quickly as you can."

The commander nodded, grasping Suyef's arm before heading off, still barking orders. Suyef's torso tensed, and his shoulders rolled forward.

"Something's bothering you."

He looked around, letting out a long breath before pointing at the flaming wreckage.

"I fear for my clan. We lost no ships in this battle, but a larger invasion places them directly in their path." His jaw clenched and one fist balled tight. "We need to change that."

Several moments later, we soared through the eastern gap. The wind whipped at my braid. The landscape, shrouded in darkness, looked even more unfamiliar, but the speeder's display provided a detailed route and terrain map. As we rode, the weariness of the day's events caught up with me, but just when sleep took me, the speeder slowed.

Shaking away the drowsiness, I saw the shell's edge several hundred meters away, the speeder aimed directly at the expanse. The darkness and nearby peaks obscured any view farther inland.

"Where are we?"

"The old man's tower is beyond those peaks," he said, pointing north and east.

"So, why are we here?

"Call it a hunch."

I looked around, noting some familiar terrain.

"This is where I came on that ring device," I said.

Suyef nodded. "This is the closest point between our shells."

"This hunch. Curious kind? Or dangerous?"

"Both."

A beep sounded from the display, a timer showing all zeros. The night shield melted away, and light poured in. Suyef's body tensed against me. As I peered into the light, my breath caught in my throat.

There, stretched out all the way to the Colberran shell, lay another massive fleet.

"So, was Quentin wrong?" I asked. "About the large ships."

"No. This fleet was different."

"How so?"

"It was a mixed fleet. Both the sleek, long attack ships and several that were bloated, heavy. Bulbous. Like giant basins creeping through the sky."

"How were these big ones staying afloat that far from the shell?"

"Never underestimate the ingenuity of the needy." Her eyes flared, jaw setting. "Especially Seekers."

She fell silent. I waited to give her the time she needed, looking through my notes and checking the device.

"They built a bridge."

As Suyef set the speeder's sensors to scan, an explosion ripped the tops off the eastern mountains. Nomad ships flowed down toward the edge.

"Help from other clans?"

He shook his head, turning the speeder north and taking off.

"My clan must have detected them and come back."

"With that other fleet, the Colberrans can trap them."

Shots from the Colberrans struck the surrounding mountains. The Nomads returned fire.

"That's the greater threat," Suyef said. "Preventing a foot-hold is easier than removing it."

The speeder shot through a pass and into a valley. I glimpsed the tower at the far end.

"Where's the other fleet?" I asked.

"Hopefully not close behind."

We slowed to a halt at the tower and vaulted off, racing for the door. It opened as I neared it and deposited us in the control room. My companion darted toward the balcony, pointing at the panel.

"Work your magic and get it started," he barked, looking out through some specs. "Call me when you have a connection."

"To where?"

"Anywhere on the shell!"

Before I could even start, the computer spoke. "May I help you, Micaela?"

"Um, Suyef? It recognizes me."

"It's working?" he asked, to which I nodded. "Send the Nomad reports first. Then we'll send another."

He tossed the padd to me, and I heard a connection chime.

"Computer, is this connected?" I asked, setting the padd down.

"Affirmative."

"Transmit these messages to the nearest Nomad station."

"Message will take thirty seconds to process and transmit. Proceed?"

"Yes!" I yelled as I joined Suyef.

The battle was clearly visible in the distance.

"What are you looking at?" I asked.

"That bridge," he muttered, handing me the specs. "How it works. Weak points."

I looked out toward the floating platforms.

"Those are gravity wells under them. Similar to the ships, only larger." I handed his specs back. "A direct attack without lasers is the only way to take them out. Rockets?"

"We don't have those. No one has for centuries." He nodded toward the room. "Did the message make it?"

"Computer, status of message?" I asked.

"Transmitted. Receipt confirmed."

"Any response?"

"Negative."

I followed him back inside.

"Will she let me access the network?" he asked.

"Suyef, identity recognized and confirmed," the computer stated.

"Okay," he said. "Computer, is there a Nomad battleship transmitting a command-and-control beacon?"

"Affirmative. Set to receive only."

His hands darted across the screen, entering columns of data.

"Computer, can you mask this signal?" he asked.

"Affirmative. Location will remain secure."

"Please send the following. 'This is crown prince Suyef, clan Bilal, calling commander, defense fleet. Transmitting platform details from shell observation. Requested support from the nearest station. No response received. Will signal once they send a response. Good luck.'"

"Confirmed receipt," the computer stated as the panel cleared.

Suyef moved back to the balcony, training his specs to the west.

"You're nervous," I said, joining him.

"These are my people. My brothers and sisters."

He continued scanning the ground to the west. I remained in the door, watching him. That stoic Nomad demeanor he wore like a mask had seemed so perfect a few weeks ago, but now I knew what to look for. A slight finger tic, neck tension, or a shift in stance. I couldn't tell you precisely what he felt all the time, but at that moment, he felt fear. That gave me pause.

"Can you see them?" I asked, moving closer and following his gaze.

"I see some dust shifting," he said, pointing. "With so few speeders, many will have to walk."

A series of explosions drew our attention to the battle. A pair of Nomad ships, one soaring above, the other below, rotated around a bulbous vessel, raking it with withering laser fire. Smaller Colberran ships darted in, but one of the Nomad ships snagged a pair in gravity beams as it swung over the transport. Helpless, the ensnared ships crashed into the top of the transport, ripping through the hull. Explosions split the ship in two, the two halves ripping apart as they fell from sight.

Suyef shifted next to me, taking in a sharp breath. Tearing my gaze from the sight, I saw that the previously well-organized ranks of Nomad ships now moved in disarray, several diving out of sight. Suddenly, a torrent of laser fire raked across the Nomad fleet.

"Water above," I whispered.

The initial Colberran fleet had arrived.

"Why do you think the Nomads attacked like that?" I asked, setting my stylus down.

"They had two choices," Micaela said. "Chase a fleeing fleet or attack the invading one." She held her hands up to either side. "Two dangerous foes. Which do you attack?"

"The more dangerous one."

"Especially when one may draw you away from the other," she said. "I don't think that commander believed he could defeat both forces."

"So, a desperate act?"

"No, a delaying one," she said. "If you can't defeat your foe, then do what you can to hold them off until help can arrive."

"But what if help never comes?" I asked. "Wasn't he risking losing ships and people he might need later?"

"He was, but that's his job," she said. "I don't envy military leaders. Theirs are the choices debated and analyzed forever, that get people killed. It's a no-win, regardless."

She frowned, tapping a finger on the couch.

"If Quentin were here, I'm sure he could give us an example," she said. "Sorry, the details of history bore me. I prefer personal stories."

"You have such a memory for it."

She shook her head. "No one realizes they're living history. It's just their life."

"So, what happened?"

"People died," she said. "A lot of them."

"You watched?"

"No, once the first refugees arrived, we left."

"Who won?"

Micaela locked gazes with me. "Does anyone ever really win a battle?"

I pursed my lips, waiting for her to continue.

"The short version is the Nomads defeated the Seeker ships, but it only delayed them." She held up a hand when I looked up. "How did they beat them?"

I nodded.

"They tricked them," she said, flying one hand under the other.

"They went under the shell," I said, smiling.

"And ships already there performed some unusual maneuvers. It was quite something to see recordings of it."

"So, where did you go?"

"To talk to old people."

The refugees, aided by speeders sent ahead, arrived a short while later. Once the tower accepted the rescue commander as an approved user, I went down to help the refugees move in.

"It's time to go," Suyef said, pulling me aside when I stepped out of the elevator. "We need to get to the Nomad council."

"Why?"

"The Seekers will not give up regardless of how that battle ends," he said, moving toward our speeder. "And we need help."

"And you think the council needs convincing?"

"No," he said as he mounted the speeder. "We need their permission to access the Sunken Citadel."

"Help is there?"

He pointed down.

"We can use the Sunken Citadel to contact those closer to the core."

I stopped just short of mounting, dreading his next words. He looked down at me.

"I don't like it, and I know you hate it, but they are probably the only force that can stop this."

"You're right," I said, climbing onto the mount. "I hate it."

"Wait, he wanted to bring the dragons into the Intershell War?" I asked, stopping Micaela.

"He believed they alone could end the conflict," she said, standing and walking toward the table. "But he had an ulterior motive."

She placed a hand on the Seeker cloak I'd brought with me.

"To look for Quentin?"

"I don't know." She shrugged. "He believed Quentin would survive. And he was very adamant about getting to that citadel."

"That's a poor excuse to come to us."

"It wasn't his only reason."

"Your water problem."

"And the network issue."

"But Quentin found your water."

She folded her arms and leaned on the table. "We still couldn't get it. That required controlling a citadel."

"The citadels can only control what's on each shell."

Micaela moved to the window and looked down. I followed her, attempting to see what held her attention. She just stood there, staring toward the core. Then it hit me.

"The Shattering destroyed that place centuries ago," I whispered.

"Making it the perfect place to hide something, don't you think?" she asked, looking up at me. "What do you think your people are 'sworn to protect' down here?"

"But that citadel perished. It's one of the few records we have from the Shattering."

"*Can* you destroy one?"

I paused, pondering things learned as a kid. "They can withstand the strongest natural forces, including gravity," I said. "And no weapon ever built has even scratched one."

"So, how was it destroyed?"

"By altering the history books?" I asked.

"Creating the perfect hiding place."

"For what?"

"The ultimate doomsday device."

My skin prickled with goose bumps, and my heart sped up.

"The one that ripped our world apart?"

Micaela nodded.

"The Queen is hiding Third Gate there?"

She shrugged.

"It's what Suyef suspected."

"And he wanted what? To use the most destructive device ever built to stop the war? That doesn't sound like him."

"It's also the only device that can control the citadels." Micaela's lips scrunched together. "According to legend."

"But that device was . . ."

"Lost during the Shattering," Micaela whispered, finishing my thought. "Just like a certain citadel."

I frowned at her. "How do you know all this?"

She took in a long breath, letting it out slowly. "I started a war."

"No, the Colberrans did."

She rolled her eyes.

"If you want to get technical about it, Colvinra started it because he was looking for me." She shook her head. "Actually, for something he thought I had."

"Which was?"

She pointed at my device.

"The key to the entire network."

CHAPTER 5

TILTED

Core-night came as we moved through the mountains. When it did, I noticed Suyef looking around more, but he remained silent when pressed. The terrain faded into darkness, and I thought about the refugees. Nidfar never came to protest against the tower's new residents, making me doubt we had talked at all. The memory felt real, as did the words he'd spoken. *Don't be alone. Bad things happen when you're alone.* With only Suyef left, the old man's words echoed loudly in my mind.

Shaking my head against that depressing line of thought, I focused instead on our route through a narrow valley. The slopes rose sharply to either side as the pass ended in a tight canyon. I pressed my neck device to speak to Suyef, his responses clear despite the wind.

"Are we climbing?" I asked, yawning to clear my ears.

"For now," he said. "We'll begin descending into the heart of the shell soon."

I frowned, contemplating underground tunnel networks beneath the mountains as I peeked at the display. Columns of symbols showed a constant flow of information about the mount, the terrain, the weather, and more.

"You can see terrain beyond what's visible," I said. "That display isn't Ancient."

We leaned left as the canyon veered right, our momentum carrying us near the left wall.

"It's a Nomad design." He tapped the side of the screen. "Seeker mounts have a very similar version."

"They stole it?"

We leaned opposite a left curve in the canyon.

"We know we built them first."

"It's an efficient design," I said.

"And they just made it identical? Including the materials?" he asked, chuckling. "Possible, but highly unlikely."

"But Seekers hacking your network and stealing the designs is more likely?"

He shrugged.

"Not impossible. Just highly improbable."

"Could someone have sent them the design?"

"That's one theory among several."

"Any suppositions on who did it?" I asked, ducking against him as a powerful gust tugged my braid.

"Several," he said, teeth clenched.

Ahead, the canyon floor rose toward the canyon's upper edge. He pulled back on the controls, lifting the nose and riding the sharp slope. The moment we shot over the top edge, he pushed down on the controls and decelerated, bringing us to a smooth halt. Looking back down, I saw how the canyon split the mountain's south slope almost to the peak. Turning my gaze north afforded me a view similar to those from Quentin's board and Nidfar's ring transport.

"Wow," I whispered.

We hovered astride a row of tall mountains running east and west, a natural barrier separating the edge from the rest of the shell. From this height, I could see how the shell sloped at an angle down to the north, a massive wilderness of mountains.

"I knew about the shell's tilt, but I've never seen it," I said. "It's so mountainous."

"The result of the collision."

"What's the angle?" I asked, tipping my head to the north as I looked east.

"It's about a thirty-degree slope."

"All the way to the sea, yes?" I asked, to which he nodded. "Such a fascinating place."

"Enjoy the view. The next good one comes when we reach the sea."

Staring toward the horizon, I frowned.

"From this height, I thought we'd be able to see the Maelstrom."

He gunned the mount, sending us shooting down the slope.

"You're not looking low enough."

I stopped Micaela with a raised hand.

"You couldn't see the shell's tilt when you first flew there?" She shook her head.

"Flying is a bit distracting, especially that way."

"An invading armada right behind you doesn't help that." She smiled.

"The view was spectacular."

"I've seen it," I said, tapping my stylus on my paper. "The shell, the tilt. Now I just go straight to Quentin's 'base.'"

"Well, what's left of it."

"Was there more before?"

"An entire structure. The Nomads aren't sure who built it, but they suspect Nidfar."

"Getting him to talk won't be easy," I said, groaning.

She laughed.

"Figured that out, have you?"

"He's dodgy, even if you can find him," I said. "He's only seen when he wants to be, yes?"

"How right you are," she said, her voice quiet.

We fell silent, her looking at the window, me my notes. After a moment, I continued.

"The Maelstrom," I said. "Can't say I saw anything deserving of that name when I went there. I mean, on that first trip. Just the landscape before landing on the edge."

"The Green Zone," she said, smirking. "I had a bit of fun with Suyef over that color choice."

"My guess is he didn't take it too well."

"'It is green for safe, nothing more,'" she said in a deep voice that broke into a chuckle. "Sorry, my Suyef impression isn't very good. Not low enough."

"Don't forget the hint of a rasp," I said.

I cleared my throat, sat up as straight as I could, and looked down my nose at her.

"'Logwyn, you're trying to fly before you've even sprouted wings.'"

She snorted in laughter, then covered her now red face. We both broke into a fit of giggles.

"Oh, that's totally him," she said between laughs.

"Did you just snort?" I asked, breathing fast.

She assumed a mocking pose, nose up, eyes wide, hands on her hips.

"A high one never snorts," she said, her voice sharp.

47

We held gazes for a moment. Then her lips twitched and her pose dissolved into more laughter.

"Seriously," she said, panting and fanning her face. "That impression was spot on. Has he heard you do that?"

"Water above, no. My interviews with him are so serious," I said, my face warming a bit. "Humor just doesn't seem right with him."

"Don't let that stoic exterior fool you. Nomads have a fondness for absurdity and heckling. Outsiders rarely see it because most misinterpret their sense of humor as something sinister or idiotic."

I nodded, making a note to ask him about that. Silence followed, an awkward pause after the levity.

"So, the Green Zone."

Micaela nodded. "Right. It runs along the shell's edge, expanding to include that entire section down from the peaks we stopped on. It's called that because it's stable."

"As compared to the Maelstrom."

"Right." She held a hand up, palm flat toward me. "If where my fingers start is that line of peaks, Quentin's outpost would be here." She pointed at her middle finger's tip. "Everything between my thumb and my pinkie is the Maelstrom." She pointed at the confluence of palm lines near her wrist. "That's the Shattered Citadel."

"Your destination," I said, nodding. "I'm guessing you couldn't just go straight across."

"Under normal circumstances, no," she said. "Nomads follow routes along the edge."

She drew her finger down her thumb to the joint, then across to the palm lines.

"If forced, they will cross the Maelstrom," she went on, then lowered her hand. "But only if forced."

"So, does the Maelstrom extend down here?" I asked, pointing at her arm just below the wrist. "This is the sea, I'm guessing."

"Yes. The area north to the citadel is stable," she said, nodding. "Most use that route, if they go at all."

"They don't use the citadel?"

"They revere the place, but the collision nearly destroyed it," she said. "The entire thing moved closer to where the sea is now."

"So, is it true north for them?" I asked.

She shook her head.

"The sea is north now."

"The entire thing?"

"Technically, it's a spot in the sea nearer the Shattered Citadel, but yes."

"The force necessary to move a citadel is . . ." I trailed off.

"Unimaginable?" Micaela asked. "Inconceivable?"

"Either of those," I said.

"Now, imagine forcing two powerful gravity generators that close together."

Her hands quivered, moving closer, then farther apart repeatedly.

"Everything between them got pulled in two directions."

"Including the citadels."

She lowered her hands, and I nodded.

"And as a result, it shredded that region."

She arched an eyebrow at me. "Shredded? It's still doing it."

"See, our records are spotty," I said, pointing at her. "You've seen it. What's happening in there?"

"Chaos."

"And you had to cross it?" I asked.

"We had no choice."

"Did you have any idea what you were in for?"

"No amount of book knowledge could have prepared me for what came next."

"And now that you know?" I asked.

"Just another reason I don't go near that shell."

We descended to the north through a small canyon, slowing just before the canyon opened up. Suyef's entire body felt tense, and he jumped slightly at my touch. My back itched from seeing him so unnerved.

"You're going into the Maelstrom?"

He nodded.

"Why?"

"It's the fastest way," he whispered.

"There's something you aren't telling me."

He tapped the screen, showing several red dots blinking all along the edge.

"Seekers," I said. "They cut us off."

"Enough that they can cause the trouble we need to avoid," he said.

"Those have to be from the original fleet," I said. "To be that far ahead of us."

"With more coming," he said, pointing at the shell's edge south of us. "They scattered along the shell's edge after the invasion battle."

"Leaving us only one way to the citadel," I said. "Through that."

Stretching, I looked down the canyon. He remained still.

"I can't tell if you're supremely confident or desperate," I said.

He shrugged but said nothing.

"Will they follow us?"

"They would be crazy to try using those ships," he said.

"And we're not? You're going to get us killed."

He turned to look at me.

"I don't know of another way."

I looked at him, then at the ground ahead.

"Fine," I said.

We traveled down that canyon as it widened for quite a while. It presented me with time to think. About my family, Quentin, the battle. The Maelstrom. All of it. Taken altogether, it was a lot to feel. Angry, sad, irritated, exhausted. I felt all of that, almost even overwhelmed. Especially with Colberran ships lurking overhead, hunting.

I blinked. A Colberran ship flew out over the canyon just ahead of us. Suyef stopped the speeder, and we remained still, hiding behind a large rock.

"Did they see us?" I asked.

He shrugged. "Maybe. They will if we move."

"Battleship? Transport?"

He inched the speeder's nose to the right, giving us a better look. "Cruiser. Not heavily armed."

"It wouldn't take much to finish us," I said.

Suyef expanded the map on the display. We hovered just north of the Green Zone, a solid red line showing our route. Dotted red lines branched down into the Maelstrom to both sides.

"That's the only ship near us," I said.

"For now."

"Are those other routes?" I asked, pointing at a dotted line. "That we could use."

"Those are more recent attempts. None repeated," he said, shaking his head. "Even this route will change, eventually."

I looked back up the canyon. "If we hug the wall, we could go back. We'd have to deal with more ships, obviously."

"No, we go forward."

"Just like that? Not even considering another option."

"I know this shell," he said, sitting up. "When I say this is our best route, it is."

"Until the route changes." I pointed at the ship. "If you're putting me in danger, I get a say."

"Three choices," he said. "Go back toward even more ships. Continue forward with only one ship to deal with."

"For now," I said, imitating him. "What's the third one?"

He turned the mount down the valley. "You won't like it."

"Worse than the other two?"

"Think of it as the 'break glass in case of emergency' option."

I looked at the ship. "I will like none of this, right?"

He remained silent. Finally, I waved him onward, wondering how much I wouldn't like option three. What I didn't know was how much he was dreading it.

"Had he been in the Maelstrom before?"

"He never talks about it," Micaela said, shifting on the couch. "Even that trip."

"But you were together there."

She shook her head. "He just won't talk about it."

"Okay," I said, looking at my notes. "This valley seemed fairly stable. Or had you not entered the Maelstrom yet?"

"For a time, it was, and it provided a bit of protection," she said. "But we were in it, for sure."

"So, Quentin's journey to the elders' council," I said, looking at some older notes. "There's no mention of the Maelstrom. Just an alien landscape, no details. Do you know why?"

"Details bore him?" she said. "Ask him."

"I can't find him."

"For now."

I looked up at her to find a perfectly serene face staring back at me. Narrowing my eyes, I continued. "Still, it seems odd he would leave that out."

"My life would be a lot easier if I could fathom that man's mind," she said, rolling her eyes. "Alas, I cannot."

"So, either he left it out, or he never saw it."

"Probably the latter," she said, looking at the window.

"Why do you say that?"

"Because it's not always in the same place."

CHAPTER 6

SCOUTS

We stuck to the canyon walls as we followed the stubbornly slow Seeker cruiser. It dragged on so much I felt like it was trying to match our pace.

"What are they doing?" I asked. "Have they seen us?"

We crept over a boulder, but the ship didn't react.

"Seen? No," he said. "Perhaps caution against what the Maelstrom might do."

"Because of just broken gravity systems? Or can the citadel alter the code, too?"

He nodded, pointing back behind him. "So we always stay near the edge."

"To keep escape an option?" I asked, leaning out to see the entire ship.

"The only survivors I know of never made it far in," he said, nodding. "And what they described." He shook his head. "Reality warped and changed."

"That's specific," I said, slapping him on the back. "How many times has it happened?"

"In my lifetime, only twice."

As we crossed over another boulder, the ship glided beyond the canyon's right wall. On the display, the large red mass kept moving north, us following.

"So, even up there, they're not safe."

"We don't know the full reach of the Maelstrom on a vertical axis," he said, nodding. "The collision happened soon after the Splitting. *How* remains a matter of controversy. Some say the dragons, others say us, and more say the Colberrans."

He edged the mount along, pacing with the now-hidden ship. "One fact we know: this has existed ever since."

"How far back do your records go?"

"I've studied the last fifteen generations," he said. "A small portion of the records."

Looking up at the canyon walls, I shook my head. "So much we don't know," I said. "Anything could happen."

As we continued, the Seeker cruiser moved out perpendicular to the canyon's edge. Suyef slowed the mount as the cruiser lowered down even with the ground above us, the wind whipping at our clothing.

"What are they doing?" I asked. "Making a bridge?"

Suddenly, several objects arced out from the ship. Long and tubular, with wings unfurling to either side, the objects soared into the sky

"Scouts," Suyef hissed, moving us under an outcropping.

"Those are small. Are they manned?"

"Yes, just a suit wrapped around the pilot," he said, stopping just out of sight of the cruiser. "Similar to Quentin's belt and board."

"So, gravity beams."

One scout shot past, flying low. It spun in a flash and soared up the far side of the canyon.

"That suit must have them strategically placed all around the body to save the pilot from the pressure. So, tight, focused beams and a lot of speed and agility."

"The suit uses internal generators to cushion the pilot."

I shook my head. "Seekers think of everything."

"Those aren't Seeker design," he whispered, leaning over to look up at the cruiser.

"Ancient?"

He nodded.

"From a matter forge?"

"Possibly," he said. "The citadel would have had some already."

He guided the mount closer to the wall and looked back up the canyon. His gaze shifted back and forth, but the scouts had vanished. I watched the cruiser.

"Scouting beyond the canyon walls?"

"Something's not right," he said, voice quiet as he stared at the display.

"Besides the Seekers 'following' us by flying ahead?"

He looked up at the ship, lips pursed. He tapped one finger on his cheek.

"Interesting way to say that," he said.

"Seems obvious to me. They can't hide that ship, so trick the target into thinking it's shadowing you."

He sat there, eyes on the ship. "Why give away the advantage?" he finally asked. "They still had us on sensors."

"Why do it at all?" I asked. "Maybe they don't know there are no 'safe' passages and followed us, assuming we did."

A whooshing sound back up the canyon drew our attention in the other direction. I looked at the display to see the scouts flying beyond the canyon walls.

"That's a dangerous game," he said, pointing at the ship. "Right now, that thing is above the canyon. That changes soon."

Looking at the display, I saw the canyon widened farther ahead.

"He has to know he's risking his ship being here," I said. "Maybe that's why he's following you. He can't ask a Nomad to be his guide. Well, not directly, at least."

Suyef remained quiet, leaning forward to look around. Then he resumed his seat, manipulating the display.

"What are you doing?" I asked, leaning over to see.

He waved toward the ship, the other hand still working. "Between my people and the Maelstrom, that ship won't make it to the Shattered Citadel. But we need to get there." He looked up at the vessel. "Somehow, we have to lose it or eliminate it."

A heavy silence fell as Suyef scanned over the terrain, muttering to himself. I pondered how many people were on the ship; might perish if it came down. The possibilities weighed on my heart.

"You don't want to just lose it. Do you?"

He didn't answer.

"Can we lose them?"

He looked over his shoulder at me. "There are two results, but only one road to either."

He tapped at the display, projecting an alternative route. He leaned back, looking up at the ship.

"You know they'll just follow us," I said. "Can we outrun them?"

"We may have to find out."

He pressed an actual button, and I felt my weight increase. Then two metallic wings flowed up to engulf my legs and lower torso. Once secured, my companion sped up. We passed under and past the ship. I looked back as one scout dove low behind us.

"Suyef, incoming," I called out.

He drove the mount toward a small crevice on our right, and I tensed, unsure if we would fit. Wind buffeted us as we entered the small offshoot, sharp, jagged rocks moving past in a blur. Immediately inside the new canyon, our path ascended at an alarming angle. The walls narrowed, so close that us crashing to our deaths in a rocky vise seemed certain.

The next instant, we shot into open air, but my relief vanished when I saw large outcroppings of rock rising up like giant fingers trying to grab us. We flew into them, dodging through the narrowing gaps. It reminded me of the Wilds: a forest of rock swallowing us the farther we went.

"Dragon's Maw," he said, never looking back.

"What?"

"Those," he said, nodding at a formation. "Teeth."

"Creative," I muttered. "Looks like fingers to me."

He grunted, leaning to the left in a sharp turn under an overhang.

"You've named places here?" I asked, leaning with him. "In a place that changes all the time?"

"Places still exist here," he said, straightening post turn. "The Maelstrom doesn't change that, just alters what it looks like."

We slowed, arcing in a sweeping angle around a large formation comprising a solid center and a multitude of arms jutting out toward the ground in every direction. On the far side, we shot off a cliff, jagged mountains splitting the sky as we followed the sloping wall down to the right. There lay the remnants of a large water pipe, pieces flung into the cliff like sticks thrown into mud. When we approached the wreckage, Suyef guided us under a sizable chunk and stopped.

"I thought the water lines were indestructible like the citadels," I said, staring at the structure. "Did the Maelstrom do this?"

"No," he said.

The havoc wrought on the world's most powerful civilizations by the ancient collision was sobering, made worse by the thought of random alterations to reality striking at any moment. I looked back up and saw one scout.

"And here they come," I said.

Suyef grunted and continued down the sloping wall, leaving the fragments behind. Ahead, the slope ended at the base of a tall mountain, forming a near perfect angle. Suyef flew left along the bottom toward another mountain.

"That angle," I said, looking back. "Doesn't seem very random."

He shrugged one shoulder. "It's not all like this."

I looked up just as the cruiser twisted down into the valley, the scouts racing after us.

"Your plan isn't working," I said, turning forward. "If you have one."

His entire torso shook with a hearty laugh.

"Actually, it is."

"You want them following?"

"They will follow us regardless," he said. "Only one thing can stop them."

He turned the mount hard to the right, and we shot down another valley.

"Are you actually looking for the Maelstrom?"

Ahead, a jagged rock lay in our path, breaking up the otherwise smooth valley floor.

"The Maelstrom finds you," he said, guiding us over the rock. "Not the other way around."

"You talk about it like it's alive."

"Maybe it is."

"What're you going to do when we find it?"

He looked back at me, one of the few times he took his eyes off piloting the mount.

"Pray we survive it."

As he said the words, the Maelstrom struck.

CHAPTER 7

MAELSTROM

"It struck?" I asked, interrupting Micaela. "Did it attack you?"

"If the world suddenly changes in ways that nearly kill you, I call that an attack."

"I don't like the wording." I scrunched my nose, staring at my notes. "Too hyperbolic."

"Then reword it later. I don't care."

"I can't. She wants it copied exactly."

"You're not gonna give her an exact transcript of our conversations," she said, eyes narrowing. "I know you creative types, particularly authors. You can't help being melodramatic."

"I'm a scribe."

"Two sides of the same cloak." Micaela laughed. "Quentin once fancied himself an author. You may write about *real* people, but I'm sure you embellish things to build tension and drama."

"I can't say what else I'll do, if even asked to do more, but she will get an exact transcript."

"Even of Quentin?" she asked, arching an eyebrow at me. "He is rarely coherent and on topic at the same time. If you can get him talking."

She looked down at the floor.

"You keep using the present tense," I pointed out.

"So?"

"He's dead, remember?"

"No, he died. There's a difference."

Micaela smiled at my look and said nothing when I waited for more. Finally, I looked down at my notes. "So, what happened next?"

"The Maelstrom struck."

"You said that already."

"Are you telling this story?"

"I will." I smiled at her. "After you've told it to me."

She looked out the window. A moment later, she continued. "The Maelstrom struck," she said, leaning her head back. "And everything changed."

Code altering causes visual ripples that, when small, remain limited and short. The more alterations, the more ripples, all overlapping each other, creating visual distortions that can overwhelm an observer.

The valley walls boiled away from us like water rippling in a tank. Waves of dirt contorted in all directions, descending on us. We had no warning. One moment, the world was normal. The next, everything changed, nearly killing us right there.

As the ground boiled, the mount's gravity beams could not compensate. The speeder surged back and forth, vibrating in tune with the cascading ripples. And that was just the first effect. Each wave of ripples changed the surrounding world. The narrow valley surged overhead into a massive overhang jutting off a mountain.

As we floundered back and forth, rolling, spinning, twisting first this way, then that, Suyef struggled against the controls. How he kept a semblance of control over it, I don't know, but he did. Sort of.

As another distortion wave approached, we shot straight up in the air at the new overhang. Suyef yanked hard, hand squeezed white on the control bars, sending the speeder into a tight, spiraling loop.

"What are you doing?" I yelled, forcing my eyes to stay open.

"Trying," he said, teeth clenched, "to steer."

Back and forth, rolling, surging forward, then yanked backward, we went, the ground shifting, then vanishing only to reappear someplace else. It was then that I noticed something odd, familiar. Something I would recognize anywhere: Ancient symbols. They appeared whenever the ground moved, sometimes before, more often after it happened. Like a premonition of movement or an echo left behind, the symbols were everywhere I looked. Sometimes, I caught only a flash of them while, other times, they remained visible for a few heartbeats. I couldn't make out anything specific, and, to be honest, I doubted what my eyes were seeing. With the Maelstrom in full effect, I couldn't be sure I wasn't just seeing things. I thought to say something to Suyef, but he had his hands full enough.

Suyef groaned as he struggled, and my stomach threatened upheaval. We shot forward for a stretch, then stopped as the ground moved, leaving us to drop into a nosedive. The ground cracked open below us and a large piece of rock thrust up right at us.

Suyef pulled the mount in a counterclockwise spin around the elevating rock. He gunned the speeder down the new formation toward the new surface level. As we neared the ground, one scout flitted across my vision, spinning out of control. It smashed into the rock face, sending a shower of rock down on us. A large chunk struck the mount, flipping us into an end-over-end spin. Another scout careened past and out of sight as it dodged the falling rocks. All around us, I saw flashes of symbols appear, then vanish. Or was it a trick of the light? I couldn't be sure.

Suyef slowed our spin and maneuvered us away from the now-crumbling rock formation. Below, the scout pulled up in a tight arc and shot away from the ground.

"I've lost it!" Suyef called out.

"What?" I asked, watching the scout.

"The valley," he blurted. "I've lost it."

His head darted back and forth as the shifting ground changed around us. Suyef spun us one way, then another, keeping us at a safe distance from each new formation.

"Where's the ship?"

I checked the sky, currently off to my left. Suyef pulled the speeder around in a flat spin, orienting us to the blue expanse. Of the two remaining scouts, I could see nothing. We shifted around a tall, thin formation as it rose and bent like folded fabric. As we passed it, I looked for the symbols, but saw nothing.

Suddenly, the surface below us dropped away, and the mount plummeted. As Suyef struggled to find purchase and hold us aloft, the Seeker ship soared into view, caught in a downward spiral directly above and behind us.

"They're above us!" I called out.

Another formation appeared to our left, giving Suyef a new anchor to point our speeder at the falling ship. Men fell off the ship's superstructures as the stricken vessel rolled in an ever faster clockwise spin.

"Their fail-safes are down," I yelled, pointing.

"Hang on!"

We shot toward the plummeting Seeker ship. Suyef piloted the speeder along the vessel's bottom edge, keeping the superstructures and guns aimed away from us.

"They're spinning so fast," I said. "Does an object's mass determine the Maelstrom's strength against it?"

"Maybe."

The vessel continued to spin, and Suyef shifted to stay along its bottom. I looked back and saw one scout fly in below us. Attempting an identical maneuver to our own, it opened fire, bolts of light lancing up at us.

"He's firing!"

Suyef spun us toward the vessel's far side. Shots streaked past, each bending in different directions. The scout tried to follow over the ship's topside, but a superstructure smashed into it. The small ship spiraled toward the ground, falling out of sight just as the ship's turrets turned toward us.

"Suyef, the ship!"

"We need a way out," Suyef yelled, accelerating in a tight turn back and away from the Seeker ship.

At that instant, the ground changed, rock materializing above as the ground below crumbled away. I barely registered that I saw a few symbols this time before Suyef pulled hard, flipping us upside down and parallel to the new formation. The ship opened fire as its bow tilted down parallel to the ground, now falling away below it. Suyef gunned the accelerator and tried to maneuver away from the shots. As he did, the ground above shifted, sending us careening toward the energy beams.

"Hang on!"

He flung us into a tight spin as the ship's blasts bent in wide arcs around us.

"Gravity's warping their shots," I said, clinging to him like an anchor against the rising dizziness.

"Warping everything," he yelled, leaning left and slowing our spin momentarily.

The Seeker ship rolled away, topside now out of view. The ground kept forming and shifting, appearing, then vanishing. Each change sent both our speeder and the Seeker ship spiraling as each tried to compensate.

"Suyef, how do we get out of here?"

He didn't answer. The ground shifted right at us, pushed us away as Suyef held us even with it. Below, the Seeker ship shuddered when struck by the same shifting ground. It fell sideways into a roll, bringing the topside into view. Every battery on the deck opened up, sending a torrent of laser blasts in our direction. Then the ship buckled, its back broken when the ground tore into its belly.

Suyef yanked the controls back and forth, trying to climb away. Laser blasts detonated on every side as we fell into a dizzying spin. I closed my eyes against the chaos.

"Can't hold it!" Suyef yelled.

We jerked hard, and I opened my eyes. Ahead, a cliff surged up directly in our path. Laser blasts peppered the earth as we spun end over end.

Squeezing my eyes shut, I thought of my family, of Quentin, of Suyef. Inertia tugged at my limbs, and I heard the mount groan. I gripped Suyef as hard as I could.

Then something hit me.

Hard.

"How did you not vomit?"

Micaela shook her head. "It all happened so fast, Logwyn. I remember feeling it coming, then changing directions."

I nodded. "So the Seeker cruiser. Gone?"

"With all hands, as far as I could tell."

"What about the other scout?"

"Never saw him again."

"So, how did you get out?"

"It threw us out."

CHAPTER 8

SHATTERED

When I opened my eyes, the light sent waves of fiery pain through my head. I squeezed my eyes shut, and that hurt. Everything hurt. Every inch of me felt bruised and scratched. I groaned and coughed, my throat dry and rough, and the pain worsened.

"Suyef?" I whispered, my voice cracking.

"Your companion will return," a female voice answered.

Opening my eyes revealed a room similar to my old bedroom. A network terminal stood to one side, a table with chairs on the other. A Nomad woman sat at the table and held out a hydration pack. I accepted with a tentative nod, noticing the bed was really just pillows.

"How long?" I asked.

"Long enough for him to carry you here," she answered, handing me a nutrient pack. "We weren't certain you'd wake."

My head throbbed in unison with my heartbeat.

"I wish I hadn't."

The woman chuckled. "Considering you survived, the pain is a small price."

"When will Suyef return?"

As I ripped into the nutrient pack, the door slid open and Suyef entered.

"Ah, you're awake. Good." He held out a hand to me. "Come, we're expected."

A wave of dizziness pulsed through me when I stood. Suyef caught me mid-sway.

"I'm okay," I said. "Just got up too fast."

"You sure?"

I nodded, squeezing my eyes shut. "Except this headache."

"That we can help on the way," he said, pulling me toward the door.

"To where?"

"The council room."

"Right now? I just woke up."

He glanced at me, then at the Nomad now following us. "The war didn't stop because you were unconscious." He waved at a passing Nomad, whispering something I didn't catch.

"Did something happen?"

He nodded. "The Colberrans established a foothold."

"They succeeded? How?"

"Their success remains to be seen," he said, grimacing. "For now, they built a bridge."

I looked at the other Nomads, "Will the other clans help?"

"Yes," he said, leading me to a lift. "But they need convincing to move before they reinforce their position."

The female turned down the hall as we boarded the lift. Once inside, I leaned near him. "Are you still hoping to, you know, get help?"

"It may be the only way to end this war," he said, jaw tight.

"Short of winning it?"

He looked at me. "Does anyone ever really win a war?"

"He said that first," I noted.

"The words stuck with me," Micaela said.

"Clearly." I scanned over the notes. "Am I going to get an explanation on how you got to the Shattered Citadel? You know, out of the Maelstrom?"

"The mount's protective shielding saved us, despite the damage it took. Suyef came to first and used the damaged machine to get us to the citadel."

"You were that close?" I asked.

Micaela shook her head. "Not when that happened, but Suyef said the shifting ground moved us closer when it threw us. Still, he said I was unconscious for several hours of travel."

"And then, upon waking, straight to the council?"

She nodded. "Barely an hour after I awoke."

"So, what'd they say?"

"The same thing most politicians say."

I arched an eyebrow, awaiting some quip. Micaela looked out the window for a moment.

"Nothing helpful."

"It's hard to want to hear what comes next with lines like that," I said.

Micaela smiled. "True, but they gave us one thing."

I waited, staring at her.

"Permission."

"When questioned, be truthful and open," he said. "About everything."

Before I could respond, he stepped from the lift. A Nomad waited for us in front of a set of large doors. He held up a hydration pack and a medicine injector.

"For your headache," he said.

I heard the injector's trigger when pressed against my arm, sending relief into my bloodstream. Nodding my thanks to the Nomad, I consumed the fluid before looking at Suyef.

"Ready," I muttered, grimacing.

The room beyond seemed out of place. Every wall bore rich, colorful curtains, giving off a warm, royal feel. A sweet-smelling smoke filled the air, and pillows adorned the floor. Overhead, orange and yellow sheers dimmed the lighting, casting shadows around the room's edge. Several Nomads sat in a semicircle on thick pillows around the room, faces shrouded in the dim light.

My heart pounded in my chest, the throbbing exacerbating my fading headache. Goose bumps crawled up my legs when those eyes turned to me. Twenty-one Nomads awaited us, heads close in discussion. Ten sat to each side and one sat across from the door. Most quieted when we entered. A few grasped something long in their hands, holding them near their shadowed faces. Puffs of smoke rose from their heads, adding to the room's haze. Suyef motioned me to him, then addressed the Nomad facing us.

"Chieftain, I bring a witness to corroborate my account," he said, then he looked at me. "Tell them of the invasion."

"All of it?"

"Leave nothing out."

As the entire room focused on me and a feeling of loneliness crept into my gut, Suyef lightly tapped my arm. When I looked at him, he smiled and nodded. I opened my mouth to thank him but didn't. Instead, I told them what happened, of our mad race from Colberra in pursuit of Quentin and watching the outpost fall with him on it. I told them about the invasion and of ships falling from the sky. Of the Maelstrom, of it swallowing us whole and spitting us out on the other end. No one stopped me or interrupted me to ask questions. Hardly anyone moved, save to inhale and puff out smoke. I've never addressed a more attentive audience.

When I finally finished, a great weight lifted from me, a burden I hadn't realized I had carried since I'd met the Nomad. Suyef tapped my arm again before facing the council.

"Her account matches my own and the reports you received."

The Chieftain leaned forward.

"Someone could have coached this Colberran well."

Suyef pointed at a padd set on the ground before the man.

"That proves she is not."

"You were recording me?" I hissed, leaning toward him.

"Standard protocol." He nodded at the council. "I make the accounts to the network so they don't have to. It is imperative that someone enter an account for the records."

"What if you aren't able to?" I asked.

"I am not the only one," he said, then addressed the council. "She is a witness to the invasion."

Another Nomad leaned forward.

"We do not question your account's integrity," a rough, raspy female voice said, head turning from me to Suyef. "Merely the motivation of some present."

"She has no reason to lie or trick you," my companion said. "She only came here at my bidding."

"It is not *her* motivation that I question," the woman said, turning toward the Chieftain and pointing at Suyef. "We all know of this one and his quest for revenge. Now it has brought war to our doorstep. I think we should stop indulging him."

"My search did not cause this invasion," Suyef said, his voice tight. "You all know the particular Questioner who did that."

"And what drew his attention? Did you avoid him? Avoid giving him cause for this cowardly attack?"

"You read my report," Suyef said, holding his ground. "Our encounter with him was random. We separated ourselves from him as quickly as we could without raising suspicions."

"Yet you purposely involved yourself with this one." She pointed at me. "Knowing he sought her."

He shrugged. "She presented a unique opportunity to find the answers you sent us to get."

"Did you find them?" asked another female sitting to my left.

"We don't know. I've yet to fully explore her family's connection to the network," Suyef said, pointing at me. "She, in particular, possesses unique coding skills." He looked back at the Chieftain. "That alone warranted further study. So, I helped her, in part, to keep her away from the Questioner."

"That was your only motivation?" the second woman asked.

Suyef hesitated before answering. "To help us and to stall the Colberrans, yes."

I looked at him, pondering the question.

"And bring war to our people," the first woman stated. "Brash decisions we paid for with Nomad lives."

The Chieftain's head turned toward the woman. "An invasion of this magnitude required much planning. Suyef may have merely sent sparks onto bonfires of war already in place."

"A paltry excuse, and the Colberrans' preexisting plans do not absolve him." She leveled a finger at me. "We already knew they planned for an attack. Was he not informed of this before he left?"

Suyef shook his head.

"I was told of their expanding fleet numbers, but nothing that showed an imminent invasion."

"As the only shell in striking distance," she retorted, "for whom did you think they built such a fleet?"

Suyef opened his mouth, but the Chieftain cut him off.

"We are not debating the policy or military decisions of a dishonorable people," he said, looking around the room. "We must decide what to do from this point forward." He pointed at me. "And one citizen does not an entire civilization represent. Particularly one that sided against her own people."

"She hardly had a choice in that," the woman said.

"That is immaterial to this meeting," the Chieftain said, voice heated. "Do you wish to call for an inquiry, Ellis?"

The woman looked at me, then shook her head.

"Then let us move on to the reason I convened the council."

"Remember," he whispered to me, leaning close.

"I never lie."

He nodded at the council. "Make sure they know that."

"And if they ask about your real motivations?"

He smiled. "Tell them."

"Won't they see it as a waste of time?"

"They will not agree if they know they are being deceived." He nodded at the belligerent councilwoman. "True feelings are more persuasive."

"I doubt anything I say will help."

"Saying nothing would be worse," he cautioned, turning to the Chieftain and clearing his throat.

"You have something to say, Suyef?"

"We request access to the Sunken Citadel, Elder."

Every member of the council moved. Some looked at the Chieftain, others leaned toward each other to murmur. The belligerent member, Ellis, I noticed, remained still, eyes on my companion

"I don't think they like that."

"It is an uncommon request," Suyef said. "The council strictly controls access to both citadels."

I watched the agitated people around me. "Why?"

"The first actual record in our history is an oath. We follow it as religiously as your people do the government's dictates."

"What oath?"

"One that we reveal when we choose," the Chieftain stated, silencing the room. "For now, know that we have our reasons." He looked at Suyef. "Why do you wish to break our most sacred of rules?"

"It's a tradition, not a rule," another female elder said.

"Traditions exist for a reason," a male replied this time. "We all know the reason for our adherence."

"The directives of old protect us," yet another female elder stated. "We all know the warnings. Our own and those from the past."

I looked at Suyef.

"Are you as lost as I am?"

He shook his head.

"We all learn the warning in childhood."

The Chieftain raised a hand, quieting everyone. He gazed at me for a moment.

"She needs to know," Suyef said quietly.

The elder considered me a moment longer. Then he looked around at the other elders, eyes stopping on a few, including the previously belligerent Ellis. After a moment, he nodded.

"She is your charge, Suyef. If you deem it important, then she will be told."

"I would know his reason," Ellis interjected. "Before we reveal our most guarded secrets to a potential spy."

"A complicated scheme planting her as a spy," one of the other elders said. "Years in the making, with layers of complexity and many parts; many people."

The Chieftain nodded and looked at Ellis.

"Making it that much harder to execute."

"We're talking about Colberrans. Seekers," she said. "Secrets follow them like dust behind a speeder."

"I'm not a Seeker," I said.

Every head turned toward me. Ellis shook her head and leaned to whisper to another elder. The Chieftain glanced at the pair, then back at me.

"You have something to say?"

Suyef nodded at me, and Ellis and her counterpart stopped whispering. At that moment, what I had to say seemed very weak. Still, it needed saying.

"Not all of us revel in secrets."

"Didn't your family conduct your altering education against your government's mandates?" Ellis asked. "She lies to our faces. Points for boldness, I guess."

"I didn't lie. I said not all of us revel in secrets. If you know my family's most *guarded* secret, that proves my point."

Ellis shook her head.

"A dance of words changes nothing. Colberrans are all well-versed in deception."

"You haven't proved me a liar, merely assumed guilt based on prior experience with people who share only my nationality." I looked at the Chieftain. "Yes, my family taught us the code in secret, but we didn't lie about it. No one ever asked." I looked back at Ellis. "Neither did this council. Failing to speak of something does not mean you're lying about it."

Ellis watched me for a moment.

"Let's test your truthfulness. Why do you want to go to the Sunken Citadel?" She nodded at Suyef. "Why do you both want to go?"

I glanced at my companion, who just watched me. I couldn't read his face, but I recalled his warning.

"To get help," I said, looking at the Chieftain.

"From whom?" he asked.

This time I looked at Suyef. This was his to answer, his to defend. He stepped forward, head held high.

"We wish to petition those who gave us the original order to intervene in this war."

Another audible hiss moved through the room, the elders leaning back and forth to speak. The Chieftain remained still, eyes locked on Suyef. After several moments, he raised a hand for silence.

"You know the danger, Suyef. You know what awaits far below."

My companion nodded.

"As does she, perhaps more than anyone here."

"Yes." The Chieftain turned to me. "What do you think of his plan?"

"It has as good a chance of stopping this as it does helping me," I said, glancing down.

"So none," Ellis said. "Even she doubts him."

I looked up at her.

"My doubts have no bearing on his beliefs. He may be right. I don't know."

"But do you have reason to doubt his logic?" the Chieftain asked.

I shrugged.

"As I don't know where we're going, yes. We all doubt the unknown."

"Not all of us," Suyef whispered.

"We can't let her enter the heart of our sacred places," Ellis said. "And we do not need the help of those whose price we are all too familiar with. The Colberrans will fall to our might."

I looked at Suyef, curious what price she meant. Another female elder leaned forward, head turned to Ellis.

"And how many of our sons and daughters would you sacrifice to do so?"

"As many as it takes," she replied. "I don't expect that total to be very high if the Colberrans are as stupid as the lot that chased Suyef into the Maelstrom."

"The mistakes of a few do not mean the rest will do the same," the other female said. "The Colberrans will learn."

"Regardless, I trust our armies over those cursed beasts. They never take an interest in anything beyond what helps them," Ellis went on. "Mark me, if they do come, they could help either side in this war."

"That's the Reds, Ellis," the other female responded. "The Greens—"

"Are more likely *not* to come, Rialla," Ellis cut her off, slicing a hand through the air. "They are even more useless."

"It can't hurt to ask," I said to Suyef.

Every head turned to face me. Clearly, I hadn't been quiet enough.

"You have something to say?" Ellis asked.

I met her gaze with a boldness I didn't feel.

"It can't hurt to ask them," I said again. "Particularly since the Greens are already involved in these events."

Everyone stirred, looking at each other and trading whispers. Suyef leaned closer to me. "I hadn't mentioned the particular shade of dragon that attacked the Seekers yet," he whispered.

"Why not? That's an important detail."

The Chieftain cleared his throat, drawing our eyes. "Please explain."

I pointed at Suyef. "He told you that dragons attacked the Seekers transporting my siblings and me. Those dragons were green. They took my younger brother and most of the Seekers and left me and my brother Donovan behind." I glanced at Suyef. "Well, we *thought* they only left us. Turns out Colvinra escaped, but he might have done that after capture."

"You're sure it was the Greens?" Ellis asked.

"Red and green aren't exactly similar colors."

"Watch your tone in this chamber," she replied.

"Don't insult my intelligence." I looked at the Chieftain. "I apologize for my abruptness. It was Greens that attacked, led by the Dragon Queen herself."

The room stilled at those words. Even Ellis quieted. The Chieftain's head cocked to one side, one hand lifting to his face.

"Are you certain?"

"She was easily twice the size of the next largest."

"Describe her," Ellis said, her voice quiet. "In detail."

"Bright, emerald green like the rest. Besides her size, the bone structure differed from the rest." I waved a hand over the back of my head. "The skeletal protrusions were reddish gold and swept along her back. They actually looked like they merged into the creature's spine. Also, her wings easily doubled the rest."

The Chieftain looked around.

"Her description matches the Queen's."

"Girl, had you ever seen a dragon before that day?" Ellis asked, and I shook my head. "So, it's possible it was just larger than the rest."

"It's possible, but he agreed with me." I pointed at Suyef. "And he saw her in the prison battle."

All heads turned to my companion, who raised his hands to either side.

"Either is possible," he said, bowing his head toward Ellis.

"No one has seen hide or tail of the Queen in over twenty cycles," the Chieftain said. "Until now, there hasn't been even a whisper of her activity. Once, she was ever-present in the world's affairs. Not anymore."

"All the more reason to go ask for help," I said. "Maybe we can find out why she's hiding."

"No one said she's hiding," the Chieftain went on, waving a finger at me. "Merely staying out of our affairs, a contrary behavior to her past actions."

"That doesn't change my statement."

The council fell silent. After several moments, the Chieftain stood.

"All in favor of allowing access, stand. Those against, remain seated."

The entire room stood except for Ellis. When I glanced her way, she shrugged.

"No decision deserves a unanimous vote," she muttered.

The Chieftain turned to her.

"Your opposition is now recorded. Will you acquiesce in the majority vote for unity's sake?"

Ellis held my gaze a moment longer before standing and looking away.

"The vote passes. May your path find much water and your journey be short." The Chieftain raised a single finger. "Remember your original mission, Suyef. Discovering that will help this war as much as getting the help you seek."

After he spoke, the council filed out. Soon we stood alone in the room.

"So, are we on our own?" I asked.

"No. Getting into the citadel requires help."

"Why?"

"Because the citadel doesn't want us to enter it."

CHAPTER 9

SEA

"That seemed too easy," I said, setting my stylus down.

Micaela interlaced her hands and stretched her arms out before her. She didn't respond.

"The decision," I continued. "That seemed too easy. You got precisely what you wanted out of them."

"The elder knew we were right." Micaela dropped her arms and shrugged. "She's an obstinate person by nature, but also very smart."

"Seems a waste of time to me."

"Don't you follow your council's proceedings?"

"Avoid it like the plague," I said, then stopped. "Sorry, didn't think that through before I said it."

She waved a hand at me. "I'd think you would want to keep abreast of your leaders' decisions."

"Even the Queen didn't bother to check in on them for over twenty cycles."

"There were good reasons for remaining aloof, not the least being the inane nature of the council members," Micaela stated. "You go when it matters."

"Precisely why I stay out of it," I said. "Same with that council. Objecting just to object with no real reason to?" I paused, pondering events. "But considering how that war ended, maybe she was right."

Micaela nodded and let out a deep breath. "Sadly, you're correct. How that ended was, in part, the result of what happened next."

"Which was?"

"To start, I nearly drowned."

We left with an escort, the Shattered Citadel's single massive superstructure vanishing into the mountainous desert. That was all I glimpsed of it thanks to our exit via a tunnel system that ran all throughout the mountains surrounding the fortress.

As we traveled, the terrain shifted, tall trees bursting forth in ever-increasing height to smother us in a blanket of leaves. The air remained dry as the sounds of creaking wood filled the night.

Remnants of Ancient technology dotted the land, shadows of the shell's calamity centuries past. A water pipe, tied via cables to the nearby trees. Abandoned control stations, tops ripped off. A water pipe fragment, lying to one side of a station.

My mind wandered, pondering the water, this strange landscape. Thoughts of my family filled my head. Of Quentin, the invasion. The Nomads. Suyef.

He remained the only familiar point. The emotional weight I bore pressed down, tears moistening my cheeks. I wept in silence, grieving for my family, my world lost. Something strong and warm gripped my shoulder. Suyef's hand.

We stopped to rest, and I sat alone, the storm inside me continuing to rage, Suyef standing nearby. I closed my eyes, uncertain I could sleep. I awoke at a touch, Suyef's hand bringing me back from a sleep free of dreams, the first I could remember having in a while.

We rode in silence, shifting back and forth through the dense forest. The air felt heavy, and an unfamiliar smell tickled my nose. Something else, more foreboding, pressed down on me, a shadow beyond that was cast by the leafy cover. My companions, I saw, kept looking back and forth, shifting on their mounts.

The foliage hickened, forcing us to slow to a crawl. The speeder's display showed our destination just ahead, obscured by the leaves. Suddenly, like a blanket ripped from you during sleep, the forest opened, and we shot out into a clearing. I stared in awe at what lay before us.

The Great Sea, a carpet of glistening blue, filled the horizon. Ripples of light danced a mesmerizing pattern on the surface, and a cool breeze kissed my skin. Glancing up, I wondered if the water shield's surface felt like this.

"Is it potable?" I asked.

"No," Suyef said, pointing at some nearby rocks. "Salty."

"Where's the salt coming from?"

"The Sunken Citadel, we surmise. Some think to discourage living here."

"I imagine matter reforgers can clean it. Insert salt water, remove the salt, and take out what's left."

He grunted, lowering the mount to a park.

"And you get reforging materials," I continued. "Ingenious."

"Necessity."

"Same difference."

After I dismounted, he tossed me a bundle. "Go put that on."

Once in the trees, I pulled out the suit. Bright blue, it stuck to my skin like wet fabric. I also found a belt with some pouches, a small light device, and three items made from the same translucent material: goggles that clipped to the bridge of my nose, earplugs, and a mouth guard molded to cover my mouth and nose. It reminded me of one I'd once worn as a child to realign my teeth.

"Must this suit be so tight?" I asked upon my return.

A quick glance at my companion and our escort showed the suits did indeed hide very little.

"Makes for faster and smoother swimming," he said, tossing me a pair of gloves. "Those will seal to your sleeves. That bulge at your neck is a hood. Your face gear will seal to it once they are in place."

"We have to swim there?" I asked. "I don't know how."

Someone snorted nearby, earning a glare from Suyef. He tapped a button on his mount's control panel. Slots opened on both sides and the front. Flat protrusions like wings slid out, joining along the front to form a platform. Everyone followed suit, each pair climbing aboard their transformed mounts.

"We don't have time to teach you," Suyef said, climbing onto his mount. "I'll give you some basics as we move, but we must leave now. Even here, the citadel might notice our presence and act to stop us."

"Why do I feel you don't expect to come back?" I asked as I climbed aboard and sat in front of him.

He looked up from the controls, eyes on the water ahead.

"You expect to?"

"He expected you to learn how to swim just like that?" I asked, stopping Micaela with a raised hand.

"No. The plan was for me to swim with him helping. He taught me what I would need to know to do that."

I looked at her for a moment, pursing my lips. "You trusted him that much?"

"It's not like I had much of a choice, anyway. But yes. I did."

"So, what happened?" I asked, making a note to bring it up later. "Were you able to swim with him?"

Micaela shook her head.

"That would require things going according to plan," she said. "They did not."

We moved out onto the water, core-night arriving soon after. I stared into the liquid substance in awe. The shifting waters danced in the dim light, swirling in a mesmerizing motion. I leaned down and hung a hand out.

"Don't," Suyef whispered.

I looked back at him, sitting at the now-transformed controls. With a twist of his hand, the craft sped up, turning left or right as he pushed his hand in the opposite direction.

"What will happen?"

He said nothing. I looked down at the water. "You act as if it's alive."

"It or something inside it."

He turned the craft a bit to one side. The other craft, formed in a line to either side and slightly behind us, mirrored his move.

"Something or someone?" I asked, looking ahead.

"Does it matter?"

"Probably, yes. An automated process just has to be stopped. We can reason with a person."

"If you can get to the citadel," he replied.

"Someone must have tried. What happened to them?"

He tapped the mouth guard hanging from his belt. "That's why you have this."

"But I thought the equipment was just necessary," I said.

He pointed at the sea, ignoring the look I gave him.

"When we are in the water, you need to be ready. Mouthpiece, goggles, earplugs, hood. In that order. Put your gloves on now."

I pulled the latter item on and watched them attach to my sleeves.

"Just like that," he said, locking the control in a set direction before lying down on the floor. "To swim, swing your arms like this and kick your legs behind you like so."

He reached out toward me, palms out, then swung his arms in an arc down to his side, bringing them back up above his head as he kicked his legs out and behind him.

"Keep your face forward," he said, returning to the controls. "Twist your body the way you want to go. Use your arms to help guide and your legs to move."

"Which way?"

"Down," he said. "Or, if you see a light below the surface, toward it. If you see a light above the surface, get away from it."

I imitated the arm motion.

"Like that?" I asked.

He didn't answer, eyes looking beyond me. Ahead, a thick fog boiled up along the surface, swallowing the horizon.

"It begins," Suyef whispered.

The Nomads slowed to a crawl as the fog loomed overhead. As I glanced back at my companion, the dim night vanished in a swirl of gray haze. Even Suyef, visible in the control lights he now leaned over, appeared fuzzy around the edges. Time slowed, the shifting water the only sound I could make out save for my breathing and heartbeat.

With the breeze gone, the only sign we still moved lay in my companion steering our craft. Turning to ask him how far out into the water the Sunken Citadel lay entombed, I paused. He moved back and forth around the control stick, head craning and eyes squinting as he looked into the thick haze.

"Suyef?" I whispered, drawing his gaze. "What's wrong?"

He shook his head. "I don't know."

That gave me pause. My limited experience had shown me that Nomads pride themselves on knowing what's going on, on presenting an air of control. Hearing him admit he didn't know what was going on set my heart pounding.

"Are you trying to see the others?" I asked.

He held up a finger to silence me, then pointed beyond me. "She's out there. Waiting."

"You speak of the citadel like it's a person."

He nodded. "This one acts like one. One that's been alone for centuries."

"How does she know we are coming?" I asked, looking down. "Oh, the gravity beams."

"Yes. She can sense vibrations in the water. Like I said, isolated for a very long time." He looked at me. "And she likes it."

Something shifted in the fog beyond his head. My hand darted up as his head spun around.

"What was it?" I hissed.

Suyef moved the control stick, and the transformed mount turned hard to the right toward the craft on that side, forcing me to grip the craft's side to stay upright. We traveled for a few moments, but found nothing.

"Shouldn't they be here?" I asked.

"We spread out on purpose. Eventually, we might come across them."

"Can't you see them on the control panel?"

"No, we turned off everything but the essentials. We don't know if she can track us using those."

"If she can detect ripples from your gravity beams, I don't think signals between mounts are going to make much difference."

He shrugged. "That's the plan. It's always been the plan. Spread out and stay above the water as long as possible."

Frowning, I looked back out into the fog, watching for the other hovercraft.

"Why leave yourselves so vulnerable? Why not group up? Defend yourselves?"

He chuckled. "You speak like we have a chance of doing so."

"Don't we?"

"No, and that's the point."

The strategy made little sense to me. I stared into the fog, then looked back at him.

"You're hoping the citadel attacks, aren't you?" I asked.

Before he could answer, she did.

I held up a hand to stop Micaela.

"They did it on purpose?" I asked.

"They hoped multiple targets would increase the odds one might get through."

"But what about the others?"

She shrugged. "Had I known in advance, I would have protested. As it was, I didn't have that chance."

I pursed my lips, staring at her. "You referred to the citadel as *she*."

"Then, I didn't. Now, I know better."

She fell silent. I waited for her to continue, but she didn't.

"So, she attacked," I went on. "Then what happened?"

She looked at me but remained quiet. I recalled her words. "You nearly drowned."

The attack came so fast. As we drifted, something rose from the water, just barely visible in the fog. Something long and thin, jointed in multiple places like an appendage and quick. The fog hid much, but not the moment it struck.

The sound of ripping metal and a distant cry of alarm tore through the air. Suyef twisted the control, and we shot forward, just dodging away from a strike. Water splashed down around us, and something thumped against our craft. I turned to see a Nomad grasping the side. Before I could lunge for him, he slipped, vanishing into the water and fog.

"Don't lean over the edge," Suyef hissed.

The craft pitched as he flung the control in the other direction, throwing me against the sidewall. Nearby, I heard the distinct sound of crunching metal. Pieces of a doomed craft splashed down around us, and I saw a body fly past. Suyef turned our craft away from every splash, every craft struck, every cry from a fellow Nomad. We sped up, then slowed, turned this way and that. I crouched low, arms out to either side, gripping the side rails. Water splashed all around us, plastering my hair to my face.

"Suyef!" I called out. "Where are we going?"

He never answered. At that instant, one appendage found us.

The deck pitched upward, flinging me high into the darkness. I flipped end over end before falling down into the water. The impact knocked all the air from my lungs as the water swallowed me. A burning sensation stung my eyes, forcing me to squeeze them shut. I grasped at my belt, tugging the mouth guard free and forcing it into my mouth. Fresh air rushed into my lungs, the burning stitch in my side dissipating. I clipped my goggles to my nose, the water draining away once they sealed in place. My eyes still burned, but at least I could see.

Not that I could see much. If the fog had been a dimly lit soup, this was a blinding stew. My hair swirled around my head, but I only felt that. The only source of light came from a dull glow above that faded as pressure built up on my body. An icy dread completely unrelated to the freezing water gripped my heart. I was sinking.

I tried to kick and move my arms like Suyef had shown me, with no obvious sign of success. Soon, I tired as the light faded to almost nothing. I stilled, conserving energy. It was then that I noticed the pressure increasing. Water swirled past me from foot to head. I was sinking.

I remembered the light attached to my belt and reached for it. The clip was empty. I checked the belt's two pockets and found only the earplugs, which I donned. I struggled against the water, trying to mimic what Suyef had told me.

The last of the light faded, and darkness swallowed me. I was alone. Lost.

And certain I would die that way.

CHAPTER 10

SUNKEN

"I can't even imagine what that must feel like," I said, setting my stylus down. "I've seen the Great Sea. Truly impressive. But to be in it like that."

I stared at her for a moment before shaking my head. "You must have felt . . ."

"Doomed? Alone? Like I was falling into oblivion?"

"Sure. Any of those. Like I said. Unimaginable."

Micaela nodded. "Everything feels so slow. And moving takes so much effort."

"What happened to Suyef?" I asked. "And the other Nomads? Did they end up in the water like you?"

"I'm not entirely sure what happened to them. I presume they made it out safely." She took a slow breath. "It's been so long now, I can't remember."

"So you didn't see them underwater?"

She looked at me.

"At first, I saw nothing."

The light faded, like echoes of music leaving my ears, leaving just the sound and feel of the water. The darkness, the isolation, reminded me of a night when our settlement lost power. My infant sister woke me with a cry, and I fumbled around in complete blackness, trying the shutter controls before stumbling to the door. I tried to pry it open with my fingers, panic gripping my heart. Then the door shifted and my father's hands appeared above mine. We pushed it open, and the feeling passed.

Vaguely, I wondered if anyone would come for me, if Suyef would find me. If his hands would grip mine as my father's had, pulling me out of this dark world. I shook my head. I hadn't waited for the door to open, to be rescued. I wouldn't now.

The freezing waters reminded me of the hood tucked behind my neck. I tugged it up over my head with fingers I could barely feel and pressed it against my face gear. A moment later, the gear sealed to the hood, pushing the water back. I flexed my hands, trying to work feeling back into them and getting my bearings. Using the blood rushing to my head as judge for up versus down, I tried to imitate Suyef's swim motion. I'm not sure I accomplished more than keeping blood flowing to my extremities.

As I struggled, something shifted ahead of me and I realized I could see my arms. The blackness, still heavy, was receding. Far above me, still very dim, a single light appeared. Suyef's warning came to mind: swim away from lights above the surface. But was it above the water or in it?

Despite his warning, I wanted nothing more than to reach it, to stay near it so I could see. I kicked, trying to get closer, but it seemed so far away. My legs were so heavy, my arms so hard to move.

The light brightened and became more focused: a small circular shape bobbing back and forth in a rhythmic pattern. Had

Suyef found me? If so, how was he doing it? Or was it really him? Could the citadel have found me? Suyef said it tracked vibrations in the water. Should I hold still? Wasn't sinking a motion?

The light came closer and closer. It wasn't big, getting smaller the closer it came to me. Or was it moving away? It was hard to judge distance, but the receding darkness had to mean it was coming at me. A sense of dread built up inside, accompanied by panic. The light was coming right in my direction. It had to be the citadel. What else could have found me?

I gyrated my body, swinging wildly to get away. The darkness continued to recede. The light was gaining on me. I pushed and kicked even harder, the coldness long forgotten in the frantic effort to flee. I could see my hands clearly now, bubbles swishing past as my limbs thrashed. Still, the light came. I blinked. Had I seen something ahead of me? Was it the arm that attacked us?

That gave me pause, and my motion slowed.

Then the light caught me.

"Why did you assume the light was dangerous?" I asked, tapping my notes. "He'd told you to go toward the light."

"You know the answer to that question."

I paused, looking up at her. "Why would I know?"

"Because you've experienced that feeling before," she said.

I watched her, pondering what she wasn't telling me. What knowledge she was keeping.

"Panic," I finally said.

She simply sat there, eyes never leaving my own. I looked away, taking a deep breath, and went on.

"When it strikes, you see yourself doing it. You can see the entire picture, what you need to do. You want to do it, but something grabs hold of your heart."

Still, she sat there, watching. Listening.

"Something cold. It grips you hard and doesn't let go. You want to move forward. Or backward. Or you want to freeze." I looked at my hands. "Anything but what you are doing."

"Exactly."

I looked up at her, pondering her knowledge of me. Of her familiarity with me. What else did she know? Why did she know it? Why wouldn't I just ask her? What was I afraid to know?

My fingers picked at the stylus, rolling it across my notes. Micaela just sat there, watching.

"So, the light caught up to you."

"Yes, but that wasn't the worst of it," she said, looking away. "Not by a long shot."

"What could be worse than being chased while sinking to your death?"

She chuckled, a nearly imperceptible sound. "Something catching you."

Few things in life are as terrifying as having your throat constricted. Sinking was scary, but it felt more isolating because of my breather. That all changed when something grabbed my throat.

The instant I felt pressure, my hands shot up. It was solid, holding against my grip. My skin tingled, and a surge of strength only adrenaline can provide coursed through me. I clawed against my assailant, bending the appendage backward. Only then did I feel the bone structure. Using my hold, I twisted around, momentarily blinded by the light. The source of illumination shifted down, revealing my attacker. Suyef.

Joy raced through me as I pulled him close, gripping onto him, to the solidity and safety he offered. The presence. After too short of a moment, he shifted, finger pointed to one side. He pulled me to his side, slipped an arm around my back, and handed me the light. Then he began kicking and swimming with his free arm. Together, we moved through the water. I held the light in front and kicked my legs with him.

We swam on, but the light revealed little. Just when I began wondering if the vast emptiness would never end, something shifted ahead. I thought my eyes were playing tricks on me, but the light soon revealed they were not.

Objects loomed overhead, reflecting the light at us. More appeared below us, and I looked around for defenses. Nothing moved, however; the citadel appeared not to notice us. That or it didn't care we were there. After all, it could attack us at any moment, and we'd be helpless. That thought left a very nasty feeling in my gut.

After several more minutes of swimming, we neared a flat surface: a walkway. To either side, tall pillars lined the path, reaching up like skeletal fingers trying to grab us. Smaller structures stood below this walkway, domed roofs just cresting the platform's level. The farther we went along the path, the larger the structures we saw. Soon, they dwarfed the pillars.

Suyef pointed ahead, and I shone the light forward. Another flat surface perpendicular to the path reflected the light back at us. Twice my height and as wide as the platform, the door looked like it stood alone, blocking the path. Then I spied a smaller, brighter reflective surface on one side of the door: a control panel. Suyef guided us down toward it, revealing the darker walls that held the door and panel. The latter jutted out enough to grab and hold against the flow of water. Suyef pushed the panel with his open palms, and it flickered twice before lighting up, revealing symbols across the screen.

I leaned to see a sequence of unstacked and jumbled code symbols shifting in a random pattern. I touched one, but nothing happened. Suyef took a hold of my hand and pressed my finger against the panel. The screen compressed, and I felt a slight click. The symbol, still moving on the screen, jumped back to my finger and held its place. When I let go, it resumed its motion. I scanned the rest for something familiar, but none were quite a match. I looked at the Nomad and shook my head. He nodded, waving a hand at the panel and then at the door. I shrugged. He held his hands up, outer edges pressed together, and slid them open, nodding at the door. I held out my hands to either side, shaking my head again.

For a moment, we floated there, the light in my hand casting our shadows back along the path. Then he leaned in toward the panel. I gripped the panel's bottom edge, pushing down to settle my feet on the platform and remain in place. He tapped on the panel twice, shaking his head. He moved the symbols around, forming a few different columns, but nothing happened. After a few tries, I grabbed his shoulder, drawing his attention. I pointed at the door, then held up both hands. With one, I formed a hole with my fingers; held out two fingers pressed together with the other and inserted them into the hole.

He nodded and turned back to the panel, shifting symbols this way and that. The doors remained sealed, and he glanced at me, shrugging. I was looking around, at a loss, when I felt his body jolt. He shifted forward, and I leaned over to examine the panel. I felt a jolt of my own.

The symbols had changed.

"Wait, they changed? How?"

"One moment, they were unreadable," Micaela said. "The next, I could read them."

"Oh, the display used the other code language."

She nodded.

"I didn't know that. Only Suyef could read it initially."

"Why do you think it changed?"

I waited for a moment. When she remained silent, I stood up. "Care for a glass of water?" I asked, moving toward the kitchen.

"Please."

I filled a pair of clear glasses, watching her. She sat, eyes staring out the window. She didn't move as I approached.

"You look outside a lot, High One," I said, stopping and holding out a glass.

"It's soothing," she murmured, taking it and sipping some water.

I sat down, glancing at the window. "Why is it relaxing?"

"Out there, it's simple," she said. "The world works the way it does. It doesn't change. Well, unless we mess it up."

I sipped my water and stared at the sky. "Regardless, it's simple. You can rely on it. Shells orbit. Citadels provide water. People live. People die."

Her head turned, drawing my gaze. "Stability is underappreciated."

"This shell has that," I said, sipping my water. "The same queen for centuries, for example."

"Yes, but even she left you. For twenty cycles, if memory serves."

I shrugged. "That was before. She's here now."

"Yes," Micaela whispered. "Yes, she is."

She sipped her water, eyes turning back to the window. She chuckled, her body barely shifting. "All things change, eventually. Even this calm, predictable world is changing."

I waved at the window. "You mean the shell once visible there? You can still see it if you're at the window."

"It's falling out of orbit because this shell is moving. In a few months, that shell will break free and fall down into the core."

I nodded, watching her. "Time is against us."

She didn't respond.

"I assume the Queen's mission has to do with what is happening out there, yes?"

"Everything is connected, it seems." She looked at me. "Even you."

After a moment of silence, Micaela stood up and raised her glass. "Thank you," she said, moving toward the far door. "I need some rest."

"High One, if I may, what's beyond that door right there?"

"Nothing of consequence," she said, pausing at it and looking back.

"Then why do you hide there?"

"We all need a place of solitude, Logwyn. Don't confuse that with hiding."

The next day, I arrived to find Micaela standing in the far door, head turned away from me. Just beyond her, I glimpsed part of a cloak.

A silver one like the one on the table.

I opened my mouth to speak, but Micaela looked over at me, stopping me in my tracks. The cloak vanished as the door closed.

"Did I interrupt something?" I asked.

"No." Her voice seemed tight. She clenched her jaw, and her clasped hands were white from her grip.

"Is something wrong, High One?"

Her eyes shot up, nostrils flaring at me. "Besides you insisting on using that moniker?"

"Apologies, Micaela," I said, bowing my head.

She looked away, and my eyes darted toward the door. I ventured a guess on the wearer of the cloak I'd seen briefly. "Why was Suyef here?"

"I told him you'd figure it out if he didn't leave." She chuckled. "Just a check in. See how we're doing. Tell me about some other things." She arched an eyebrow at me. "He has a vested interest in your work."

"Why does he care so much about my work?"

She moved toward the window as I sat down. "Maybe he doesn't. Maybe he's only interested in you. Or maybe he thinks it will help me."

I contemplated her words. "Help you with what?"

She placed a hand on the window, then turned to look at the wall of images. When she spoke, I almost couldn't hear her.

"Healing."

CHAPTER 11

ENTOMBED

Suyef waved me toward the screen. The floating symbols made sense now: a simple open command with some very intricate symbols for the door and its internal mechanisms. The sentence structure appeared identical: primary noun at the base, ascending up to the secondary and tertiary nouns. This structure only had one noun, which should have simplified the column. Still, it took me a few attempts to complete the column, opening the doors just a crack.

Suyef grabbed one door's edge. I grabbed his other arm, and he pulled us inside. My head bumped the doorframe, and the closing doors hit my feet. Next, the water shifted, swirling down until my head emerged near the ceiling. Suyef pulled his breather out and twisted it to release, then tested the air before nodding. The device tugged at my face before the locking mechanism disengaged with a pop. Goose bumps sprouted on my face as I sniffed the stale air.

"Oh, it's cold," I said, floating down as the water drained out. "No heating?"

"Maybe. Or it just takes too much energy to heat every compartment and room at this depth."

"Ye-yeah, probab-bly true."

I wrapped my arms around my torso, rubbed my hands against my arms, and kicked my legs to keep the blood flowing.

"I thought this suit would keep me warm."

"It does," he said, moving toward the far wall.

Flexing my fingers, the joints aching, I shook my head.

"And I'm still freezing," I said, voice shaking. "Is that another door?"

I moved closer to the far wall. Suyef ran his hand down an identical split in the wall.

"So, this chamber keeps the water from getting inside," I said. "A water release room?"

"Maybe," he said, nodding.

A smooth, solid surface met my foot as the room continued to drain. Strands of my hair wrapped around my face, the rest sticking to my back. A vicious shiver tore through me, and Suyef shook his head. He moved close and wrapped his arm around me.

"I hope it's warmer on the other side of that door," I whispered.

Behind us, the water finished draining. A soft click preceded the hiss of some machinery coming to life. A light flickered on overhead, and the interior door slid open to reveal a long hallway, more lights blinking on in a receding wave.

"Have you ever seen Ancient lights do that?" I asked.

"No. But I've also never been in a building underwater, Ancient or not. Maybe it's normal here."

"What now?" I asked. "Control center?"

"Yep," he said, pointing up. "Unless something destroyed it, it's at the top of the central structure."

"Where are we?"

"I don't know. Assume the bottom and hope we get there sooner."

"How tall is this place?" I asked, looking down a side hall.

"Citadels are all identical," he said, continuing on the same path. "With one exception, or so our records tell us."

"For'a Dal," I said, my eyes roaming around.

"More forbidden information your father shared with you?"

"My mother, actually."

He stopped at another intersection and stared at the wall.

"The control citadel was larger than the others."

I joined him and stared at a column of symbols just before the wall ended.

"Location marker?" I asked, brushing the markings with my fingers.

"Yes," he said, pointing at the base symbol. "This . . ."

"This tells us which superstructure this is." I pointed at the symbol above it. "The floor. The next one is the floor's quadrant. And the top one is the junction or intersection."

I pointed back toward our entrance. "There was another one on the doors, but it had another symbol. Room number?"

"Correct," he said. "And the junction or intersection symbol shows which one is nearest."

"We're halfway up, if I'm reading this right." I peered closer. "Primary structure."

He nodded, pointing back down our hallway. "That came from another superstructure."

The size of the citadel gave me pause. "This sea of yours is massive to hold this thing."

"This isn't even the deepest part," Suyef said, moving on. "The central shaft is this way."

As I hurried to catch up, something dawned on me. "Wait, we both could read those."

My companion grunted.

"But you can read the symbols from my shell. So, how did symbols from my shell end up in this citadel?"

"Were they easy to read?"

I thought about it. "Actually, no. It took a moment."

He continued walking as I thought about it.

"So, we were reading the actual Ancient symbols?" I asked.

"Eliminate the impossibilities and the truth will remain."

A pleasant feeling warmed me inside. "My father used to say something similar. Said he read it in a novel once."

"I don't remember where I learned it. Maybe a book. Or someone said it. Still applies."

He peered at more symbols. I examined the markings more intently this time. The differences were subtle but still there. Shifts in lines, an unexpected wide curve, a flourish or two. Just enough to make it a challenge to read.

"It's that way, yes?" I asked, pointing.

Suyef nodded, and we moved toward a set of closed doors. They slid open at our approach, revealing a platform extending into an open expanse. Rails lined the pathway's edge and, as I passed through the doorway, I saw more platforms crossing the open space.

"Nearly halfway," he muttered, pointing down at even more walkways.

"Who builds such a tall, open place like this inside their facility and then fills it with walkways?" I asked. "It's a waste of space, not to mention hazardous."

"At least they put in railings," Suyef said, looking behind us.

A smaller platform jutted out to one side of the door, accessible through a small gate in the railing.

"What's that?" I asked as we moved nearer.

Suyef pointed at symbols on the wall.

"A lift."

"How do we use it?"

He touched the gate, and it swung open. We stepped onto the lift, and the gate closed behind us just as the lift rose straight up along the wall. Once higher than the door, it glided up along the wall at a diagonal angle.

"I guess it has a preprogrammed destination," Suyef said, looking around the open space.

"Up, at least," I said.

"Yes, toward the control room, and maybe the communications controls."

"But you don't know for sure."

"I've never been in the Shattered Citadel's control room," he said. "But it makes the most sense."

"I don't disagree with you," I said, looking at the walkways we passed. "But there's no guarantee we'll be able to use it, let alone find anyone willing to listen."

"Or be in range to do so," he added. "All valid points. But we can still try."

I looked toward the citadel's top. "If this place doesn't want us here, why do you think it will cooperate with us?"

"I don't. But someone let us in."

"*Let us in* is generous," I said. "We don't know why that happened. It could still be a trap." I pointed up. "An elaborate one designed to bait us into going to the control room."

"Also possible." He leaned back from the rail, eyes locked on something above us. "It's a chance we have to take."

"Do we?" I followed his gaze. "What are you watching?"

"Our destination."

"Wait, the first lift took you directly to the control room?" I asked, holding up a hand to stop Micaela.

She chuckled. "No, we rode several and crossed several walkways before we reached the top."

"So, he was just looking ahead?"

"No, he was watching the next platform," she said. "You should know by now that Suyef stays focused on the next step."

I shrugged, staring down at my notes. "Just seemed very convenient for you. Like someone was giving you exactly what you needed at each turn."

"Don't assume someone wasn't doing that."

I paused and looked up at her. "Someone was helping you?"

"It wouldn't be the first time."

She watched me. I said nothing.

"Already forgotten the bit of timely help given us when darkness swallowed us?"

"No, I remember. The voice from the panel. Your face." I tapped my stylus on my notes. "You never explained why you were talking to yourself."

"Because, at that point, I didn't know what was actually going on."

I brushed a strand of hair from my face.

"And do you now?"

"Mostly."

"And you will not tell me."

"You wouldn't believe me if I did."

"Try me."

Her blue-green eyes stared at me, eyebrows furrowing, hands clasped on her lap. Then she shook her head. "What I can tell you is it wasn't me. I'm not nearly as cruel as her."

"Cruel?" I asked. "She was helping you."

"If there's one thing I can say about the person on the other side of that screen, it's that she does nothing that does not benefit herself."

She locked gazes with me.

"Nothing."

I made a note to come back to that topic.

"So, why help you this time?" I asked.

Her jaw tightened.

"As I told Suyef, it was a trap."

"This is a trap," I said as we exited the lift.

"It was easy," Suyef said, nodding. "Even with the swim."

"No, that was hard," I said. "But what kind of defense doesn't even go after us in the water? We were most vulnerable then."

"No one else made it down," Suyef said, looking back at the now-closed lift doors. "Maybe it didn't want them coming with us."

I took a few deep breaths, stilling the voice in my head screaming to run and calming my racing heart. "I'm trusting you won't intentionally put us in danger."

He grunted and stepped across the platform where two closed doors stood, blocking our way to what I assumed was the citadel's control room. Suyef approached the doors, and I grabbed his arm. "Are we sure we know what we're doing?"

"No, but we have little choice."

He nodded at the room before moving toward the entry, which opened to reveal a large, well-lit space. Warm air rushed out, soothing my chilled skin. Suyef stopped in the doorway and looked around.

"The lights aren't flickering," I said. "No power issues here, apparently."

A platform similar to Nidfar's dominated the center of the room. Opposite the entrance stood a wall of windows looking out into the dark water. A ring of unfamiliar network stations lay around the edge of the room, just under the windows. I moved into the space, examining the stations. Each station possessed a different interface: multiple small screens, keypads, a set of spectacles with ear inserts and curved glass lenses.

"This place is clean," I whispered, running a finger along a pristine surface. "Look at these. So old."

I leaned over the spectacles.

"I haven't seen a set of these outside of a museum holo."

"Remember where you are."

I looked over my shoulder to see him staring at the platform. "That's your way down, isn't it?"

"My way down?"

I nodded, standing and waving at the interfaces. "In case you can't communicate from here. You're thinking of using that to go down to the dragons to get help."

"The thought had occurred to me."

"You expect me to believe you didn't know it was here?"

"I suspected," he said. "But I didn't know for sure."

"If we can't communicate, what makes you think that will work?" I asked. "A carrier wave has a longer reach."

"Under normal circumstances, yes. But this is an Ancient citadel. The rules are different here."

"Physics is constant," I said, picking up the spectacles. "Well, if this is a trap, let's spring it. If memory serves, this creates a virtual interface."

Donning the spectacles, I felt them shift and the inserts go into my ears.

"That's a strange feeling."

"What is?" he asked.

"They automatically adjusted to fit my head." I looked around for an activation switch or node. "They're not turning on, however."

My companion leaned over the station and pressed a hand to a panel. He stood there for a moment, then shook his head.

"Everything is on," I said, moving toward another station. "The stations aren't responding."

A flashing light appeared just before my left eye.

"Wait. Something's happening."

Suyef spun away, his staff unfolding into his hand.

"No, no, here." I pointed at my face. "I see a flashing light."

The Nomad didn't move. The light blinked again, then scrolled up the glass, a column of code following in its wake. It shifted, building a connecting symbol before starting a new column. Other lights appeared across my vision, building column after column.

"Script columns," I whispered. "Activation structures, power up signals. I think everything is turning on."

"Do you know which interface is what?" he asked, tucking his staff away.

I moved, looking at other stations. The columns shifted and highlighted different structures. "Power flow and climate," I said, pointing at two stations behind him. "Here. Communications."

Suyef moved close to the station nearest me. I approached the panel, and it turned on. The glasses cleared and a series of status displays appeared. The screen mirrored the device.

"Backlit, touch screen displays," I whispered. "I've never seen a working one before."

"Can you bring up the array?"

I looked at the interface before my eyes.

"The array is online. Power's good. But nothing is being sent," I said, glancing up at him. "No carrier waves. No emissions. Nothing. The power is going to the array, but it's dissipating. I'm not sure where or why."

"Show me," he asked, pointing at the panel.

The display shifted when I looked back down.

"Is the power dissipating at the array?" he asked. "Or before it gets there?"

"Who knows? The diagnostics all say everything is working." I tapped the display and the transmission controls appeared. "But a test signal doesn't transmit."

"How are you able to just bring up the right control on the right panel?"

I tapped the edge of the spectacles. "When I focus on a panel, I see the data and interface options before my hand gets to the glass."

"Convenient," he whispered, looking at the platform behind me.

"If we can't send a signal, how do you expect to get that working?"

"Because it's a different system," he said. "The citadels keep tight control on intershell communications. Even Nidfar hadn't managed it, but his platform still worked."

"That's still a much shorter distance to travel." I pointed down. "Those shells are much farther away. By several orders of magnitude."

He frowned at me. "Is that the correct usage of that phrase?"

"What?"

"Order of magnitude. Are you using that correctly?"

"The point is the distance between your shell and the deep core shells is easily a hundred times the distance between our shells."

When he opened his mouth, I cut him off. "We don't have time to argue the math. You get the point."

He bowed his head, hiding what looked like a smirk as he moved toward the platform. "Can you activate it?"

"Probably, but what's the point?"

"To get help."

"You don't even know where you're going."

"We have to try."

"And what if they aren't there?" I asked, waving at the floor. "Or worse, they are there, but they don't want to be disturbed."

My companion stiffened visibly.

"The Greens have a very well-defined sense of decorum. Even if disturbed, they will treat us warmly."

"You say this from experience?"

"No, from our archives."

"And nothing has changed since then?" I retorted, ignoring the dancing symbols shifting quickly across my vision.

"They always treated us well in the past."

"Suyef, I'm not trying to be difficult here." I touched his shoulder, drawing his eyes to my own. "Please, listen to me. This just feels off. This whole thing." I let my hand fall. "If you recall, I said something felt off before we left Nidfar's tower in the Wilds and look how that turned out."

A tight, twisting feeling gripped at my gut when he glanced at me, and I felt my face redden. "I'm sorry. That was too far."

Before I could say more, something beeped in my ear. The symbols all blinked, shifted into a new configuration, blinked again, then vanished. For a moment, nothing happened.

A soft hum filled the room as the platform began to glow and spin open from the center. Another ring, identical to Nidfar's, appeared and hung suspended, parallel to the elevated surface. A line of light traced down one side, and, with a resounding pop, the ring slid open. A set of stairs rose from the floor, leading up to the platform.

"You?" Suyef asked.

"Not intentionally." I tapped the side of the spectacles. "It's possible your proximity activated it."

Suyef looked at the ring, then rushed up onto the platform

"What are you doing?" I hissed, trying to grab his arm. "You don't know where it goes."

"Time to find out," he said, holding a hand out to me. "Coming?"

With a scowl, I tried to pull him down. "No, and neither are you."

With a nod and a tug, he pulled me up with him. My momentum carried me into him, and I hoped we might fall off the other side. He stood like a pillar, his arms wrapping around me.

Before I could move, the floor opened up below us, and we dropped into darkness.

CHAPTER 12

TRAPPED

"You hoped you'd knock him over?" I said, setting my stylus down.

"I had the thought," Micaela said, nodding. "But you've met him. He's built like a column."

I chuckled. "And you like a dust cloud. Clearly, he didn't listen to you."

"No, he did not."

"Can you blame him? Even telling me now, you didn't sound really convincing."

"I didn't need to be. My position made complete sense."

I arched an eyebrow.

"Regardless, it worked. Partially."

"How so?" I asked. "Didn't you say this was a trap?"

"Yes, Logwyn," she said. "But not all traps are bad ones. Or set by the wrong people."

"And this one was a good one?"

"No, this one was indeed a bad one."

"You're confusing me now."

Micaela chuckled.

"That trap lay inside another one. And both lay across the path to your destination, Logwyn."

"My destination?"
"Answers."

For a few moments, we fell through the heart of the shell, my hair flapping above my head, before we shot out the bottom of the Nomad shell and down into the expanse below. The only saving grace of this trip came from the wet suit, which proved as aerodynamic as it was hydrodynamic.

Even though I knew what to expect, flying by a ring is disconcerting, especially straight down. As we descended, my skull ached and my ears popped. I grabbed my breathing apparatus, Suyef following suit, and shoved my hair into the hood. Once finished, I felt the changes in the surrounding air vanish. I gave Suyef a thumbs-up, which he returned.

Unlike the first trip, where the ring had spun around me, this one remained on a fixed plane. As far as I could tell, it kept parallel to a surface below us. Specifically, our destination. Looking back behind us, I caught sight of what could have been more Ancient symbols trailing after the ring. Even along the ring, I could see some fading in and out of sight in the bright core light.

The unshielded core made it hard to see anything below, which didn't make me feel any less helpless. Above, the Nomad shell receded, the shape reminiscent of a figure eight with jagged edges. Off to one side, I saw the smaller Colberran shell and the three floating islands the Seekers used to stage their invasion.

Suyef grabbed my arm and reached over to tap my mouth apparatus. The light dimmed to a slightly orange hue, allowing me to look down. There, orbiting between us and the core, lay three relatively enormous masses. They appeared in a straight line, the largest slightly to my left, another nearly the same size to my right, and the smallest directly in between.

We fell through the sky at an alarming rate, now measurable by the rapidly approaching shells, and I pondered the approach. With no sign of a citadel on the surfaces, would we be entering from below or from the side? Or was there a shaft straight down the middle? The smaller shell, much larger than it first appeared, seemed to be our destination. Or was the ring using it as a point of reference before turning toward one of the larger shells?

The ring sped down one side of the smallest shell, then darted along the underbelly, dipping from its flat plane toward its destination. At the center hung a mountain-sized stalactite reaching out toward the core like an arm. I spied a small cave at the peak that our ring oriented toward, approaching without slowing. The air buffeted us as we shot up into a tunnel, the cave closing and plunging us back into darkness. After a moment, a door spun open above, and the ring slowed.

We entered a dome-shaped room adorned with a few light sconces and a single door. The floor closed, and the ring lowered us to the platform before opening and vanishing into a slot around the surface's edge. We removed our apparatuses and looked around.

"Um, this isn't a control room," I said, tucking the device away.

Suyef stepped down off the platform. "I don't like this."

"*Now* you get wary," I muttered, pulling my braid free of the hood.

The door slid open and two men, whispering together, entered. They wore cloaks similar in cut to a Seeker's, but blood red with black fringe. Each bore a staff similar to Suyef's in black-gloved hands. They wore no hoods, their heads shorn of hair.

They froze, conversation dying, when they spied us. Suyef they glanced at, but their eyes widened when they saw me.

"It's her," one hissed just as the other shoved him back out the door.

"Go!"

Suyef lunged, trying to grab at the retreating guard. The other guard charged at the Nomad, and the pair fell in a heap at the door's entrance. The fleeing man called out an alert as he vanished. Suyef rose and struck the guard's head twice, rendering him unconscious.

"Can you get that platform working again?" Suyef asked, pulling the limp guard into the room.

"There isn't an interface," I said, looking around.

Suyef moved near the door and peered down the hallway. I tapped at the spectacles, trying to toggle them on.

"These don't work, either."

"We need to move *now*." He darted down the hall.

"What's going on? Why did they recognize me?"

I chased Suyef down when he slowed at an intersection, hand held out.

"I'd rather not stick around to find out."

Suyef waved me to the left, and we rushed onward, the sound of voices behind us. Another guard appeared at the intersection, pointing at us and yelling. Suyef cut down a hall to the right, and I followed to find a set of doors sliding open. We stumbled to a halt on a platform, a double-barred railing standing just opposite us.

"Oh, my word," I whispered.

Before us stood a massive cavern, giant stalagmites soaring up toward equally huge stalactites sweeping down to their stony brethren. The ceiling above dwarfed the largest mountain I'd

ever seen, and the far side was a blur of colors and dim lights.
But I barely even noticed that magnificent spectacle.

All I could see was the massive city.

"More amazing than our city?" I cut Micaela off.

"No, Logwyn. But remember, I hadn't been there yet. So,
this one made quite the impression." She nodded slowly. "More
so than even I understood."

I scanned my notes.

"Two other shells used to orbit near ours until just a few
cycles ago. So, the larger shell was probably this one."

"Yes, it was."

"Did you ever visit the other one?"

For several moments, Micaela sat in silence. I moved to
speak, but thought better of it. Eventually, she looked over at
me. "I'm sorry, lost in memories I'd rather forget."

"Part of this story?"

A single nod followed, a small smile tugging at one side of
her mouth. "You'll understand soon enough."

"Soon?"

"Soon, actually."

"This trap you mentioned. Was it in that city? On the
other shell?"

"No, we already triggered the trap long before that."

I looked back up at her to see her eyes on the window.

"We were just too blind to realize it."

The city lay spread out in concentric tiers, each smaller than the one above. Block-shaped, single-level buildings jutted out from the rear rock face of each level. We stood on a tier halfway up, buildings shrinking in size farther up behind us. A jumble of large, multilevel buildings rose from the bottom center, each adorned with ornate carvings above the entrances and tall windows. With each tier, the carvings became less ornate, vanishing entirely a few floors above us.

On each level, thousands upon thousands of people moved about, all wearing floor-length robes similar in color to the cave: dull and mute. Those far below wore robes adorned with contrasting, but still dull, fringe and ornate belts. Each tier's clothing became progressively simpler, with those several levels above wearing robes lacking fringe with simple rope belts.

The people shuffled along, their eyes low, shoulders sagged, their voices quiet when they spoke. Every male kept their hair short or nonexistent, and the women pulled their hair into a single tight ponytail that hung halfway down the back.

"Who are these people?" I asked, feeling very out of place in our outfits.

"Core-dwellers."

"We aren't on the core."

"My people call anyone that lives below our shell core-dweller."

I nodded, looking around. "So, have they always lived here?"

"I don't know," he whispered, moving to one side of the door. "Maybe."

Before I could respond, someone shouted from the hallway. We drew back from the door, trying to hide in the crowd. The people shuffled past us in silence, never once looking up. Even when jostled, they kept moving, eyes down, faces blank.

"What is wrong with these people?" I asked as we paused near a structure carved from the cave so he could look back. "It's like we don't exist."

"Beaten people rarely notice when someone steps on them."

"Beaten?"

He pointed at the passersby.

"Look at their shoulders, faces. They are a broken people."

"What a horrid way to live," I whispered, seeing no emotion at all in their eyes. "And no color, you notice. On them, on the walls. Anywhere."

"Seems the farther down you go, the more variations in color you see," Suyef said, pointing down into the city. "A sign of power or rank, maybe."

"Even that seems dull."

"Your hair stands out even more than our clothing," he said, moving along with the crowd.

"Blonds and brunettes everywhere," I said as I avoided a young girl barely older than my sister. "Everything is dull here."

"Except those guards."

We ducked into an alley. A set of doors blocked the exit, a single panel jutting out on the right.

"Can you access it?" he asked.

I rushed over, tapping the screen. Symbols I could read appeared.

"Maybe," I whispered, searching for the activating structure. "Well, it's not a common command. That would be too easy."

Suyef stood near the alley's opening.

"Anyone coming?"

"Several," he hissed. "Work faster."

Symbols shifted up and down at the touch of my finger.

"Hissing at me doesn't help."

"The threat of imprisonment might," he said, moving close and pointing at the screen. "Try putting that large one on the bottom."

"I'm trying to open the door, not blow it up." I waved at the symbol in question. "Where it is makes the most sense."

"Using Colberran grammar," he countered. "It's different here."

"All the more reason to be careful."

"Fine, just figure it out." He rushed back over to the corner. "Quickly."

I tapped the large symbol and moved it up one slot against my better judgment. You can imagine my surprise when the panel flashed, and the doors opened.

"Suyef, you were right."

"Good work," he said, rushing through the doors.

I took a step, but movement caught my eye. The young girl stood near the corner, eyes locked on me. She held up a hand, a furrow cutting through her brow as her head shook. Her mouth opened partway, but Suyef pulled me through as the doors closed, cutting her off.

To this day, I wondered what she would have said, wondered what I would tell me in her place. The look in her eyes hinted at it, but I didn't put it together. How could I? I didn't know what lay beyond those doors. I didn't wait long enough to hear her warning.

The warning I'd have said in her place.

"Run."

CHAPTER 13

NIGHTMARES

"Bit hyperbolic, don't you think?" I arched an eyebrow at Micaela.

"When you write it, Logwyn, change it however you wish."

"I don't think I get to change much of this. I'm supposed to record your words and reproduce them on paper."

"You and I both know full well that if you did that with Quentin in his current state, it would be unreadable." She stood up and moved toward the kitchen. "Water?"

"Let me, High One," I said, setting my stylus down.

"Just for that, I'll even grab you a snack," she called over her shoulder.

"Sorry, Micaela. It's just what's expected."

"For those of a higher status." She set out two glasses and filled each with crystal-clear water. "Of which I am not."

"I don't know what your status is," I said, picking up a glass and nodding. "You left that detail out."

"With good reason," she said, setting a bowl of green-skinned fruit slices next to the water. "I just don't like terms that denote power over others." She grimaced and picked up her glass. "In my experience, people demanding terms like that are trying to inflate their own egos. I don't need that, I assure you."

"Sounds like you've met our council," I said.

I took a piece of fruit and popped it into my mouth. Micaela's grimace turned to a frown.

"I employ the same tactics as your Queen with the council."

"She avoided sitting in council for almost twenty-five cycles," I said, taking up another slice of fruit. "Most did not know *why*. Many debated how long she would do it, almost as much as why she eventually went back."

She paused, her hand holding a slice of fruit partway to her mouth. "To stop them from continuing blindly down the wrong path," she whispered.

I wondered again how much she knew of our leader. "Toward war?"

"War is a direction that council would never go willingly. Complacency? That's a path they choose way too much, even when faced with a war they can't avoid." She moved to her seat, glass in one hand, the slice of fruit still uneaten. "Regardless, they choose that path a lot, I assure you."

"Meaning what, exactly?" I asked, grabbing the bowl and my glass and returning to my seat.

"Meaning the Queen had to return. If she hadn't, it's likely we wouldn't be having this conversation."

"Because she wouldn't have brought me in to hear it?"

She shook her head. "Because I wouldn't be here to share it."

"Where would you be?"

"Trapped in a nightmare."

We found ourselves in a smaller, tunnel-like cave directly under the city's sloping cavern. Its ceiling flowed up and away at a sharp angle, widening from the floor as it went. The tunnel opened up into a small channel cut into the floor to either side of the door, its opposite wall sloping up and back to match the cave ceiling. Veins of eerie light glowed from the rock walls.

Suyef rushed to the right. The gap between the channel walls remained narrow, the far reaches of the cave shrouded in blackness. I heard nothing save for my companion and saw little more. Still, the air felt heavy, thicker.

"Suyef, we're under the upper portions of the city."

He nodded, continuing down the crevice. "Maybe this leads to another door."

"Or a larger opening to the center."

We moved as quickly as we dared in the low light but found no more doors. The farther we went, the more the air felt like something was pushing it down toward us.

"Suyef, we have to go back," I whispered, turning my head to look into the darkness. "Something's not right with this cave."

"Until we figure out what that is, we're better off here than in the hands of those guards."

I looked behind us, the dim light barely illuminating the path in the distance. Then it hit me.

"They didn't follow us." I stopped and grabbed Suyef's arm. "Why didn't they?"

"Maybe they didn't see us," he said. "Come on, keep moving."

I remained there, feeling something was wrong. Something in the air. "There's a reason they didn't follow us."

The air pressed down, and I thought something shifted in the darkness.

"Suyef," I whispered. "We need to go back."

He didn't answer. Instead, he stared into the blackness, a single finger held up. I looked around, squinting to see through the dim light.

"Shadow assassins?"

"No," he whispered. "Something bigger."

Those familiar words echoed in my head. Words he had said once before. I crept toward him, barely letting myself breathe.

"Like at the prison?"

I felt him press back against me. He shifted, his wet suit creaking.

"Maybe."

"We need to move," I said, pulling him toward the doors.

He grabbed my arm and yanked me around, nodding in the opposite direction.

"I think it's between us and where we came in."

My heart pounded in my chest as we moved. One hand gripped his cloak, the only familiar thing left to me. I kept looking back, not wanting to be surprised.

As I turned my head, something hit me square in the back, knocking the wind from my lungs. I slid across the slick floor, stopping when I collided with something that crunched. My lungs struggled as I collapsed onto my back, convulsing until I coughed and air rushed back in. Eyes watering, I rolled over to get up, but my hand landed on something smooth and long. I froze at the sight.

Under my hand lay a human bone.

"Just lying there?" I asked.

"And it wasn't alone," Micaela whispered.

"Which bone was it?"

"Femur."

"And there were more?"

She nodded.

"Many, many more."

Thousands of white, clean bones lay in a pit at the end of the crevice. It opened up into the middle of the cave, the far end vanishing into the darkness. Every single bone appeared to be human.

A split second later, Suyef grabbed my arm. "Come on," he whispered, pushing me up and onto the pile of bones. "Walk carefully."

"Are you insane?" I asked, pushing back.

"It's the only way out," he hissed, stepping carefully. "Come on, before whatever that was returns."

I looked back, but the dim light revealed nothing. Suyef called, urging me forward. Still, I held back, wary to step on the grotesque pile. Clenching my jaw, I moved, but something above stopped me.

From the darkness, something long, lithe, and scaled whipped out and knocked Suyef flat into the bones. I spun around, but something struck my head. A burning sensation ripped across the back of my neck, and all feeling left my body. The room tilted, the floor racing toward my face, but I never landed. At the last moment, the floor shot away under me.

Suyef lay below, one arm reaching up toward me. My arms dangled out of control, my head lolled around, and I couldn't speak.

"Micaela!"

I heard him cry out. Just as I tried to call back, something falling back down caught my eye.

A single braid of red hair.

"So, what attacked you?"

"I think you know, Logwyn."

"What color?"

"Blood red."

Her jaw tightened, her fingers twisting a strand of her red hair.

"Have you ever worn it that way again?" I asked, pointing at her hair. "A braid, I mean."

She shrugged, holding up the strand and looking at it. "That was a different time."

"So, that city," I went on, thinking better of asking more. "A Red was hiding under it?"

"Not hiding," she said, hand dropping. "Ruling."

"The Reds ruled those people on their shell?" I asked. "I don't remember hearing anything about that."

"Does your council tell you everything they know and do?"

"Still, keeping that a secret is a big deal."

"They were following an order."

"From the Queen?"

She nodded, and I frowned, looking back at the Queen's chamber.

"Why did she give that order?"

"Because of what happened next."

"Which was?" I asked.

"The Reds put me on trial."

I chuckled, waiting for her to say something else. "On what charge?" I asked when she remained silent.

Her eyes locked on the door behind me.

"Shattering the world."

CHAPTER 14

BRAID

A sound drew me from my quarters into an empty hallway.

"Nidfar? Is that you?"

Silence. I frowned, looking at the balcony.

"If you're waiting for him to turn up, Logwyn, you'll be here a while."

My heart jumped, and a tingling sensation traveled up my spine, along my neck, and into my armpits.

"Don't do that," I exclaimed, rounding on Suyef. "Give me some warning."

"I just did," he said.

He moved back into the living quarters, and I followed, travel sack in hand, stopping just inside the room. Suyef waited near the table, watching me.

"Where have you been?"

"Chasing a ghost."

"Quentin."

He chuckled. "He is . . . a handful."

"So is that old man," I muttered. "And impossible to talk to."

"And here I thought you were well-versed in getting troublesome people to talk. You know, with all this practice."

I ignored the comment, mind drifting to the box in my sack. I wanted an explanation, some answers. I reached inside the bag, and he arched an eyebrow, head tilting a bit. I paused, his and the Queen's words, their reasons for it remain secret, bubbling to the surface. The object scared them, and that alone gave me pause. Instead, I pulled out my notes and the recorder.

"This isn't easy. None of them—Micaela, Quentin, or Nidfar—none of them tell their stories coherently. Hers is the most linear and thought out, but even she tunnel-wanders and doesn't always make sense." I waved a hand over my notes. "This is a glorified mess. I'm probably the only one who can make head or tail of it, and even I'm daunted by it."

"She believes you can handle it," he said. "From what I see, she placed her faith well."

"Thanks, but faith doesn't help," I said, glaring at him. "Especially with less-than-forthcoming interviewees."

"Everyone tells their story in their own way." He pointed at me. "You, of all people, should understand that."

"Yes, but I know a lot more than you realize," I retorted. "You know she's shared more than either of you."

"Micaela will tell you what she wants when she wants to. And not before."

"This time she stopped because of what happened to both of you."

He nodded. "A lot happened."

"And I need you to fill in some gaps," I cut in before he could go on.

He stopped, jaw shifting, eyes moving to me. After a moment, I pressed on.

"What happened in that cave?"

His eyes narrowed. "Bones. Braid."

He shifted, reaching into his robe and pulling something out. He stared down at the object hidden just below the table's edge in silence for several moments. His chest rose and fell in a deep sigh, and he looked up at me. His eyes narrowed, watching me as he set the object on the table between us.

A braid of red hair.

I looked up to see his eyes locked on the braid. "You kept it?" I whispered.

He nodded. I reached over and picked it up. Still soft, the braid was heavy. Twine around each end held it tight, and the faint scent of spices and something earthy tickled my nose.

"She is very important to you," I said, setting it down.

"Because I kept that?"

"You scented it with her perfume," I said. "She still wears it."

"I would think by now you'd understand."

"You are friends." I waved at the braid. "But this shows something more."

His eyes remained on me. I picked up the braid again to inspect it further.

"How long have you had this?"

"Not as long as this story might lead you to believe," he said.

"Is this the only thing you have of hers?"

He shook his head.

"Care to share?"

"Not yet."

I ran a finger down the braid, watching him. "This is more than mere friendship, Suyef."

"We've established that," he said, holding out his hand. "Family always is."

I frowned, shaking my head and holding the braid out. "That's more than family, Suyef—"

"No," he cut me off, emphasizing each word. "It's not."

He took the braid and tucked it away, standing up and heading for the balcony. The message was obvious. He did not

want to talk about it. He didn't want to bring up a painful
memory. One that hurt him deeply.

One that still hurt.

Suyef returned a short while later and resumed his seat. I
remained silent until he waved at my notes.

"So, what was that cave?"

"A mass graveyard."

I stopped writing, looking up.

"How do you know?"

"Guards," he said.

"Who was guarding it?"

"Not who." He looked at me, face expressionless. "What."

I inhaled, my heartbeat speeding up. "You found a Red
mausoleum and walked away unscathed?"

"Losing her is unscathed?"

"No, physically. Reds are very territorial."

"Regardless," he said, shrugging, "I escaped."

"How?"

"On the back of a Red."

Now I sat in silence. Suyef watched me, eyes narrowed.

"You're joking, aren't you?" I asked.

He shook his head. I tapped my notes.

"Go on."

"I told you. It was a Red mausoleum. They told me, and
one helped me leave."

"But why? What happened to Micaela? Why didn't they
take her with you?"

I sat back, hand paused over the paper as I glared at him.

"You asked questions, and I answered them," he said. "If you want more, be specific."

"You're being obtuse."

"How am I supposed to know what you want if you don't state it clearly?"

"Enough," I said, slamming my notes down on the table.

He cocked his head to one side, eyebrows raised. I leaned back and took a deep breath.

"Sorry," I whispered. "I'm tired of wild tunnel chases."

"Then you are really going to hate where this is going," he said.

I glared at him, taking several calming breaths as he watched me. When I stopped the exercise, he leaned forward, nodding.

"Details. First, the bones lay in a strange arrangement for a mausoleum. All piled up, as if tossed aside." He paused, lips jutting out in thought. "What I didn't know then was that they tossed them aside ritually. It's the culture. The people there seem simple. Emotionless." He pointed at my notes. "How did Micaela describe that city?"

"Mostly straight lines, cut from rock, little decor. Some doors bore ornate carvings based on the tier."

"And the people?"

"Drab colors. Some fringe and jewelry farther down, none toward the top. Hair nondescript."

"Not their appearance. Their eyes."

"Listless. No emotion," I said, pointing at my eyes. "Nothing alive."

"From the outside, all true." He pointed at his chest. "But not here. Faces remained controlled, calm, but not inside. And not inside those buildings. The carvings, fringe, the jewelry, they were functional."

"Societal rank," I said.

"But not obvious ones," he continued. "First, Initiates. Those newly come to the society, all living in the upper tiers until they join the next rank. The Accepted."

"Those chosen to join?"

"No," he said, smiling. "Something I didn't know then was that no one leaves once you come to that place."

"Ever?"

"Ever," he said, nodding.

"But you left? Micaela?"

"And you're getting ahead," he said, shaking a finger at me. "So, no one leaves. To join the next tier, they had to make a choice."

"Accept that they weren't leaving?" I asked. "That they had to join."

"Precisely. And that group filled the tiers from the upper levels almost to the bottom."

"Let me guess. The top rank lived at the bottom. The leaders."

He nodded but said nothing more.

"The Reds?"

"Those chosen by the Reds," he said. "A tiny, select group."

"But there are so many Reds," I said.

"They live everywhere else on that shell except that city, in every cave and crevice. Every tunnel. Filling it like dirt poured down a hole."

"And this mausoleum?" I asked, tapping my notes with my stylus.

"No one lives there. They rarely even enter it. And no human may enter it alive."

"Why have a door?"

"A sealed door," he said, folding his arms and leaning back.

"And those people wouldn't think to unlock it, I'm guessing."

"Why enter the place you keep your dead? Particularly one so well-guarded?"

"Why guard it?" I asked, glancing at my notes.

"Some vestige of their past they never explained, and I didn't ask."

"If humans can't enter, how do the bones get there?"

"A series of long shafts reach down from the top level into the mausoleum," he said, hand held above the table. "When someone dies, they hold a ceremony before dropping the body into one of those."

"That's different." I swallowed, my stomach twisting. "What if someone accidentally falls in?"

"They built a field emitter a few meters into the shaft. It's tuned to only let rigid mineral deposits through to the cave."

"Bones," I said. "It strips away everything but the bones, letting those fall down into a pile." I looked back down at my notes. "Doesn't seem very respectful."

"It is their tradition," he said. "I may not understand, but it is what they do."

I nodded. "So, you stumbled onto their graveyard, and they took offense and captured you."

"They captured her. I turned myself in."

"Why do that? To stay with her?"

"Because no one hides from a dragon," he said. "Especially not on their turf."

"Why just turn yourself in?" I asked, ignoring his comment. "How did that help?"

"How else could I follow her?"

"They could have taken you somewhere else," I said. "Or killed you."

"Neither happened." He leaned on the table. "I'm sure you know that, unlike your Greens, factions split Red society asunder long ago."

"The Greens only seem unified," I countered. "Especially compared to the Reds."

"Yes, your council. They made things difficult for us."

"They specialize in difficult," I said, looking up from my notes. "Especially when dealing with the Queen."

"Not entirely unhealthy for a society."

"It is when they prevent anything from being done. And that isn't what we're discussing."

"That may be so," he said, bowing his head slightly. "But it is pertinent to this story."

"How so?"

"Because the Red I turned myself in to was a traitor."

CHAPTER 15

TRIAL

"They did what?"

"You heard me, Logwyn," Micaela said, grimacing.

"What were they thinking, putting you on trial?"

"They weren't," she said, her face twisting into a forced smile. "Well, they weren't thinking of having a fair trial, at least."

I arched an eyebrow at her. "Even a sham trial would need evidence."

"This was about revenge, not justice." Her eyebrows rose and fell, and she sighed. "That's not fair, honestly. I may not agree with their justifications, but, from their perspective, it makes sense."

"No," I interjected. "It doesn't. The Shattering is Ancient history."

"Literally."

Micaela chuckled, and I smiled, nodding.

"Yeah, and you are barely thirty cycles old."

She bowed her head, the chuckle fading.

"Why would they blame you for that?" I asked.

"Easy, really. They believed I was someone else."

"Who else would they be after?"

Micaela motioned with her chin at the door behind me. The door I had first entered when this all began. The Queen's door.

"Her."

I awoke on a flat mattress lying in a small chamber with a single ceiling light and a washbasin on one side. When I turned my head, pain jolted through me.

"Ah, you're awake, High One," a female voice said from above.

Squinting, I saw a black sphere mounted near the light.

"Your attire is inappropriate for your station. Please change."

A door to the room near my head opened enough to allow someone to drop a satchel before closing. It contained simple pants, a blazer, and a pair of soft-soled shoes. Prisoner attire from my shell.

"I'm not wearing that."

"You cannot appear before the tribunal wearing *that*," the voice insisted.

"Then I won't go," I said, leaning back and crossing my arms. "I don't even want to."

A guard holding a tray of food and water entered through the same door. He glanced at me, set the tray down, and left me to my meal.

"Thank you," I said to the closed door.

I ate my nutrient pack, pondering the situation. This tribunal wanted to talk to me. I looked at the clothing, thinking of the woman's use of the *High One* moniker juxtaposed with the prison wear given me. I sipped some water. "Where's my companion?"

"You are alone."

"In here, yes. But I had a companion there with me."

"No one else is here," she said. "You alone trespassed on sacred ground."

I frowned.

"Sacred?"

"Our burial grounds. You dishonored our dead."

"I'm sorry. We didn't know."

"As if that would matter," she scoffed. "Compared to your other crimes, dishonoring our dead is trivial."

"Other crimes?"

She chuckled.

"And you will pay for them."

"High One?" I looked at the camera. "You're mistaking me for someone else."

The sound of metal dragging on rock filled the room. It took a moment to realize she was laughing.

"Oh, you are a funny one," the woman said. "Soon, you will pay for what you've done. Then who will laugh?"

I turned back to my meal, thinking about Suyef.

"Where is my friend?" I asked.

No answer, not that I expected one. If they had caught him, why tell me? Or maybe they hadn't caught him. Or worse. That thought filled me with dread, so I tried to put it out of mind.

That proved impossible.

The door slid open as I finished eating. The guard, pulse gun in hand, waved me to follow, clearly not caring that I had not changed clothes. Six more guards with guns waited there. The first one moved down the hall, and I followed, the rest coming after us. We passed several more doors on either side of the drab hallway.

"Where are we going?"

No one responded, so we marched in silence. As we passed more doors, I thought of my brothers. Of Suyef. Had they been here? I opened my mouth to ask, but stopped when we reached a set of sealed doors. The first guard muttered something into the door's panel. After a moment, they slid open, and the guards pushed me inside. They stared at me until the doors slid shut.

I found myself alone in a narrow, circular room. Light panels shone up from the floor near the walls, and a series of lines divided the ceiling into pie wedges. In the center sat a single chair carved from stone. Overhead, I saw no ceiling in the dim light.

"Hello?"

No answer came, so I sat down to wait. When I did, a loud whirring sound filled the room, and the ceiling slid open to reveal a tall, dark shaft. The chair vibrated, and I gripped it as the floor rose. The lighting revealed walls carved from a smooth stone surface but little of what lay above. With my gaze cast upward, a sense of dread filled my stomach.

Light shot down as I heard another panel slide open. I blinked my eyes to adjust but saw nothing beyond the bright light. However, my vision was not the only sense suddenly assaulted.

A cacophony echoed down, a deafening roar that rumbled my core. Screams and cries, both human and beastly, filled my ears. I craned my neck to glimpse more, but the bright light concealed it from me. I closed my eyes and took a deep breath to steady my heart rate. The roar grew to a crescendo, shaking every inch of me.

It just got louder the higher I rose.

"This sounds ominous," I said after Micaela fell silent.

"Very much so. I didn't know then, but nearly every member of Red society filled that chamber or watched via broadcast."

"They meant to make a show of you," I said, shaking my head and shifting my papers around. "Probably won the ruling party a lot of points with the populace."

"True. The Reds have made it clear they believe their way to be the one true path and the Greens stand in the way."

"We protect this world from vermin like them," I hissed, my neck tensing.

She looked at me, a small smile tugging at one side of her mouth.

"I know what you believe, Logwyn. What you all believe." She nodded, closing her eyes for a moment. "Trust me, I know."

I took a deep breath as I watched her.

"This is where you learned about their perspective, isn't it?"

"A twisted one, but yes."

"How did you know that?"

"I don't know. Probably because the Reds were putting me on trial for actions I hadn't committed."

"Yeah, that'll do it," I said. "You must have felt very alone."

She nodded. "At that moment, I felt almost as alone as I ever had."

The platform came to a halt, depositing me in a large, rectangular space surrounded by walls easily three times my height. Before me stood a stage upon which five empty chairs sat just before a set of tall, closed doors. Above the walls lay row upon row of balcony seating set behind half-walls built along the outer edge, the rows climbing to the top of the cavern. People sat in every row, with sizable gaps left empty among the rows of seating. The people screamed, many shaking fists at me, while others threw pieces of torn cloth down onto the floor around my seat. Some slammed their open palms on the half-walls; still others spat in my direction.

A massive tone shook the chamber, and a large door opened in the ceiling far above, letting in light that illuminated the upper reaches of the cavern. The crowd fell silent, their vitriolic cries gone, angry visages twisted in hatred wiped clean. A passive calm flooded over the cavern, a quiet that chilled my bones. Only one thing could cause that kind of reaction. A shadow moving into the light above confirmed my fear.

A massive red dragon, large wings tucked against its long serpentine body, dove into the chamber. Its bone structure stretched down its back and nearly rivaled that on the Green that had taken Maryn and dropped me in the Wilds. The beast swept down and landed on the large platform before me, shrinking in size so as not to disturb the chairs. Only then did I notice the others with it; many more, in fact. None equaled the first Red's initial size, though all were large in their own right. Dozens poured into the chamber, some landing in balcony spaces left clear for them, the rest in a ring around the arena. Four more alighted with the first beast, two on each side. Every one of them looked down at me, tongues smelling the air, smelling me. Did they smell my fear? Doubt? Uncertainty? Refusing to be intimidated, I held my chin up and returned their gaze. No one came to sit in the chairs. I remember thinking that then, that the chairs remained empty.

"Even now she sits full of pride and arrogance," the lead Red hissed, craning its long neck to look at its counterparts.

I blinked, staring at the beast's mouth. It had opened, and a hiss emanated from it. How that hiss translated to words in my head was unknown to me.

"She doesn't even deign to respond, seeing herself as so far above us," the Red leader went on, raising its neck to look down on me. "She refused to appear in attire appropriate for her position."

"At least she doesn't come to us in her abomination form," a Red on the leader's left stated, nodding at me. "In that, she shows some tact."

The leader's entire body shook, a low rumble emanating from its gut.

"In that, she shows intelligence, of which most would not consider her blessed." The beast dipped its head down toward me. "Wisdom. Foresight. Those she is sorely lacking and always has. Thus why we are here."

"For a farce?" I said, drawing every eye in the chamber. "A sham? What is the meaning of this? Why am I being held prisoner? What crime have I broken besides trespassing on an unmarked burial ground?"

My voice echoed off the cavern walls. No one moved until the Red leader laughed. Soon its counterparts followed suit. In waves, the other dragons joined in. After a few moments, everyone, dragon and human alike, was laughing. Everyone but me.

When the noise finally died down, many a human spectator sat wiping their eyes of tears, and the Red leader held its head up high. Its voice boomed, but I noted it did not echo.

"What crime have you committed?" it called out. "Dare you insult this esteemed audience?"

"I'm not trying to insult anyone. I'm just trying to understand what's going on."

"Your feigned ignorance is merely a veiled insult," the Red hissed. "Don't think by doing so you'll have any hope of avoiding justice."

I frowned.

"If the verdict has already been determined, why are we doing this? Particularly as I don't know what I'm being judged guilty for."

"You're being judged for your own actions, High One," the dragon to the leader's right said.

The Red leader nodded at its companion.

"And she does not need us to remind her of that which she has already done." It looked at me. "To us and to the world."

"Fan of hyperbole, are we?" I whispered.

The Red leader's head shot up.

"The perpetrator will remain silent!"

I looked around, marveling at a streak of defiance uncommon in me.

"Seeing as there isn't one present, that's an easy ask," I said, glaring at the Red leader.

"Read the verdict," the leader said.

The Red on the far left shifted, moving its head to look at a panel glowing in the floor.

"We find the accused guilty of the charges levied against her: namely, knowing participation in the sabotage of the citadel network, conspiracy with known fugitives to unleash evil on this world, and the planned murder of millions of innocent people."

Murmurs rushed through the crowd as the dragon continued reading.

"We also find the accused guilty of sedition against the Red society and the attempted genocide of the same."

"Oh, yes, High One," the Red leader said, looking back at me, "not even your assumed rank will save you now. You've avoided justice for thousands of cycles, but we have a long memory. Now you will pay for your attempts to destroy our most sacred of possessions."

Its head moved down as close to me as it could reach.

"This world."

The inanity of it all left me dumbfounded. These beasts seriously thought I had something to do with events that occurred several thousand cycles before my birth. Worse, they'd held a trial without me present and found me guilty of it. The absurdity left me only one thing to do.

I burst out laughing.

"Really?" I asked Micaela. "A bit cliché, don't you think?"

"Write it however you want, Logwyn," she said. "That's what happened."

"You laughed?"

"What else could I do?" she asked. "It was absurd."

"I bet that went over well."

She chuckled, shaking her head.

"I'm sure you can imagine."

"Can we go back for a moment?" I asked, looking at my notes.

Micaela nodded.

"The speaking. You said that it was—how did you put it? 'Unknown' how you understood what the Reds were saying."

She nodded again.

"I take it this was the first time you'd ever spoken to a dragon, then?"

"Yes. The first three times I encountered them were under very different circumstances."

"But now you know how it works? Did someone tell you?"

"In a manner of speaking, yes."

"Why? Our societies frown on divulging the method of communication, particularly to outsiders. It's one of the few common traits we still share."

"Such an interesting turn of words, that phrase," she murmured, head cocked to one side and eyes narrowed. "And who made that rule?"

"It's not a rule," I said, shrugging. "Just an, um, a code of conduct? But not official. More informal."

"A guideline?" Micaela offered.

"Yeah, like an unspoken rule."

She nodded but said nothing.

"Who told you how it works?" I asked

"You mean with scribing?" she asked. "No one. I figured it out on my own."

I could tell by her reaction I didn't hide my thoughts about that statement. She smirked and chuckled again. "You figured it out? Care to explain how?"

"I know how it works. And, so you won't doubt me, here you go." She held up a single finger. "The dragon is not talking in a language we understand. The hisses and other sounds I heard? Their language." A second finger. "Through a complicated bit of scribing, they converted the sounds to words for the listener and piped them directly into their ears, which explained the lack of echoes." A third. "It's translated into whatever language the listener needs."

She dropped her hand and looked at me, one eyebrow raised. I was unsure what to say.

"Shall I continue?" Micaela asked, nodding at the recorder.

I glanced back down at my notes.

"Sure, my other questions can wait."

"Good, because what happened next is probably going to make you forget all about those."

"I'm not sure at this point you could surprise me," I muttered, jotting a note down to myself.

"Don't be so sure," she stated, her voice lowering. "Particularly where Seekers are concerned."

Her jaw clenched as she hissed the next few words.

"Especially one persistent Questioner."

As the leader's last hiss and my laughing echoed in the chamber, the gathered audience erupted in cries of delight and anger. This drowned out my laughter, which soon died down. I'm sure they saw me, but only the council looked quite perturbed by my reaction. Most of the audience, however, seemed not to care. Many shook fists at me, and almost every one of them nodded in agreement with their leader. One thing was clear: this society had decided about me. At that moment, I made the choice not to engage them anymore.

The lead Red raised its head, and silence fell in the chamber. The sounds echoed in the sudden quiet, all eyes on the Red, which stood with its head cocked to one side. After a few moments, it looked up at the audience.

"We will achieve justice today, but only a justice of the highest order."

Murmurs shifted through the audience.

The leader went on. "We will not sacrifice that which makes us who we are in the name of revenge. Our laws, our culture, that is what we fight to preserve." It turned its gaze back to me, tongue darting in and out. "High One, you know the laws better than anyone here. They forbid the punishment your crimes are worthy of."

I wanted to speak but remained silent.

"You won't escape the consequences," the Red went on. "Our laws do not allow it, but those of the shell you claim to be from do."

The creature's words reminded me of the warden, Mortac. The Red acted like it knew me, had met me and interacted with me. I looked around the chamber. No, this *entire* society believed they knew who I was supposed to be.

"This tribunal will hand you over to the authorities of your claimed shell and let them do with you as they please," it said, raising its head high. "So rules this court."

"So rules this court," the other four echoed.

The sound of doors opening filled the chamber. A single figure, wrapped in a black cloak and hood that hid its face, stepped through an entry in the chamber walls directly left of me. Its long shadow reached out almost to my chair. A rumble boiled through the crowds above. Whether in anger or pleasure, I wasn't sure. The cloaked figure walked toward me.

"You thought you'd escaped," its voice whispered.

Goose bumps raced across my skin as I recognized the voice.

"Thought yourself so clever," it continued. "So clever."

The figure stopped a pace from the chair. The audience began shouting, the noise melting into an unintelligible, yet angry, roar. They clearly disliked this stranger.

I looked back at the hood. No, not a stranger. The man removed his hood, a wicked smile splitting the last face I wanted to see.

Colvinra.

CHAPTER 16

DANCING

"Wait, one of the Reds was a traitor?" I asked Suyef.

"Hard as that may be to believe, some disagree with their ruling class." He pointed at me. "The Greens have some of the same issues."

"Nothing traitorous," I protested. "Oppositional, yes. Defiant, maybe. But not treacherous."

"You can believe that. There are always elements unhappy enough to want change."

"So, a traitorous Red. That doesn't explain how you convinced them to help you."

"True, but that wasn't so hard," he said, a small smile tugging at his lips. "I offered them something they couldn't resist."

At my arched eyebrow, he continued. "Control of the citadel network."

"How could you possibly offer that?"

"It was quite simple, really," he said. "They'd seen Micaela. I realized they thought she was someone she wasn't. Someone powerful."

"Yes, the Queen. The one creature everyone knows can control the network," I said, nodding. "They put her on trial because of that bit of mistaken identity."

"They did, indeed. Once I figured out their intentions, I assumed she'd be in prison long enough for me to get help." He grimaced and looked away. "That almost proved to be a mistake."

"You wouldn't have asked your people."

"Not my people," he said. "They had their hands full repelling the Seeker invasion."

"You asked the Greens to help free her?" I asked, then sat upright, a thought tickling at my focus and drawing it away from Suyef. "Wait. Wait, I remember this."

The Nomad sat quietly as my memories fell into place.

"There was a fight. An 'incursion' is what our leaders called it," I said, waving a finger at Suyef. "That was just a few cycles ago, back before—"

"The Intershell War?" he asked, to which I nodded. "Technically, Colberra was already invading my shell."

"Sorry, I don't pay attention to current events. The past is easier to dissect and figure out."

"It's also not threatening," he countered. "It's safe when all you have to do is interpret or talk about events."

"Yes, yes," I said, waving him off. "Are you trying to tell me you instigated those events? That your plea for help convinced our council to risk open war with the Reds just to save Micaela?"

"I'm not trying to do anything. I'm telling you what happened. Look it up."

"I can't, and you know that," I retorted, pointing at the recorder. "The Queen air-gapped this thing."

"Such is the limit of a paperless society."

"Nobody, not even your society, has kept a paper record of anything in centuries. Maybe since before the Splitting."

"Thus, a limit."

I watched him, pursing my lips.

"So, you didn't answer my question." When he didn't speak up, I continued. "About how you convinced the Greens to rescue Micaela."

"The same way I got the Red traitor to help me," he said. "I offered them something I knew they couldn't resist."

"Control of the citadel network?" I asked, frowning. "By convincing the Greens she was the Queen."

"You Greens have worked hard to foster the belief she controls the network."

"It's served most of the world well," I pointed out.

"Those that know and those that agree with you, yes."

"And those that haven't," I added. "Even the Reds."

"They would argue that point, but I would not. You know where my people stand on this."

"With us, as you have for centuries," I said. "For as long as our history records."

"And how far back does it?" he asked, eyebrows raising.

"Longer than your records," I said, eyes narrowing. "Why?"

"And for all that time," he continued, holding up a finger, "the story you've told the world is that the Queen controls the network, yes?"

"Yes, why?"

"Because it's not true, and you know it isn't."

"What are you talking about?"

"Your Queen has never controlled the network," he said. "Merely been on good terms with the party that does."

"What?" I asked, shaking my head. "Everyone knows the Queen can control it."

I paused, recalling what the Queen had told me.

"Well, she *did*."

"Until recently, yes?" He nodded at the recording device. "Until she gave you that, you had no reason to doubt your education. Now, ask yourself this: Who could wrestle network control away from the Queen?"

"Are you saying Micaela broke the network?"

He shook his head.

"Well, what then? Enough double-speak."

"I'm not trying to deceive you," he said, leaning forward and pointing at my notes. "But you already have the answer in here."

I opened my mouth to protest, but he cut me off.

"A face talking to us from a panel."

"The prison. Micaela's face."

"But not her," he stated.

"According to her. She could be lying."

"Why lie?" he countered.

"To hide what you're doing?"

He stared at me for a moment.

"Why would she do that?" he asked.

"I don't know, but I'm not saying she did. Just that it's a possibility."

"Normally, yes, I would agree. But not this time."

"Why not?" I asked.

"Because I know who controls the network, who has always controlled it," he answered. "And it's not Micaela. Nor the Queen."

"Then who is it?"

"For now, that's not important, but it will be soon enough," he said, holding up a hand to forestall my protest. "What is most important right now is that both the Greens and Reds were mistaken about who did, and that played out to my advantage."

"How?" I countered. "By tricking them into thinking Micaela controlled it?"

"In both cases, yes, but in different ways."

"Meaning?" I asked.

"That each side believed what it wanted about the situation, specifically about her, and I took advantage of that."

I stood, setting my stylus down.

"I'm done with your games. You're just talking in circles."

"I beg to differ," he said. "We've discussed a lot, just not what you want to talk about."

I leaned over the table.

"The point of this is to inform me so I can tell this story, not confuse me with half-truths designed to create fake drama and tension."

"You're being told the story, but you want to jump to the end," he replied, arms folded and head cocked to one side. "We've discussed this before."

"This is different," I said. "You want me to know this part, but you never say what is actually going on." I took a deep breath and lowered my voice. "I'm not trying to be difficult, Suyef. Just trying to do my job."

"And I'm trying to help you. Why act like I am fighting you?"

"I don't think you are," I muttered. "I'm just getting frustrated at this process. It's taking a long time to compile everything, and all of you taking your own approach in how you share your stories isn't making it any easier or shorter."

"We're not trying to make this difficult for you," he assured me. "It's just a tough story to tell."

"Particularly with this many moving parts," I said, nodding and picking up my stylus. "And we've gotten off track."

"That we have."

I took in another long breath and let it out slowly.

"If it helps, Logwyn," he said, pointing at my notes, "you are privy to a lot of details we didn't know."

"Yes," I agreed. "And in terms of storytelling, you all get top marks. Lots of drama, tension, cliff-hangers." I frowned at that last word. "Anyone who reads this is going to tire of cliff-hanger moments."

"Well, when you write it all down, take them out."

"What, and lose all the drama and tension?" I asked, laughing.

"You realize that, if you include all these interludes, you're really tearing down that fourth wall," he said, waving at an imaginary wall to my side.

"Are you kidding? I can't leave this stuff out. It's my only opportunity to talk directly to them."

"And to think you didn't want to do this," he said, smiling and shaking his head. "You were wrong, by the way."

I graced him with a glare before picking my notes up.

"So, you played each side by using Micaela as bait."

"That sums it up."

"How did you convince the traitor to help you right off?" I asked. "I mean, it must have taken some convincing."

"It didn't happen right away," he replied. "They locked me up at first. Not in the same prison Micaela was in, mind you. I think it was just a guard shack. Anyway, they kept me there for a while, refusing to even talk."

"Kind of hard to convince someone to help you if they refuse to talk," I pointed out.

"Which I think was the intention. They avoided me completely."

"So, how did you do it?" I asked.

"I didn't," he said, shaking his head. "When he came to me, something had convinced him. I just offered him an opportunity."

"Wait, what?" I asked, frowning. "The traitor Red already wanted to help you?"

"No, he wanted to help Micaela."

"By helping you escape? To do what? Get help?"

"Precisely—and from the one force able to do so."

"The Greens. Which is how you got from one shell to the other. But then you used the same logic to convince them to help." I shook my head. "I can hardly wait to see how you pulled that off."

"Do you think we were the only ones confused by the face that talked to us during the prison attack?" he asked, pointing at my notes.

"You all thought that was Micaela," I said, nodding. "We haven't discussed who you think it really is."

"All you need to know is that control of the network lay in that entity's hands," he said.

"Wait," I whispered, holding up a hand and shifting my notes around. "Wait."

Line after line, page after page, I scanned through until I found it.

"Here," I said, holding out a page for him to read. "Does this name mean anything to you?"

"Who told you her name?" he asked, looking up at me.

"Who do you think told me?"

He looked back at the paper, nodding and smiling when he saw the answer. "Nidfar," he whispered. "Of course he'd tell you about Celandine."

"He didn't tell me anything about her," I said. "He shared a conversation he'd had with Colvinra when she came up."

"Either way," Suyef said, shrugging, "you know her name."

"Who is she?"

"I think you know. Rather, I think you can guess."

"The one controlling the network?" I asked, receiving a nod. "Why would the Queen stand for that?"

"You assume she had a choice," Suyef countered, sitting back in his chair.

"If she lost control," I said, glaring at the Nomad, "I for one would expect her to get it back."

"That's assuming she had it to start."

"Why pretend she controlled it if she never did?" I asked, shaking my head. "It makes little sense." I paused, eyes narrowing. "Unless the point was to trick everyone."

Suyef waved me on.

"I mean, if no one else knows the truth and the one person who does isn't saying otherwise . . ."

"Or is playing along," Suyef added. "For whatever reason."

"Why set up the ruse in the first place?"

"The same reason someone might leave something in a stranger's possession without telling them what it is."

He glanced at my travel sack as I snapped my fingers at him.

"That's the first time you've brought that up."

"I don't know what you mean," he said, jaw clenched, eyes returning to me. "I'm talking about tricking people as a comparison."

I protested, but Suyef continued.

"The point is *why*. Why do such a thing?"

"To keep it a secret, why else?" I asked, conceding the point for the moment.

"Precisely," he said, pointing at my device. "It's hard for anyone trying to take control of something to do so if they don't know who is actually controlling it."

"So, you used confusion about that control to trick the Red into helping you and the Greens into rescuing Micaela," I said, pointing at my notes. "By making them, what? Think Micaela was this other person? This Celandine who Nidfar and Colvinra discussed?"

"The Red believed Micaela was your Queen," Suyef said.

"And the council believed she was Celandine," I said. "Wait, you got an audience with the council? Without the Queen presiding over it?"

"It didn't hurt that I arrived on the back of a Red." He held up a finger. "The first they'd seen willingly come to the Green shell in centuries."

"Yes, that would warrant an appearance before the council," I said, nodding at him. "And there you tricked them into believing the Reds had taken this Celandine prisoner."

"That was my goal, yes," he said. "But they responded oddly when the Red showed them security footage of Micaela's trial." He frowned, faced twisted in thought. "Shocked, maybe? I didn't know it, but the council didn't need convincing. She needed to be rescued." He shook his head. "But that wasn't why they allowed that strike."

"Why do you think they did?"

"I wasn't sure then," he said. "I thought they were just surprised the Reds had conducted the trial. Now I know differently." He pointed at my notes. "Other things, which became clear soon after the raid happened, motivated them."

"Wait, wasn't it successful?" I asked, confused by his words. "The way you said that came across like you weren't successful."

"She didn't need rescuing," Suyef stated. "We thought she did, and the Greens raided the Red shell to free her. But she freed herself from her captive's control. We just helped distract them."

"*We* being you and the Greens?"

"And a few others," he said, smiling.

"The Red traitor and his cohorts, assuming he wasn't alone," I guessed.

"And one other person." When I said nothing, he smiled. "Can't you think of anyone who might be interested in saving Micaela from the Reds?"

"Mortac?"

"A good guess, but no." Suyef shook his head. "He didn't come to that part."

"Meaning he comes back later?" I asked.

"Maybe."

He grinned at me, and I rolled my eyes. "All right, I give up. Who helped?"

He nodded toward the hallway.

"Him."

CHAPTER 17

TORTURE

The proceedings ended soon after Colvinra's appearance, but not before the council placed some restrictions on the Questioner. The Reds required a guard be present and that Colvinra use their own facility rather than taking me away. Otherwise, they kept their own claws clean by giving him the freedom to make me pay for the crimes they believed I'd committed.

Thus, I sat in a large room with a single chair and one human guard beside the door. Colvinra, I knew, would arrive soon to do whatever he intended with me. As far as I knew, his only issue with me pertained to stealing water, although that involved some serious network hacking. So, two things.

The fact they chose him as the representative from my shell troubled me. It could show a more complicated relationship existed between him and the Reds. They had been at the prison attack along with Colvinra. Were the two—Seeker and dragons—working together? To what end? And why put me on trial for crimes of paramount importance to the Reds, only to hand me over to a Seeker? Nothing made any sense to me, but one thing was obvious: Colvinra and the Reds were now working together. To what end, I would one day find out. But not that day. That day, the best I can say is I let confirmation bias mess with my logic. The fact it proved correct later was beside the point. Father would have given me quite the lecture for that.

Father. I missed him. I missed my siblings.

Colvinra strode in, glanced at the guard, and chuckled. He now wore his normal silvery robes adorned with the black trim of his rank.

"You see him, child?" the Questioner asked, pointing at the guard. "If you think his presence will make me go easy on you, lose that thought right now."

I wanted to respond, to find out what was going on, but something in his eyes gave me pause. His face appeared feverish and intense. Eyes laced with enlarged blood vessels stared back at me from a face twisted in a battle of emotions. Lips parted, then closed, his tongue licked back and forth, and his nostrils flared with his rapid breathing. His hands clenched together, his knuckles white.

"You know what will make this easier," he whispered, staring down his long nose at me. "Stop pretending. I know you have it."

"What are you talking about?"

"Don't patronize me, ketch," he hissed, smacking his hands together. "Just give it to me."

"I don't know what you're talking about, Colvinra," I said, nodding at the guard. "Even less than I know what's going on with the Reds."

The Questioner leveled a finger at my face, leaning closer.

"Don't try my patience, girl," he whispered. "They want you punished. Severely."

"Then I have little motivation to help you, do I?" I asked. "You already clarified where you stand, remember? Back in Mortac's office."

His head twitched to one side, and one eye closed.

"Leave that fool out of this," he said, squeezing his eyes shut.

"That fool made it clear you're not to be trusted," I said, leaning toward the Seeker. "Not that I required much convincing."

"I think you've forgotten the precarious nature of your current predicament, my dear." He straightened, a smile twisting his mouth but not touching his eyes. "I am your only hope."

"You'll forgive me if I don't find solace in those words." I grimaced at him. "Or safety."

"For the last time, give it to me, ketch," he said through clenched teeth. "Or I'll make you suffer more now than you ever have in your all-too-long life."

An image danced through my memory. An armored face, red light emanating from the eye slit, leaning close and whispering the same thing.

"It was you," I whispered, eyes widening. "At the prison. You attacked the facility."

The grin returned, still leaving his eyes untouched.

"I see old age hasn't addled your mind," he said, standing upright. "Or are we still carrying on this ruse of youth and ignorance?"

"I don't know who you think I am," I said, folding my arms across my chest. "But you're wrong."

He considered me for a moment, then nodded.

"We shall see," he whispered. "We shall see."

"So, yet another person convinced you were someone else," I said, interrupting Micaela's narrative.

"Technically, we already counted him, but yes."

"Did it ever occur to you they might actually believe it?"

"Yes, but I didn't know why," she said. "Or comprehend what it meant."

"But you do now?"

"Very much so," she replied.

I waved at her to continue.

"Now I completely understand their reasons," she said, shrugging.

"But were they right?"

"That's getting a little ahead of ourselves," she countered.

"You didn't deny it."

"I don't have to prove a negative. You've got to prove a positive."

I pursed my lips, staring at her for a moment.

"I'm not sure that fits in this context."

"Maybe, maybe not." She grinned at me. "Either way, it doesn't matter at this point in the story."

"Why not?" I asked.

"Because Colvinra believed it was," she answered, face twisting in a grimace. "They all did, so what they did next is what matters."

A sense of dread gripped at my gut. "And what happened next?" I asked, my voice low.

She glared at me.

"Torture."

Something gripped my body just as Colvinra's words finished. I tried to lift a finger, but it didn't move. The Questioner loomed over me, shifting his head to one side. Whatever held me lifted my body and forced it to lie hung in the air, face up to the gray ceiling. Colvinra stared down at me, and my heart pounded, thudding in my ears. I felt the urge to move, to run. The only thing I had control of was my face, which I forced to stay calm, masking my fear and panic.

"Yes, there's that stoic face," he said, leaning closer. "It will do you no good."

I gritted my teeth and glared at him. I felt my face beginning to twitch as the muscles in my back and neck tightened, sending waves of excruciating pain through my body. My eyes dampened, and I blinked the tears away.

"Ah, yes, it's beginning to dawn on you," he whispered, leaning even closer. "And we haven't even made you suffer." He chuckled, tapping at my forehead. "I really don't understand why you're doing this. Just give it to me. I know now you didn't have it before." He wagged a finger at my face, then flicked my nose. "But there is no way you unlocked a travel gate from an upper shell down to this level on your own. You have it, and I want it."

"I don't know what you want," I whispered through barely open lips. "I have nothing. Just this clothing the Nomads gave me."

His eyes flickered to my torso, then back to my own.

"Yes, this ingenious suit they've designed. Well, modeled on something Ancient. How they got a prototype to duplicate is a bit of a mystery." He shrugged. "More questions for Celandine. But not until you give me the key. I can't control her without it."

"I don't have any keys."

"You know it's not a literal key," he hissed, scowling. "But it functions the same way, and I know you have it, my dear. Now, out with it."

"Do I look like I have anything?"

"Oh, you're too clever for that," he stated, returning to a stand. "Yes, brilliant, like Celandine."

He tapped a finger on my temple.

"You're both too crafty, if you ask me. Why make a device with that much control? Then again, *crafty* does not always mean *intelligent*."

I just stared back at him. He shrugged and shook his head. "It's why I wasn't too sad to see her go. Now, if only she'd stay gone."

He contemplated me, eyes darting up and down my body. A single finger tapped at his lips.

"That suit is unique," he said, leaning down and prodding me on my side. "Made of a very interesting blend. I imagine this kept you perfectly dry. And if it kept water out . . ."

His head moved near my own, eyes on my torso. He touched my neck, and something warm flowed down the inside of the wet suit. At first, it felt like warm, soothing water washing over my skin. That changed after a few heartbeats. The soothing flow shifted, prodding and squirming like something was crawling on my skin. Colvinra held his hand in place a moment longer, more warmth pouring down around my hips and to my feet. Soon, they covered every inch of me, filled every crevice, and my skin itched.

"You enjoy that little present," he said, moving toward the door. "I hope you're not allergic to any kind of insect bite. I'm not really sure what all I let loose inside your suit."

He stopped, snapping his fingers.

"Wait, I forgot something."

He walked back, his hand moving past my face. A helmet made of clear glass closed down around my head. Colvinra smiled at me, his voice muffled when he spoke.

"We can't have them escaping, now, can we?"

He laughed and turned away just as something crawled up my neck. I heard a small clicking sound and felt something move up onto my face.

My heart raced as I struggled to control my breathing. The creatures moved across every inch of skin, and the sounds filled my ears. I squeezed my eyes shut just as they began swarming the helmet. The itching persisted, and I squirmed in my restraints, struggling to wipe my skin clean. The muscles in my back clenched tight, adding to the assault of sensations. Bugs, the sounds, and the pain threatened to overwhelm me. I vaguely recall feeling something strike the back of my head. Bright light shot through my vision, and I fell into it.

"Bugs bother you, don't they?" I asked, and Micaela nodded.

"Particularly spiders," she said, eyes wide. "But, on the skin, it doesn't matter what kind it is."

"I couldn't agree more," I said, tingles coursing through my body. "This kind of attack seems, I don't know, specific? Intentional?"

"Personal."

"That's it," I said, snapping my fingers. "Like, he knew exactly how to get to you."

"I think it's obvious he knew."

"Where would he find that out?"

"I asked myself many times since then," she said, looking over at the window.

I followed her gaze. The core shone despite the time, as this shell lacked a night shield.

"There are several answers," she continued. "Someone told him willingly. He forced someone to tell him."

"Or he actually knew you."

"Or that," she agreed, nodding.

"So, when did he meet you?"

Micaela turned to glare at me, causing a strand of red hair to fall over her face. "In the water control station," she said, scrunching her nose and pushing her hair back.

"I know, but before that. I mean, since he's acting like he knows you, when did he say you met?" I asked.

"He didn't say," she said.

"But do you know?"

She nodded.

"But you're not saying because it isn't time yet?"

She sighed. "Logwyn, I'll tell you the answer when we get to me discovering it."

"Fair enough."

Her eyebrows rose and fell, and Micaela looked back at the window.

"So, you lost consciousness?" I asked.

"Yes, but it was hardly an escape."

"I wouldn't think so, but how?"

"Besides the nightmares of bugs crawling inside me and eating me alive?"

She favored me with a wry grin. I shuddered despite my best efforts.

"Yes, besides that."

She stared at me for a moment, her mouth opening and closing a few times. Then she looked away. "Because I found my father deep in that blackness," she whispered.

CHAPTER 18

ILLUSIONS

At first, the blackness brought relief that proved short-lived. After all, if I were truly unconscious, would I know it? Would I feel relief?

That simple fact wiped all the respite away as I looked into a void. A new feeling stood out: one of floating in that void. It seemed especially odd to me, as it felt like I stood on something. I tried jumping, but it moved with my feet. I felt my body tense, my legs coil, and the thrust upward as my body responded. The surface never left, reminding me very much of Quentin's board.

Thinking of him brought other people to mind. Suyef. My siblings. Father. It fanned a primal urge to not be alone, a heat building up inside until I spoke into the blackness.

"Help!" I called, cupping my hands around my mouth. "Help me."

The sound vanished as soon as it left my lips without even an echo. The air felt thick, like the water I'd sunk into before. For a moment, I wondered if I was still there, sinking into oblivion. That everything since had been just a dream.

The sensations now did not resemble the water, though. I recalled other feelings when I'd sunk into the sea: pressure and

the water shifting as it moved. My own body moving. Here, I
didn't feel or hear anything, even when I moved. Only then did
it dawn on me I could move again. When had that happened?

I hung in that void and lost all sense of time. It could have
been an instant or a chron, I'm still not sure. Just when it felt
like nothing would happen, something finally did.

A voice called to me. A familiar one, that voice. One I
longed to hear.

My father's.

"Micaela," the voice whispered, tickling at my ears.
"Sweetheart."

I turned my head toward the sound.

"Micaela."

The sound touched at the other ear.

"Sweetheart, can you hear me?"

"Father? Is that you? I can't see you."

"I'm right here with you," he answered. "Always have been."

I frowned, staring off into the darkness.

"Don't get all sentimental on me, Father. Remember what
you used to say? 'Memories are a poor replacement for the real
thing.'"

I heard him let out a long breath.

"Yes, I know," he whispered. "But right now, that's not
what I meant."

"You're not making any sense, Father."

"Does any of this make sense, Micaela?"

"No, it doesn't." I frowned. "Particularly this conversation.
It's not possible."

He chuckled. I continued looking around, but saw nothing new.

"Isn't it?" he asked, still laughing.

"I don't see what's funny about this," I said, feeling my
cheeks heat. "You're just a figment of my imagination helping

me cope. You're not here. And if you are a part of me, I'm insulted. I'm laughing at myself."

I paused, thinking over what I'd just said. It sounded odd; still does.

"Levity may be your only hope," he said. "And, while I commend your logical explanation for us talking, I can assure you that I am actually here."

"No one is here but me." I waved a hand about my head. "And this blackness."

"No, you're sitting in a room, leaning against a wall thinking you're somewhere else," my father said.

"I was in a room . . ." My voice trailed off. "Wait, how do you know that?"

"I told you, I'm here, watching you," he said. "Right in front of you."

I shook my head, trying to think. "Why would you be there? And why aren't you helping me?"

"There's only one way to help, and you know what it is."

"I don't know what you're talking about, Father," I said. "I don't understand what is happening, how you are here. What . . ."

My words ran out. A single tear rolled down my cheek.

"It's okay, sweetheart," he said, his voice calm. "Take a deep breath and think. Try to remember when it happened."

"When what happened?" I asked, jaw clenching in frustration.

"When you found the device. The one this man is after. Just think back, and you'll remember."

I shook my head a bit too hard and shut my eyes, a sharp pain in my neck.

"I found nothing. No device. No key, nothing," I insisted. "He's lying to you, Father."

"Search your memories, my dear," he continued. "You must have it. He wouldn't insist you did if it weren't true."

I opened my mouth to argue, then paused. He'd called me *my dear*. My father never did that. His pet name for me was *sweetheart*. The only person he'd ever called *dear* was my mother, and he hadn't used that in a long time. But someone else had called me that, done so recently.

"Stop the act, Colvinra. I know it's you."

"This isn't an act, Micaela," my father's voice said. "It is me."

Gritting my teeth, I glared into the blackness.

"Stop these games, Colvinra," I continued. "I don't have it."

The darkness changed from a complete black to a gray hue.

"See that light, Micaela?" my father asked. "It's right overhead. Just open your eyes. I can see them stirring."

"Whatever this is you've stuck me in won't hold me, Seeker." I jutted my chin out and stared straight ahead. "I can't tell you what I don't know."

The darkness faded, revealing blurry images. I blinked, trying to focus. It looked like the room I'd been in before. A figure stood off to one side and another farther away. Colvinra and the guard, I presumed. However, a third figure was present, closer to me and kneeling. He had fading gray hair. I blinked again and my vision cleared, bringing the man before me into focus.

"Father?" I whispered, hardly daring to hope.

He smiled.

"You're awake." He nodded over his shoulder at Colvinra. "I was worried he'd killed you."

"So, it was you I heard talking?" I asked, frowning.

"No, you were out cold," my father said. "I told you, I thought he'd killed you. You were hardly breathing. Then you began murmuring, and I knew you were at least alive."

My eyes narrowed as I looked at the Questioner.

"So, you were planting those words in my head, making me think he was saying them."

Colvinra shrugged.

"You made yourself black out to get away from the illusions. It wasn't just your mind that shut down to protect itself from damage." Half of his mouth twisted into a grin as he pointed at me. "In my book, that means you're hiding something. I'd hoped hearing Daddy might coax you into sharing your secret. Alas, it did not."

Colvinra squeezed his hand into a fist. My father grabbed at his neck, his eyes bulging. One hand reached out toward me and stopped, fingers spread and pushing hard against a glass-like substance. I lunged toward him, my hand slamming into the same wall near his. Climbing to my feet, I pressed near the glass, eyes on my father. His face turned red as he pawed at his neck with his other hand. Every time his hand smacked against his neck, a light shimmered and, for a split second, I saw the symbols again. It was then that I first suspected what was actually happening: I was seeing the code when someone altered it.

"Colvinra, what are you doing? Don't do this. Please."

"Give me what I ask for and this will all end."

My father's face darkened, mouth opened.

"I swear I don't have it," I said, sliding down to my knees. "Please, don't kill him."

My father's face turned purple, and he slumped against the glass. His eyes fluttered, mouth open, chest heaving with each gasp.

"Give it to me, Micaela," Colvinra hissed, voice rising. "This doesn't need to happen this way. I know you have it."

My father stopped moving, and I slammed my fists against the wall, trying to wake him.

"This has gone far enough," the guard bellowed, his voice thundering in the room.

Colvinra spun to face the guard, who strode toward my father. The guard sliced his hand through the air, and whatever held my father in place vanished. His limp body collapsed down onto me, and we fell against the wall. He gasped for air and clutched at my arms. I held him tight, cheek pressed against his head.

"You may not harm this civilian you brought along." He moved between us and the Questioner. "I'll have to ask you to leave until I can inform the council of your actions. I'm sure once they clear this matter up, you can continue with the traitor."

Colvinra's fists clenched tight, and he glared at the guard.

"You impertinent fool," he growled. "This man is her father. Hurting him *is* punishing her."

"If the council agrees," the guard said, shrugging, "then they will return him to your . . . care as soon as possible."

The man pointed at the door.

"For now, please leave and return to your quarters."

The Questioner shifted his stance, hands dropping to either side.

"I'm not leaving until I'm finished," he said, voice low.

"So be it."

He started toward the Questioner, hunching over as he moved. He jerked to a halt after one pace. For a split second, the lines of his body blurred, like a tuning fork being struck. Symbols coalesced all around him, smashing into each other before vanishing. He stumbled one more step before falling to his knees. Colvinra's face broke into a grin.

"Did you think that would work?"

The guard fell to one side, leaning on his arm.

"How are you doing this?" he asked, his voice tight. "How did you stop me?"

I frowned as the Questioner moved toward the confused guard. What had I missed? What was the guard trying to do? Did it have to do with his body blurring?

"I know better than anyone else what you're trying to do," he whispered, kneeling before the man. "I'm the one who brought that knowledge to this world, you uneducated cur."

Colvinra grabbed the man by the throat and lifted him up to his feet. Pulling him close, he glowered down as the man struggled against his grip.

"Did you really think the man who taught the world how to take that form wouldn't know how to stop someone from changing into it?" he whispered, shoving the man away and turning toward me. "Now, where were we?"

The door hissed open and more guards rushed in. Colvinra spun, throwing up his hand. The air rippled in front of him and then moved in a wave across the room to knock the charging men to each side. One guard crossed his arms before him and held his ground, the rippling air only knocking him back a few inches.

"Ah, someone who knows what they're doing," the Questioner said, hands dropping to either side.

The guards fanned out, hands in a defensive posture. Something peculiar happened just around Colvinra's hands. For a split second, the Ancient symbols coalesced and I could make out structures. I glanced at his face and then his hands, but the symbols were gone.

"I'm not leaving," the Questioner said.

"You will leave the prisoners alone," the guard who had held his ground said. "I revoke your authority in this matter."

"Over your dead bodies, it has been."

Colvinra shifted, arms raising to head level. The guards all moved into similar positions, hands in varying places around their heads.

"This will not go well for you," he said, head turning to take each of them in.

The guard opened his mouth to respond just as the door slid open to reveal a man in gray robes with ornate markings all along the edges. A loud sound echoed into the room, elevating and dropping in tone in a repeating pattern. He barked something unintelligible as he stepped in, the door shutting behind him. The guards lowered their hands, but Colvinra didn't move.

"Hold!" the man said, hand out to the Seeker. "Bring your prisoners to the council chambers at once. Guards, escort him, but do not provoke him."

"Why should I cooperate?" the Questioner asked.

"If you don't, this entire room will detonate before you can lift a finger." The man waved an arm at the room. "Taking all of us with you."

"That doesn't give me much reason to trust you," Colvinra muttered, lowering his hands.

The man stepped near the door. It opened, and the loud sound returned.

"We need your help," he said, pointing at a red flashing light.

The Questioner's head cocked to one side, but he said nothing. The man pointed at me.

"Her people are attacking us."

"You said the guard vibrated?" I asked, earning another glare.

"Yes, like a tuning fork. I thought that was a straightforward description," Micaela said, frowning at me.

"I agree. That's not what I'm curious about." I cocked my head to one side. "What do you think he was trying to do?"

"Something I didn't understand then," she replied. "Something that involved his entire body. That's why his entire body shook when Colvinra stopped him." She shuddered. "I can't imagine what that must have felt like."

"Neither can I," I said, contemplating her for a moment before continuing. "But at that moment, you didn't understand."

"Not in the slightest. But I was starting to understand; put it together like puzzle pieces falling into place. It took more time before I could fully comprehend what each of them had done, understand the scale of what Colvinra had done." She looked over at the window, a lock of her long red hair falling down over her chest. "Once I did, I never underestimated that man again."

"But you realized then?" I asked. "When he did this to the guard?"

"Not enough to appreciate his power," Micaela said, shifting in the seat and pushing her hair back over her shoulder. "I mean, I had an inkling after the battle at the prison. However, at that moment, I didn't have a clue. I also didn't fully appreciate the extent to which he would go to get what he wanted."

She turned her eyes back to me, and they looked hollow; hurt. She'd carried that pain for so long that it sometimes overwhelmed her. Yet, this time, I only saw hints of it. Yes, the hurt was there, but she'd mastered controlling it; hiding it. I doubted anyone would ever accuse Micaela of being hysterical. Not anyone with half a brain.

"And that proved to be a fatal mistake for many," she whispered, drawing my attention back. "Including some I hold dear."

"For one of them?" I asked, pointing at Quentin and Suyef in the Queen's pictures.

"Them and others."

I looked over my notes, then up at her.

"So, Colberra came to rescue you?"

"Excuse me?"

"What that man in the ornate robe said. His words were 'her people are attacking.' I presume he meant Colberra got bold enough to attack the Red shell."

Her brow furrowed, head cocking to one side.

"You track history as a part of what you do, yes?"

I nodded.

"Have you ever heard of an upper shell force coming down to the lower shells to attack? Not just against either the Reds or the Greens. Any force ever?"

"No, but this is your story. I'm just trying to make sense of it."

"Well, prepare to be confused, because I was," she said, shifting and crossing one leg over the other. "It wasn't Colberra that had him worried."

Micaela leaned an arm on the back of the couch and rested her head on her hand. She stared at me, waiting. I looked at my notes, then back at her.

"It was the Greens?"

CHAPTER 19

STRIKE

"So, Quentin survived the fall in the outpost," I said, watching Suyef across the table. "Of course he did, as I've talked to him. But how?"

"That's his story to tell, if he ever continues," Suyef said, shaking his head. "And trust me, it's quite the tale to behold. I wouldn't have believed it myself, but there were witnesses."

"Who could have witnessed that?" I asked, frowning.

When he just stared at me, I ventured a guess.

"The Greens?"

"An interesting conclusion," he said, pursing his lips. "Please, explain your logic."

"The outpost crashed one shell in the Green and Red cluster. Plus, we're discussing the Green raid on the Reds, which you've already said he took part in." I spread my hands out before me. "It stands to reason they witnessed his survival."

"I can't argue with your logic."

"There's a *but* coming, isn't there?" I asked, glaring at him.

A small smile tugged at his mouth. Suyef leaned forward, hands pressed flat on the table.

"Unfortunately for you, yes. Neither the Reds nor the Greens witnessed his antics."

He fell silent, eyes on me. I searched my memory, trying to remember the details. Just as I reached for my notes, I got it.

"The people he went back for," I said, snapping my fingers. "They witnessed it because he saved them."

"Their testimony kept him from serious trouble later," the Nomad said. "But we're getting ahead of ourselves. The only part that matters for now is that the shell in question wasn't next to the Green shell, then."

"The Red shell," I surmised.

"And," Suyef said, raising a finger, "somehow, they didn't notice the outpost's crash. That, or they assumed no one survived."

"Meaning Quentin and the survivors were safe from the Reds' attention. So, when the raid happened, he was already there." I glanced up from my notes. "Interesting confluence of events."

"If you only knew."

"So," I said, looking at my notes again, "your strike wasn't a complete surprise."

When he arched an eyebrow at me, I went on.

"They knew you were coming."

"Ah, yes, they clearly knew the Greens were up to something," he said, nodding. "But to say they were ready for us is an overstatement. They were so caught up trying to decide what to do if the Greens did something that they were totally unprepared for an actual strike."

"Wait, they knew you were coming, and you still tricked them? How?"

"By coming from the one direction they didn't think to protect," the Nomad said, pointing at the floor. "The core."

The alarms still echoed everywhere when Colvinra, my father, and I returned to the arena, guards in tow. Reds now filled the chamber, with nary a human in sight in the rows above. The council, still on the platform, conversed among themselves as we approached. The leader lifted its head, and the group fell silent. Its head twitched, and the blaring alarm stopped.

"You know why we summoned you," the Red leader hissed. "Our spies report the Greens are up to something."

"I don't care," the Questioner stated, stopping ten paces from the platform. "This is your fight, not mine."

"You have a vested interest in helping, Colvinra," the leader countered, nodding at me. "You are in as much danger as the rest of us."

"If the Greens mess with me, it will be their mistake," the Questioner said. "This is your mess. Clean it up."

Another council member spoke up. "We can't entrust our prisoners' security to you alone."

"You want her tortured, and now you're concerned about her safety?" Colvinra asked, pointing at me. "She may be an enigma to your society, but still."

"We will carry out her sentence on our terms, not anyone else's," the Red leader said, rising to its full height. "Not yours or the Greens."

"The Greens aren't here to punish her, you fool," Colvinra yelled up at the Red. "They're coming to rescue her."

My father moved closer to me, putting his arm around my shoulders. His hand trembled, so I reached up and gripped it.

"If they do, we'll be ready for them," another council member said, earning a glance from the Red leader.

"Wait, they aren't already on their way?" Colvinra asked the council member. "Then what's with the alarms?"

The leader looked at the offending council member another moment before turning to the Questioner.

"We are in preparation. Intelligence hints at the possibility."
The Red leader's head first shifted side to side, then bobbed up
and down. "We're taking precautions."

"You can't possibly have spies among the Greens," the
Questioner said, looking around the room. "Despite their differences, they would never even think to do that. They lack
imagination."

He fell silent for a moment, still contemplating the council. He looked back at me; at my hair.

"No, you have traitors here. Traitors you've been watching."

As he finished speaking, the entire structure rocked. We fell
to our knees as the dragons above took to the air. The alarm
resumed, more frantically this time. Colvinra moved close,
grabbing us by the arms.

"Time to go," he said.

"What's happening?" my father asked as I pulled him up.

When Colvinra didn't answer, I did.

"The Greens are already here."

"You attacked from the bottom of the shell?" I asked Suyef.

"It was the Red spy's idea. He said there was a passage no
one used."

"And was he right?"

"It was unprotected when we got there. Still, the strike
leader, Gul, didn't want to just charge in."

He raised a cupped hand, palm up, and pointed at his middle knuckle.

"The passage entered the lowest and most central outcropping. Gul positioned us to one side and sent only six Greens

and the Red to scout it out. Once they signaled it was clear, we followed them as they went ahead as a screen."

He held up a single finger.

"Now, before I go on, do you know anything about Green battle tactics?"

"Enough to follow, but explain it anyway for anyone who reads this."

"Right. The basic Green strike unit," the Nomad explained. "Six dragons in a pentagonal formation, five at each point and the leader in the center. They all carry one or two human riders wielding pulse cannons and wearing grav-belts like Quentin's."

"To stay mounted," I said. "Also more range of motion, right?"

"Exactly. Increased firing vectors."

"Also, the spinal structure keeps them on," I said, waving at my back. "Sorry, I know I said I didn't know it well. Actually, I just try to avoid the subject."

"I'm sure you studied at length as a child."

"To a point, yes," I said, smiling at him. "Everyone here does."

"To prepare you in the event it's needed."

"Yes," I said, nodding. "Please, continue."

Suyef watched me for a moment, then shook his head.

"The human riders are completely responsible for their own safety when outside the dragon's spinal structure," he said.

"Yeah," I said, waving a hand over my chest. "Because down around the torso, the spinal structure's effect loses focus."

"Particularly on smaller Greens," he added.

"The smaller the mass, the less pull it has," I said. "Simple physics."

"Hence the belts. But staying on the dragon isn't their only concern. Wings, appendages, and, sometimes, other structures. Also, projectiles."

"Wouldn't the spinal structure's effect deflect most of those?" I asked, frowning. "No, no, I remember now."

When Suyef said nothing, I went on.

"The structure's force only reaches a certain distance around the spinal column itself. It cancels the effect of other gravitational forces, rendering the dragon weightless. Particularly helpful for intershell travel."

"Which is why the dragons, both Red and Green, have been the dominant power since the Shattering," Suyef said, holding up a single finger. "One fact that survived the lost era before our historical accounts begin."

"We've gone a bit off-shell," I said, trying to refocus. "I realize some of this was for anyone who reads this, but I assume reviewing Green tactics matters in the narrative."

"Very much so. The details make certain parts of the story even more amazing once you hear them."

"Is this when you learned about the strike formation?" I asked.

"Yes. That screening force? I was riding as the lead dragon's front rider."

"Why would they risk you in that position?" I asked, furrowing my brow. "You had no experience."

He smiled. "A friendly face."

"Right, Micaela would see you," I said. "But couldn't they have brought you in with a different strike force? I assume they sent several."

"Five teams. Thirty dragons plus about sixty gunners. And the insurgents."

"A number you didn't know, and you couldn't tell them apart from the other Reds."

"Yes," he said, nodding. "That would prove interesting later."

"Interesting for whom?" I asked. "The Greens or the Reds?"

"Both, but we're getting ahead of ourselves—again," he said. "To answer your question, I went in with the first team, whose mission was finding and rescuing Micaela."

I frowned at Suyef.

"So, what were the rest doing while the first team did that?"

He smiled at me. "Distracting the Reds."

The alarms continued to blare as a couple of Reds soared out through passages above. Most remained, eyes cast to their leaders below. The council hissed at each other, ignoring us.

"Time to move," the Seeker said, shoving us toward the door.

"Where do you think you are going?" the Red leader said as the guards moved closer.

"To do what you aren't," Colvinra muttered.

As the guards approached, the Questioner flung out his hands to either side. The guards flew backward and slammed into the arena walls. For a split second, I saw something coalescing near his hands again, but it vanished when I tried to focus on it.

"Father, did you see that?" I asked, pointing at the Seeker's hands.

My father didn't answer, but he looked between me and the Questioner. His eyes narrowed, and he opened his mouth to speak, but Colvinra rushed forward and shoved us toward the door. Behind us, the guards lay strewn about like dolls tossed on the floor.

"You dare attack us?" the Red leader's voice boomed behind us.

Colvinra spun around.

"No, the Greens dare do that," he yelled. "And you dared to attack me."

Another tremor rocked the chamber. He pointed at the council.

"You've got other creatures to skin before you lose control of this shell. Again."

He spun away from the council with that last word. The Red leader looked ready to launch itself and strike the Seeker, but a large tremor shook the room, making me stumble and my father fall to his knees. Colvinra kept his balance, but only just. The council exchanged looks before nodding at the lead dragon.

"This is not over, Colberran," the Red leader hissed. "If anything happens to her, you will share in her punishment."

It rose into the air, wings flapping in a flurry.

"Reds, to your stations. Today, we fight. Tomorrow, we get justice!"

Every dragon in the chamber roared and took to the air, soaring out in a massive blur of red and gold.

"Come on," the Questioner bellowed, rounding on us. "Better to vanish before our reptilian friends grow a spine." He favored me with a hideous grin. "Either the crimson or emerald kind."

I helped my father to his feet, and the three of us rushed out into the long hallway. At the first intersection, Colvinra shoved me to the right.

"Keep moving, ketch," he said. "And no funny ideas, or I'll just kill him now. I've got other ways of convincing you to talk."

My father moved closer to me as the three of us fled the arena.

"Did you see something, Micaela?" he asked me. "When that Seeker was fighting the guards?"

"Yes," I said, leaning close as we moved. "Symbols. Like on the computers."

Behind us, the alarms echoed, and we could hear distant cries of battle. Then the hall shuddered, knocking us all into the walls. I barely registered the sound of cracking rock before the entire structure collapsed on us.

CHAPTER 20

DISTRACTIONS

"When we entered that passage, I wasn't sure what to expect," Suyef continued. "Resistance. Or maybe a hideout of insurgents." He shook his head. "Nothing. The insurgent led us to a large chamber and said that we would encounter Red patrols beyond that point."

"How far below the city were you?" I asked.

He held a hand up above the table as far as he could reach.

"If that's the top of the shell and the table is where we entered, the city would be about here," he answered, holding his other hand almost as high as the first.

"So, a long way," I stated, jotting a note down. "Did the insurgent have a plan to get past the patrols and up into the city?"

"Not what I'd call a plan," Suyef said. "He wanted to help but really just got in the way. Still, he proved useful in one way."

"How so?"

"Distraction," he said. "He fooled guards while other insurgents drew the patrols' attention, all so we could incapacitate them. But once the real distraction began, all pretense of sneaking went out of the tunnel."

"What did the rest of the strike force do, exactly? Besides the obvious."

"Precisely that." He smiled at me. "They gave the Reds exactly what they expected. A frontal assault on their outer structures. They attacked from five different directions."

"So the Reds couldn't focus their defenses," I said, nodding. "Still, only thirty dragons and sixty gunners. They hopelessly outnumbered you."

"The Reds proved less dangerous to us in the end," he said, voice lowering.

I frowned at him and shrugged. The Nomad let out a breath I hadn't realized he'd been holding.

"Once past the initial patrols, we made our way up a labyrinth of tunnels. Even I would have a hard time navigating that on my own. The sheer number of tunnels and caves made me wonder if the cavernous network was natural. Either way, it took a lot longer than expected to get to the shell's inhabited parts. We continued up into the shell. The plan, shared with me once inside, was to get to the inhabited portions before the attack so we would face less opposition in the prison." He grimaced. "But you know what they say about plans."

"They're useless once things take flight?"

"Exactly. We barely made it to the lower sections of their city."

"Then the attack started?" I tapped my notes. "Something that shook the city?"

He frowned. "No, the only way we knew it had begun was the alarms and the Reds appearing everywhere. The initial response seemed more precautionary, but it meant Reds taking positions near the ceiling of each tunnel, giving them full view in both directions. So, we moved into smaller passages."

"To avoid detection," I said. "Makes sense."

"Eventually, we ran out of those tunnels," he continued. "I wasn't sure how far in we were, but our ability to remain undetected soon ended. We entered a large cavern partway up the side. They had carved many structures out of the rock face. Dim lighting emanated from stalactites and stalagmites, providing a soft luminescent glow to the entire space, including every Red guarding the cave."

He placed one hand at the edge of the table, then moved the other away from it at an angle up to the ceiling. "Our squad leader, Set, ordered a quick move like this to the next tunnel, with gunners targeting the light structures to hide our movements."

"Wouldn't that be moot once clear of the tunnel? They'd see you."

"Yes," he said, "but it adds confusion, a boon in a fight."

"But they could see your path when the lights went out."

"We spread out to reduce that effect."

"Did that work?"

"It proved unnecessary," he said, shaking his head. "Before we could act, tremors rocked the cavern, and the alarms returned. The attack had begun, providing us with plenty of confusion." He pointed up. "Pieces of the cave broke free, crashing down into the structures. We could hear screams everywhere, and the Reds abandoned their posts."

"If they were ready for an attack, why would this bother them so?" I asked, frowning.

He shrugged.

"Maybe they were unprepared for what happened. Maybe they were expecting something else. I don't know. All I know is, when the cavern shook, they abandoned their posts."

"Making your progress easier."

"Not entirely," he said. "Some held their positions. Inconveniently, the ones nearest our target passage."

"So, you had to attack them?" I asked, eyebrows rising at the thought. "Not sneak around them?"

Suyef shook his head. "They spotted us almost instantly."

"So much for that."

"We expected it," he said. "We just hoped to minimize any fighting."

He paused for several heartbeats, staring at his hands.

"So, what happened next?" I asked, stylus in hand, watching him.

"Our team darted out of the passage," he continued with a shake of his head. "We kept a tight, flat formation: two dragons front, two each side, and the leader, Set, in the middle with one behind him."

He moved his hand across his body and then up toward the ceiling. "A column just above our planned exit dashed our hopes of slipping away. It hung down to either side, forcing us closer to other light structures. So, our two lead dragons launched small bursts of fire to destroy the column. As their fireballs detonated, the alarm intensified in the cavern. Reds began dropping from above, heading for us. Our formation flew out from the wall, shifting back to a vertical pentagon."

"I assume vertical means along your flight trajectory?" I asked, and he nodded. "And you planned that move?"

"Yes," he said. "All of their formation shifts were so coordinated that I assumed they'd trained on them a lot. Of course, they only told me about a few."

"Thanks. Please continue."

"As the Reds fired at us," he went on, "the five dragons expanded and contracted around the leader. They returned fire, forcing the charging Reds to dodge instead of focusing their fire. As the two forces neared, the gunners moved into action.

"The Greens shifted back, parallel with the ceiling, and moved into a diamond pattern. The rear gunners slid under the racing dragons, pulse weapons drawn, while the lead gunners all jumped up toward the ceiling, grav-belts keeping them tethered to their mounts. Just as the Reds and Greens reached each other, the latter dove away from the ceiling. The front gunners followed them and, as we flew under the Reds, I heard rocks cracking. Overhead, entire swaths of stalactites broke free and shot down like missiles. The deadly projectiles smashed into the Reds, sending them crashing down toward the city below. What debris remained raced after us up into the passage. A few Reds moved to follow and, just as they reached the passage opening, the rear gunners unloaded their pulse guns into the following debris. The large chunks of earth shattered into a shower of smaller pieces. The instant the rocks exploded, the lead gunners flung the mass of debris into the pursuing Reds."

"Brutal," I whispered.

"But effective," he said. "That group stopped pursuing us."

"An attack probably just stunned or disoriented them," I said, nodding. "After the initial shock, their instincts would kick in and their spinal structure would save them from a fall." I grimaced and waved a hand at him. "Still brutal. What happened next?"

"We raced up the passage, certain only that we were moving up," he continued. "That tunnel proved very short, and the Reds lay in wait for us."

"How did they know you were coming?"

"Someone warned them, probably," he said. "Regardless, they were waiting for us. When we entered the next chamber, a volley of fire struck the passage, showering us with debris. My mount jerked to one side along with the other two on that side of the formation. The three opposite us took off in the other direction. The Greens unleashed a return volley as they split, striking rock formations across the cavern. Reds hiding there scattered and returned fire. The gunners all jumped toward the ground, throwing more projectiles at the Reds."

"How were six dragons causing this much havoc?" I asked, cutting him off. "The distraction was that effective?"

"Indeed," he said. "They looked uncertain and maybe a bit surprised we were that deep in the shell. Most likely, they thought they were too far from the exterior to face any attacks. Especially that early." He arched an eyebrow at me. "Our sudden arrival appeared to fluster them, making hit-and-run tactics much more effective."

"Still, I'd expect a better, more organized defense."

"Maybe, maybe not. Either way, they weren't ready for us, and we took advantage of that. As the attacking Greens outside drove inward, we pressed on. Up to that point, the plan seemed to work."

"Seemed?" I asked. "So far, this plan *seems* to have gone perfectly."

"Like I said, it seemed fine." He let out a sigh and shook his head. "That lasted until the battle truly started. We made it to the central portions of the city before that happened."

"The defense was stronger there, I'm assuming."

"That, and they had a secret weapon." Suyef leveled a gaze at me. "A powerful one with a nasty predilection toward Green dragons."

I frowned at him.

"And toward Micaela," he added.

Realization dawned.

"Colvinra," I whispered.

CHAPTER 21

DEFENDER

The dust covered everything when I opened my eyes to look around. My father lay behind me, arms curled tight over my torso and head. His hair, gray with age, now looked chalky white. Colvinra, his arms out to either side, stood over us like a protective shield. The rubble of the smashed hall lay in a ring around us, and far above through where the hall ceiling once stood, I saw the distant roof of a massive cavern.

The Questioner blinked and pulled his arms back. As he did, something shimmered around us, and the Ancient symbols I'd seen before flickered into view. The entire construct wavered, then dissipated like smoke. With the construct gone, dusty air flowed in, tickling my nose and causing me to sneeze.

"Get up," the Questioner barked, grabbing at us. "This structure won't hold much longer."

Gaining my bearings, I puzzled over what he'd done. Looking at the rubble, at how it lay in a circle with only dust in the middle, it was clear he had shielded us. He still valued me, or, rather, something he thought I had. Considering our circumstance, trapped on an enemy shell with no one around to help us, I decided that not arguing against his delusion about said object was in our best interest.

I grabbed at my father and rushed back the way Colvinra pointed. As we rounded a corner, two guards nearly collided with us. One had a nasty gash on his forehead, and the other held his arm tight to his torso.

"Don't go that way," the cut guard said, nodding over his shoulder. "Structure's compromised. Arena's in ruins."

"What happened?" I asked, gazing in that direction.

"Greens blew out the top," the other guard said, grabbing his companion with his good arm. "Come on, before they come this way."

"Stand and fight, fools," the Questioner ordered them.

The two men exchanged glances, then turned and ran away from the arena.

"Cowards," he muttered, rounding on us and pointing after them. "Move!"

He shoved me in the same direction, away, I noticed, from the battle he'd just ordered the guards to go fight. Not that I wanted to be involved in a fight between dragons. One could say a person need only experience that once to fully appreciate it. As events would play out, I could only avoid that experience for so long.

Colvinra herded us through a maze of hallways, finally stopping us before some sealed doors. He pushed one open and peeked through. After a moment, he stuck his head out. I shifted around behind my father, then saw the Questioner's hand, a single finger pointing at me.

"Don't even think about it," he threatened, his hand balling into a fist. "Try anything, and I promise you'll regret it."

I stood close to my father and took his hand, grateful to have him back. The only family member I had left. I had so much I wanted to say but couldn't just then. He favored me with a smile before he resumed watching the Questioner.

"If you can see the symbols, Micaela, it means you can change them," my father whispered, eyes never leaving the Seeker's back. "You can make the constructs like he's doing."

"How?" I asked.

Colvinra, his search finished, cut off our conversation with a shove to the door. He beckoned us to follow.

"Move quickly, before any of the infernal creatures come around," he said.

"Which are we hiding from?" I asked as I looked around.

A series of glowing stalactites illuminated a large tunnel that extended out of sight around walls of rock in both directions.

"Take your pick," the Questioner said, moving left. "The Reds don't like you, the Greens me. Running into either would be bad."

"The Reds seem angry with you, Seeker," my father interjected. "You may have more to worry about than us."

"You go on telling yourself that, old man," the Questioner said, grinning. "We'll see who's in the most danger here."

We continued down the tunnel as sounds of battle echoed through the passage. Every moment, I expected the battle to come crashing down on us or for something to shake the structure loose. I kept a wary eye on the rock overhead, pondering what to do if it cracked or came down on us. With my attention on the ceiling, I didn't see a crack in the ground and tripped. My father tried to catch me, but my momentum pulled him with me.

As we fell, an explosion detonated right overhead, sending a shower of rock and debris all around us. Shielding my eyes, I looked back at the tunnel. Red faction guards, just visible in the dim light, rushed toward us with pulse guns drawn. Colvinra yelled something just before the rocks lying strewn about rose and flew down the hall at the charging humans. One guard fell from a blow to the head, two others slammed

face-first into the ground after a boulder took their feet out.
The rest kept coming.

"Get behind me," the Questioner called, hand up toward
the guards.

Symbols shimmered around his hand and didn't fade away.
Pulse shots from the guards' weapons smashed into an invisible
wall, making only a thud against our captor-turned-protector's
shield. With a shove, the Questioner flung the entire construct
down the chamber, knocking everything, guard and debris,
back. I jumped up, grabbing my father as Colvinra shoved him
down the hall.

"Do that again, old man, and I'll leave you behind."

"He fell helping me, idiot," I hissed.

"Whatever. I have little reason to keep him either alive or
with us." He moved ahead as we approached a fork. "Keep
going. Any more trouble, and this will be your tomb."

"Colvinra put up quite the defense for you two," I stated when
Micaela paused in her narrative. "Threats against your father
notwithstanding."

Micaela shrugged.

"That man was a mystery. One minute intent on making
my life either difficult or painful, the next fending off waves of
Red guards." She grimaced. "His motivation wasn't confusing."

"He wanted the key device," I said. "Which you didn't
have, let alone even know what it was yet."

Micaela smiled at me.

"Are we dangling a net over the shell to catch something?"

"You'll tell me when you tell me."

"Nice try, Logwyn," she said, chuckling. "You want to know, and now."

I favored her with a grin.

"Yes, but you've rebuffed me enough. I know better."

Micaela pursed her lips and narrowed her eyes at me but said nothing.

"So, you were fleeing the guards?"

Another squad ran into view as we approached the fork. Colvinra grabbed nearby debris and struck each of the guards in the head, and the men fell. Only one raised his weapon. We rushed down the left fork, voices echoing behind us. A tremor shook the passage, knocking me toward a wall, the Questioner into the other, and my father to his knees between us. Another tremor rocked the shell, dust falling down onto our heads.

"What was that?" I whispered, looking around.

"Dragons firing at each other," Colvinra muttered, pushing himself off the wall. "Keep moving."

Just as I moved, a pulse shot ripped into the rock face behind me. Colvinra pulled his own weapon from inside his robes and sent several pulses back the way we'd just come. I heard several shouts and a thud, followed by more shots at us. The rock wall to my right detonated in a shower of tiny debris, raining down on my father's head. The tunnel vibrated and shook as more dragon strikes missed each other and hit the shell. Those blasts felt closer, possibly right overhead. However, in that space, I couldn't tell.

We stumbled our way to the end of the passage, Colvinra standing his ground and firing shots. My father and I took cover to one side of the tunnel exit, which led into a decent-sized cave that ran perpendicular to the passageway we'd just left. Massive, glowing stalactites illuminated the entire cave. We stood on a wide, smooth, artificial platform carved from the stone about halfway up one side of the large cave. As before, buildings jutted out from the wall in either direction, with rows of the structures lining the cave above and below us.

A blast of rocks ripping out of the tunnel brought my attention back to our pursuers. Colvinra still held his ground, launching volley after volley from his pulse guns. Shots from the guards detonated all around, one striking the Questioner. It should have knocked him backward, but, just as it hit, the telltale shimmer of his scripted shield blossomed into view. The bolt of agitated air struck the leading edge of his triangular-shaped shield, slicing in two and dissipating. The Questioner unleashed two more shots into the tunnel. In the distance, I heard a thud, then nothing. Colvinra grinned as the last of our pursuit fell. He turned and moved near the platform's edge, my father and me following.

"We can't be in the open space," the Questioner said, looking around. "The guards are one thing. Out here, we're like fragments adrift from a shell."

"Lost?" I asked.

"Defenseless," he said. "The residents might come out, and you're not exactly a welcome sight. They'll just as likely turn on us as run away. More so inclined to attack is my opinion." He looked up at the cave ceiling. "And let's not forget the other issue."

I followed his gaze and pondered the outcome of a Green dragon finding us. Would it harm us or just take out Colvinra? Why were the Greens attacking at all? Could they really be coming to rescue me? If so, why? So many questions with no answers. Even the Seeker confused me. Despite fending off the guards, I didn't trust him. Nothing he'd said eased that feeling. Were we really any better off with him than anyone else here?

A group of men wearing drab clothing came out from a nearby building, all brandishing weapons. They froze when they caught sight of us, and, after seeing me, they screamed and charged. Colvinra spun into action while we dodged behind a building to take cover. A section of the rock face ripped out and soared toward the platform's edge, taking three men off with it. The others converged on the Questioner. He downed one with a pulse gun and sidestepped an attempt at his head with a nasty-looking blade attached to a long staff. Colvinra swept his leg and took that man down as he shot a third square in the chest just as he was preparing to leap toward the Questioner. Another piece of rock flew up and knocked the last of them to the ground. Colvinra turned to face us, sweat glistening on his forehead.

"Keep moving," he said, rushing closer.

"Do you know where we are going?" I asked.

"Anywhere they aren't," he hissed, waving a hand at the dragons overhead.

More people appeared from the structures. Colvinra fired his pulse guns at the first few and threw chunks of the walls to take out more. My father and I dodged around a fallen guard and darted back toward the structures on our left as another rolled to the ground from a stone to the head.

"Get down!" the Questioner cried out.

I dropped into a roll, knocking my father in the legs to send him down in a sprawl. A chunk of wall ripped free just behind us and soared past, dropping debris all around. I watched the former wall collide with a pair of men, knocking them off the platform. Another man dove under the flying rock, only to fall to Colvinra's pulse gun. The Questioner spun into view, one gun firing back the way we'd come, the other aimed beyond us.

"Get up," he hissed. "Hurry."

My father hesitated, his face flushed, his brow glistening, and his chest heaving.

"He can't keep this up," I said, putting my arm around my father.

"He'll do so, or he gets left behind," Colvinra said, turning a pulse gun on my father. "His choice."

"I'm fine, Micaela," my father said, putting a hand on my shoulder. "Really."

He pushed himself up, head high, and stared back at the Questioner.

"Let's go."

Uncertain my father spoke the truth, I moved alongside him, giving the Questioner a nasty look. Our situation was precarious enough without our self-appointed guardian exacerbating it. My father and I moved in the direction he had pointed.

Just as we cleared the ripped-out wall, a roar echoed through the cavern. All three of us halted, my head spinning to find the source of the earsplitting shriek. Colvinra shifted beside me, but I ignored him. A swish of air danced past us as another shriek filled my ears. A flash of green caught my eye off to the left, then another and another. Each sent a ray of hope through me like an electric shock.

The Greens had arrived.

"I want to feel proud that my people made it to you before Colvinra did something nasty."

"Waiting for the other shoe to drop, Logwyn?" Micaela asked, standing and stretching.

"It seems to be the pattern," I said, standing and shaking my legs awake. "Two flaps of the wing, then fall back a bit."

"I find your use of such colloquialisms interesting, considering."

I shrugged. She smiled and moved over to the kitchen, retrieving a glass of water I'd prepared for her before starting that day. She sipped the water and stared at me, her eyes sharp and intent.

"Your demeanor is different today." When she arched an eyebrow at me, I nodded at my notes. "Whatever comes next must not all be bad."

"Compared to what?" she asked, frowning.

"Previously, these pauses occur after you tell me something bad has happened, like when something happened to your family members." I nodded at the picture frames. "Or Quentin, in one instance. So I watched you and, with the benefit of hindsight, your demeanor showed what was coming." I pointed at her. "You're carrying yourself differently this time. Your head is high, shoulders back. You're looking at me instead of out the window."

She favored me with a small smile. "You're very observant."

"I've had a lot of chances to watch you."

"Don't sell yourself short, yet," she stated, moving around the counter. "Life will do enough of that."

"So, if whatever is next isn't as bad as the rest, what was it?"

She stopped, eyes locked on mine for several moments. "I learned something."

CHAPTER 22

SHIELDS

"So, when you finally encountered Colvinra, was Micaela with him?" I asked Suyef as we resumed our seats, hydration and nutritional packs in hand.

"To be honest, I didn't know he was there until it was too late," the Nomad said after sipping from a pack. "A lot of what happened when we made it into that portion of the city was a blur."

He consumed more of his pack, then continued speaking. I downed the rest of one nutritional packet, then ripped into another.

"Our tactics changed little: dart, dodge, confront only when pressed, and keep moving up. Tunnels made us easier targets. In those, the world spun around me as the Greens constantly changed spots in formation. The passages offered one advantage: a steady supply of rocks to grab and throw at our pursuers. Between our breakneck speeds and the barrage of missiles sent behind us, the pursuit rarely fired any meaningful shots."

Suyef moved a hand under the table, then brought it back up, fingers pointed high at the ceiling.

"Then we entered the first major cave, twice as large as any so far. Steep walls surrounded an oblong-like space, with a city lining those walls in a standard cavern city layout: tiers of platforms carved from stone forming shelves all the way up the sides." He held a hand over his head and waved the other above it. "The lower structures lay in sight. The darkness obscured those above, but I could see them on the opposite side. Initially, we stayed near the wall, darting along one tier. I tried to look for people in the city, but they were hiding or not present."

"Could you just not see them owing to speed?" I asked.

"Maybe. Either way, the cavern seemed empty, but not for long," he said, grimacing a bit. "Not that we stayed in the air." He held up a single finger. "Rather, *I* did not stay in the air. Nor did my mount."

"Reds took you out?"

"We might have dodged that kind of attack." He leaned forward on the table. "We re-formed the flat pentagon and flew over the city. Nobody was in sight initially. Just as the cave curved, though, Reds began emerging from all over the city. Dozens of them flew in close, but never fired."

"Because of the city. They didn't want to damage it."

"We thought so, too, and we took advantage of that."

He held one hand flush with the table, just a few centimeters off the surface. Then he moved it from left to right.

"As close as we dared for fear of surface fire. That proved our mistake. So intent on avoiding attacks from above and below, we missed what was in front of us."

"How could you not see something coming right at you? Your point dragons should have had that assignment, yes?"

"Now you're an expert on the formation?" he asked, one eyebrow raised.

"No, it's just obvious. If you're in front, that's your responsibility."

"You're correct, and they should have been more careful. But remember: we were really moving, so seeing people on the ground was difficult. Still, I think they should have seen it coming."

"So, what was it?" I asked, waving at him to continue.

"I'm not sure what *it* was," he said with a shrug. "But I know the source."

"Colvinra," I said, tapping a page. "You said that before."

"None of us saw him do it, but the investigation later revealed it was him. Whatever he did, it caught all of us—dragons and gunners—by surprise." He leaned back, head cocked to one side. "Have you ever flown before?"

"How do you think I got here?"

"Right. So, you understand the precarious nature of it. Now imagine something forcing your mount to a sudden stop."

A shudder shook my torso.

"I'm not fond of heights as it is. That would be terrifying."

"When he struck, *terrifying* is the perfect word. We were flying at top speed, and I remember looking behind us for any pursuit that was maneuvering to fire at us." He held up a single finger. "One moment, I was staring back at our two trail mounts." A second finger joined the first. "The next, my mount just vanished, and I flew, feet flipping up over my head. My grav-belt tried to keep me tethered, and I had just enough time to lock on to something below me before I crashed down onto a hard surface."

"And the dragon?" I asked.

He brought the hand down onto the table. "Right on top of me."

I felt mixed emotions when the Greens flew into view: partly glad, hoping for rescue, partly angry over them taking my brothers, and a bit confused surrounding their presence. Were they even there to help? They'd helped before, and it turned out badly for us.

I felt all of that in a few heartbeats. Five Greens flying in a flat pentagon formation with a sixth larger dragon in the center soared into the cavern. I just made out a pair of humans riding atop each creature. How had such a small contingent made it this far without being stopped? Then again, how deep into the shell were we? At first, they were alone—but not for long. Dozens of Reds eventually followed them out, joined by many more from the cavern.

Another tremor shook the city, knocking us down. I looked around for the source, as none of the dragons in sight had fired on each other, let alone the city. Were more Greens attacking elsewhere? That would explain how this small force got here.

Just as they flew directly over us, something went wrong. The center dragon jerked downward. Its body convulsed and contorted, and I could see its scales compressing around the middle. Something had grabbed it. The two riders flew clear and fell down onto a platform below us. A twinge of fear gripped me until I saw one of them flip and slow his descent. The riders seemed to have something like Quentin's belt to stay on their mounts, a precaution that just saved them. For the moment.

A grunt drew my gaze to Colvinra, who stood with an arm outstretched toward the captured Green, the hand gripped tight into a fist. He flung his arm down, and the Green fell down toward its riders. The collision that followed shook our platform and sent a cloud of debris across the cavern.

Shouts rose all around us, some cheers, some cries of concern. People rushed out from the buildings to look down at the spectacle. I heard more noises below: people crying out for help and others for those needing it. Guards appeared nearby, rushing to look over the side while giving Colvinra a wide berth. Several formed up facing him, most brandishing staffs with a few carrying pulse guns. Those guards fired at the Seeker, one striking him square in the chest. He stepped back from the impact, and I saw Ancient symbols shimmer around him. Another hit him in the leg with the same result.

"He's shielding himself," I said as we huddled near a wall. "You can see it, too, can't you?"

My father looked at me, then at the Questioner.

"I see pulse shots hitting something and having no effect."

"You don't see the Ancient symbols?" I asked.

He looked at the Seeker, turned back to me.

"Micaela, are you certain you can see him scripting?" he asked, his voice quiet.

When I nodded, he put a hand on my shoulder.

"Did you ever wonder why we taught you to read those symbols?" He looked at the Seeker, still defending himself. "It was so you could script if you ever figured out how to see the code."

"You knew all along, didn't you?" I asked. "That I could do this."

He shook his head. "No, but we knew you could never learn how if you didn't know how to read and write them."

"How did you know that much?"

He shrugged. "We had an excellent source, that's all I'll say for now." He pointed at Colvinra. "Focus on what he's doing. See the constructs he's using. It's just like coding. Once you can see the construct, you can make it and do the same thing."

"How?"

He chuckled. "Yes, I remember that reaction my first time seeing the symbols."

"Wait," I said, pointing at Colvinra. "You just said you couldn't see them."

The Questioner ripped another chunk from a wall nearby. He threw it at a passing Green, just missing.

"No, I said I saw the shots hitting something," he said. "Stop assuming."

Before I could respond, a pulse shot blasted into a nearby wall. I dove away as debris spread in every direction. Nearby, Colvinra fended off more guards armed with projectile weapons. My father grabbed my shoulder, nodding toward a wall chunk. We crawled behind the protection it offered.

"We can't stay here. There's an alley." I pointed at it as I looked back to find Colvinra surrounded. "Quick, while he's distracted."

My father grabbed my arm before I could stand.

"Wait. Do you recall your structures?"

"Seriously? A grammar lesson?"

"Do you remember them?" he asked, and I nodded. "Well enough to see them in your mind?"

"Depends on how complicated the structure is," I said.

A peek around the chunk revealed most of the guards down, Colvinra still fighting the others.

"Why—" I paused, looking back at my father. "You're kidding."

"I'm dead serious."

"You want me to do what he's doing?" I asked. "I don't know how he did it, let alone the column structure necessary to make that code."

"Look closer."

Colvinra held out his right hand and squeezed his fist shut. A guard running at him jerked to a halt, a burst of symbols appearing around his neck. The man, his face reddening, clawed at his throat as Colvinra focused on something below. A moment later, he flung his arm across his body toward the edge. The poor guard flew off and collided with an ascending Green. The mighty beast didn't even flinch, but the tumbling guard struck one rider. Both men fell from sight.

The Questioner turned toward us, but more guards rushed him from the opposite side. Several pulse shots found their mark, enough to push him back. With each shot, the structures formed, pulsed out in a wave, then vanished.

"It's not one structure," I said. "It's a lot of them overlapping, the same column over and over."

"Close enough to make it all out?"

I squinted and watched the columns appear and vanish. Then I shut my eyes and imagined drawing the column on a piece of paper, tracing the symbol on the platform beneath me.

"It reads *window* in the center. It also has some dangling adjectives." I opened my eyes. "That's it! Impenetrable glass. The central column reads *glass* and the modifiers add the elements to make it impenetrable. He's wearing many small chunks like a cloak, overlapping like an arch. That must be where it gets its strength from: multiple pieces supporting the other. And air must pass through the cracks so he can breathe."

"Try to form one in your mind. Remember your scripting lessons," my father said, pulling me back behind the fallen wall. "Build it in your mind."

I closed my eyes and drew the structure in the air before my face. I could see it in my head easy enough, but the battle nearby distracted me, and the construct fell apart. Covering my ears, I hummed to block the noise, singing the strokes as I drew the imaginary column. With the construct nearly complete, something finally dawned on me.

"Mother made us memorize all the notes that match those structures for this." I looked at my father. "Both of you were teaching us to do this all along."

"And training you in Ancient technology," he said, grinning. "Did it work?"

"It fell apart when I had that thought," I said.

"Did it?"

I closed my eyes, and the structure reappeared.

"Well, it certainly came back faster than before." I waved in front of me. "Something's missing. It lacks solidity."

I looked back over the rock at the struggling combatants. More guards lay strewn about the Questioner, but more kept coming. I concentrated on his shield.

"Oh, I see it," I said, settling back down. "There's another symbol at the bottom." I held up one hand, flat with fingers up, and pointed at my wrist. "Here. It's a weird one. I think it means *solidity*."

"Confirmation bias," my father said. "You thought that word, so you translated it that way. It means *foundation*."

I snapped my fingers. A guard flew past us and smashed against a wall and fell to the ground, grabbing the back of his head. We both moved away from the poor man to hide behind another rock.

"That stupid line. You always made us put a line on the bottom when we drew these. You called it the foundation." I lightly smacked my forehead. "Why didn't you make it that symbol?"

"Drawn incorrectly, it can change an entire construct. We put that off until later." He looked down. "Then things happened."

"Focus," I said, placing a hand on his shoulder. "Worry about the past later." I looked over the rock to see Colvinra still holding his own against yet another wave of guards attacking him while their dragon brethren focused on the Greens above. "So, if I start with that at the bottom, does that make it solid?" I looked at him. "No, you made us draw the line of the column."

"Exactly," he said, pointing at his wrist. "Unlike here, make the hand first, then connect it. Don't build out from the wrist."

I closed my eyes and pictured the column. It returned even faster, but I added the foundation symbol at the bottom this time. Something felt familiar about this structure, like I'd seen it before today.

"This is very similar to that firewall program you had us make," I said. "No, not similar. It's exactly the same." I opened my eyes and looked at him. "That's why the Colberran government forbids learning computer coding on the Ancient systems. They're the same thing."

He nodded. "And why we had to keep it a secret." He looked over at Colvinra. "Did it work?"

I nodded. "I place it sideways to prevent it from connecting?"

"Precisely," my father said.

I closed my eyes and looked at the now-completed structure. The entire construct came into focus, feeling solid, something I could grab. I imagined touching it, then opened my eyes.

"Well?"

"I constructed it right in front of my face."

My father reached toward me and his hand collided with something inches from my nose. The telltale symbols pulsed, and I cried out.

"I did it!"

My father reached out again and touched my face.

"And lost your concentration. It's not permanent."

I repeated the process, keeping my excitement contained when my father reached out. Then, my father punched my face. At first, the shield held, but it startled me, and the construct fell apart. It slowed his hand, but he still struck my forehead, knocking me on my back.

"Sorry, sweetheart," he said, pulling me back up. "But you have to be prepared for the unknown." He peeked over the wall. "Try again. He's still fighting half the city."

I repeated the exercise several more times, with my father doing his best to distract me. After a few attempts, I held several of them together despite the battle's cacophony and my father's annoying pokes mixed with throwing small debris and an occasional punch.

"You've always had a knack for this stuff, but I did not expect you to learn this so quickly. Especially such a complicated construct. Everyone's got a specialty. Time will tell if that is yours." He moved to the far side of the rock. "Now, I believe you wanted to escape?"

I peeked around and saw another guard flying off the ledge. Several more closed in on Colvinra, who kept looking over at us.

"Does he ever tire?" I wondered aloud, straining my neck to see down the alley. "I'm feeling exhausted just from what we did."

"He's well-trained, so it requires less effort," my father stated. "Still, he can't last forever."

"We should try to get away while he's distracted," I said.

When the Questioner spun to face a charging guard, I pushed my father toward the alley and followed. Just as my father made the alley, Colvinra cried out, his voice filled with rage. I looked back and saw him fling his hand at us. Ancient script coalesced and shot toward my father.

"Down!" I yelled, rushing in front of the pulse.

Facing the attack, I formed as many structures as I could imagine right in front of me. It shimmered as a large shield materialized. The collision of charged air particles detonated against my shield with unexpected force, pushing me into the alley. I leaned into the shield, but my feet tangled, and I tripped. As I fell back, Colvinra launched multiple air pulses into the sides of the alley. Debris sprayed everywhere, and both walls collapsed down on my shield, burying me.

CHAPTER 23

EMERGENCE

"Right on top of you?" I repeated Suyef's words. "Bit dramatic?"

"No, the Green landed right on me, but momentum carried it past before overwhelming my belt's gravity beams."

"Was it hurt?"

"It took off again, so I assume not." He grimaced. "The other gunner? Not so much."

I pursed my lips and looked down.

"You made it that far with no casualties. It couldn't last."

"Our success made me think we had dodged the worst," he whispered after letting out a breath and nodding. "Foolish thoughts of the young."

"Hope springs eternal," I said.

"Once the dragon was clear, I moved to avoid detection. I heard fighting above, but I saw no more Greens down on that level." He cocked an eyebrow at me. "Then the bodies started falling."

I chuckled, drawing a confused look. I tapped my notes. "You're not the only one I've interviewed who said that."

"Said what?" he asked.

"'Bodies started falling.' Micaela said 'Bodies began to fall from the sky' in her account of the prison battle."

He actually *tsked* at me. "Still, it is hardly funny."

"Of course, it's not funny," I retorted. "But the fact you both used the phrase is amusing. To me, at least."

Suyef dipped his head.

"As I was saying, bodies started falling."

"Human ones, I presume?"

"Yes, all wearing Red guard uniforms," he said. "It was equal parts confusing and depressing. Still, it served as a needed distraction."

"To help you hide?" I asked, frowning.

"And move around and find where they held Micaela." He pointed above his head. "Also to signal the squad leader, Set, where I was."

"What happened with the other Greens after Set went down?"

"They avoided the same fate at first, although one had a guard flung at it." He grimaced. "The poor man hit one gunner."

"Using people as projectiles." I grimaced. "Disgusting."

Suyef nodded but said nothing.

"So, did Set pick you up?"

He shook his head.

"What happened next?"

"I started following guards as they moved to react. Eventually, they noticed me, forcing me to defend myself," he said, shrugging. "No deadly force, of course. The fight above drew most of their attention."

"I can imagine seeing their comrades falling distracted them," I said.

He nodded.

"I dispatched those who noticed me and followed the others, thinking they would lead me to the next level up."

"Why go toward a fight?"

"Something up there was bothering the Reds. I figured finding out who warranted the risk."

"Did you suspect what you would find up there?"

"Part of me wondered if it had something to do with Micaela, as the Red insurgent had told us she was in this part of the city," he said. "But no; no clue what was actually happening."

"So, I assume you figured it out when you made it up there," I said, but he shook his head.

"I never made it up," he said. "The entire fight came to me."

I learned one thing when those walls fell on me: constructs such as that stay attached to you if you keep your focus or know how to tie them off. Through desperation alone, my focus held, and the shield protected us from the falling chunks. This also hid me from the Seeker's view.

Peeking through a gap in the debris, I saw him fighting through guards and moving closer. Looking the other way, I saw my father from around the corner, having dodged the falling rubble. Colvinra's shots had only struck the first part of the alleyway. He moved to help me, but I waved him off. Looking back at the rubble, I contemplated how to move it without letting it all fall down on me or breaking the illusion for Colvinra that we remained trapped. I didn't figure it out.

As I thought about it, my concentration wavered and the shield shook, rubble tumbling to either side. Acting on instinct, I flung my hands up. The shield shot upward, knocking the shattered wall chunks off. I crawled out, looking back to see

Colvinra still engaged with guards. He glanced at me, and a wicked-looking grin crossed his face. I didn't wait to see more.

I rushed over to my father, and we ran down the alley. Behind us, the Questioner cried out, no doubt struggling to extricate himself and pursue us. We fled, taking the first turn and finding the cavern wall. It rose to our left, and the alley continued just between it and the city structures.

"Where are we going?" my father asked, looking over his shoulder.

"Away from him," I stated, looking the other way.

"But how do we know we're moving away from him?" He pointed out into the cave. "This alley goes the same direction as the principal thoroughfare."

"Just keep moving," I hissed, looking over my shoulder. "Whoever finds us most likely won't be friendly."

The alley widened at the next intersection and shifted out from the wall at an angle. Small buildings lined the rock face on our left. Shouts sounded behind us, and I looked back to see a still-empty alley. My father bumped into me as I stumbled a bit, and he reached out to catch me. Just then, movement above caught my eye. A guard peered down over a small roof outcropping. He reached out and aimed a pulse gun, but his arm wavered. I reached for my father as the gun fired. The shot missed left, tearing into the alley floor.

Acting on instinct, I built the structure directly above my father. It fell into place an instant before a second shot narrowly missed him. The shield deflected a third shot up at an angle to strike near the roof of a building ten paces in front. The force knocked my father toward me. I caught him, but we fell against the building. Pain shot through my back and head. I gripped my father and looked up just as the man fired a fourth time. The shield held, and the shot careened back down the alley to hit the rock wall.

"Keep moving," I yelled, shoving my father ahead.

The shield shifted with him, and I realized my instinct drove me to tie the shield to him. I could still see the construct at the core of my creation and, upon further inspection, I saw a second one wrapped around the primary. That one looked like the word *rope* or *knot*; *anchor*, maybe. More shots followed, giving us all the encouragement we needed to run.

Colvinra would eventually find us, not that our escape appeared to have much of a chance of success without him. The Reds made it clear they saw me as a threat. One they intended to eliminate.

"If I may interject," I asked, cutting Micaela off.

"First time for everything, I see," she said, favoring me with a small smile.

"Apologies, High One," I said, feeling my face flush.

"It's fine, Logwyn. What's your question?"

"You took to scripting quickly," I pointed out. "From what I know, that's not typical."

"My father worked with my brother and me on Ancient constructs a lot," she said, shrugging. "Memorizing them and forming them in my mind became nature to me."

"Yes, but doing that on paper or on a screen differs from altering the building blocks of our universe." I frowned at her. "You went from being unable to even see the base code to suddenly forming elements into useful things, all the while being chased. To say that was fast is understating the matter." I looked at my notes. "I'm not sure anyone who reads this will buy that. It strains credulity."

Micaela nodded in a slow, deliberate fashion.

"I don't disagree. It seemed easy. However, I struggled to duplicate what I did that day for a while after." She pointed at the wall behind me. "What's beyond there?"

I glanced in the indicated direction.

"A study? A large cavern? Rock wall?"

"All correct, but you can't see them. So, are they still there?"

"I know they are," I said, turning back to her. "You can't just make them disappear. That's not how altering works. You may create the illusion they aren't there, but that's not changing reality."

"So, you're holding on to the notion that reality prevents it from being changed." She nodded at the wall. "Such faith is key to altering. You must know and believe it will happen, or the construct falls apart. You can build constructs all day long, but it's all for naught if you lack faith in what you do."

"And you lacked that after these first attempts?"

"Protecting my father left me highly motivated. Confidence in altering helps a lot with alterations imposed on reality." She pointed at her eyes. "A wise person once said 'Faith is belief in sights unseen by eyes.' I don't think that person lived to see the Ancients discover how to alter, else he or she might have chosen different words."

Micaela nodded at the wall.

"We can't see what's beyond that wall, but our knowledge and experience tell us what's there." She waved a hand around the room. "Unless we focus, most of the time, the code remains invisible to us. To those who haven't learned yet, it's always invisible." She held up her index finger. "But it's still there."

"Did everything altering-wise come as quickly to you?"

"Most definitely not. Only things that keep people safe, especially shields. I'm quite adept at shielding. Healing took longer, but not as long as the rest." She inhaled and let it out slowly. "This sequence of events started it all. I probably began already inclined to alter protectively, but Colvinra and the Red guards motivated me."

"By threatening your life," I said, jotting a note down.

"No," she said, her voice quiet but firm. "Threatening my family."

As we raced down the alley, I struggled to keep a shield over me, let alone duplicate my father's. Several pulse shots told me more guards had made it onto the rooftops and found us. With each shot, unease grew over the quality of my shields.

As we passed another intersection, an explosion of rock erupted from a building to our right. Acting on instinct, I fabricated more shields all around us. This time, I included the hook construct. I heard men cry out in anger as their shots deflected off my new shields. Still, the shock wave knocked my father to the ground.

"So, you *can* script," a familiar voice growled.

A tall figure stepped toward us through the dust. I kneeled to help my father stand, then stood, our backs to a wall.

"Nice bit of coding," he continued. "Crude, but effective." He frowned at me. "Why this game, woman? Why hide this way?"

"I don't know what you're talking about," I insisted, moving between him and my father. "I've told you that already."

The Questioner spat.

"You, who bested me in combat, who escaped me in the oceans above. Why do you hide, ketch? Why don't you face me as before?"

"You've got me mixed up with someone else, Colvinra," I said, shaking my head. "I had never seen you before the prison. Ever."

"Enough!" he yelled. "Your games bore me. Mortac may believe your act, but I see through you."

He flung a hand toward us. I shoved my father free just before the attack struck. Each shield shook, vibrating my body. Colvinra didn't let up, firing his gun at my stumbling father. For a split second, I saw part of the pulse shot's script: symbols showing an electrical charge. A myriad of symbols spread through the air, from the gun to my shield. Then everything changed.

All around me, I could see the code layered over everything. I backed up, trying to handle the overwhelming amount of information, tripping over my father's feet. We both fell just as Colvinra's shot ripped past, leaving a charged feeling in the air. The Questioner took aim at my father as he crawled away.

Still overloaded with information, I tried to narrow my focus. Colvinra's weapon seemed to excite the air particles with a static charge along a direct path in front of the weapon So, I did something stupid. I grasped at the moisture in the air, altering the code from a gas to a liquid. As the excited particles moved past me, a wall of water coalesced. The pulse shot struck the water before it could fall, and electricity arced back at the Seeker. The electric blast sent the column of water flying all over my father and knocking him to the ground.

"Run!" I yelled, not looking back at Colvinra as I helped my father up.

My father fled down the alley, trailing water. Colvinra fired another shot, but my original shield held. I followed him and saw Red guards ahead on the rooftops, all taking aim at us. A torrent of pulse shots struck all around, some aimed at us, most at the Questioner. Colvinra slowed to defend himself while we fled. As we did, I continued trying to make shields around my father and me. Most failed, but I kept trying, hoping for success. Desperation to save my father drove me.

Ahead, the alley ended at an intersection opening to the right and left. My father went right, and I followed just as more shots ripped into the wall over my head. Guards shouted and continued firing. I did not see Colvinra.

The alley turned left and opened up onto a plaza. My father stumbled to a halt, and I collided with him. Ahead, standing on balconies and rooftops, waited about a dozen guards, all with weapons drawn.

"Freeze!" one said. "Hands where we can see them!"

We did as ordered. I peeked back past my arm to look for Colvinra. Sounds of combat echoed, but I saw no sign of the Questioner or his foes.

"Move to the center," the guard said, waving at us.

We moved forward at a slow pace, and I looked around. My first count had been off by half. More stood overlooking the plaza on either side, all with weapons aimed at us. The guard giving orders held up a device and spoke into it. He shook his head twice, and he waved his weapon at us. After several moments, he put the device away.

"You four. Take them to a secure facility," he called out, pointing behind us. "Everyone else with me. Let's take out the other Colberran now."

A tremor shook the plaza. Part of a building to my right collapsed, knocking several guards off the roof while still more guards fell from sight. Another tremor ripped through the structures, and more men fell. The platform split beneath my feet, one section elevating. I grabbed my father's arm and staggered toward another alley.

Just as we reached it, a shriek split the air behind us, chilling my spine and halting us in our tracks. Behind us stood

Colvinra, arms lifted overhead toward a writhing and twisting Green dragon suspended in the air. Colvinra clenched his fists and slung them at the ground. The beast fell from the sky like a piece of cloth ripped from a hanging line.

We fled but did not make it very far before the impact. The poor creature crashed down, sending out a punishing shock wave of air and debris that knocked us down. Only my muddled shields saved us from the flying chunks of rock. A cloud of dust settled around us, traces slipping through the shields' cracks and belying the fragility of my hastily made constructs.

I squinted at the edges of the shields' coding. There had to be a gap, but I couldn't see it. Closing my eyes, I drew smaller versions between the various columns, trying to create a webbed protection. The flecks of dust slowed to a halt. I let out a small breath but inhaled sharply as the shielding merged and shrank, stopping inches from our bodies. A thought occurred to me, a dangerous decision I might not have made in other circumstances.

"Father, roll over."

When he complied, I duplicated the web wrapping around his back like a cloak, one made of impenetrable material. After finishing with him, I did the same to myself.

"I think we have shields around our bodies," I said, peeking through the dust hovering near my face to see what was going on. "It will keep your skin safe, I hope."

"But it's solid," my father whispered. "A large enough rock striking that web shielding will move you. Energy doesn't just dissipate when it hits this. You saw the Questioner getting knocked back."

"It's the best I can do. I'm messing with something I don't fully understand in ways I didn't know I could." I pointed the opposite direction. "Let's use this dust cloud to move."

We crawled to another alley. Most of the structures remained intact, albeit damaged. Once around the corner, I stood and helped my father up.

"That way," I said, pushing him forward. "Hurry."

The alley opened onto the primary thoroughfare that ran along the platform's edge. We turned left, staying close to the structures. My attention roamed all over the rooftops, the platform, and the cave above.

"Stop!" a voice cried out from behind.

Three guards ran after us, pulse guns drawn. More guards rushed out from ahead to cut us off." to make it clear the guards are not the ones from behind running ahead, but new ones.

"To the edge!"

I grabbed my father's arm and moved away from the buildings. Pulse shots hissed past now that they could fire without hitting each other.

"Micaela! What are we doing?"

"Something stupid."

I gripped his hand and leaped from the edge.

CHAPTER 24

CONVERGENCE

"The fight came to you?" I asked Suyef. "How?"

"I kept following all the guards, monitoring the commotion above. Guards continued to fall off the ledge—"

"Or something threw them," I interjected.

"Yes. Some were, obviously. The trajectory of others showed they either fell or got knocked off. Whatever it was, the Greens were in the wrong position to be doing it," he said, holding up a finger. "Also, where the bodies were falling showed the fight above was moving.

"Then the ledge's base shook, cracks started forming, and the surrounding guards panicked, fleeing away from the cave wall. A second, much stronger tremor followed the first, reverberating through the walkway beneath me. Part of the ledge overhead cracked, and the guards became so focused on the impending disaster above that they stopped chasing me."

He let out a deep breath. "Then the ledge cracked."

"Did any of it fall?"

"Not at first. The crack knifed out to the outside edge, and the far side lifted. Small pieces of rock fell all around me. Despite all the damage, the ledge stayed in place. I raced along the walkway, dodging stopped guards. In the distance, another

Green flew toward me, and I tried to flag it down, but it never made it to me."

I grimaced. "It fell?"

"More like yanked from the sky," he said. "The beast just stopped, midair, body writhing."

He balled his hand into a tight fist.

"Like something was squeezing it. Then it moved"—he pulled his hand down—"toward the ledge, twisting and writhing the entire time as it fell. An instant later, another tremor shook the platform, and several large chunks fell off."

"From the dragon's impact?" I asked.

He shuddered. "With the force of that impact, it was a wonder the beast ever flew again."

I felt a tension in my shoulders loosen. "So, it lived?"

"Luckily, yes. Not that I was paying much attention, as something else caught my eye that, understandably, made me forget about most everything else."

He sat in silence for a moment before continuing.

"As I began, I saw two people jumping from the platform. One I didn't recognize, but the other"—he held up a finger—"I did."

I stopped writing and looked up. When he remained silent, I filled in the obvious blank.

"Micaela."

Who jumps off of something without knowing for sure what would happen next? I blame the situation, which called for something desperate. A sufficient reason, I suppose. Either way, only one thought filled my mind as I did: get away. Only one escape route remained, and I took a gamble on my new ability to escape.

As I leaped, I envisioned a row of shields sloping down from where we jumped off. I imagined a long row of the constructs, forming the code for each. As we fell, fear of failure gripped my heart and caused my breath to catch. Several eon-like heartbeats passed before all the wind exited my lungs as we collided with my constructs. The surface tugged at my wet suit, which grew warm as we slid on the invisible, yet very solid, surface. I gripped my father's hand, my eyes locked on our destination: a platform identical to the one above.

At that moment, I realized one of my many mistakes: angle of descent. Our path would carry us to the platform's edge. Out of obvious options, I did the only thing I could think of: I let the shields go. The bottom fell out of my world, and thoughts of a very painful reunion with solid ground filled my head.

It didn't disappoint.

"My first thought upon seeing Micaela jump was that she must have been desperate to do so," Suyef said, leaning forward onto his elbows. "I wondered about the man's identity, but only briefly."

"So, what did you do?"

"Besides stare? What could I do? I didn't know what she was thinking." He tapped his waist. "I considered using the belt from the rooftops to slow her fall, but falling under that dragon had damaged it. Jumping toward the roof only got me halfway up the wall."

"You didn't use it before that? Seems like it would come in handy in such situations."

"I think you know my view of using technology for everything," the Nomad said, leaning back and crossing his arms.

"Your first instinct is to do it yourself, I know. Then you use what you have to when needed, but only after exhausting other options." I nodded at him. "Since that didn't work, what did you do?"

"Watch, at first. Micaela and the man fell several paces before they hit something." He held up his right hand in a fist, then lowered it a bit, opened it to a flat plane, and moved it down across his body. "Their arms and legs spread out, and they started sliding along something I couldn't see."

"But you knew what was going on, I presume."

"I recognize altering when I see it. Which made the man with her even more interesting to me."

"You thought he made that escape route?"

Suyef smiled.

"Micaela had never altered in front of me. I was aware of her training but, as far as I knew, she hadn't connected to take that next step."

"So, you thought he was doing it?"

"Only for a moment." He cocked his head to one side as he stared at me. "Considering their angle of descent and acceleration, you can imagine where my concern was."

"On stopping them."

"The same guards I'd followed were moving again. Toward Micaela and her companion." He spread his hands. "That left me very few options."

"Two people out of reach, fleeing something powerful, and guards all around you. So, what *did* you do?"

"The only thing I could. I ran right at the guards to distract them. Before I made it two steps, the two of them dropped like a rock onto the rooftops." He grimaced. "From that height, it was going to hurt. They were lucky it wasn't worse."

My body shivered, drawing his gaze. "I fell once when I was younger. Not an experience to repeat."

He watched me for a moment, lips pursed. "Related to your failed test attempt?"

"We're off topic." I shook my head. "So, Micaela and the man with her fell. What did you do?"

"Nothing," a familiar voice said from behind me. "Well, not without my help."

Standing there, a big smile on his face, was Quentin.

Hitting the slide nearly knocked the wind out of me. When we hit the rooftop, the shock left me numb and seeing white light. My lungs clenched just before the pain struck, my entire body feeling on fire. When I gasped, that just aggravated the pain.

"Micaela," my father said between coughs. "Are you all right?"

I nodded and regretted doing so.

"*All right* is optimistic."

"What happened?"

I tried looking around, and the pain worsened.

"I let the shields go," I said, hands pressed to the sides of my head. "Maybe not the best move, but it stopped us from going over this platform's edge."

"That was dangerous."

"We made it in one piece," I said, rolling over and looking at my father through my hands. "Can you move?"

He leaned against a small wall, hand grabbing at his hip. "I have to."

"Anything broken?" I moved closer, teeth gritted against the burning pain.

"I can't tell." He shifted and grimaced. "My tailbone feels broken. How did we not break anything more serious?"

"My shields from before absorbed the impact, I think."

I pushed myself up and grabbed his arm to help him stand.

"They're still working?" he asked, groaning as he steadied himself.

"I think so."

"Well, that's good."

I looked for any guards.

"Appears safe, for now." I looked up at the level we'd just left. "Until they follow or signal someone on this level."

My father kneeled down, one hand massaging his lower back.

"Either way," he said, "we won't stay unnoticed for long."

I pointed left. "There's an opening in the wall."

"Do we want to be on the ground?" he asked. "Seems safer up here."

A Green dragon streaked by, two Reds in hot pursuit.

"Well, mostly."

"We need to hide, Father."

I pulled him up, and we moved on shaky legs, my father leaning on the half-wall to keep steady. With one arm around his waist, I kept watch for anyone following us. Voices echoed around the cave, but no pursuit appeared. It was a matter of time that would run out soon enough. My father's injuries worried me as I watched him struggle. The fall hurt him more than he seemed willing to admit. We needed a moment and a place for respite, but both seemed impossible to find.

Just as we approached the opening, a pulse blast ripped into the rooftop, spraying rock everywhere. Grabbing my father, I lunged through the opening, ducking into a roll just as my father cried out in pain. Another shot sent several chunks of wall around us.

I shouted "Keep down!" as I scrambled up after my dad. We moved away from the opening toward another wall ahead.

"Are you okay?"

"No, but I can move."

We approached a gap in the next wall to find stairs leading to an empty alley. I pushed my father ahead of me, glancing back. Guards rushed across the rooftops, and more guards pointed at us from above. I hurried over to find my father leaning against the wall.

"Someone is down there," he said, pointing at the alley.

"So we go the other way."

I grabbed his hand and pulled him back up the alley. A shout followed us as we turned a corner. I saw guards rushing at us as the others descended the stairs from the roof we had just left.

"Keep moving!"

Pulse shots ripped through the air after us, one deflecting off my father's shielding and bouncing back to detonate in the wall. Another struck me squarely in the back, knocking me into the wall. We kept moving, dodging back and forth to avoid the shots.

"Which way, Micaela?"

Ahead lay an intersection with three paths: one left, one right, and one ahead at an angle to the right.

"Whichever one is clear!"

He got to the intersection ahead of me, looking left and right before taking the angled exit. I glanced each way, seeing guards rushing forward, weapons drawn but not firing. We ran on, the alley angling back to the principal thoroughfare.

"Father, wait!"

It was already too late. He tried to stop, but his momentum carried him clear of the alley. Two guards approached from the left, weapons drawn and aimed. Another figure moved in from the right. I ran into my father, tackling him down and rolling with him away from the guards. I tried to form another shield around us and saw the third figure leap over us. He leveled one guard with a roundhouse kick to the head. The other guard stumbled, bringing his weapon around, but never finished the move. The figure spun again, sweeping his leg to take the man's legs out. As the figure finished his spin, I glimpsed his face.

"Suyef!"

I got up but saw another guard behind the Nomad. In a flash, I finished the shield and flung it at the man as he fired. The pulse struck the shield and deflected back into his torso. The moving construct hit him next, carrying him into an open door we had just run past in the alley.

"Micaela, behind you!"

I spun just as a guard fired at me. The wave of electrified air struck my shielding around my neck, the force staggering me. Two guards joined the first, all three firing at me. The pulses hit my torso, knocking me backward. As I fell and the three men fired again, something moved overhead. I looked up, expecting a dragon, and saw the last thing I ever expected.

Quentin.

CHAPTER 25

REUNITED

"Where have you been?" I asked the returning Quentin as he seated himself.

"Fine greeting, that is." He wagged a finger at me. "Mind your q's and p's, or I'll just leave."

I let the comment with its inverted letters go.

"You left on purpose?"

"I what?" He looked between Suyef and me. "Where?"

I pointed at him. "Don't play dumb, Quentin. You left me here on purpose."

He stared at my finger and said nothing.

"Are you even paying attention to me?"

"Look at her face when she's mad," Quentin said, leaning toward Suyef. "Stands out against her hair."

"Quentin, that is rude," the Nomad said, his eyebrows drawn together. "Answer her questions."

"Which ones? I can't keep track because she asks so many."

Suyef reached over and tapped my notes. "She's trying to help, remember? She talked to Micaela, and now she's talking to you."

"Didn't she leave?" Quentin frowned at me. "You get around for someone restricted by your own mistakes."

I closed my eyes and took several deep breaths. Suyef said something to Quentin in a low voice. When I opened my eyes, the Nomad watched me.

"My apologies," I said. "That will not happen again."

Quentin stared at his hands, eyes wide open as he examined them. Whatever had happened seemed to do two things to him: mess with his memory and cognitive functions or send him into an uncontrollable rage. As annoying as he was, this state was preferable to his other moods. I addressed the Nomad, hoping to draw Quentin out.

"Shall we get back to your story?"

"So, Micaela and the man with her fell from sight," Suyef said.

"You keep saying the man with her. I know it's her father."

"I didn't see where she and her father fell," he said, dipping his head at me, "but I presumed on a rooftop. Guards scrambled everywhere, calling out for orders. Two near me made it two steps before I used their distraction to dispatch them. Another pair saw me and turned to defend themselves, but I didn't want to waste time on them. I grabbed one of the guard's pulse guns and fired off several shots first. One fell, but the other ducked behind his compatriot. He took longer to dispatch."

"You're being modest," Quentin interjected. "I saw your fight." He leaned toward me, grinning and lowering his voice. "He made it look easy."

"And what were you doing while he did this?"

He leaned back and smiled. "Coming to save the day, of course."

Quentin's appearance astride his grav-board caused several emotions: confusion, elation, shock, to name a few. The two men's sudden appearance restored something to me: hope we could make it. What we were going to do or how remained unclear, but their presence, the three of us converging at that point. Yes, I felt hope.

As I fell, and Quentin, grav-board up and head hanging down, soared overhead, something pulled me up into the air just as three more shots whizzed past. I flipped upside down and around to land beyond my father, staggering a moment as Quentin landed next to me, and saw more guards rushing toward us, weapons firing. I raised my hands, made a shield, and shoved the construct at them, but nothing happened this time. The construct dissipated instead, forcing us to the ground as shots sizzled the air. I tried again, but the construct faded before I could finish it. Suyef and Quentin jumped up as I tried a third time, this time succeeding. I shoved a wall of impenetrable glass right at the guards, knocking them left and right.

A guard spun in from the right, a staff wreathed in flame in hand. Suyef's staff, also ablaze, met the other with a resounding crack. Beyond, a guard fired at the Nomad, and I tried to make another shield, but the shot never found its mark. Just before it struck, the shot bent into a curve and careened past the Nomad's head. Quentin floated into view, his hand held out toward Suyef. At first, I thought he'd scripted, then realized he'd just used his grav-belt.

The shrieks of Red and Green dragons battling overhead filled the cavern, but I barely noticed all that. More guards joined the rest, and I spun in every direction, throwing up a shield here, flinging another one there. Quentin flitted back and forth, grabbing weapons from the guards and shoving them aside with his belt. Suyef defended my father, his staff a dizzying blur of spun fire keeping the guards at bay. Around and around we went, but this couldn't last forever.

"We need to move!" I yelled and pointed toward the far end of the platform. "That way."

My father stumbled as Suyef pushed him forward. A guard rushed toward the pair, but Quentin downed him with a pulse gun. He carried two, each constantly firing as he circled us. I considered trying to encase him in protective shielding but wasn't sure I could with the surrounding battle. The guards kept coming, leaving me to wonder what protected the city elsewhere. That led briefly to thoughts about the actual citizens, but only for a moment.

We fled along the thoroughfare, Suyef spinning and dispatching guards with his blazing staff, Quentin darting around overhead, pulse guns felling guards before they got close. All the while, I flung up shields as fast as I could make them, shoving some away, tying others in place so the guards would run headlong into them. Still, they came with no apparent strategy beyond just overwhelming us, which made no sense. However, I couldn't dwell on that, merely took advantage of it.

"Quentin!" I called as he backflipped over me.

He shoved a guard away and landed, facing me. I wanted to give him protective shields, but more guards came from just beyond him. I began making a shield, my eyes on the men. Quentin jumped up in the air just as I threw the shield at the charging guards, knocking them flat.

"Do that everywhere!" he called out, waving his arm in a sweeping arc.

Nodding, I focused, struggling to form a large shield around us, a difficult enough feat without all the commotion. Quentin and Suyef kept the guards at bay as I worked. When finished, I called out and grabbed my father, who looked winded.

The surrounding guards all cried out, drawing my gaze. Quentin hovered overhead, arms outstretched. All the guards lay knocked down in a ring, the closest ones unconscious. Those farther back moved a little, some raising pulse guns. Suyef, a pair of pulse guns in hand, joined Quentin in dispatching those few still awake and, for the moment, we had a bit of respite.

"You're alive!" I said when Quentin landed near me.

"And you can make shields," he replied, grinning, then stopped dead in his tracks. "What happened to your hair?"

I grabbed at the hair hanging around my face. The hair lacking the braid. "Long story."

He nodded and looked around. "So, learned to script, huh?"

"How did you survive?"

"I assume you know these two, Micaela," my father said.

"Sorry! Suyef, Quentin, this is my fa—"

Beyond the edge and far overhead, a large Red shrieked. Several more rose into sight, all looking down at the four of us. The first Red let out another cry, and they all unleashed an onslaught of fireballs, not at us, but at the platform beneath us. A thunderous roar split the cavern's air as the stone cracked and shook. A few shots strayed near us, and I erected a large shield over our heads, angled down toward the now-unstable surface.

"Look out!" my father yelled.

Guards, now conscious again, resumed their attack. Quentin and Suyef moved in a circle, firing shots at anything that moved. I made some small shields to block shots, shoving some at our assailants.

"Why aren't they running?" I called out. "Those beasts are a threat to all of us."

The stone surface dipped down, and I stumbled. My father fell to his knees and grabbed me. The guards, ignoring the risks, continued their attack even as the platform trembled. With a resounding, heart-stopping crack, accompanied by more reverberating explosions, the surface sheared off and the outer edge dipped down, sending us, the guards, and the remnants of the thoroughfare falling toward the level below.

CHAPTER 26

FALLING

"Why do you think the guards kept attacking?" I asked when Micaela stood to stretch.

"They weren't afraid for their lives. I didn't realize it then and thought they were pretty stupid to just keep following orders." She moved toward the window. "There is a big difference between mindless and fearless. Add determination, and it's a different equation." She paused at the window. "And pulse guns aren't usually fatal. Well, unless you get knocked off something or into something with enough force."

"Charged particles can overload the nervous system," I said, joining her and looking down at our world's bright core. "Still, that single-minded pursuit of a target reminds me of soldiers. But you said these were all guards?"

"Very much so."

"So, not Seekers or Nomads, all trained to fight like members of a military unit."

"That they lacked training is the only reason we made it as far as we did before Suyef and Quentin arrived."

I looked back at the recorder to make sure it was still active. The light shone, so I continued.

"But pulse guns weren't the only danger you all faced," I said. "The Reds and Greens were doing a lot of damage to the city."

"It seemed indiscriminate," she said, nodding. "Except most of the people weren't there, as they'd known the attack was coming and had fled to shelters in the cave walls."

"And they can build another city instantly with altering," I said. "Still, it put you in a lot of danger."

"The Reds' distaste for my demise at their own hands seemed to fade when they realized I might get away," she said. "Which forced Colvinra into his weird protective role since he thought I had what he was looking for." She chuckled. "That all ended when Quentin and Suyef arrived."

"That convergence was quite impressive," I said, watching her reaction. "The three of you fought together pretty well."

"Singular determined focus, albeit on different things. Me on my father. Them on me." She chuckled. "All of us on getting away."

"Suyef once described you and Quentin as the greatest force this world has ever seen when you are together."

She frowned, but I went on.

"Just you two, I mean. He never mentioned himself in that equation."

A small smile tugged at her lips.

"Suyef is many things, including modest. He's a rock of stability, a central point of focus in any situation you can count on to do precisely what's needed or expected. That can push you to be more creative or risky." She looked at the pictures. "For Quentin, too, but sometimes that's a bad thing. Most times, it's very good."

"And for you?" I asked.

"At first, a good thing. Something I could rely on. Even need."

She paused, taking in a deep breath and letting it out through her nose.

"And soon that proved to be very painful."

"Did Suyef stop being that rock?"

"No," she whispered, a tremor shaking her throat and head. "I let him die."

A heavy silence followed. I pondered her words. Was everyone in this story going to die and come back to life? Would she answer if I asked? I doubted it, as she didn't seem willing to talk about it just now. Then again, when did she look like she wanted to talk?

"But I'm getting ahead of myself," she said, cutting through my thoughts. "First we need to get out of that cave. Yes?"

I stared at her, lips pursed as I contemplated pressing her for more, but thought better of it. If I pushed too hard, she'd send me away. So, I tabled those questions.

"What happened after the platform broke?"

She shrugged. "We fell."

My first thought was for the people below us soon to be crushed. As we slid down the smooth surface, another thought came: we were going to fall off before we even made it to the next level.

A boulder smashed into the falling platform to my right, rolling past. I could see more chunks breaking free and tumbling down, a large one crashing into the platform directly above us. Acting on instinct, I flung up a shield, and a horrific vibration shook my entire body. My feet and knee warmed as I leaned into the shield: friction from the stone pushing me. I shoved back, trying to throw the boulder away, but the rock's weight proved too much. I pushed harder, hoping to stop the thing from crushing us.

The next instant, the boulder lifted and tumbled off the edge. Quentin dropped into sight next to me, spinning to face my father as he did. Suyef clung to a crack in the platform, gripping my father's arm in a clenched fist. Before we could move, another boulder smashed into the platform near Suyef. I shoved the shield at the boulder as Quentin moved near the Nomad. The chunk lifted with the shield, and both tumbled to one side. With the rock gone, I saw a guard sliding feetfirst with a staff pointed right at the Nomad.

"Look out!" I screamed, pointing.

Quentin felled the guard with a pulse, and he slid past, unconscious. More chunks of rock landed, forcing me to construct shields to deflect them even as I wondered where they came from.

"How far is this drop?" Quentin yelled.

He dodged a large rock and moved below my father and Suyef. I wondered also, but I didn't look. The need for shields took all my focus. Sweat beaded on my brow, and I felt a weariness creep into my core. I needed something different, like what Quentin had done at the prison. Forming a much larger construct, I duplicated it and erected two shields in a wedge above us. The falling debris hit the shields and deflected to either side.

Suddenly, the entire platform trembled, and the floor dropped away from us. Above, the platform's jagged edge rose, tipping out into the cavern and turning from an unstable floor into a falling wall. Below, we spied a massive tunnel at the bottom of the cave. The next instant, the remains of the platform fell over. Suyef lost his grip, and he and my father slid off the edge and into the air above the tunnel entrance.

"Did you figure out where the rocks were coming from?" I asked.

"Some broke away when the platform split and broke off." She grimaced. "Others were being thrown at us by smaller Reds."

"Wait, where were the Greens during this?" I asked, stopping Micaela. "Why didn't they prevent them from attacking the platform?"

"I didn't know this then, but they were helping us," she replied. "When the platform broke free, several of them flew under to slow its fall using their spinal structure's control over gravity and keep it from crushing the occupied levels."

"So, they pushed the platform to the bottom of the tiered city. But why let them attack the platform in the first place?"

"There were six Reds for every one Green, and that's just from my distracted count during our escape."

"So, we know you survive," I stated. "What happened next? Quentin and his board?"

"He and that device played a huge part in it, yes. But so did something else."

The left side of her lips tugged up in a half smile.

"Or should I say someone?"

I frowned. "Colvinra?"

She laughed, shaking her head. "The Greens."

Quentin's board compensates for most of momentum's effects, but not all of them. Particularly when you're not the one wearing the belt. When we fell, my stomach felt like it exited the opposite direction of the fall. We began to spin, making it hard to focus. For a split second, my father spun into view, then vanished as I turned to find Quentin closing in. Only then did I realize the fall threw me clear of him.

"Gotcha! Keep your shields around us!"

I nodded, all of me grateful for the stability his board offered. I wrapped my arms around him and saw chunks of the platform breaking free to fall toward us. One came directly at the tumbling figure of my father. I threw up another shield, shoving it to knock away as many chunks as I could. More fell, forcing me to make more shields as we plummeted down into the tunnel. As an enormous chunk crashed into the tunnel wall and spun out past us, I saw Suyef tumble toward it, plant his feet, and vault in our direction.

"How is he doing that?" I yelled at Quentin but got no answer.

Taking my eyes from the debris, I saw Quentin with both hands outstretched. One reached toward my father, who somersaulted in the air nearby, and the other at Suyef, whose leap carried him past us. It was all surreal, with the walls of the cave rushing quickly by.

The Nomad whipped out his staff, igniting and swinging it in a wide arc in one smooth motion at a guard standing on the cliff wall, weapon drawn. Suyef drove the end of his staff into the guard's hand, knocking the weapon free. His momentum should have carried him into the wall, but Quentin's hand clenched and yanked back. As the Nomad soared toward us, I wondered how many of those blue beams that belt could produce.

A flash of green drew my eye up and my attention to the debris. My last shield still held, moving with us as we fell. Quentin's arms never slowed as he kept my father under that shield, prevented us from hitting the wall, and moved Suyef around to dispatch any threats. As the rocks continued to tumble past, I glanced down. The bottom of the tunnel remained obscured in shadow, making me wonder how far we might fall.

A rock smashed into the wall near us, spraying us with debris. I erected another shield, halting most of the rocks, but one got through. Quentin flung out his hand, shoving the chunk away, eyes never leaving Suyef. I looked back up, trusting Quentin to bring us down. I had little other choice.

Another flash of green flitted into view. I squinted through the rain of rocks and spied it again, moving fast. It took a moment to register what it was and, when it did, another blossom of hope emerged.

It was a Green, diving after us.

"So, Quentin, flying down that tunnel must have been stressful for you," I commented, drawing his blue eyes away from his fingers.

"Flying is fun," he said, grinning. "Falling is not."

"And was that falling or flying?"

"Neither. That was surviving."

I clenched my jaw, reminding myself to be patient.

"You didn't answer my question."

"Yes, I did. You just didn't like the answer."

"All right. Was it stressful? Difficult?"

"Of course it was." He shook his head and gave Suyef a look. "Can you believe this one?"

"Answer the question, Quentin," Suyef said, glancing at me. "She's trying to understand."

Quentin's eyes widened and his nostrils flared as he looked at Suyef and then at me.

"Flying is always difficult. It's not natural. This is easy," he said, moving his fingers. "You don't even think about doing it. Flying requires more thought, more focus."

"But aren't you better at scripting when there's a lot going on?"

"Scripting, yes. But using those two devices is not the same. It's built on the same principles, but it's very different."

"How is it different? Explain that to me. It's altering, yes. But a machine is helping you do some of it."

"All of it, actually. But I'll concede the point. Yes, it's a lot like scripting."

"So, what made this difficult for you?"

"One of the hardest things I've ever done."

"I asked what made it difficult."

His eyes squeezed shut, and his nose whistled with a large inhalation of air.

"Quentin," Suyef said. "Easy. She doesn't know how it works."

I waved at the Nomad, never looking away from Quentin. He leaned forward, hands pressed to either side of his head.

"It's not important," I said. "So, Quentin, how did you manage it?"

He looked up at me, eyebrows raised.

"How did you manage all of that?" I asked. "You said it was difficult. How did you manage it?"

"Motivation," he said, nodding at Suyef. "My friends' lives were at stake. Succeed, we live; fail, we die."

I nodded, lips pressed together. For the moment, Quentin looked to have calmed.

"So, you're falling down that tunnel," I continued. "Micaela's shielding everyone, you're holding her tight and sending Suyef around to keep guards, who must all have had grav-belts as well, from attacking. What happened next?"

Quentin chuckled. "Things got messy."

Someone once said bad things happen for good reasons, or
something like that. I never really agreed, making me short-
sighted or something. As we fell down into that tunnel, it hit
me hard. A moment of clarity that the events that brought me
to that shell that day had forced me to learn how to use that
board and use it well. Otherwise, that fall would have ended a
lot messier than it did. Instead, I trusted my instincts, pushing
myself to a whole new level. You know, where it becomes second nature.

Still, we were falling into a dark space, with building-sized
chunks of rock tumbling down after us, and four different bodies to keep track of in the mess while avoiding both falling
debris and pieces of the tunnel wall jutting out. Oh, and let's
not forget the Red dragons and all their fireballs smashing into
the tunnels ahead. Or below. Whichever works best.

So, I danced the difficult dance, pushing us out from the
wall when needed, pulling us close, shoving boulders Micaela
wasn't able to deflect, and keeping us all as close together as
possible to make her job easier. All the while, I kept peeking
down the tunnel, trying to see where it led and make a plan
for what to do when we reached the bottom. I was confident
I could prevent a fatal impact and, with Micaela's amazing
shields, that we'd make it unscathed. Only those blasted Reds
and their guards proved unpredictable, complicating it all.

Moving Suyef around so he could keep any guards we
encountered busy was the hardest part. The ones on the walls
were easy enough: most of those we moved past so fast they

couldn't get a shot off. But the ones who fell with us or, worse, jumped down after us, proved peskier. Not that Suyef couldn't handle them, but they never came from convenient angles. This forced me to move him everywhere, leaping from boulders occasionally and once even running down the tunnel wall with us when I let him drift too near it. The look he gave me after that one.

When that Green dragon appeared, I was thrilled. The Green glided down with ease, boulders moving away instead of smashing into it. The creature performed a majestic spin around the tunnel, sweeping away the boulders before approaching us.

"Quentin!" Suyef called out. "Push me closer!"

Nodding, I used the belt to throw him to the other side, even making a throwing motion out of habit. A falling boulder nearly hit him, but Micaela deflected it just as I twisted him around to dodge it. Micaela's father screamed a warning, pointing down at an outcropping racing closer. I pushed us all out around it and, in desperation, grabbed Suyef and threw him hard at the dragon, counting on the creature to grab him. A jolt shook me, and I saw a large boulder crumbling against Micaela's shield. Her whole body shook and slumped against my back. If we didn't do something soon, she'd wear out from the exertion.

"Quentin!"

Suyef sat safely astride the Green's back, one hand outstretched at Micaela's father.

"Him!"

I maneuvered us around another outcropping and used the momentum to throw her father toward the Green. As he grabbed Suyef's hands, I spun us down alongside the Green. Suddenly, the rain of debris lessened, and I looked back up the tunnel. The debris still fell but not near the creature.

"We need to get out of here!" I felt my face redden from stating the obvious.

"How?" Micaela asked.

More Green dragons appeared around us, with the Reds in close pursuit.

"Where does this tunnel lead?" I asked the first Green.

"To a tunnel hub," the creature answered, its mouth never moving. "Many likely routes of escape."

"Don't you think they know that?" I pointed at our pursuit. "This could be a trap."

"They couldn't have known we'd come this way," Micaela said, tugging at my shoulder.

I glanced back and saw the Reds flinging several boulders at us. Micaela pushed a shield out to get a couple, the other Greens a few more, leaving some for me to redirect. Instead of just tossing them aside, I tried flinging them back at the Reds. The Green nearest me shifted, drawing my attention to the tunnel, so I never saw if I hit my targets. The Greens tightened their formation as the tunnel turned in a direction other than down. Ahead, the enclosed space opened up and, as a group, we shot out into a cavern, another tiered city lining the walls. Tunnels around the cave opened like black maws that ripped up the otherwise regimented city levels.

Not wasting any time, our formation dove for the nearest tunnel, but a barrage of fire forced us away. We veered at another, only to find a flight of Reds coming out of it and forcing us back up into the open space.

"Told you this felt like a trap," I called over my shoulder.

Micaela pointed up. "That one, it looks empty."

Pulling the grav-board around under the Green, I looked where she pointed.

"Seems too obvious." I looked over at Suyef. "They want us to go that way. All the rest blocked, except that one."

Suyef tapped the Green with this staff.

"Set, it's your call."

The formation arced in a wide circle. The Reds surrounded us, but held their fire, most likely to avoid hitting each other with crossfire. Around and around we went, a dizzying dance of Red and Green, with us caught in the middle.

The next moment, Set decided.

"Form up, tight diamond," he ordered. "We are going in."

CHAPTER 27

BLACK

"So, did you agree with Quentin?" I asked, drawing a frown from Micaela. "About it being a trap?"

"Of course, but what could we do? It was the only exit. Besides, that tunnel proved just as much a trap to them."

"How so?"

"Green riders," she said. "The tunnel forced us into a tight formation. The Reds had to follow, and they did fire at us, but from as tight a formation as our own."

"So, only the lead ones could fire at you."

"And it made them easier targets," she said, nodding.

"For what? Pulse guns wouldn't faze a Red."

A small smile tugged at her lips. "You're forgetting the walls."

When I just stared at her, she leaned forward and mimicked a throwing motion.

"The Green riders used their grav-belts to rip those walls into a debris cloud that trailed behind us, and the Reds flew headlong into it. It was decimating to them. Not completely, mind you, but it gave us some breathing room." She cocked her head to one side. "And for what came next, we needed it."

"What was at the end of that tunnel?"

A long breath followed, her chest rising and falling. "A monster."

The Greens closed their formation as we entered the tunnel. Air currents buffeted us and Quentin tensed as he maneuvered the grav-board up and over the Green Suyef called Set. The Reds continued the pursuit, the front creatures opening fire on us. Only a few shots zoomed past before the Green riders unleashed their attack.

The Greens on the edge moved closer to the walls, and I heard a shattering sound for an instant. Rocks, ripped free of the walls, smashed into the Reds. The lead Reds fell back, crashing into those behind. Fireballs gone awry detonated all around us as the Green riders continued their attack.

The barrage and their falling compatriots didn't slow the Reds. Instead, they sped up, closing on our rear. Rock projectiles poured into them, but still they came, still firing shots at us. One fireball smashed into a column far ahead, sending debris flying right at us.

"Look out!" I yelled, throwing up a shield to block the debris.

Quentin moved closer to Set, bringing the shield in front of Suyef and my father. A rider astride a Green nearby wasn't so lucky, his cry ringing out for a second as he vanished.

"Keep those shields ahead of us!" Quentin called out, flipping us over to the far side of Set.

A shower of debris followed us, with the riders pulling more rocks free. Some flew at the Reds, but most soared up into the cloud of rocks. The Reds continued firing, but the rocky cloud absorbed most of their shots.

A sudden lurch, the result of a sharp turn in the tunnel, brought my head forward as my stomach complained. A few shots careened by and detonated ahead of us. I threw some shields at the debris as we flew by, deflecting the loose rock back against the tunnel.

"How much farther?" I called out to Set as we moved near the Green's head.

"I do not know."

A blast of light exploded nearby, drawing my attention to the walls. The walls that seemed closer.

"Is the tunnel getting smaller?"

Another sharp turn and another stomach flip followed my question. Quentin pointed ahead.

"Yes, and look."

The tunnel spun, bringing Set over above us, or below. I lost track somewhere in that tunnel. Where before it had been mostly dark, light now flickered on the walls.

"An exit?"

"From the tunnel, maybe," he answered, shifting us back around and down the other side of Set. "From the shell, though? I doubt we're that lucky."

The cloud of rocks following us began smashing up against the closing walls and masking the Reds from view. We could hear and see the effects of their fireballs, though.

"That's a fairly effective shield against their shots," I said, pointing behind us. "It may block them from following us."

"Maybe, maybe not."

"There's the exit!" Suyef called out as the tunnel rounded a curve.

A shattering sound drew my eyes back before I could really see the exit. Lights flashed from behind the rock cloud even as the riders flung their hands left and right, ripping more and more of the tunnel wall free. The cloud, packed tight in the closing space, now bounced and deflected off each other, some shattering, most hitting in a cacophony that filled the chamber. Light flooded down from ahead, making it hard to see. Just as I put a hand up to block the light, we shot free of the tunnel. The cloud of rocks smashed closed behind us, and the edge of the tunnel collapsed. With a resounding crash, the passageway closed, preventing our pursuit from following.

The formation slowed, turning in a wide arc around the now-blocked passage. Below lay dozens of glowing rock columns, the structures lining every inch of a cavern empty of a city. The formation slowed to a halt, hovering over our recent exit. Looking up, I caught sight of what had stopped the Greens.

Overhead flew the largest dragon encountered yet. Easily four times as large as Set, with a wingspan nearly double that of every creature I had seen, the beast dominated the cavern. The same jagged bone structures protruding along its spine sprouted along the front edge of its wings. Its torso was thicker than the lithe forms of the Greens and Reds, with large, muscular legs tucked up under the monster. Its head was wide and flat, with a thick bone structure rising from a massive jaw line to form a grotesque crown of sorts that resembled jagged teeth. Large red eyes stared back at me, sending chills down my spine.

But that all left less of an impression on me than the most obvious difference between this monster and the other dragons. Of all the horrific creature's frightening, jarring, and disconcerting features, of all the differences between the majestic-looking creatures chasing or helping me and this abomination flying above us now, only one stood out in stark comparison.

The dragon wore scales of complete black.

"Black?" I asked, tapping my notes with the end of my stylus. "A black dragon?"

"Darker than I've ever seen. Light just vanished into that monster's scales."

"History doesn't record there ever being black dragons," I pointed out. "Only legends."

"And where do legends come from, Logwyn? Human fancy? Are legends never based on some truth?"

"Do you believe that legend?"

"Of a black dragon that united the world in a reign of terror that ultimately led to the downfall of all civilization?" she asked. "It's melodramatic, but yes, there is some truth to it."

"Like what?"

She frowned at me.

"Well, your own records show that the world was at war before the Shattering. Every nation fighting, using weapons built by those sworn to protect everyone."

"The Ancients. I've read what exists in history books." I waved a hand at the device between us. "People so afraid of altering that they ostracized anyone who could do it but had no issue using devices like this recorder."

"And once built, the same people had no issue taking them apart and figuring out how they worked," she said. "And it didn't take long for them to figure out how to make weapons out of them."

"Yes, the scant records of the last great war show a brutality beyond anything history ever recorded." I looked up at her. "Well, until the Shattering."

"Even then, the history books lack much of what happened. The Ancients wiped the records of certain events to prevent them from happening again."

"But how did they justify that? I mean, without history, how do we know what mistakes to avoid?"

"No one ever accused them of great foresight," she said, looking at the door behind me. "I've been told they acted out of fear."

"So, now we don't even know what knowledge we lost."

"For one, your race almost lost the blessing," Micaela said, shifting in her seat. "The council deemed that knowledge dangerous and wanted it purged."

"She wouldn't have allowed that, would she?" I asked, pointing over my shoulder. "I mean, that's an attack on her."

Her head tilted a bit to one side, and she shrugged.

"They saw it as their duty to protect the world. A duty they believed they'd already failed to do. There's some logic there, all things considered."

I eyed her for a moment, hand on my shoulder. My mind pondered this woman and the Dragon Queen.

"She confides a lot in you, doesn't she?"

"Why do you say that?" Micaela asked.

"You have this knowledge, or seem to at least, that just isn't in the history books." I waved my stylus at the recording device. "Outside of people like me working to preserve what we know from memory, that era vanished into time, lost in that purge."

"The Ancients weren't alone in fearing the past," she said, pointing up. "The people who eventually created the Colberran Dominances erased much of their history prior to the Seekers keeping their own records in defiance of the Colberran government. All from some misguided attempt to prevent the world from ever fighting like that again."

"See, that right there," I said, pointing at her. "That's what I mean. What misguided attempt? How do you know it was misguided?"

"I read the legends, Logwyn," she said, "and I don't ignore them because they're fanciful. That's what started this little tangent, remember? The black dragon?"

"Yes, yes, I know. It's an old story told to kids of a black dragon that came when the entire world was fighting and bickering and tricked them all into letting him rule the world. He promised them safety if they swore allegiance to him. Some did, most didn't, and many kept fighting. So he killed them all and nearly wiped human civilization from existence. Or something like that. Depends on who's telling the story."

I shrugged, then held up a finger.

"However, that's just meant to scare kids. I don't recall it being discussed much in scholarly circles."

"Yet, a black dragon was right there in the middle of that battle. The Greens corroborated my story." She chuckled and nodded at my device. "Too bad she's blocked you from looking it up."

"Don't need a device to remember the stories my parents told me to keep me in line."

"Not saying you do," she said, her voice quiet. "Just that not all legends start in the imagination."

She leaned forward, pointing at the door behind me. Her eyes remained locked with mine. "Some are very real."

At first, the shock of seeing such a monstrosity prevented me from noticing what else was there. When I did, the feeling didn't get any better. Surrounding the mighty beast flew a massive army of Reds more numerous than I cared to count.

"Trap," Quentin muttered.

I smacked him on the shoulder. "Not the time."

"I'd say now's the perfect time for some humor," he said, elbowing my side.

The black dragon moved forward, his wings sweeping out and his long torso creaking.

"Enough of this madness," the monster growled. "Hand her over or die."

"I don't doubt they kill us all anyway," I said.

Set's head shifted in my direction. "The Reds would not. This one"—he nodded at the black dragon—"will not hesitate to do so."

"Delay much longer, and I will rescind the offer," the black beast called out.

Our leader shifted above the rest of the Greens.

"We know how good your promises are," Set called out. "And those who ally with you should know better than to trust you."

Set directed that last part while looking around at the surrounding Reds. The black beast made a rumbling sound and shook in the air.

"I like your spark and defiance." It moved closer, and Set moved back into the formation. "Typical, as well. You take after your pathetic excuse for a queen."

The Greens all shifted at his words, but Set growled and they calmed.

"Speak or act," Set said to the black dragon. "Don't do both."

The beast's mouth split, revealing wicked teeth. "Spunky, as well. I do like you. Too bad it will be the last thing you ever hear."

The beast unleashed a giant fireball at us. The Greens, ever ready in their formation, didn't hesitate. Before the beast could even get the shot off, we were on the move. The Reds added their own volley, a torrent of fire that followed us. So many attackers left us with few options. The formation dove low along the cave wall, dodging back and forth around glowing pillars as shots detonated all around us. Uncertain what else to do, I held a shield in front and another angled just above and behind, hoping to deflect some shots. I felt a tremor go through me and my strength wane with every deflection.

"I can't hold these up much longer," I called up to Quentin.

He flipped us up over a chunk of exploding pillar, forcing me to grip tight to his cloak. A shriek nearby preceded a blast of air and debris that struck just as Quentin spun away. When we finished the flip, I saw what had made the sound. One of the Greens was out of formation and had crashed into the surface of the cave. I saw no sign of its riders.

"We can't survive this much longer," Quentin yelled.

"Keep moving," Set called out, not slowing down. "We all knew what this mission entailed."

"*I* didn't," my companion muttered, diving under the Greens and around another chunk of rock.

The wall rose and forced us out into the middle of the cavern, where the fire from the Reds slowed. The Black dragon closed as we flew up and unleashed a massive fireball at us. It ripped through the middle of our formation, and another Green fell in a shriek. The remaining Greens scattered, looping around and reforming. They fled away from the black monster, closing on the many Reds.

The creature followed, shifting in a wide arc to come down on top of us, its giant maw opening to unleash death and destruction. Just as the light built up in its throat, a blast of fire smashed into the creature's face from beyond us. There, I saw one more thing to give me hope.

An army of Green dragons pouring in from another entrance.

CHAPTER 28

HELP

"Was that the plan all along?" I asked Suyef as Quentin stared at the wall. "For the other Greens to come to you?"

"Technically, yes," he said, nodding at Quentin. "He was correct about the trap. We expected one and planned to bring the other Greens to help."

He pointed at his wrist, and I nodded.

"Riders wear bracelets set to send a beacon if something separates them from their dragon," I said. "Standard protocol."

"For that mission, we set them to a persistent ping state."

"Allowing tracking. What about the Reds detecting the signal? Seems like they might have."

"The others needed to know our location." He held up a finger. "And all we had to do was alter the signal, and they could come to us."

"So, when did you change it?" I asked, glancing at Quentin and marveling at his stillness.

"The moment I saw that Black dragon."

"Not when you fell from your dragon?"

The Nomad shrugged. "We hadn't found her yet."

"What about when you had?"

"The plan called for us to signal only if necessary to get back out," Suyef said, shaking his head.

"Someone had confidence in your success."

"There were doubts," he replied. "But we only expected two results: returning with her or not at all." He arched an eyebrow at me. "Remember, those with me wanted to succeed. The council may have doubted the mission's success, but the Greens who did it did not."

"Yes, they sounded very motivated," I said, looking back over my notes. "What was it you said? 'Control the network'?"

"Controlling the network gives unequaled power in this world. The council just didn't believe Micaela represented enough of a threat," he said. "The Greens with me disagreed. In fact, most of the Green strike forces did. It's the only way I could get help. Gul made the choice, and he didn't give the council much say in the matter."

"I know. The Queen is the only one that can overrule both the council and the strike force."

Suyef spread his hands to either side. "They were at a stalemate. So, the council washed their hands of our 'foolhardy mission.'"

"They were right," I said. "You're lucky you succeeded."

"Not everyone came back."

His voice was quiet, drawing my eyes. He stared at the table.

"Many riders and not a few Greens fell in that raid."

"But you came back," I said, then nodded at our silent companion. "And he did. Also, what's gotten into him?"

"His mind isn't here. More so than usual, I mean. Maybe he's remembering. I don't know. Are you complaining?"

"No, it's just . . . different." I shook my head. "So, you two made it out. And Micaela."

"And she would say the lives lost were not a fair trade," he stated. "That no one's life is worth her freedom."

I took a deep breath, letting it out slowly. "They went on that mission by choice."

Suyef nodded.

"Then they knew what they were doing and what might happen," I said. "It doesn't justify it or make it easier. I can see why she carries that burden. Considering what I know of her."

Quentin slammed his hand down on the table.

"Curse you, fool," he blurted. "Why did you hurt her?"

I sat back, goose bumps rippling on my skin. Suyef had jumped up, staff unfolding in his hand.

"Why?" Quentin whispered, face twisted and tears in his eyes. "Why did you hurt her?" He leaned forward, and the tears hit the table. "Why?"

I glanced at Suyef. "Did I say something wrong?"

The Nomad held up a hand, eyes on Quentin. He just stayed there, head down, weeping.

"I don't think it was you," Suyef said. "I think hearing of her in pain bothers him."

"Because he hurt her?"

The Nomad nodded.

"How?"

"That is their story," he said, shaking his head.

"But you know what happened?"

"You already know that."

He folded up his staff and put it away before resuming his seat. I glanced at the still weeping Quentin.

"So, how did you make it out of that cave?"

Suyef pointed at Quentin. "The two of them pulled off something amazing."

The Greens' arrival threw the entire Red army into disarray. While I know they knew more Greens were present, their sneak attack on the Reds sent them into confusion. And we took advantage of it.

Set barked out orders, and our formation dove under the oncoming Greens just as they opened fire. Quentin spun down in an arc below Set, and I saw the black dragon hot on our tail, ignoring the fire from the reinforcements. The Reds' confusion proved short-lived, and more fireballs chased us along the bottom of the cave and up into the center of the arriving Greens. The consistent fire forced Quentin to keep moving around Set.

"Is it me, or are they firing at us now?"

Quentin stopped his turn short, pulling up alongside Set's head as a crossing shot whistled past.

"Maybe," he grunted.

As we moved above the Green, a blast of light detonated ahead, forcing my eyes shut. When I peeked, I saw Greens and Reds falling down, sparks of electricity arcing among them.

"What was that?"

The answer followed in the next instant. The black dragon soared above us and opened its mouth. Instead of fire, a ball of crackling electricity shot out and detonated ahead. The impact forced Quentin below Set, as bolts of lightning leaped around, hitting Reds and Greens alike. Set veered to the right and Quentin stayed close, flying tight to its left. I kept a wary eye out for any bolts, unsure what my shields might do. I just wanted to be ready.

Another detonation, this one much closer, ripped through the air, buffeting Quentin and me. Set jerked up but was too late. A large bolt arced into the Green, engulfing its underbelly and wings. Its body curled into a ball, convulsing. Quentin shifted away in a tight turn around the dragon and, as he brought us around, my heart stopped.

Suyef and my father were not on Set's back anymore.

I gripped Quentin's torso hard and craned my head, trying to find them. Electricity coursed down Set's body, jumping from one spinal protrusion to another as the creature lost altitude.

"Quentin!"

"I know!" he yelled, spinning around the falling beast. "The blast threw them off. I saw them, but—there!"

He pointed across the dragon as we flew under it. When we cleared Set, I saw the pair soaring through the air, Suyef clinging to my father's arm. They flipped end over end as they fell toward the cavern floor. Quentin sped up, aiming to one side just as a shadow swept over us. A giant Green dove through the chaotic battle, approaching the pair from above.

"Hang on!" Quentin called.

We jerked down below Suyef and my father. As we approached, their descent slowed. The pair, twisted in an awkward sprawl, soaring in a high arc directly over the passing Green. Quentin flew us under the creature, and I lost sight of the pair.

"Did you do that?"

He nodded, bringing us up to the other side.

"Hope it worked."

We came up next to the large Green, but I didn't see them.

"Where are they?"

Quentin flew higher, and I looked around, wondering if they'd gone too far.

"There's Suyef!" I exclaimed, pointing at the dragon. "And my father."

The Nomad lay hanging between two spinal structures, legs spread wide and one arm grasping a protrusion. My father's leg dangled just beyond the Nomad. Quentin slowed our climb to allow the dragon to move below us, and my father came fully into view. Suyef gripped his arm, and my father's face appeared ashen.

"Help them," I said, but Quentin was already moving.

As we approached the pair, something shifted to our right: a Red flying right at us.

"Look out!"

I grabbed Quentin's shoulder and threw up a shield.

We dropped straight down at an angle from the charging Red before it could shoot. Another fireball whizzed past us from a different direction. Our descent stopped with a jolt as Quentin flew up the other side of the Red. Fireballs targeting us flew past. I threw up more shields to deflect what I could.

"Was that you?" Quentin asked after a fireball exploded in midair.

"Yes," I said through clenched teeth. "I'm trying. Moving targets are hard." I grunted as another fireball slammed into a shield. "Doing it while moving more so."

Quentin moved up alongside the giant Green where Suyef pulled my father into the bone protrusions. I let out an enormous sigh, but the relief didn't last. Quentin turned us to reveal the mighty black dragon hovering nearby.

"Give her up, Gul," the black beast called out to the large Green.

"You know, I don't think Suyef and your father are in any danger," Quentin said, voice quiet.

"Except by association."

I glanced back at Gul, and something beyond caught my eye, something that made my heart skip a beat. The giant Green blocked most of the view, but I knew I'd seen something. Something that might be our best shot.

"Quentin, lower us down below Gul."

He did so, and I kept my eyes locked on the wall beyond. When he'd brought us far enough, I inhaled, gripping his torso.

There, up a tunnel close to where we hovered, I saw the sky.

CHAPTER 29

SKY

"Is that the tunnel the reinforcements came down?" I asked. "When they arrived to help?"

Micaela raised her eyebrows, nodded, then shook her head.

"I'm sorry, you confused me. No, that was from the other side. I'm not sure what was up that tunnel."

"Well, had the other Greens infiltrated the shell or had they remained on the surface?"

"I don't remember that part. Suyef told me something about them causing distractions so the other Greens could sneak inside to find and rescue me." She scrunched her nose. "I remember saying what I thought about that plan, and it wasn't pleasant."

"It worked," I pointed out.

She glared at me. "Only because Colvinra went power-hungry mad, acting like he was defending us. Without him, I doubt they would have found us."

"But they did," I said, then glanced at my notes. "Details on the Red shell's interior are scarce, even after this incursion. The Greens got debriefed, I'm sure."

Micaela shrugged.

"Maybe the council hid the information." She pointed at the cavern behind me. "Or she did."

"That's illegal. No one owns information except personal identification data." I waved a hand at my notes. "Details on that shell don't fall into that category. Our laws are very clear about that."

"And who made that rule?"

"The Queen issued an edict on it several centuries ago," I replied. "She countermanded the council's decision to limit access to certain data. They made some excuse about national defense or some other nonsense."

Micaela nodded.

"In this edict, did she specify a time frame? A type of information? Any restrictions?"

I opened my mouth, then paused. The Queen's edict countermanding the council had contained some restrictions.

"Time," I said, snapping my fingers. "It began on a certain date and went forward."

"Did she choose that limitation?"

"No, I think they forced her to." I frowned, closing my eyes to think. "By necessity," I blurted out, eyes opening. "The information prior to a certain date was lost."

Micaela tapped a finger to her lips. "Lost? Can anything really be lost on the computer controlling the network?"

"No, that's impossible. All the data put in always exists. But some of it is missing," I stated, pointing behind me. "Why else bring me in to help?"

"Missing. Hidden," Micaela said, smiling at me. "We're quibbling over words. The point is the data may be there—if we knew where to look."

I bowed my head. "We're a bit off-shell. My apologies."

"Conversation for the sake of it is not always a bad thing, Logwyn." She sipped water from her crystal glass, eyes on me. "But we are off topic."

I tapped the paper. "So, you saw sky."

The glimpse of core light sent a jolt through both of us. Before I could say anything, Quentin shot away from Gul, pulling up around an attacking Red. Gul raced after us, diving at another Red to drive it off. As the Green dove, the Black dragon rushed at us, his mouth opening.

"Quentin, dive!"

The entire cavern flipped upside down as he did. The Black's shot, crackling with charged power, ripped past just above us. Quentin pulled back up and pressed on toward the tunnel. Another sizzling shot narrowly missed us, and fireballs struck the surrounding cavern. Every Red, it seemed, opened fire at us.

"Is it me," Quentin groaned as we spiraled around a small Red trying to ram us, "or are they aiming just at us now?"

He was right. The fire from the Reds intensified as we approached the tunnel. Fireballs from every direction detonated across the cavern walls, knocking the glowing columns free. Others smashed into dragons, both Red and Green.

We arced into a wider spiral around the tunnel entrance. Another massive lightning ball came right for us, and I yelled a warning. Before he could react, the shot sizzled through the air directly overhead and slammed into the top of the tunnel wall. A large chunk of rock broke free and fell.

Right at us.

"All that moving and spinning. Did you get tired at all, Quentin?"

Quentin sat in silence, staring at a nearby wall. Suyef gave me a look, then shrugged.

"Quentin?"

The Nomad reached over and touched his arm, an act that seemed very out of character. Either that or it was a symbol of their bond.

"Through all of this, you've become quite close," I said.

"Yes. Surprising, I know, considering the start and what's still to come in this story. It wasn't always easy, but yes. He is my brother now." He shrugged, half smiling. "And family sticks together."

Quentin shook, a tremor jerking his entire body.

"I'm-I'm sorry. What was the question, Logwyn?" he asked, frowning. "Still this?"

"You were telling me what happened during the cave escape," I said, smiling at him. "Specifically, when the black dragon knocked that enormous piece of rock in your path."

"Was I?" His brow furrowed. "I . . . I . . . we were talking about that?"

"That is where she is," Suyef said. "Remember, she's not just talking to you."

Quentin's eyes narrowed as he looked at me.

"Getting nosy, are we? People sending you away? Asking the wrong questions?"

"You led me to this part of the story—through a very convoluted path, mind you—and I asked what happened next. How is that the wrong question?"

He shrugged. "Um, I . . . I don't remember. Sorry. Ask it again."

"The chunk of rock—"

"Right!" He cut me off with a finger snap. "Lightning balls, fireballs, and dragons all around. Tunnel out of the cave."

He nodded and fell silent.

"So?"

"Micaela saved us from it."

When the chunk of rock broke free, I wanted to slow down, pull up, and fly over it. Halfway through a spiral, I focused the grav-belt's blue beams on the chunk. As our spiral slowed, fireballs peppered the rock's edge. Micaela's shields blocked the falling shards of rock, but the fireballs did their job. I hesitated, and that gave the Reds time to move above us.

"Quentin, dive under!"

Nodding, I propelled us down using the rock chunk and felt her arms tighten on my torso. As we dove, something shimmered just beneath the rock chunk. That meant one thing: Micaela had scripted a shield. A very large one.

Knowing the strain scripting was putting on both of us, I grabbed the shield and yanked hard, angling us away from the debris. The enormous chunk smashed into her shield as we went under, and she let out a loud groan and sagged against me.

"Hang on!"

The shield shimmered overhead, lines splintering across it. I grabbed the cave floor and pushed us up the far side. Micaela's head fell against my back just as a resounding crack echoed behind us. I assumed it was the shield breaking but couldn't look. Large chunks broke away, falling down either side of the shield. I used the pieces, pushing us higher, changing their trajectory, and speeding up as much as possible to get to the tunnel. Ahead, the gap between a sizable chunk closed fast in front of us—faster, it seemed, than we could move.

"Micaela, drop the shield! Move it over us."

"I can't," she said, her voice trembling. "It's . . . it's too heavy."

Her arms shook as she clung tight.

"Stop holding on to me," I yelled, flipping upside down and under a chunk of rock. "I've got you."

Her arms loosened but didn't move. I pointed ahead to show where I wanted the shield, but also to help me focus.

"The gap!"

Momentum carried us near the far wall, offering a counterbalance to push the rock chunk. I split the beams between the wall and the chunk just as a shimmer appeared in the gap. Spinning counterclockwise on our axis revealed the opposite side of the chunk dipping when Micaela's shield moved. Our spin brought us back to face the tunnel, where I saw the gap widening slowly.

"Keep it up!"

The space between the wall and the rock couldn't have held a dragon at that point, and I could feel the air buffeting the two surfaces. I reached down and gripped Micaela's hand.

"Hold on to your stomach!"

A smaller piece ripped free from the far edge of the chunk, swinging down toward us. I sent us into another under-flip, moving my feet and the board up in front and over the top of my head as we passed under the falling piece. I stopped our momentum on a flat plane relative to the tunnel entrance, Micaela lying on top of me. Micaela's shield shimmered around the gap, a perfect acceleration anchor.

"Hurry, Quentin, hurry."

Her whole body quaked, her breath raking my hair in quick gasps. I saw cracks tunneling across the shield and fragments of Ancient symbols fall away. Her waning strength, coupled with its size, meant the shield would fail. Soon. I shook my head, focusing forward and squeezing every ounce of speed the board and belt possessed. Just as the shield fractured near the bottom edge, a beam shifted and locked on to the tunnel wall beyond the entrance. In the next instant, our speed increased significantly. We shot through the gap just after her shield failed, the rock chunk crashing down behind us.

The rock chunk compressed my shield, making my body vibrate as the weight pressed down on my torso. The pressure increased, my body trembled more, and I couldn't breathe. I buried my face in Quentin's back, eyes squeezed shut, willing him to move faster, for the tunnel to be there, the chunk gone. The tremors ripped through me, pain filled my head, and I tried to scream. Just as my ribs felt sure to crack, the weight lifted. I managed one deep breath before Quentin pulled us up hard and my stomach shifted into my loins. Air continued filling my lungs, allowing a look back. I regretted doing that.

The rock chunk fell through my unraveling shield and down into the cavern below. As it fell, the black dragon swept overhead, barreling toward us. Our angle pulled us up across the creature's central plane of flight, forcing the beast into a twist. Just as its mouth opened, the world tilted, spinning the black dragon upside down. Beyond, Greens and Reds swarmed into the passage. Looking ahead, one side of the tunnel loomed close. We flew along the wall and up toward the light. There, sweeping down the tunnel, the sky illuminating them from behind, flew more Green dragons.

"Hold on!"

We flew in a large spiral along the tunnel walls. The arriving Greens unleashed a torrent of fire into the space behind us. The two flights of dragons sped up into a headlong collision. Fireballs shot past, detonating in the tunnel above. One landed nearby, showering us with deadly rocks.

"Quentin!"

He threw us out into the tunnel center as I brought a shield up overhead. The tunnel spun as we flew past the falling rocks and up the passage. Several Reds gained, so I moved the shield below us. The Greens gave chase, smashing into the creatures and sending them all crashing into the tunnel walls. A fireball from a falling Red collided with the shield. I clenched my jaw, gripping the construct with all my remaining strength. The force of the impact pushed it up at us. Quentin, continuing our spin, reached toward my construct and used it to ride the shock wave farther up the tunnel.

"Where's the black one?" I asked, twisting my head and looking around.

Quentin pointed left in answer. The black dragon flew up the far side of the tunnel. As we shifted around the passage, it kept pace. Quentin altered our direction, rotating back around the tunnel.

The creature followed suit. A smattering of fireballs tore past and detonated ahead. Quentin shifted through a shower of rocks, some smashing against a new shield, most missing.

"It's matching your every move," I called out, peeking ahead. "Is it going to block the passage?"

"That or collide with us."

He grunted, moving the other way to avoid more fire from behind. A Red almost caught up, but a Green slammed into its tail, knocking the creature into a vicious spin back down the passage.

"Micaela, the strongest, largest shield you can muster," Quentin said, nodding at the black dragon. "If he strikes, can you block him?"

"It would send us flying in the opposite direction."

He chuckled. "Precisely."

"Are you insane?" I asked as we twisted around more falling rocks.

"Maybe!"

A series of detonations almost stole his words.

"Just get it ready."

Taking in a deep breath, I closed my eyes and imagined a large, impenetrable wall between us and the black dragon. Once I could see the constructs, I multiplied them, attaching descriptive offshoots for strength and mass. Finally, I tied them to us, stringing shields around us like a belt.

Something smashed into the wall nearby, the air buffeting us into a slight spin. Below, another Red twisted in an ugly crash, fighting with a Green as it did.

"Are you ready?"

"I don't know. Maybe. We'll see."

"Yes, we will," Quentin said, pointing. "We're almost there."

Ahead, the wide expanse of our world shone brightly after all the time in the dark. I shielded my eyes from the light and squinted to spot the Black. When I found him, an icy feeling gripped my heart. The black dragon no longer matched our course. Instead, it shot at an angle across the tunnel, heading right at us.

"Get ready!" Quentin yelled, head shifting back and forth between the exit and the approaching danger. "Almost there."

The Black creature loomed large, its mouth widening to unleash more terrifying and deadly electrical shots. I lifted a hand to set the construct in place, but Quentin grabbed it.

"Not yet!"

"It's almost on us!"

"Not in here." He pointed. "The walls. We have to be out."

The black dragon was not cooperating. It sped closer, and Quentin held a hand out at the creature. The wind speed picked up around us. Had I still had my longer hair, it no doubt would have whipped my face.

"Now!"

Shaking my head, I pushed the construct forward, my hand outstretched for focus. We shot clear of the tunnel into the expanse, but before I could look, the most violent tremor yet struck, rattling every bone in my body. Something struck me from the side, knocking me free of Quentin and into a tumbling flip into the expanse.

CHAPTER 30

ESCAPE

With the black dragon matching my moves, we needed something between us so that, when it struck, we'd have some protection. But the laws of the universe didn't change just because humanity discovered scripting. I felt the push from every strike against Micaela's shields. The falling rock chunk had required considerable force from the grav-board to keep us from being crushed. The black dragon would come at us much faster than that. So, at the moment of impact, we needed to clear the tunnel to avoid becoming one with the rock face.

I saw the tall columns of intricate symbols appear, then fade from sight. I wondered if our pursuer could see them and would just attack before she finished, but I couldn't do anything about that. Just go faster. It was a delicate dance of speed versus time for Micaela versus keeping the monster at bay—all while dodging attacks from below. Those remained many, despite the Greens' keeping them off us. Why they did this, I did not know, but they proved a worthy foe despite being outnumbered.

A shot detonating below us, followed by a Red crashing into the wall, brought me back to the moment. Maneuvering through the debris, I saw the edge approaching fast.

"Get the shield ready!" I yelled at Micaela. "Ready? Ready? Hold it."

I looked between the beast and the tunnel's end.

"Almost there."

The monster opened its mouth just as Micaela reached out, and the shield shimmered into existence.

"Not yet!" I called out, grabbing her hand.

"It's almost on us!"

I pointed up.

"Not in here. The walls. We have to be out."

The black dragon chose that moment to attack. As it sped closer, I locked a beam onto the creature. When it latched on, the wind picked up as a surge of energy pushed us forward. The edge loomed, the expanse beckoning beyond.

"Now!" I screamed.

A shimmer wavered before my eyes, warping everything I could see. My beam locked on the dragon dissipated, defusing against the smooth, invisible surface. Squinting, I pushed toward the shield and not a moment too soon.

The giant monster slammed into the shield the instant we cleared the tunnel, smashing it up into us. Micaela's construct held, although the symbols flickered into sight for a split second. The impact knocked almost every beam free of their purchase. Only one locked on to the shell remained. The world spun, and a sinking feeling grabbed my stomach.

I was alone.

"Micaela!"

I spun around, trying to focus. The shell spun in and out of view as I flipped and fell.

"Micaela!"

Something smashed into the shell behind me, and my next rotation showed the Black dragon crashing onto the surface. A wave of dizziness coursed through me, forcing my eyes shut and me to focus on that remaining beam. I pushed more beams out to slow my spin.

I opened my eyes and saw Micaela falling toward the shell's edge, her body caught in a tight, flat spin. My rotation, though slowing, carried me away from her. I tried catching her, but couldn't reach.

I dropped the extra beams and fed power through my anchor beam, pulling myself around and back toward the shell. Something flashed to my right, something Red. One of the Red beasts dove at Micaela with much greater speed than me. With few options, I reached out to grab the Red, but, just as the beam gained purchase, the Red dropped hard and fast.

"What are you doing?" I called out.

The Red moved between Micaela and the shell, and I changed the beam's angle to approach her. The creature leveled off beneath Micaela and her descent slowed relative to the dragon's movement. Both, however, still fell toward the shell's edge. I raced closer, trying to lock on to her, but the beams remained stubbornly unfocused.

The next moment, the Red shrieked and Micaela flipped up, away from the shell and my beam. A crash echoed as the Red smashed into the shell, rolling toward the edge and the massive drop to the core.

"Quentin!" Micaela called as she passed me.

I grabbed at the shell, seeking anything the beams could grasp. Micaela flipped away from the edge, speeding toward the point of no return for either of us. Without hesitating, I launched after her. A hint of despair that I would fail started filling me, but something shoved me from below. I fell into a flat spin right under Micaela just as a Green flew above us.

"Quentin!"

Micaela extended her hand. I reached out, and our hands collided but didn't lock as my rotation carried me past her.

Behind me, a shriek split the air, but I kept my eyes on her. I tried to lock on to her, but my spin didn't allow me to focus.

"Stop grabbing for my hand! Use me to stop yourself!"

I opened my mouth to yell that she would fall with me. Then I realized what she meant: the Green had caught her, and that gave me an anchor. Closing my eyes against the fall, I let the Ancient technology do its job. Within a few heartbeats, it latched on.

Laughing, I halted the deadly spin and pulled myself closer while targeting beams to lock on to the dragon. Once done, the creature released her, and we moved alongside it. The Green bellowed and pulled away from the shell. Behind, a swarm of Greens flew after us, Micaela's father and Suyef still astride Gul. The Red that saved Micaela hung limp among the Greens.

A loud shriek drew our eyes to the shell. The black dragon hovered over the landmass, mouth split in a gaping maw. The other Reds scattered back into their shell.

"We did it!" Micaela exclaimed, hugging me.

I settled us down on the Green's back for the trip to our destination, just visible in the distance. At that moment, my body shook with violent tremors. Micaela leaned close, tears streaming down her face. She smiled and looked at the approaching Gul. Her father waved, which she returned just before collapsing against a spinal structure.

"Did that just happen?"

I looked at the black dragon, still hovering over the Red shell, and nodded.

"Y-yes," I said. "I-it . . . it did."

She laughed, a cheerful sound that warmed me. A smile tugged at my lips as she fell into a fit of laughter. A chuckle rippled up from my still-trembling gut. My skin itched, and tingles ran up my spine, but still I laughed. It felt great.

After several moments, Micaela quieted, head resting against her makeshift backrest. She looked at me as I fell silent, extremities still shaking.

"So," she said.

"So," I said back.

She cocked her head at me.

"You broke your promise." When I frowned, she added, "About not going anywhere."

"I fell off the shell," I said, pointing up.

"Yes, and you survived." Her eyes never left me. "How?"

I took a deep breath, closing my eyes as another tremor shook my torso. "By doing something harebrained."

"The Red that saved them," I said, looking at Suyef. "Your friend from before?"

"Not quite a friend," he said, nodding. "It shadowed us the whole time. When we made it to the cave with the black dragon, it must have avoided the battle. Because it never engaged them in the cave or tunnel, the Greens ignored it."

"In the tunnel?" I asked. "No one noticed it, then?"

"It didn't fire at them, I guess," he said, pointing at Quentin. "Even he didn't notice it just behind the black dragon."

Quentin scoffed at the Nomad.

"You try doing all that I was doing while also catching every little detail around you."

"That's not the point," Suyef said through clenched teeth. "Nor is it relevant."

"Did the Red come back to the Green shell?"

Suyef nodded.

"So, where is it now?"

"I don't frequent your shell, save for a brief visit or two recently," he said, glancing at me. "You know something about that."

Quentin looked back and forth between us. "You two need me to leave? Let you have this private chat in peace?"

"I'd rather hear how you survived that fall."

"I told you. The Green used Micaela to give me an anchor."

"No, from before. In the outpost."

His eyebrows both raised, and he nodded. "Yes, I could see why that might be important." He held up a finger. "But this part isn't over yet."

"What's left?" I asked. "You and the strike force got off the shell and brought a traitor Red with you."

Suyef cleared his throat. "No, he's right. Much more about those events matter." When I nodded at him to continue, he said, "Our welcome on the Green shell."

I looked at both of them. "Considering they helped rescue Micaela, I'd assume you were met with great fanfare. Well, as much as expected."

The pair shared a glance.

"What?" I asked, drawing their gaze. "What happened?"

Suyef shook his head as Quentin stood up. "The Greens arrested us."

"Wait, what?"

Micaela looked up at me.

"Why would they do that? It makes no sense."

"Logwyn, are you assuming politicians make sense?" She frowned. "Really, I thought you more intelligent."

"They sent a strike force to rescue you," I said with a glare. "Why arrest you?"

"Not me," she said, pointing at the pictures. "Them."

"Why? What did they do to warrant that?"

"We weren't told." She shook her head. "When we landed, guards detained them while others took me to quarters clearly prepared in advance."

Her brow furrowed.

"I'm still not entirely sure how they knew I was coming, considering the council's position on rescuing me."

"Gul or Set probably sent word en route," I suggested. "But why not detain you?" I pointed behind me. "Because you're her friend?"

Micaela looked at the door behind me. "No, I didn't know her yet."

I perused my notes, going over the details.

"Wait, when was this?" I asked, looking up. "After the strike, yes?"

She nodded.

"Something about all this feels so familiar. You know, like when you're at an event, but your mind is elsewhere?"

"A very familiar feeling," she said. "One I get a lot when listening to politicians."

I nodded, not really listening to her. I tapped the stylus on my lips, then stopped and pointed at her.

"There was a celebration after the strike. I remember thinking it was silly." I frowned, focusing on her. "Well, no, I wasn't there. That's more what I thought later, after the fact."

My eyes, still on her, narrowed. She just watched me.

"But I remember it happening. I came late. Buried in interview notes from another project, most likely."

"Did you see us ride in on the Greens?"

"No. I missed that part. Everyone cheering made it hard to work, so I went outside. But the crowds were dispersing."

I looked down, trying to hide a small smile.

"What's so amusing, Logwyn?"

I waved a hand at her. "Just remembering what someone said when I came out and asked what happened. 'Oh, Logwyn, so buried in your stories you miss all the best ones.'" I shrugged. "I guess they were talking about your arrival."

Micaela looked away, head shaking.

"Considering our welcome, I'm not sure I'd call that one of the best stories." She chuckled. "Still, small world. Just a little sooner, and you might have seen us."

"So, you weren't told why they arrested them?"

Her head tilted to one side.

"Even knowing why later made no sense."

"What was the charge?"

She stood and moved to the window. "Breaking the network."

CHAPTER 31

INFLUENCE

I arrived at the Queen's chamber early in the morning. On most other shells, the night shield lifting signaled the day's start. This shell, however, lacked people living on the surface. No cities, no settlements—not even the Ancient waterlines bringing life to its residents.

On this shell, all citizens, regardless of form, lived below-ground. I stepped near the window, contemplating what Micaela enjoyed about looking out. I shook my head. Micaela didn't enjoy doing so; it allowed her to escape the memories dredged up by this process. Leaning near the glass, I looked at the smaller landmass floating nearby, one I'd visited in gathering this story, piecing together this mystery. Looking for something the Queen wasn't even sure existed.

Barely visible on that small shell lay the ruins of an outpost: a relic of a war now over. A ruin that nearly took the life of one of my interviewees. An incident Quentin still needed to explain to me. I gritted my teeth at the thought of that man and his infuriating condition. Suyef insisted he hadn't always been so fractured of mind, that something had changed him. Even Micaela confirmed this. But when pressed to tell me the cause, both balked, telling me to wait, bide my time.

I closed my eyes and leaned my forehead to the window, wondering when everyone would stop saying those words. If ever. *It's okay, Logwyn, my dear. Just be patient. Bide your time. Your chance will come.* My father's words echoed from the past, repeated so many times by those lacking better ones. I took in a deep breath and let it out slowly.

"It's very calming, that view," Micaela said from behind me.

I opened my eyes and looked down at the world's core: four singularities, built long in the past by minds far more advanced than mine, locked in a deadly dance.

"I'm not sure *calming* is the word," I said, pushing away from the window. "But it helps to clear the mind, to focus."

Micaela wore a long gown of dark green, her hair swept back behind her shoulders. Her blue-gray eyes looked out the window.

"What are we focusing on today?"

I turned and pointed. "That shell. The outpost on it, specifically."

"That tracks." She moved next to me. "Has he told you yet?"

"No. But you're acknowledging he exists."

"Sometimes it's less painful to pretend he does not." She bowed her head, eyes closed. "But that only works for a moment. Then the memories return. And the pain."

"What did he do to you, High One?"

She looked at me, eyes sparkling with tears. "Only what those dearest to us can do."

She fell silent.

"Before we continue, may I ask a question, High One?"

She waved a hand at me.

"Quentin. What happened to him? Why is he, um, broken?"

Her head dipped, eyes closing.

"Logwyn, I want to tell you everything." She opened her eyes and pointed at the shell. "But some secrets are just not mine to tell. When it's time, when he's able, he *will* tell you."

"So, this dancing around certain topics is just you three not wanting to tell everyone's secrets?"

She nodded, a tear creeping down her cheek.

"Just because you know the answer does not mean you can share it. Too often, people get mad at someone because that person kept something from them. They call them a liar when it was just not that person's secret to share."

I chuckled. "You just described the conflict in every work of fiction ever written."

For a moment, I thought she might laugh. A smile tugged at her lips.

"So, Quentin is dear to you," I said. "And what of Suyef?"

Her chest rose and fell. "That is a different story. The same one overall, mind you. But a distinct part that I do not relish telling you."

"But you're about to?"

"Soon," she said, nodding, "you'll know all about what happened between Suyef and me."

"You speak in the past tense?" I asked as we moved away from the glass. "As if you no longer see him, let alone interact like cohorts, friends even, in this venture. The two of you are working hard to help Quentin, yes?"

She nodded, eyes on me.

"That doesn't seem like it's ended."

"Some relationships stand the test of time. Of trial. Of death. They blossom and flourish through all the above. Some fade and then blossom again. Over and over." Micaela held my gaze. "Then there are those that simply exist, stuck where they are because of things beyond our control."

"I think I'm more confused now than when we started."

"You'll understand soon." She sat down and waved for me to sit as well. "Where were we?"

"Breaking the network." I activated the recording device and sat down.

"Ah, yes. The tribunal before the council."

"Wait, they faced a tribunal?"

"The law is clear," she stated. "When the Queen recuses herself from the proceedings, the council has complete autonomy and authority to do such things." She held up a finger. "The Queen alone can overrule them. But, when that tribunal began, her seat in the ruling chamber stood empty. No one could find her."

"So they were alone," I whispered. "I assume no Green acted as their counsel?"

"Only one person helped them that day," she said, looking at the pictures. "Me."

Moments after we landed in the main cavern, the council ordered Suyef, Quentin, and my father taken for debriefing. An escort guided me to another cave to be bathed and pampered for the next hour. However, my companions and my father remained on my mind. Now, I should be clear: I had no reason to mistrust the council and their lackeys. I didn't know of all the inner workings of the Greens' governing bodies—namely how much the council and the Queen disagreed on things. So, I couldn't really pinpoint the cause of my unease. Possibly my previous experiences with dragons. All I knew was that, until I knew what was going on, relaxing was not happening.

I extricated myself from the female attendants as soon as I could and demanded to see my companions. At first, the guards rebuffed me, citing the council's orders on keeping my companions isolated until the debriefing ended. When I insisted, the stubborn, obstructive guards transformed into compliant escorts. That was my first inkling that something was off. Regardless, I took full advantage of it and followed them to my companions. Where we found them served as my second inkling that something was not right.

The guards led me into a prison. They deposited me in a hall, my three companions locked in cells to either side.

"What's going on?" I asked.

"We've been here this whole time," Quentin said, shrugging.

"Didn't they question you?"

All three of them shook their heads.

"This makes no sense. Have they accused you of anything?"

"The guards mentioned something about his last visit," my father said, pointing at Suyef.

When I looked at the Nomad, he frowned. "The council and the strike force commander disagreed over whether I spoke the truth about your need of rescue," he said. "With the Queen absent, neither could overrule the other."

"Doesn't sound like a reason to detain you," I muttered, moving near my father's cell. "Are you okay?"

"They tended to us before putting us here. Actually, the nutrient packs were some of the best I've had in cycles."

I stepped closer to the entrance and felt the air crackle. As it did, lights around the edge glowed.

"I'd be careful," Quentin muttered. "That energy shield packs a punch."

I looked at him. "You've still got your belt. The board?"

He reached behind and pulled out a small rectangular object. "It shrinks down. Well, folds in on itself. Pretty amazing piece of engineering."

"And your staff?" I asked Suyef, looking at him.

"They left that," he answered, pulling it out. "They don't consider us much of a threat." He glanced at the wall between his and Quentin's cells. "Or a flight risk. All things considered, a humorous use of that word in this context."

My eyes moved back to Quentin. "You never explained what happened."

"I told you, something harebrained." He shifted and shrugged. "Nothing that exciting."

"How about you let me be the judge of that?" I looked back up the hall. "Guards!"

"What are you doing?" my father hissed, stepping near the shield.

"Testing a theory," I whispered. "Guards!"

The same two men rushed back around the corner.

"Are these men bothering you?" one asked.

I glared at them, pointing at the doorframe. "Why are they locked away behind that? I want them released and escorted to my quarters."

The men exchanged looks. One spoke, but the other grabbed his arm while bowing his head at me.

"As you wish, High One," he said. "Let us arrange an escort."

"Be quick about it."

That served as the third inkling.

"Okay, how did you do that?" Quentin asked as the men hurried away.

"I'm not sure," I said, shaking my head. "These people act like I'm someone of influence. That"—I waved a hand down the hall—"clinches it."

"Who do they think you are?" my father asked.

Suyef cleared his throat.

"Someone the three of us saw talking to us from a screen."

I stared at the Nomad, lost at first.

"In a dark room," he added.

"The woman on the screen at the prison?" Quentin asked, waving a hand at me. "The one that looked like her?"

"That wasn't me."

"I didn't say it was." He pointed behind me. "But I think your father knows about her. Why else go pale over us mentioning her?"

My father did indeed look as white as a set of freshly cleaned linens.

"What's wrong, Father?" I asked, moving toward his cell.

"You saw her?" he whispered, eyes darting between us. "All of you did?"

I paused midstep.

"Wait, you know about her? Who is she?"

"She showed herself to you all?" he asked, avoiding my eyes. "Why would she do that? Why reveal herself now?"

"Seems there's more to this story than a familiar face," Quentin said.

"Father, who is she? And why does she look like me?"

"She doesn't look like you." He waved a hand at me. "Just very similar." He finally looked at me. "Her name is Celandine."

"I've heard that name before," I said, cutting Micaela off.

"Yes, and soon you'll know a lot more about her." She frowned. "I am curious where you heard of her, though."

"From a strange old man wearing a robe with many colored swatches of cloth sewn to it," I said, suppressing a grin at the memory.

"Ah, Nidfar," she muttered. "Made an appearance, did he?"

"I went back to ask Suyef some questions and continue interviewing Quentin," I said with a nod. "You told me to, earlier in this process. Well, no one was there, so I spent some time, um"—I looked at my bag, the box coming to mind—"going over my notes. That's when the old man showed up."

"How was he?" she asked, a twinkle in her eye.

"Mostly coherent, particularly when talking about you," I answered, watching her. "He told me about coming to you after the settlement battle."

She shook her head and pointed at the pictures. "To this day, Suyef still insists he saw no one there."

"He's free to believe what he wants," I said, shrugging. "And to be wrong."

"So you believe me?" she asked, one eyebrow lifted.

"Three different people recounted the same events to me." I shrugged again. "Suyef's account confirmed most of the same details, save one part, which Nidfar's account confirmed." I waved a hand at the papers before me. "I've seen and written stranger things than an old man hiding his presence from people, which this old man seems adept at doing."

"You seeing him at all is a good thing. I haven't seen him in, well, a while."

"Who is he?" I asked.

She shook her head. "That's his story to tell, his secret to reveal."

I pressed my lips together and smiled.

"Worth a shot. But I understand the secrets thing." I looked over the last of my notes. "So, Celandine. Nidfar mentioned her. Something about the network and a man named Rawyn."

Micaela's entire expression twisted when I said that name.

"A name I hoped to never hear again, but I suppose that was unrealistic." She shrugged. "I don't know what Nidfar was referring to."

"He recounted a conversation with Rawyn just after you left his tower."

I scanned through my older notes until I found the conversation, then handed that part to her.

"Just some musings and highlights."

Her eyes looked my notes over. "Your shorthand is superb," she said. "A learned skill?"

I nodded.

"Impressive." She handed the paper back to me. "Yes, no surprises there."

"Staying on topic, Celandine has full access to the network," I prompted her.

"No one can truly control that much computing power or data. It's more accurate to say she controls access to it."

"Might she cause the problems the Queen mentioned?"

"Maybe. She's impossible to talk to. Very reclusive. A bit on the arrogant side."

"You seem to know a lot about her," I stated, jotting down a reminder on the topic.

"We've never met in person, but we share a connection. Some common interests. Acquaintances by circumstance."

"But you have met?" I asked.

"In a manner of speaking."

I waited, then realized she wasn't going to explain that, yet.

"So then, where did you *meet*?"

She nodded out the window.

"Down there."

I looked out, thinking she meant the other shell. Then it hit me.

"Wait, you went *there*? The forbidden citadel? No one may go near that place."

"Because it's too dangerous," Micaela said, nodding. "Yes, I've heard all the same things. But I was there." She looked back at me. "And so is she."

"Okay, so how did you get there?"

She smiled at me. "I broke Quentin and Suyef out of prison."

CHAPTER 32

REASONING

The conversation ended abruptly when the guards returned, this time with an escort. Soon, we stood in my quarters, Quentin, Suyef, and my father staring around at the room.

"So, we get prison cells, and you get luxury." Quentin grinned. "Tell me again you're of no importance to them."

"The question is why," I said, sitting at the table and looking between Suyef and my father. "You two seem to know something about it."

"I gambled based on what happened at the prison," the Nomad said, sitting across from me and pointing at my father. "Clearly, he has some information about the person on that screen."

"I know little." My father frowned. "She's very reclusive. She only communicates using the network panels, and I'm still not sure why she contacted your mother and me." He shrugged. "Something we did got her attention."

"Perhaps your secret projects?" Quentin asked. "Or some research on the Ancient code?"

"Maybe," he said. "As we never pinpointed where or who she was, I was a little wary of her at first. She might have been a Seeker or a Colberran spy."

He waved his hand at one wall before nodding at Suyef.

"Or working for the dragons or the Nomads. Or she could have been one of them. Although," he said, bowing his head at Suyef, "I wasn't aware of your people's complexion."

"It's a common trait in my clan, but not in all Nomads," Suyef said, then nodded at Quentin and me. "Also in the clans currently leading the council."

"My mistake," my father said. "Regardless, I didn't trust Celandine right off."

"What changed your mind?" Quentin asked.

"She put me in contact with someone dear to me," he said, resting his hand against his forehead. "On the condition I keep it a secret until that person revealed themselves to me."

"Did you meet this person?" Suyef inquired, drawing a headshake. "So, why speak of it now?"

"She only forbade the identity," he said. "Not the contact itself. But, all things considered, it's not wise on our shell to reveal you're secretly communicating with people on the network."

Anger welled up inside me, and words poured out before I could stop myself.

"Someone found your conversations, didn't they? And that brought the Seekers down on us?" I glared at him. "That's why they took our family away."

He frowned at me. "No. She warned us they were coming. Your mother didn't like taking advice from a stranger but, with Jyen how she was, we had no choice." He looked down. "Not that it helped in the end."

The anger fell to a simmer.

"That doesn't mean they didn't know about your conversations with this Celandine."

"I don't think they know she's there. I think they suspect someone is controlling the network, causing issues with it, but nothing certain. From the questioning I got when they detained me, I believe they're as stumped about it as everyone else."

"So, why come for us?"

"The illness," he said. "That got their attention. I don't think they were even watching our settlement before that."

"That's not entirely true," Quentin interjected, "and you both know what I'm talking about."

"The water," I said. "But we never pinned down who did that exactly."

"Yeah, neither did we," Quentin said, nodding at Suyef. "We only stumbled on it while looking for something else."

"That was the second reason they came," my father went on. "Well, after they took your mother."

"Why did they take her?" I asked. "She wasn't ill."

He shrugged. "They suspected she was, and, with an outbreak already striking the settlement, they acted quickly to isolate her for observation." He looked at the floor. "At least, that was their story. Celandine informed me otherwise."

An icy hand reached inside and wrapped itself around my heart.

"You knew they did not take her to a hospital?" I whispered. "And you didn't tell me?"

"No, I didn't know that until after the Seekers took me." He pointed at a panel across the room. "That thing appears offline, but Celandine can activate them anywhere, anytime. While the Seekers held me, she told me your mother was not on the shell."

"So where did she go?"

My father's face twisted into a pained look.

I answered my own question. "Celandine doesn't know."

"I'm sorry, sweetheart. I wish I had an answer."

Anger and sadness welled up inside, but I suppressed them. It proved a lot harder than expected. I glared at Suyef.

"So, them thinking that I'm Celandine explains their interest in me. I'm sure that will complicate things," I said, then looked at Quentin. "But none of this explains how you survived."

He laced his fingers behind his head.

"I told you, I—"

"Did something harebrained. I heard you," I stated, folding my arms and staring at him.

"No, but it's a good start," he said, head bobbing up and down, tilted to one side.

"So, what was it you did?"

He grimaced.

"I jumped off that speeder."

Quentin and Suyef sat at the table when I entered. I took my seat, set my stuff up, and then looked at Quentin.

"So, what were you thinking, jumping off the speeder?"

"Doesn't miss a beat, this one," he said, chuckling and looking at Suyef.

"Answer her question."

He frowned at the Nomad, then moved his eyes back to me.

"I'm pretty sure I wasn't thinking."

To this day, my reasoning eludes me. The blow to my head probably played some role. But that would imply I was unaware of my actions, which isn't true. I knew what I was doing and, worse, knew it was foolhardy.

As the speeders passed one of the settlement's damaged structures, movement caught my eye. When the speeder turned alongside the crashed Colberran ship, I craned my head for a better look. A gap in the smoke revealed two children struggling out of the tower. I didn't hesitate at all before leaping off, relying on the grav-board and belt to catch me. The Nomad called out, but the battle noise and roaring blaze soon swallowed his voice.

As I sped back toward the structure, the scene became clear: a teenage girl, brown hair braided like Micaela's, tugged at a small boy pinned under a twisted wall piece. The girl screamed for help, face red and knuckles white. The boy cried out in pain.

"Look out!" I called, landing next to her.

The girl jumped, falling back. I approached the boy.

"Are you hurt?"

"My foot feels strange," he whimpered, tugging his trapped leg. "I can't move it."

I pressed him down with one hand, holding the other out toward the wall, and tried to shift it without dislodging it. The entire structure trembled and groaned above us. The boy looked back and forth, watching me.

"What-what are you doing?" he said. "What are you doing?! Are you scripting? Stop that! Get away from me!"

I used the belt to give the structure some stability, flinging a powerful beam behind me as a counterbalance.

"Stop!" the girl yelled. "You'll bring it down on us."

The pressure on my body increased. After a moment, the structure moved up and away from the boy. With a cry of relief, he pulled his leg free and began crawling away.

"Stay away from me. Don't come near me!"

The girl grabbed under his arms and helped him move back. Once they were clear, I set the wall back down. Metal creaked, but the structure stabilized, allowing me to release it.

"Come on," I barked, turning toward them.

The girl stumbled, falling down and clutching the boy to her chest. Both stared at me with wide eyes, and the boy held a hand up at me. Breathing hard, I kneeled down and tugged at my belt.

"I'm not scripting. Look." I held up the grav-board, folded into its smaller form. "It's just technology that lets me push and pull things."

Before either could respond, a deafening explosion tore through the air, a flash of white light blinding us. The ground shook, knocking me to my knees. I squinted, trying to see.

"What's happening?!" the girl screamed.

The sound of earth cracking echoed around us, drawing my attention to the flaming wreckage. There, cutting across the ground like a zipper on a coat, the ground ripped apart. As it did, the surface beneath us dipped back away from the shell. I looked past the burning ship but saw no sign of Micaela or Suyef.

"Help!"

I turned back just as the ground dipped farther, knocking me down and sending the children sliding toward me. Grabbing at the ground behind them, I yanked myself forward, flinging my body across theirs. The settlement shook violently before tipping our world upside down. I looked up and saw the blinding light of the core beckoning to us.

And down we went, outpost, chunk of shell, wrecked ship, and all.

"Why did the kids' reaction surprise you?" I asked, cutting Quentin off and earning a glare for my effort.

"This would go faster without interruptions," he muttered, leaning down and tapping his head against the table. "So hard to focus."

"Just following my instincts. Imagine how it is for me, trying to piece all this together from the fragments you're giving me." I glanced at Suyef. "All of you."

"Writers," Quentin blurted out, turning his head to look up at me. "Picky and have to have it all just right. Got to know it all before you do anything. Just go with it. Let the story tell itself." He waved a hand at my notes. "Let your questions answer themselves."

"That's not how I work," I said. "I'm a scribe, not a writer."

"Sure," he said, tapping at my papers. "Dreading the chance to publish this. You probably can't wait to blab to anyone who will listen and make your mark."

"Anticipating? As opposed to dreading?"

"Whatever."

"So, you fell."

His eyes narrowed at me, then he sat upright. "Don't think I don't see what you're doing here."

I glanced at Suyef, who remained silent, watching us.

"I'm just getting the story," I said, shrugging. "Now, shall we continue, or must this diatribe go on?"

"Diatribe?" he blurted out. "Fine! Get on with it."

He fell silent, nostrils flaring, arms folded across his chest. I waited, giving him time to cool down.

"So," I prompted him after a moment. "You were falling."

"With a giant chunk of shell and an outpost right on top of us." He looked up at me. "I didn't have a clue what to do."

"It's not a common situation."

"You think? And then, just because that's not enough to deal with, the entire outpost turned on us."

"Wait, what?" I asked.

"The gravity system went haywire." He flung a hand out to the side. "It tried to throw us off it."

I frowned at him. "It was still working after being disconnected from the shell's network?"

"Yeah, I don't know, either," he said. "The pieces of network hardware must be self-contained. Or just that system." He pointed down. "The dragon shells don't have citadels, and they have access to the network plus gravity and water systems."

"They have a form of a citadel, just different." I waved my hand at him to continue. "So, what did you do?"

Quentin took in a deep breath and let it out. "I learned how to fly."

CHAPTER 33

STYLE

One thing I gained that day was a genuine appreciation for the intricacy of Ancient technology. Most of us don't think about it at all, you know. Most Colberrans, for example, don't even ask how it works. That would require thinking, something they seem allergic to. Well, according to my father. My experience, though small, proves him true. However, I digress.

My knowledge of the gravity generation system grew in leaps and bounds that day, first learning of the flat plane pulling the water under the shell, then with how it broke as we fell toward the core. No, before that day, I didn't truly appreciate what the Ancients built for us.

When the outpost shook free from the shell, it fell into a spin. The inertia pinned us at first, but I kept a firm grip with my belt on both kids and the ground. A useless precaution when the system went haywire.

A whimper drew my gaze to the kids, eyes squeezed shut and arms wrapped around each other in a vise grip.

"Are you okay?" I called over.

The girl nodded but kept her eyes closed. One arm held the boy's head to her chest while the other gripped his torso. Something moving through the expanse overhead drew my gaze. In the distance, the Nomad shell raced across the sky. Even farther away, I spied Colberra before the spin took them both from view.

"I feel like I should be sick," I muttered.

I couldn't pin down why I didn't feel sick. My first thought was the empty sky, void of reference points. Only the core and the two shells broke the sky's calm.

Whimpers drew my eyes from the sky back to the children. Tears poured down the girl's face and I could hear the boy screaming into her chest.

"It's okay," I said. "I've got you."

The boy shook his head and squeezed the girl tighter.

"Help us," she said, eyes still shut. "Help us."

The core spun into view, slower this time. Shielding my eyes, I pondered the results when we got there. The surface at my back rumbled, and hundreds of small cracks split the ground. The boy fell into an apoplectic fit, and it took everything the girl had to hold on to him.

"Hey!" I yelled at him. "Stop it. You're going to hurt her."

That got his attention. He looked at the girl, then glared at me. Her eyes never left me.

"Help us."

A shadow drew my gaze toward the core, where I saw something that compounded my already growing sense of dread: a pair of giant shells directly in our path. Looking all around, I gauged what remained that I could use the belt to grab and hold us away from the falling fragment. Without knowing which side might smash into the ground, this offered the only chance at avoiding certain death.

I pushed up to stand, still gripping the children and the shell with the belt. Something yanked my feet away just as I made it upright, throwing me skyward. The beams, still gripping the ground, stalled my momentum just over a body's length in the air.

The children were not so lucky.

"Something pulled you?"

Quentin placed two fingers on the table, then grabbed them with his other hand and pulled them up.

"Just like that. An odd feeling, mind you, despite my time on the board."

"I assume it flung more around besides you and the children?"

"Oh yes," he said, eyes widening. "Rocks. Glass. Pieces of building. All that debris shifted about in patterns, and I thought it was random at first. However, after a few moments, the pattern became visible."

Quentin set his hands flat on the table. He took in a deep breath and let it out.

"I had little more time to think about it," he said, his voice quiet. "The next moment, it ripped the children away."

The children, arms stretched out, gripped each other's hands as they flipped end over end. Before I could grab them, the boy shot away to the side, then his whole body twisted as he rose straight overhead. The girl flew in the opposite direction just long enough for me to grab and pull her in. However, she shot toward me much faster than expected, forcing me to seek a better anchor as a counterbalance for the belt. It was then that I realized the ground wasn't there anymore. As the girl passed below me, I mounted the board and tried to pull myself toward the shell. This sent me into a spin down around the girl, who I grabbed and pulled close.

"Gotcha!"

She clung to me, head spinning around, eyes roaming the sky.

"My brother!"

"I know."

As we spun, the boy came into view, flipping over and over in a high arc above us relative to the shell. Any attempt to move into his current path pushed us farther away.

"Blast it!"

A new tug flipped us over, heads toward the shell, and sent us careening toward the ground. The weight of my limbs grew heavy as we fell. I focused every beam I could on the ground. My stomach twinged despite the board's counter-effects. Wind whipped us, and the girl's grip tightened, making it hard to breathe. We fell to within a few paces of the ground before the force tugging us vanished and we shot back up into the air, all the weight in my limbs vanishing.

The respite proved short-lived as the broken gravity system, as best I could guess, yanked us toward one of the ruined structures. Instead of fighting the pull, I pushed to one side, riding it in a wide arc around the structure.

The girl grabbed my head, pulling my gaze to her.

"My brother!"

She pointed back behind me, where the boy was falling toward the shell. Then I lost him as the core spun into sight. We were getting closer to it, and fast.

"Hang on!"

Riding those currents proved very tricky. I tugged hard at the structure, hoping to swing back around and into another eddy of weird gravity. Instead of moving toward him, we shot down at a hard angle, jarring my neck. I flung out a beam at the last moment to deflect us around another structure. The boy soared high above us, and, tracking him, I caught sight of something else.

The two large shells below floated relatively close to each other. In between, but closer to the leftmost landmass, a smaller chunk of rock orbited, one much too small to be a shell. And it was toward that object the plummeting settlement now raced.

"Please help him!"

The girl tightened her arms around me. Momentum carried us around the tallest remaining structure, giving me an idea. Latching on to it, I tried to alter our trajectory. A sudden lack of resistance surprised me, and we overshot the mark and flew up into the sky. The smaller shell loomed large as we slowed high above the settlement, but still short of the boy.

"Tomas!"

The girl reached out as I did, however none of the beams latched on at that distance. I looked back at the settlement where a few of my beams remained locked on. Pushing along them gained us some speed.

"Keep your body tight to mine!"

The girl nodded and gripped me tight. I pulled my arms in and shifted the board parallel to my legs. We fell through the air. Turbulence shook us, making maintaining our rigid up-down form difficult, but we gained on the boy. However, the distance to the small shell also shrank rapidly. Shoving back against the outpost caused the beams to diffuse, losing their grip. Tears flooded my eyes, forcing me to blink to see anything. The beams refused to lock on to the boy as we fell toward the small landmass, the nearby shell looming above.

I looked back and, latching one last time to an outcropping, pushed hard along that beam. The burst of momentum nudged us toward the boy, flipping head over heels just beyond my reach. Frustration battled with my growing fear. The girl screamed against my chest, feeding the frustration. I looked back, hoping for one more outcropping, and saw the ruined settlement roll into view. I eyed the tallest building, trying to guess its rate of rotation and angle. A shadow fell across the settlement as the smaller of the three lower shells loomed large. An unending scream twisted the boy's face, barely visible now.

The structure reached a usable point, and I bent my legs and kicked away with one last desperate shove, my eyes targeting the boy. I'm still not sure to this day if it helped, but the speed we gained exceeded any prior attempt. The wind howled as we fell, and the beam behind me defused. I gripped the girl tight, staying as aerodynamic as possible, my eyes still on the boy, my body tense. Beams would coalesce around him but never sharpened in a lock. My jaw hurt and my back tightened as I strained. The shell raced ever nearer; settlement closing fast. The girl trembled but held tight to my torso.

"Come on!" I screamed into the howling wind. "Lock on!"

The shell looked massive now, the boy a speck falling toward it with alarming speed. I gripped the girl with one arm and reached out with the other. My stomach lurched and my vision wavered.

Just a little more speed, I thought. *Just a little more.*

The girl yelped, head jerking against me. Behind us, the outpost closed fast, twisting in a death spiral. Desperate, I flung a series of beams back, this time using them to push against whatever they could find. This produced a series of surges that accelerated us toward the boy. My outstretched hand gave me focus against the nausea as I tried to grab at him. Panic swelled in my gut, and my skin tingled. Soon, the two landmasses would smash together with us in between.

With another surge from behind, I stretched out my fingers, willing the beam to grab the boy. My eyes filled with water. The inertia of our spin kept increasing, making it hard to concentrate. Too much rotation meant we might not hold our course. The next problem.

Shards of pain stabbed through my head and down my neck as we accelerated toward the boy. Just as thoughts of failure filled my head, one beam brightened. I blinked, but it stayed bright. We had him.

I carefully pulled back, trying not to harm him. The slight tug sped up our fall downward. The shell loomed large, the settlement right behind us, leaving few choices and less time. I had one idea to save us, and it was going to be close.

"Reach out and grab him!"

The girl turned her head, arm toward her brother. We spiraled closer, and she grabbed his shirt. I wrapped an arm around him, securing the sibling to my side. The shell, close enough now for me to see different rocks, remained just beyond the beams' reach. Above, the falling settlement closed the gap. Seizing an idea, I pulled us out of our tight spiral dive and reached back up toward the shell. Outcropping after outcropping slipped by as the falling rock rotated, but none came close enough to lock on. Without purchase, we fell into a flat spin, our rotational speed climbing beyond what I could control. A spinning, dizzying array of input flooded my senses, making it difficult to focus.

Closing my eyes, I reached out, trying to grab the chunk of rock. The outer edge brushed against my reach, like a soft breeze shifting a cloth across my skin. Below, the approaching shell tickled the same senses. The two children tightened their

grip on my body. I took a deep breath, trying to clear my mind.
Trying to see only the shell and grab it.

The next instant, two things happened. A beam grabbed
something above, and a burst of speed pushed us down. The
next moment, another beam latched on below. Using both, I
shoved, knocking us out of the flat spin in a stomach-turning
flip. The children groaned and the throbbing in my head
intensified. More beams locked on as the shells closed on each
other. Overhead, the tallest structure swung down ahead of us.
I grabbed it and yanked hard. A chunk broke free, but a second
beam locked a split second later, creating the counterpoint we
needed.

My body shook to the core as we careened through the air.
Chunks of the shell filled the surrounding space. A blast of
wind buffeted us from behind as we raced past our counterpoint. Several beams now latched on above and below, giving
us more speed. A cacophony detonated behind us as we shot
out from under the falling shell. My former home disintegrated
in a mighty explosion of dirt, metal, and kinetic energy.

Pulling us above the now-shattered outpost, I cried out in
triumph. The girl laughed and hugged me tighter.

"You did it!"

"Yes," I whispered, every inch of me quivering. "Yes, I did."

I landed on this new shell as quickly as I could, let the children go, and promptly collapsed.

CHAPTER 34

COMPLICATIONS

"Well, I can't believe I'm saying this, but I agree with you."

Quentin looked over at me, eyebrows furrowed.

"It was harebrained."

Suyef chuckled.

"But still impressive, Logwyn." He pointed at my notes. "I'm sure you have a lot of that already, but that one should land high on your list."

Quentin glared at him. "It's not a contest."

"Of course not. I would win that."

I stared at the man, and my mouth fell open a little. "Did you just make a joke?"

Quentin snorted.

"Yes, he's a riot." He jumped up, moving toward the hall. "Complete comic!"

"And that was the most calm and normal exit he's made," I said, nodding after him. "Period."

Suyef let out a deep breath.

"I told you that you're having an effect. Making him remember who he was." He looked down the hall. "Of course, when Micaela makes an appearance, that will be the test."

"Of what?"

"His recovery." He looked back at me. "She means more to him than anyone or anything. More than he can admit right now."

His eyes locked with mine, one eyelid twitching, his jaw twisted. His nostrils flared and his gaze returned to the hall.

"And he hurt her."

"How?"

Suyef took a deep breath. "He's not the same person anymore. Something . . . broke him."

"Something?" I asked. "You don't know what? Or you just aren't telling me?"

"No, I wasn't there. I only know some details." The Nomad nodded toward the departed Quentin. "He's different now and doesn't want to be. He's had a hard time accepting that."

"And is that what hurt her?"

He stared at me for a moment.

"He has to tell you. And her."

He fell silent.

"She's important to you."

"She is my friend. Family." His head inclined slightly. "All family matters."

"This is more than family, isn't it?"

"What matters is she is important," he said. "Particularly to him."

"No, you don't get to dodge that question," I said. "You matter in this, as do your feelings. They affect your judgment, cloud your choices." I pointed at my notes. "And unless I've missed the mark, that began before the rescue mission."

He stared at me. His lower jaw shifted first to one side, then the other.

"What I feel doesn't matter anymore," he whispered. "That dust spread across the expanse."

"It matters to you," I said, leaning forward. "And it matters to me. And anyone who reads this. You're not just a side character. A companion. You have a story, too, and it's a part of this one."

"Stay focused," he said, shaking his head. "He's the one who needs your help."

I pondered his words, eyes locked on his. After a moment, I nodded.

"I'll let it go for now. But your story is important. To me, if no one else. Don't you forget that."

He grunted. "We humans are such odd beings. We place so much value on a person. A companion. A friend. We'd do anything for them.. Quentin learned how to fly just to get back to her."

"I'd say he did that to survive."

"Surviving that fall wasn't flying. I heard a recording once on a Colberran station. Some clip from ancient history. I don't remember it all, but I recall one phrase. 'Falling with style.'" He pointed toward Quentin's room. "That feat? Falling with style."

"So, when did he learn to fly?"

Suyef leaned back, staring at my notes. "How do you think he got off that shell?"

When I arrived for our next interview, Micaela stood in the kitchen, her eyes cast down to the counter.

"Good morning."

"Welcome," she said, not looking up. "I hope you slept well."

I shrugged, stopping across the counter from her.

"Spent the evening reviewing my notes, and I have some questions."

She looked at me for a moment before going back to her work.

"Are you preparing a salad?"

"The Queen allowed me the use of her reforger," she said, nodding. "I'm not in the mood for a nutrient packet today." She paused, looking up at me. "Are you allergic to anything?"

"No," I said, looking over the plethora of vegetables. "That's a lot of reforge credits."

"Do you really think the Queen needs reforge credits?"

I opened my mouth to rebut, but stopped. The Queen limiting herself thusly was an interesting thought. "To set an example."

Micaela nodded at the far door while slicing a large, sharp knife through a red, bulbous vegetable I didn't recognize. "If she uses her reforger, who would know?"

"We wouldn't. What would it matter?"

"You asked where all this came from. So, does it?"

I watched her cut the strange-looking vegetable into smaller chunks, then slide them into a bowl using the edge of the blade. "What is that?"

She held one by the green handle protruding from the top, the bulbous end pointed at me.

"This is a bell pepper," she answered. "Red means it's ripe. They start out green, then go yellow, orange, and, finally, red."

"Sorry, I'm not much of a . . ." My voice trailed off.

"Horticulturist?"

"That. Yeah, sorry. So, that part. Is that a . . ." I pointed at the handle. "Stem?"

"You really know nothing about plants?"

"I've seen them in botanical bays, but I spend little time there." I pointed at the other vegetables. "Most of those I know, but that's a new one. What does it taste like?"

"This one will be sweeter," Micaela said, tapping the end with her finger. "There's an old wives' tale that four bulbs instead of three makes it even sweeter." She chuckled and shrugged. "Purely a mental thing, I think."

"But red is riper than green?"

She nodded at me.

"Are plants a hobby?" I asked.

"No, but I enjoy them fresh. Particularly compared to nutrient packs."

"They're efficient, not tasty."

She grimaced, then waved a hand as she continued working.

"They could have made them taste better. I'm sure you didn't come here to discuss my eating habits or the finer points of horticulture."

I smiled.

"No, I came to discuss Suyef."

She paused, eyebrows furrowed, lips pursed, partway through cutting a long, green vegetable called a *cucumber* if memory served.

"What about him?"

"He's more than just a companion. My notes reveal a lot when looked over." I cocked my head. "Especially when I have the advantage of talking to him as well."

She paused in her preparations—knife, tip on the counter, held just over the tomato—and glanced up at me. "How are they doing?"

"They or him?"

"You heard me," she answered, her voice quiet.

"Suyef is Suyef," I said, shrugging. "He talks more with each visit." I grinned at her. "He even made a joke the last time we met."

A small smile tugged at the corners of her mouth.

"He has a . . . unique sense of humor." Her eyebrows rose and fell. "Well, all Nomad humor is."

She stared at the tomato, then resumed cutting. After scraping it into the bowl, she looked at me. "And Quentin?"

"It depends on the day," I said, watching for clues to what she was thinking or feeling. "More recently, he's been calmer. Lucid. Fewer side tunnels in his story. He's even become less erratic. You know? Dropping me midsentence and running out."

Her head shifted so slightly I would have missed it if I wasn't watching.

"He even asked for his grav-board."

"What?" She looked up, pointing the knife at me. "Please tell me Suyef didn't allow that."

"Actually, he let him have it for a day." When Micaela's mouth opened to respond, I held up a hand. "Suyef told me he'd kept the belt."

The knife lowered.

"Good." She shook her head and picked up the now-full bowl of vegetables. "Let's just say that last time he left quite a mess to clean up."

Micaela carried the bowl to the table, where two bowls with matching forks and tall glasses of water awaited us. She set an unmarked bottle next to the bowl of vegetables.

"What's in that?"

She twisted the cap, which unsealed with a resounding pop of pressurized air. A tangy scent tickled my nose, making the sides of my tongue water.

"It's called dressing, and it goes on the salad." She frowned at me. "There are places on this shell that specialized in pre-pared foods like this. Have you never gone to one?"

I shrugged. "I don't get out much."

"Don't you ever get invited out? By friends or family?"

I looked at the fork, running my index finger along its smooth handle. "I don't have many friends, and my family . . . they're around, but I am busy."

"Busy or hiding?" she asked as she spooned the salad into each bowl.

"Those aren't mutually exclusive. Work, best done alone, often keeps me busy." I waved my hand around the chamber. "The Queen didn't hold court for over twenty cycles, probably hiding down here."

"She wasn't hiding," Micaela said as she poured some dressing on her salad.

"Excuse me?"

"The Queen. She wasn't hiding, per se."

"Then what was she doing? She needed to be leading."

Micaela took in a deep breath and let it out. "How long do you think she's been doing this?" she asked, handing me the bottle.

"Doing what?" I took the bottle and set it next to my bowl. "Hiding?"

"No," she said. "Leading your people. How long?"

She took a bite of her salad, the fresh vegetables crunching.

"We don't know, exactly," I stated, memories of my chat with Nidfar surfacing. "But quite some time now."

"Longer than you've been alive?"

I nodded, pouring some dressing over my food.

"Longer than the eldest person alive today. In fact, do you recall a single record in your people's history that doesn't mention her or the fact that a Dragon Queen was in charge?"

"No, she's always been there."

I stabbed some of the salad and put it in my mouth. The vegetables crunched, releasing moisture that spread the dressing across my tongue. It tasted tangy, with a hint of sweetness.

"Leading. So," she said, pointing her fork at me, a small red tomato speared on the end, "don't you think it's entirely possible she might not need to be involved in every single act of leadership?"

"Maybe, but twenty cycles of absence?"

"You're assuming she remained involved?"

I considered her words as she resumed eating. The Queen could lead from down here, assuming she had been here. Some historians surmised the Queen formed the council to avoid the need for her to lead our people. Others insisted the people demanded a say in their governance. Either way, one thing was always clear.

"The Queen and the council haven't gotten along, particularly in recent cycles."

"That's putting it mildly." Micaela looked up from her salad. "And it's been a lot longer than a few cycles."

"But what exacerbated the problem? Not the strike on the Reds."

She snorted a laugh as she finished swallowing her last bite.

"No." She sipped some water. "Those fools on the Green council had their minds made up before the strike brought us back."

"So, why do you think the Queen didn't intervene? Why stay down here?"

Micaela looked up from the remnants of her salad. "Because of me."

That answer caught me off guard. "What issue did she have with you?"

"No issues with me." She shook her head. "But she knew that something was coming. That my arrival signaled the beginning of something larger. Something worse."

I snapped my fingers.

"You know, I think I remember your arrival." She frowned, but I continued. "I wasn't sure what was going on, but everyone kept cheering, so I went out to the platform's edge. By the time I got there, however, all I saw was some people I could barely make out entering the central hall." I pointed at her. "That was you four, wasn't it?"

When she didn't answer, I went on.

"It had to be. Someone I asked said we had rescued someone important from the Red shell." My eyes narrowed as I looked at her. "So, either that was you, or that's the largest coincidence I've ever seen."

"And what happened next?"

I shook my head, then stopped. That hadn't been that long ago. Several months at the most. Maybe a cycle.

"The Intershell War ended. That was what happened. Someone took control of the shells and ended the war." I pointed the fork at her. "Was that you?"

She set her fork down, and her shoulders sagged.

"It was all of us."

"You stopped the war, yet you look like that was a bad thing."

Her head lowered.

"We stopped nothing but let someone else do it. We thought we knew what needed to happen, and we were wrong. And that cost thousands of people their lives and handed power over the shells to the last person it should have gone to."

"Colvinra," I said, my voice quiet. "But how did he manage that?"

"We led him right to what he'd been looking for all along."

"The key to the network," I whispered.

She nodded. "Then we handed it right to him."

"I don't understand."

Her gaze locked with mine. "Remember how I said we were walking into a trap?"

"Yeah, on the Red shell. And that it was part of another one."

"Yes, one step of many," she stated. "All designed for one purpose: lead us to a destination."

"Where?"

She pointed at the window. "Down."

"And then, Micaela, I collapsed on the ground," Quentin said, hands spread wide as he smiled. "It took a moment to register where we were, let alone contemplate doing anything about it."

I stared at him. "Where are the kids?"

"That's what you ask?" he asked, frowning.

"You're here. I'm sure how you got from there to the Red shell is another amazing tale," I said, pointing into the hall. "But I don't see any kids. So, where are they?"

His entire frame sagged. "They wouldn't come with me."

"You left them there?!"

"No. Well, yes. But not for good."

"Are they still there?"

"As far as I know. I found a place for them to hide and plenty of supplies from the ruined settlement." Quentin shrugged. "They wouldn't come with me. I wasn't even sure how I was going to get off that shell." He held up a finger. "I did promise I'd send help."

I shook my head, stood, and approached the door. The guards stepped forward when it opened.

"High One? Do you need something?"

"My name is Micaela, not High One. Do you know anything about the shell piece that fell from above?"

"News feeds showed it."

"There are news feeds?" Quentin called out from behind me.

"This man," I said, pointing at Quentin, "saved the lives of two kids when that fragment fell from the sky. He left them there to find help."

The taller guard glanced at the other, who raced off.

"We'll tell our superiors," he stated. "If they are still there, we'll bring them back." He looked behind me at Quentin. "Do you know their names?"

After getting the names, the guard stepped near a panel and spoke into it. I nodded my thanks and returned to the table, doors closing behind me. "Well, that's taken care of."

"You clearly have some power here," Suyef stated. "They didn't even question you."

My eyes narrowed as he spoke.

"Yes, and I think there's more to it. I doubt an entity living in the network commands that much power and respect. Something else is going on."

"At least the mistaken identity is helping us this time," Quentin stated.

"This time?" my father asked, looking at me.

Before I could answer, the doors slid open to reveal a squad of unfamiliar guards.

"High One," one guard said. "My apologies, but the council requires your companions."

"All of them?"

The man shook his head. "The Nomad and the board rider."

None of us moved. Oddly, neither did the guards.

"What are you waiting for?" I asked.

The man bowed his head. "Our orders require we get your permission before bringing them."

"Why?" Quentin asked.

The man didn't even look at Quentin.

"Answer his question," I said, testing this strange authority.

"Ours is not to question orders," the man stated, head still bowed. "I do not know the reason."

"But you can tell me why you all keep acting like I'm someone else."

He shook his head. "They instructed me to request your permission and say nothing else."

My eyes remained on them, but they all avoided my gaze.

"And I suppose you can't stop me if I choose to go with them?"

The man looked up. "They said to invite you if you did not come on your own."

"Let's go."

The guard's hand twitched at his side, but he remained silent and still.

"What is it?"

"Your companions must remain secured when moving about," he said, words rushing out.

I glanced at Suyef, then back at the guard.

"Secured?"

"Yes, High One," he went on. "Here are the orders."

He held out a padd, which I took to look over. Quentin and Suyef moved up on either side.

"Well?" Quentin asked.

I felt my breath catch in my throat. "You're being arrested."

"On what charge?" Suyef inquired, leaning close to look at the padd.

"Breaking the network."

CHAPTER 35

THEATER

"Wait, I remember that."

Micaela cocked her head to one side, lips pursed and silent.

"Apologies for interrupting you, but I remember some of this," I went on. "About someone on trial for kidnapping the Queen."

"Not a trial. Just charges brought before the council."

"Yes." I tapped my stylus on the paper. "They issued two statements, if memory serves. One informed us that the Queen, presumed safely in personal exile deep inside our shell"—I glanced around—"which I assume meant here. Anyway, they said the Queen vanished, and they weren't sure where she had gone."

I pointed at Micaela.

"I'd wager anything that the first statement came before the raid. But I don't remember, exactly."

"And the second?"

"They announced two men being taken into custody on charges of network sabotage. Sorry, the details are fuzzy." I glanced down at the recording device. "Usually, I just look this stuff up."

"And this time you can't," she said. "Do you remember anything else?"

I frowned, searching through my memories.

"It was about a cycle ago. I don't recall the trial's result. Or if there was one. The issue just died, which seemed odd considering it involved claims of kidnapping the Queen."

"There wasn't a trial," Micaela said, leaning forward. "That would have required a jury, and the council wanted to keep this quiet."

"Why? They record all their sessions and store them in the public database."

"All of them? How would you know?"

"If I had network access," I said, waving at my device, "I'd show you the archives."

"But is it a complete record?"

I paused, considering her question. Only one entity could overrule the council, and she, until recently, had been in seclusion. "It would be a matter of them abiding by the law."

Micaela's lips curled down in a frown. "And governments never falsify records?"

"That would violate our most basic principles of governance," I said. "Some sensitive records need protection from mass consumption, but the records exist."

"And do you think you would find a record regarding those two men appearing before the council on accusations of sabotaging the network?"

I thought for a moment, then shook my head.

"Before this conversation, I would have thought so, but they might deem such information too sensitive to store publicly." I held up a finger. "I'd want that information saved and secure. That information could prove dangerous, if true."

"And what of the people involved?"

"I'd want them to remain in custody to protect the information further." I frowned at her. "So, how are those two still free?"

"Because someone needed them to spring the trap. For us and everyone else."

"I'm not sure I follow."

"Someone broke them out of prison."

"You?"

She shook her head. "The same person who broke the network."

I nodded.

"Celandine."

The council members stood together talking when we arrived. A high, domed ceiling soared above the circular room, pristine and white. Three tables—two of equal size—carved from stone rose from the floor, forming a semicircle opposite the entrance, the smaller table directly opposite the door. The council, all adorned in floor-length green robes edged with brightly colored fringe, stopped talking and moved behind the longer tables. They stood in silence, looking at the empty chair behind the smaller table. After a moment, a woman, her head covered with black locks and her robe fringed in bright yellows and pinks, moved from the left to face us.

"This session is now convened. The accused persons stand before the council." The woman nodded at me. "A reputation witness graciously agreed to join us. All parties submitted pertinent evidence prior to this session. Session bylaws prevent submission of any further evidence, except that which is already in this chamber." Her voice moved at a steady, monotonous clip. "With the full council now present, we await Her Highness, if she joins us."

The woman stepped back, head turned toward the door, the entire council following suit. I stood in silence, waiting. Quentin shifted next to me, but Suyef remained still. After a moment, I realized they weren't looking at the door. They were looking at me. I opened my mouth to ask what was going on but never got the chance.

"As Her Highness has absented herself," the woman continued, "the responsibility for these proceedings passes to the council chairperson. Council, please sit."

Everyone took their seats save for the woman, who stared down at a padd, jaw clenched tight. When she looked up, fire lit her eyes. Dread gripped my gut and, keen to its prior warnings, I did not ignore it. Regardless of the result, one thing stood out: we were not in friendly territory. Not in this chamber.

"Quentin. Suyef." The chairperson looked at each of them. "Please step forward."

The Nomad did so, but Quentin remained still. Suyef looked back, waving him forward.

"Be respectful," the Nomad hissed. "It will help."

Quentin glared at him but stepped forward. I joined them in a united front.

"You stand accused of sabotage," the chairperson continued. "Of actions detrimental to the network and thus to our society. Our civilization currently faces immeasurable levels of risk that, even now, consume a large amount of resources to combat the problems. How do you plead?"

Quentin glanced at Suyef.

"What problems?" the Nomad asked.

The woman looked at each of them.

"How do you plead?"

"I'm with him," Quentin said. "What problems?"

"The accused persons enter a plea of no contest," the woman said, turning her head to our left.

"We did no such thing," Quentin stated.

Suyef grabbed his shoulder, but Quentin shrugged him off.

"No. They accuse us of something we didn't do and ignore us. I would expect more from a legal body seeking the truth."

"Do you wish to enter a plea?"

"Not guilty," he said, nodding. "We just got here. Well, I did." His head jerked toward Suyef. "He's been here once before, and I'm pretty sure you didn't let him out of your sight."

"Your companion has not entered a plea," she said.

"Not guilty."

"The accused persons enter a plea of not guilty," the woman stated, her voice flat. "Let the official record reflect the pleas."

Suyef motioned at Quentin, then stepped forward.

"I believe the laws require the council to present all evidence from the accuser in person for rebuttal."

A man with a head shaved bald leaned over to whisper in the chairperson's ear. She nodded, eyes still on Suyef.

"The council stands as your accuser," she said. "As to the evidence, the council deemed it too sensitive to reveal to outsiders."

As she spoke those last words, several council members at the opposite table shifted, casting glances at each other. One pair leaned close and traded whispers. It seemed the decision didn't sit well with everyone.

"If you don't present the evidence, it doesn't exist," Quentin said. "Thus, we are innocent."

"The evidence exists but, if shared with you, you would become a security risk."

"And I'm guessing we won't be able to leave anyway," Quentin retorted. "So much for a just society."

The whispering among council members continued. Quentin turned to Suyef, who held up his hand.

"The council has decided," the chairperson said, looking around the room.

The whispering went silent, everyone turning to look at her.

"You are a security risk because of your actions. If we share the evidence, you become a greater risk."

Quentin looked at Suyef, who waved him off.

"That logic doesn't hold," Suyef said. "We are not the only ones who have interfaced with the network." He pointed at the padd. "Access to the network does not equate guilt. Nor does access equate action. Without evidence of action, your accusation is 'you have access to the network.' Like each of you and most of your entire society, plus several others on distant shells."

The whispering among the council resumed.

"You also have no actual control over the network," he continued, "as its hub is located elsewhere and interfaces with each shell separately. Can you protect information stored on a network whose primary hub you don't control? Finally, we know of the entity using the network, as she has contacted our companion and her father multiple times. That entity has access to everything on the network, including your secrets. An entity you have no control over. All things being equal, if you are experiencing problems, is not that entity more likely to blame than either of us? Thus exists reasonable doubt. Without evidence to the contrary presented by the accused for rebuttal, the evidence does not exist. So say your bylaws. If the council ignores those bylaws, then the council abdicates its authority to accuse anyone, as they violate the same rules that govern its existence."

"How do you claim to know so much of our bylaws?" the bald man asked.

"The same bylaws control the ruling bodies of Nomad society, as both are based on Ancient society."

His words sent a wave of movement through the room. The chairperson cleared her throat, never taking her eyes from Suyef.

"The members of this council possess the proper authority to access sensitive information." She nodded at her counterparts. "We all swore an oath to protect this society, including its secrets." Her lips pursed and her eyes narrowed. "As to this entity you speak of, we have no evidence such a being actually exists."

"Her name is Celandine," I said, causing every head to turn toward me. "I've seen her."

The chairperson shifted, looking around the room, at the council members, everywhere but at me. After a moment, I noticed her eyes kept glancing at the empty table.

"I'm sorry, High One," she finally said, head bowing repeatedly, eyes cast down, "but as you are not occupying a seat on this hearing, we must ask you to wait until directed when to speak. Decorum and all."

"Why do you people keep calling me that?" I asked, stepping forward. "My apologies for violating your decorum, but you brought me into this. I want some answers that this farce of a proceeding isn't providing."

"Their innocence or guilt has not been determined," the woman began.

"Oh, I think it has," I went on, cutting her off. "And I think that's why you want to keep the evidence secret." I pointed at the other table. "A decision that is not unanimous, if I interpret their reactions correctly."

No one at the other table confirmed my suspicions, but they didn't deny them, either. Instead, they remained still, eyes moving back and forth between the chairperson, who stood and moved around the table, and me.

"The vote occurred prior to the summons. A majority agreed the evidence must remain secret." Her head shifted toward the opposite table. "Only one person can overrule that vote. But as she recused herself and has taken to"—the woman glanced at me and then my companions—"other interesting activities, the council must act without her."

"According to the treaty between our peoples, you must contact my people before you can try any of our citizens," Suyef stated, then pointed at Quentin. "As he did not arrive here until your dragons brought him and he has been in your custody ever since, the council either misinterpreted any evidence of actions as his"—he dropped his arm—"or intentionally attributed it to him." He took a step forward. "Your people have always conducted themselves with the highest regard for the law and the sanctity of life."

The woman chuckled.

"What would you know, Nomad? You're barely old enough to have mastered a trade, let alone know anything about us."

"We keep very detailed records," he said. "Particularly when it involves those from other shells." He glanced at the council members on either side. "Especially when it's your kind we're dealing with."

"Your people's records have no consequence here," she stated. "What matters is the decision of this council to secure that information to guarantee the security of this shell."

"The treaty has consequence here," he said. "By holding this trial, you are already in violation of it."

On a hunch, I stepped forward, drawing every gaze toward me. Two of the council members sitting to my right leaned forward a bit. The chairperson clenched her jaw, and her head twitched to her left. Toward the empty table. Glancing around, the strangeness of these people's behavior struck me again. Now, though, was not the time to ponder such things.

"I think it does matter," I said, nodding to my right. "I think some members present disagree with the majority decision. And if you fancy yourself a body founded on justice, you owe it to the truth to let the evidence speak for itself."

"The decision stands," the woman said, shaking her head. "The time for debate on this issue is over." She leveled a glare at my two companions. "We will confine you two to quarters until—"

Quentin stepped forward. "No, you will not judge me guilty of something I didn't do without showing proof it happened."

Suyef grabbed at him, but he shook free.

"Stop, Suyef. I've had it with these councils." He leveled a finger at the woman. "You are lying or are being lied to. Prove me wrong with this evidence only you claim exists. Defend your position fairly and let us defend ours. If not, this body is a farce and has no authority to confine any of us." He pointed at the table to the right. "And if none of you will stand up in the face of this travesty, then resign and let people who will stand for the rule of law take your place."

I held my breath as the woman approached Quentin. None of the other council members moved.

"The decisions and processes of this body are not subject to your whims."

Quentin took a step toward her. She held her ground, craning her head up to look at him.

"Since you plan to confine us anyway, your claims of us not being able to leave if we hear your secrets rings false," he said. "You have no evidence, so I don't see a legal body before me. I see either a group of liars or people who believed a lie without fully examining the proof and who refuse to admit they might have erred."

"The evidence is—" the chair started, but he cut her off, one hand pointing at the doors.

"You have an entire strike force of witnesses to testify that I wasn't with them when they left here. Where are they?" He pointed at Suyef. "You are stating on the record that you let him out of your sight when he showed up with a Red traitor, despite witnesses that will testify that's not true."

She said nothing.

"With no evidence, he remained under guard and touched nothing here. So, the council is intentionally blocking witnesses from testifying to the truth, contrary to your assumptions." He pointed at the padd on the table. "And I'll wager your problems started before he got here. So, put your evidence on the table, let it speak for itself, bring in the witnesses, defend your actions before your own people who probably disagree with your definition of justice and security, or call an end to this bit of theater, and let's get to the real issue."

"And what is the actual issue?" the woman asked, her eyes never leaving his.

"That your network has been getting worse slowly for cycles," he said, looking around the room. "Probably close to twenty of them. Before we ever got here."

The council members all shifted. The chairperson shook her head.

"So, you admit to knowledge of the problems and how long they've been going on?"

"Knowledge of problems does not equate guilt." He pointed up. "The Nomads and the Colberrans both know the problems exist, which is why we are here. Correlation, causation, and all that." He pointed at her padd. "Now, get that thing and verify my age because, unless you're claiming we sabotaged your network in primary school, that should paint the lie to whatever bill of goods you bought without question."

"Your cleverness with words and twisting of details notwithstanding," she stated, "the decision to seal the data is final."

"Truth is not cleverness with words," Quentin went on, his face reddening. "Your data is nonexistent until you present it here in front of those you accuse."

"As is the decision of this council," she continued, ignoring him. "We confine you two to separate quarters until you either admit to your guilt and help us fix the problem or we extradite you back to your shells."

"We'll help you regardless," Suyef stated. "As he said, that's why we are here. To get help. We'll share what we know, and you can do with it as you please."

"An admission?" she asked, looking at him.

"Do not play me the fool. It is a request for and an offer of help. Had you actually presented your case instead of conducting this bit of theater—"

"With no audience," Quentin interjected.

"—you'd already know we have the same problems on our shells." The Nomad glared at Quentin before continuing. "On his shell, it's potentially leading to a water shortage. You took his things when we arrived, and he has the evidence you need to verify what we say."

"Enough," the woman said, returning to the table. "We will give your possessions to your elder companion. He may visit, but not to bring them to you. When you either admit your guilt or we extradite you, we will return your possessions to you." She looked at each of us. "Your interaction with us is over. We will not interfere with your choice. We will not coerce you into action."

"Imprisonment without a fair trial. Ultimatums. That is coercion," I said. "As my companion said, this council abdicated its authority by violating its own bylaws. You are a shame to your own society."

Everyone shifted, heads bowed. The chairperson shook her head and looked at my companions.

"We hope you make the right choice."

"We have no choice to make," Suyef said. "The choice to make is yours. Until you will work with us, there is nothing we can do." He pointed at me. "Her assessment of this council is correct." He looked at the table on the right. "Until courage returns, tyranny now exists. I will make certain to warn my people that you have violated the treaty."

"Communication with your shell will only come when you admit guilt."

"Or you extradite us," Quentin blurted out. "Or was that just for show?"

The chairperson clapped her hands, and the guards removed Quentin and Suyef.

"And am I to be imprisoned?" I asked.

"What you do is your own choice, High One," she answered, avoiding my gaze. "We would never think to stand in your way."

"Why are you calling me that?" I looked around but none would look at me. "Treating me like I'm one of you? Giving me such nice quarters? Attendants?"

They all avoided my gaze.

"And why aren't you looking at me?"

No one answered. After a moment, the chair stood up.

"I'm sorry, High One," she said. "But we can't answer your questions now."

"Now. Meaning you can at a different time?"

She held her gaze on me, but it took effort. The twist in the jaw, a flicker in the pupils. She was clearly nervous, either by my presence or the interaction. I shook my head and turned to leave but stopped.

"Will you stop me if I speak the truth of what you did here?"

Everyone shifted, clearly uncomfortable with my words. No one spoke.

"I don't know who you think I am, but I know one thing: you all are a disappointment. Your people would be better off without you." I turned, then paused.

"I will contact the Nomads and Colberrans myself and tell them of this council's betrayal and abdication as ruling authority. Until you fix your error, do not interact with me. Ever."

I walked to the doors, which slid open.

"Good luck, High One, with whatever you seek," the woman called to me.

I paused in the doorway and looked to one side. "Until you fix your error, you do not exist."

"We hope you find it soon."

I stepped out without responding, the doors closing behind me.

CHAPTER 36

TRIANGLES

"That didn't go well."

Quentin stood staring at the wall. Not moving or speaking, staring. It was the most still I'd ever seen him. And it unnerved me. Suyef coughed and leaned forward.

"Hardly anything ever turns out how he hopes, Logwyn. He just didn't care. Eternal optimist, he claims. No mistakes, only—how did he put it? 'Happy accidents.'"

"What does that mean?"

"I don't think he knows," the Nomad said. "Not anymore. It meant everything happened for a reason, if you rolled with it. If not, whatever happened was your fault. Or something like that."

I tapped the stylus on the table.

"A narrow-sighted way of looking at things."

"Maybe." Suyef shrugged. "He means well but acts rashly sometimes. More often than not, it worked out fine. Other times . . ."

His voice trailed off as he looked at Quentin. His whole frame shifted, and he shook his head. "Other times it did not turn out well at all."

"So, what happened next?"

"They locked us up in separate cells in different wings. Micaela went back to her quarters."

"Yes. And then?"

Quentin turned from the wall.

"Someone broke us out."

The guards deposited me in a cell identical to the one I'd been in before. The entire wing stood empty, leaving me alone with my thoughts. They left my belt and board and the padd with Micaela's father, assuming the council told the truth. Clearly, they believed we would try to escape. Not that those items would have helped in those chambers.

The Ancients designed them as the ultimate prison. They lacked any straight lines save for the bed jutting out from the wall. The room even lacked the simple panel interface present in my previous cell. I assumed this wing's design expected the worst prisoners to live there. It was quite boring, with only the shield's hum as company. I soon felt antsy.

I had no clue where they put Suyef as they separated us when we exited the council chamber. When I looked back, Micaela stood outside the doors looking at the hall Suyef had vanished down. And standing in my cell, pacing, thinking, shifting, pondering, something bugged me. Something about how she looked after him and not me. The strange feeling ate at me, a gut-wrenching feeling that sent tingles up my spine. My pacing increased and my agitation intensified with the feeling.

Why wouldn't she look at me? Had she done so, and I missed it? Did it mean anything? Had she done it on purpose?

Had she just not thought to look at me? That last question cast a long shadow of loneliness that gripped my heart.

Those thoughts and feelings so dominated my mind that I almost didn't notice a pair of numbers flashing on the energy field. Illuminated in white light, the two numbers hovered in the air, etched into the force field. I moved my hand as close to the shield as I dared, heard the humming rise in pitch and volume. The two digits—a six and a zero—hovered inside the shield, completely flat, with no visible source. I lowered my hand, puzzled.

The next instant, the numbers changed.

"When I left the council, I saw the guards leading Quentin and Suyef down different halls," Micaela said, shifting on the leather couch. "Quentin right, Suyef left, both bracketed by guards. I pondered their destination and when I'd be able to visit."

"What about you?"

"They escorted me back to my chambers. They did not order me to stay, but I didn't feel like leaving. So, I ate and waited." She shook her head. "I'm not sure how long I sat in silence. At some point, guards arrived with Suyef's staff, Quentin's belt and board, and their padds. When I asked where my companions were, the guard shrugged and exited, never looking at me."

"Why would they give you their stuff?"

"It made no sense to me, either. A prison like that would have storage for a prisoner's personal items."

"No, instead of your father, as they said they would."

"Not sure, but they did."

"Usually, the only time they release those items is upon release or death and someone comes to claim them. Or for unplanned prisoner departures."

"You mean escapes."

"Not just that," I said, shaking my head. "They have randomly released people in the past. I'd check the records to be sure, but I can't."

"No one has ever died while imprisoned on this shell."

"How do you know that?"

She smiled and nodded at the door behind me.

"The Queen told you." I nodded, glancing at my notes. "So, what happened next?"

She looked away, the edge of her mouth nearest me curving up.

"Quentin's padd turned on."

My curiosity piqued the instant the device activated. *The guard must have turned it on by mistake*, I thought. *Or it turned on when I moved*. I dismissed both ideas, as the device required tactile interaction, and Quentin employed a screen lock on his.

The screen lay blank save for the digits six and zero: *60*. *Why that number? Who sent it?* I flipped the device around to check for a tether to a nearby terminal, but the connectivity light remained off. Frowning, I flipped the padd over. *Was it a timer that hadn't started?* That seemed likely. I tapped the screen, but nothing happened. Tapping in the middle, along the sides, and in the corners achieved nothing. I slid my finger across the screen from left to right, but nothing changed.

"What's going on?" I asked, my voice loud in the empty chamber.

The next instant, the screen changed. The numbers became translucent, and an image lay just behind them. I peered closer to find a schematic. My fingers moved on instinct, touching the screen and sliding apart. A second later, it zoomed in, enlarging the section in the middle. A small light blinked in a room just off a hall, one with an identical pattern to this one. I tapped the blinking light and a series of smaller lights appeared, brightening in succession away from the room, beckoning the viewer to go that way.

"But where do you lead?"

My facility knowledge remained limited, but I knew enough to see this led to the lift. Tapping the light blinking at the end of the trail changed the image. The floor plan rose and faded from sight, replaced by another. That one also vanished, as did another. The pattern repeated seven more times.

"Ten floors! Go down ten floors."

On that last floor, the line led to a large open space some distance from the lift. And even more curious, two lines joined it on that level.

"Two people join there maybe," I whispered, tapping my finger on the screen. "Quentin and Suyef."

The device beeped, returning to the starting level. The number changed, decreasing. Counting down the seconds. *But who is counting down and why do they want me to follow this route?* I looked at the room's access panel and remembered I hadn't contacted either the Nomads or the Colberrans. Looking back at the padd, I saw the counter approaching zero.

Deciding, I donned Quentin's belt, attaching Suyef's staff to it, and grabbed both padds before rushing out the door.

"So, a counter appeared for both of you?"

They nodded.

"Right on the force field," Quentin said, stretching where he stood. "I would've missed it if a guard hadn't coughed."

"What did you think it was?"

Suyef chuckled. "I wasted no time contemplating it. I assumed it was a trap."

"But did you know what might happen?"

"What else could it mean?" He shrugged. "I assumed the shield would drop."

"And did it?"

"The instant it hit double naughts," the Nomad stated, pressing his hands together and then splitting them apart. "I got away from that room as fast as possible."

"What about the guards?"

"There were none in the immediate hall, nor at the exit from that wing where at least two guards should have been."

"Abandoned their post?"

Quentin chuckled and smiled. "More like removed from it."

When the shield dropped, I wasted no time jogging down the empty hall, eyes watching for movement. The wing appeared empty. At the end of the hall, I slowed as voices reached my ears. Pressing myself up to another cell, I spied the sleeve of one guard around the opposite wall's corner, his voice a murmur as he talked with the other. I stopped, as moving closer risked them spotting me.

As I contemplated the situation, the guard yelled. Something smashed into the wall beside me and slid past. The guard. The other lay crumpled against the wall.

"Suyef?"

"No, but I'll take that as a compliment." Micaela walked into view, smiling and waving me forward. "Hurry."

"Sorry. I just figured . . ."

". . . that the only person who could take the guards out was him," she cut me off, nodding. "The thought that I might have helped you didn't occur? So, either you don't think I can, or you just didn't think at all."

She arched an eyebrow at me as we moved on. "I choose to believe the second." Micaela held out my board and removed my belt with her other hand. "You might want this. It's handy."

"I thought it was dangerous."

She glared at me as I put the belt on. "It's both." Micaela pulled out a padd and glanced at a schematic. "Come on."

"What's that?" I asked, staring at the device.

"Did you have a countdown showing anywhere?"

"Yeah, on the . . . wait, you had one, too?"

She nodded as we moved, eyes darting from the halls to the padd and back. "Yes," she said, "and this escape plan appeared with it."

She handed me another padd, which I tucked away.

"How do you know it's an escape plan?" I asked. "It could be a trap."

"Possibly. But someone helped us before."

"Someone who looks a lot like you."

Her hand shot up at an intersection. She glanced at the padd before moving to the left, hurrying as she responded.

"Regardless, someone helped us like this before, so I'm willing to play this out. Now, let's go get Suyef."

That gnawing inside returned at the mention of my friend's name. No—not his name, at how she said it. Something about it felt wrong, like a pressure in my chest. Swallowing didn't ease it. I shook my head, telling myself it was silly. Letting something bug me that shouldn't.

None of it helped.

"You were jealous," I said, tapping my stylus against my cheek.

Quentin flushed, looking away. Suyef shifted, the most visible sign of discomfort I'd ever seen from the stoic man.

"And this . . . *thing*," I said, waving my hand for emphasis. "Is it still there?"

Quentin glanced at Suyef, whose jaw clenched, eyes locked on me.

"The answer to that question will come in due time," the Nomad said after a moment.

For the first time that I could recall, I saw something in his eyes. They widened and glistened with moisture. Then he looked away, and the moment passed. When he looked back, whatever had been there was gone. I jotted a note to remind myself to ask Micaela about it, to get her side of this strange triangle of friendship I'd stumbled on to. To get some answers.

For once, I didn't have to wait long.

CHAPTER 37

LINES

We went down two floors to where I assumed Suyef would join us. Approaching a cellblock wing, we slowed, Quentin shifting to the front. I prepared a shield construct, but it proved moot. Suyef stood over a slumped guard, and we saw no sign of a second.

"Glad to see you didn't need our help."

He frowned at me. "Why would I need help against an unarmed guard?"

"Never mind. Here."

He caught the staff.

"Did you deactivate the force field?"

"Did you have a countdown on yours, too?" Quentin asked.

Suyef nodded. Quentin glanced at my padd.

"That way," he said, starting down the hall.

Suyef glanced at the padd, then at the moving Quentin.

"What's that?" he asked, falling in with me as I followed Quentin.

"An escape route." I held up a hand. "And no, I don't know who is sending it, but I have a theory."

He walked in silence as Quentin marched on ahead. "The face on the prison screen."

"She's helped us before." I waved Quentin through an intersection. "Stands to reason she might again."

"That's a tall leap of logic." He pointed at Quentin. "Even for him."

"She's helped so far," I said, watching Quentin hover near some double doors. "But, as we aren't sure of her motivations or if this help now is even her, we should be wary."

"To what end? All the help so far just landed us in more trouble." He pointed down the hall. "And when the guards regain consciousness, this will anger our hosts. Even with their predilection toward you."

We arrived at the doors. Quentin glanced back and forth between us.

"Everything okay?" When no answer came, he continued. "Are we in the right place?"

"I'm not sure what it is," I said, nodding. "But it's a large space."

"Only one way to find out."

The doors slid open at Quentin's approach, revealing a small platform with a waist-high wall opposite the doors. Beyond stood an enormous cavern, massive stalactites reaching down several hundred paces. The platform proved to be a walkway at this level of the structure.

"Now this makes more sense."

Quentin pointed down at a large facility. Below, massive rectangular containers lay in neat rows and, beyond those, dozens of bulbous objects that reminded me of a beetle I'd once seen in a holo. They were nearly half the size of the containers, and each sat on four small legs jutting out from the bottom. A flat rectangular gangway extended out the fatter end to the ground. A rounded protrusion jutted out of the narrower end along the upper edge, glistening against the object's surface, which otherwise absorbed the light.

"Are those—"

"Ships," Quentin said, leaning over the wall. "If we stay close to the wall, we might get down unnoticed."

A hollow feeling filled my gut. His belt still bothered me, his complete trust in a device he'd only really just learned to use. Still, I could not deny its usefulness. Quentin's apparent prowess helped ease the feeling, but only a bit. I pointed at several figures moving among the objects.

"What about them?"

"I could land us on top of a container without them seeing."

"And what will we do once down there?" Suyef asked. "Where would we go?"

"To one of those ships," Quentin said, frowning. "To leave."

"This shell was where we hoped to find help. If we leave now, we go back with more questions than answers."

"We can't stay here," Quentin said, deploying his board and hopping on. "One step at a time. Get down, get on a ship, then figure out the next part."

He held out a hand toward each of us, and my feet lifted off the ground.

"Quentin, the lights," I said, pointing toward the walkway.

Lights shone out from below us, illuminating the wall in massive columns. He nodded and spread his hands wide. We moved, first shifting into position above the platform, then moving down just below it, him in the middle, us to either side. We settled against the surface in the shadows between the lights, helping conceal us from eyes below. A bout of vertigo gripped me, and I pressed my hands against the wall. The feeling worsened when we started moving down, accelerating.

The floor raced closer, and images of us crashing into it filled my head. I clenched my mouth, stifling a cry and bracing for the impact. Then our momentum slowed, and the wall vanished behind me as Quentin altered our trajectory, bringing us out at an angle to land on a container. The flat surface had folds spaced evenly along the surface, like ribs on a gaunt body.

Quentin moved toward me, but Suyef touched his shoulder and pointed to his left, where a guard moved between the containers. Quentin leaned near the edge and, with a flick of his finger, shoved the guard into the opposite container. His head thumped with a resounding crack, and he fell motionless on the floor.

"Hope you didn't kill him," I whispered.

Eyes widening, he jumped off, landing silently next to the man. He pressed two fingers to the man's neck and paused. Then he nodded and waved us down. Suyef jumped and Quentin caught him, bringing him down in silence. I followed suit.

Suyef grabbed the man's pulse gun and moved to the end of the containers. He glanced each direction, then waved his hand for us to follow him farther from the wall. Ahead stood the bulbous shape of a ship, just visible beyond the containers. At each crossing path, Suyef checked for guards.

We encountered two. Quentin flung them up against a container, but the impact failed to incapacitate them. Suyef charged them, and I erected shields to trap the noise. A few small sounds leaked out as the Nomad dispatched them.

"That was mostly effective," Quentin said, nodding at me as we moved on.

"I had to layer shields to make it work."

"It worked," Suyef said as he joined us. "Celebrate small wins like you do grand ones."

He tossed the pair of pulse guns to Quentin as we approached the edge of the containers and stopped. I stared at the oddly shaped ships.

"They like clean lines, I guess," I said.

"They must feel secure here. This close together, one shot takes out several at a time."

"I doubt they have much to worry about here."

"A single stalactite falling would knock out a dozen of these ships," the Nomad muttered, leaning out to look around. "Ten guards in sight, but there are more."

He pointed at the nearest ship. A guard stood on the vessel's far side.

"That one," he said.

"You sure?" I whispered. "You just said we shouldn't leave."

"I got outvoted," he said, shrugging. "Besides, it's safer inside that than out here." He glanced at Quentin. "Can you reach him from here?"

Our companion stared for a moment, then nodded.

"On my mark, grab him and fling him back behind us. Micaela, place a shield here between the containers, please. If he's still conscious after hitting that, I'll dispatch him."

"She gets a *please*, but not me?"

Suyef waved Quentin on. His eyes shifted and narrowed, and his hand raised toward the guard. I leaned close to Suyef.

"Are you sure this will work? What if he cries out?"

"It's a chance we have to take. Ready?"

I watched him for a moment, contemplating saying more, then nodded. Quentin's thumb twitched upward.

"Now," Suyef whispered.

Quentin clenched his hand, and the unsuspecting man grunted. I formed the construct, which shimmered into existence just as the man whipped past me. He slammed into it and crumpled down into Suyef's arms. He laid the man down gently, checking his head.

"Let's go."

We rushed out, Quentin and I heading straight for the ship, Suyef sweeping out to the left. The short distance felt much longer now that we were out in the open, our footfalls sounding like booms to my ears. To the right, I spied a guard's legs under one ship, heading for the same open space. I extended my stride, accelerating, as Quentin lunged ahead of me, no doubt using his belt. Quentin leaped up, the board materializing under him, and a tug on my torso yanked me forward. We landed at the foot of the platform and ran up into the ship. I saw no sign of Suyef.

"Not big," Quentin muttered, looking around.

The cramped interior contained two benches along either side, with compartments above and below for storage. Beyond that stood a single chair, which I sat in. Surrounding the chair lay a semicircular window, affording a good view of the ship's front and sides. A single, solid clear interface similar to the network stations lay just below the window. The interface flashed once and turned on at my touch. A myriad of control interfaces appeared, and a display similar to the speeder's materialized on the glass window just above.

"So, we can operate it," Quentin said, moving up next to me. "What's that?"

An icon flashed on the surface nearest me, a tap opening a window on the panel. A circular image appeared, a round object in the middle and a solid line at the outer edge. Between those, several smaller objects lay spaced at different intervals around the center object.

"That looks like a picture I saw once," Quentin said. "A piece of art etched in metal. My father said it represented our world."

"Yes. Water shield here, core there, shells in between."

My finger brushed the image, and it flashed before zooming in on one of the small objects near the middle. The image rotated, bringing the object to a flat plane as its shape came into focus. A single light blinked in the middle of it.

"That's a shell, all right," Quentin said. "And I'll bet it's this one."

I tapped the blinking light, and the image zoomed in to show a top-down view of the surrounding ships and containers. One ship blinked, so I tapped it. The image dissolved, revealing an overlay with script flowing into columns. Quentin leaned close, one hand on the seat just above my shoulder.

"Looks like your ally is here as well," he said. "Flight plan, maybe?"

"But where to?"

"Can you get this thing airborne?" he asked, standing and looking back at the hatch.

"Maybe," I muttered, eyes roaming over the panel. "I'll try."

"Do it. I'm going to help Suyef."

"This thing might just take off," I said, turning to look back at him. "The hatch might close."

Quentin stopped and grinned over his shoulder at me. "Then I'll just have to be awesome again."

"You did not say that," I stated, staring at him.

Suyef snorted and shook his head. "You would say that."

Quentin leaned back, hands behind his head, smiling. "It sounded good in my head, Logwyn. And, hey, I am awesome on that board."

I groaned, looking at Suyef. "So, where were you while they boarded the ship?"

He shrugged.

"Let *Awesome* here tell you."

Quentin hooted, jumping up.

"Yes. Let me," he exclaimed. "And I'll start by taking those words back."

Those words filled my head as I left the ship. *Why did I say that?* She'd just think I was boasting, showing off. When I said it, I thought it was funny, maybe disarming. Now it just seemed silly. Shaking my head, I focused on the task.

Staying on the ground, I ran over to another ship and looked for Suyef. Movement to my left proved to be a guard walking beyond another ship. Squatting afforded me a better view under the ships. Several guards moved about, but I saw no sign of the Nomad. Micaela could have that ship moving any moment.

A hissing sound behind me filled my ears. Goose bumps covered my skin as the sound echoed in the chamber. Jets of steam shot out small ports on our ship's lower side. A guard rushed closer, and Suyef dropped behind the man and struck him across the head. More guards approached as the sounds increased in frequency.

"Suyef!"

I pointed at the ship, and he nodded, running in the opposite direction toward an onrushing guard. Suyef twisted, bringing his staff up to drop the man. He spun to the ground, pulse gun in hand, and shot another guard. I looked around for guards trying to flank him. A pair rushed in opposite me, ignoring the Nomad and heading for the ramp. I grabbed them, stopping them dead in their tracks. One of them cried out, drawing Suyef's attention.

As he looked, another guard lunged at him, knocking him to the ground. I dispatched the guards with my pulse guns.

"Halt!"

Several guards rushed in from every direction as the ship lifted off, the hissing sound increasing in volume. The legs folded up inside, but the walkway remained out.

Firing several shots toward the approaching guards, I leaped onto the board and soared up next to the ship. Below, Suyef and the guard struggled toward a dropped pulse gun, more guards surrounding the pair.

"Sorry, Suyef."

Dropping closer, I fired on the struggling pair, knocking both of them out. I grabbed the pair, separating them as they rose. I tossed the guard at his companions and yanked Suyef's limp form toward me. As he soared closer, I flipped up toward the open hatch, now moving away from me. Pulse shots whizzed past us, my belt bending the pulses away. One struck Suyef, knocking him into a flip.

"Oh, he's going to kill me for that one."

I moved him up into an arc over me and pulled us both inside the ship's hatch. Micaela remained in the chair, head down, looking at the panel.

"We're in!"

She pressed a flashing icon on the left, and the plank retracted as the hatch closed, cutting off the exterior sounds. Muted thuds struck the ship's underside as the guards continued firing.

"Figured out how to fly this?" I settled Suyef down on the bench and activated a harness field to hold him.

"Not exactly," she said, her voice tense. "But we're moving."

I grabbed her chair as the ship dipped to the left. The belt reacted, keeping me balanced, but I still placed a hand on her chair. Old habits never die, or something like that.

"Where are we going?"

"There's an exit on the other end of this cavern," she said. "But it's closed."

"So, why are we flying toward it?"

"I'm not actually controlling it." She shook her head and pointed at the panel. "It's on autopilot. All I did was activate it."

"What's that, then?" I asked, looking where she pointed.

"Activation sequence." She waved at a visual display of the surrounding terrain. "That turned on once the program activated. It had a preprogrammed course out of here to a point under the shell."

"So, no control."

She glared at me, and I nodded at the Nomad.

"He will not like that."

The ship zoomed over the other ships, arcing toward the cavern's far end and a large, octagonal opening set a few-hundred paces above the hangar floor. It remained sealed by a set of massive doors, shut along a diagonal line. Lights flashed along that split, once yellow, then twice red.

"That can't be a good thing."

Micaela tapped on another display, bringing up a translucent image.

"That's the door. I can't activate it or unlock it or anything."

"But the ship is flying at it, so whoever did this must have planned for that."

"Planned for what?" Suyef asked.

The harness shimmered as he sat up. Micaela tapped a flashing light near me, turning the harness off.

"Getting out of this hangar," she said, not looking back. "Are you okay?"

"You shot me," Suyef said, looking at me.

"No choice. I needed to get you on board."

"Good thinking," he said, touching the side of his head. "Next time, take better care of me."

My face warmed and the back of my neck tingled.

"Sorry about that," I said.

"We're approaching the doors," Micaela called out. "Which are still closed."

Suyef moved up to her right, and I shifted over to the left. He tapped an image, activating another translucent screen. A solid vertical and horizontal line slid across it in succession.

"No one is pursuing us," he said. "Curious."

"That seems the more pressing matter." I pointed at the doors. "I'm pretty sure the plan isn't to fly into them."

Ahead, the lights flashed green, and the doors separated. A chime sounded, followed by a surge in acceleration. A series of lights set in circles lit the passage beyond, giving us an idea of our speed. The tunnel dipped down in a sharp turn, revealing another door. As we approached, the doors slid open, a shaft of bright light slicing into the dark space. I squinted instinctively, but the glass, detecting the change in light, darkened, allowing us a view of the shell's underside as we soared out into the expanse.

I looked at my companions.

"Now what?"

CHAPTER 38

REINFORCEMENT

"So, was it Celandine?"

Micaela, wearing a blue dress today instead of her usual green, rolled her shoulders back against the couch.

"Yes. That's what we suspected, at least."

I tapped a nearby page. "Her name has popped up a few times. Notably, after the prison escape."

"I gave up trying to understand that woman."

"So you've met her?" I asked.

"As much as someone can say that." Micaela smiled. "Of course, she met my father first."

"Did you meet her through the network?"

"No." Her head tilted to one side. "Yes? Technically, maybe."

"That's as clear as rock."

"You'll understand soon enough. I can say that I'm one of the few people who have met her." She paused. "Well, interacted with her directly."

I watched her in silence.

"What?" she asked.

"Are you being cryptic on purpose? Just say what you mean."

"I did."

"Where is Celandine?" I asked, glaring at her.

"Somewhere where she's a threat to everyone. At the center of this entire thing," she said, looking down at my padd. "Where she can control it all."

"She's in a citadel?"

She said nothing, held still.

"That citadel? The one lost in the Shattering?"

She remained still, watching me.

"The Breaking destroyed it. Didn't it?"

"How do you know?" She waved a hand at my notes. "Do you have any actual evidence?"

"We learned about it in primary school."

"Without evidence, any claim can masquerade as truth. Quentin would say the same thing, but he'd mess the words up," she said, grinning. "Well, probably."

"I think that's the first time you've smiled when talking about him."

Her brow furrowed, and she looked away. I returned to the previous subject.

"Why keep that a secret? That *the* citadel is still around?" I held up a hand. "No, don't answer that. I already know the answer."

She watched me, hands folded just below her chin.

"National security."

"World security, but yes."

I watched her for a moment.

"Where is it?" I asked. "Citadels aren't easy to hide, especially that one."

"You don't think it's here, do you?" Micaela asked, frowning.

"No, out there," I said, pointing at the window. "Where out *there* is it?"

"The only unreachable place left. Unreachable, save for those blessed with the form."

When I said nothing, she pointed at the floor.
"Down there."

We're falling into the core.

When the ship left the tunnel, our world's glowing heart bright in our faces, those words reverberated through me. Just as the glass dimmed, the ship spun to the left and flew along the shell's underside, darting between massive stalactites similar to Colberra's. Gripping the panel, I looked down to see our destination.

"We're going to the center axis."

Quentin looked out the window.

"Any pursuit?"

Suyef scanned the area. A large blip flashed up near the screen's bottom edge.

"They are now," he said, zooming in. "Three ships."

Our ship flew into an alcove between three stalactites, dipping down toward the core and stopping. A low hum I hadn't noticed suddenly quieted, and the lights dimmed.

"What's happening?" Quentin asked.

I scanned the displays, but nothing stood out.

"Hiding? I'm not sure."

Suyef tapped his display, changing views.

"We reached our destination."

"Yes. So, now what?" Quentin asked. "There's nothing here."

A bulbous shape raced past us.

"Except them," Suyef said, leaning near the window. "Maybe this is intentional. Hiding here to lose any pursuit."

"Then what?" I asked.

He looked at me, one eyebrow raised.

"Get away and find help."

"There isn't another flight plan loaded," I said. "So, if we leave, where are we going? Plus, what help are you hoping we'll find?"

"I doubt anyone here will want to help us now," Quentin stated. "Beyond answers, what were you hoping for?"

"Help with stopping the war," I said. "We thought the dragons might help."

"I don't think they care," Quentin muttered as he sat on a bench. "If that council is a good measure, I think the Greens care only for the Greens."

"Leaders are not representative of the people at large."

"You're from Colberra. You know that's not true."

"Having spent more time there than you, Quentin," Suyef countered, "I can say that most Colberrans do just fall in line, but not everyone." He pointed at the rear of the ship. "Their decision was not unanimous, merely governed by rules."

Quentin shook his head, laughing once before saying, "Rules they make up or ignore as they see fit."

"We have bigger problems than politics here," I said, tapping the panel. "We must be missing something."

My companions fell silent as I glared at the displays, watching for any changes. Out the window, another ship flew past.

"Shouldn't their scanners pick this thing up?" Quentin asked.

"When the systems shut down, maybe the ship becomes untraceable," I said.

"I wonder how long they'll keep looking," Quentin said, staring out the window. "This is such a weird view." He stomped his foot on the deck twice. "Must have a gravity emitter."

A thumping drew my gaze, and I turned in the chair. Suyef tapped a bulkhead overhead that lay between the compartments. He pointed at more running down to merge with the deck.

"They reinforced this ship," he said. "And a gravity emitter is not standard on a ship like this."

"Why's that?" I asked.

He held his arms wide. "They are massive and costly to fabricate." He moved a thumb and forefinger close to each other. "The tinier something is . . ."

"The more expensive it is to make," I said, finishing his statement. "So, what is this ship for?"

"It's not a fighter," Quentin said. "No weaponry controls."

I tapped a portion of the panel to my right. "But it has armor. A lot of armor."

"So, no weapons, but heavily armored with reinforced structural integrity," Quentin said. "I'd also wager on short-range use, judging by this compartment." He looked at Suyef. "But you saw all those ships. If they are that expensive, why build so many?"

"It would be expensive for us to build them," he said. "The Greens have better resources and technology."

"So, what are they for?"

I pondered Quentin's question. Where would a small, heavily reinforced ship with a small crew need to go that would require armor plating and structural reinforcement, but no weapons? I examined the walls, the deck, the panel behind me, the window. The window facing down.

"The core!"

I glanced around at my companions. Quentin looked at the window for a moment, then at Suyef.

"It makes sense," he said. "We know little about the core beyond speculation, but if any of what we know is true, anything going down there would need reinforcement against the gravitational forces there."

"Or be immune to them," the Nomad replied. "Remember: we may not know a lot, but the Greens do."

"That doesn't change my statement," Quentin said. "We can surmise what a ship like this would need to have to survive down there. They could build them."

"If they could go there in the first place," Suyef said, nodding at the panel. "None of that helps us now. We don't even know that's our destination, let alone what to look for."

"What we know is whoever helped us used this ship," I said, pointing out the window. "Going to the core seems the best use for this ship. That must be our destination."

"If you're right," Quentin said, approaching the control panel, "what's the next step?"

"Maybe it's preprogrammed to hide here first," I suggested. "To wait until it detects no ships in pursuit."

Suyef stepped up on the other side.

"Or for us to do something."

"What do you mean?"

"Maybe there's a trigger." He nodded at the panel. "Something we must start."

Quentin laughed, still examining the interface.

"I thought you were against this."

"I merely stated that we were leaving without help or answers." The Nomad glared at Quentin. "That remains true."

"If there's a trigger," I interjected, "it could be anything." I tapped a finger on the edge of the panel. "If it were me, I'd make it something obvious. Or connected."

Quentin pointed across to the other side of the controls.

"The armor. That's what you noticed."

"Why does that matter?"

He looked at Suyef, then back at me.

"Because someone knows you well enough to predict your actions. And how many people have we met acting like they know you?" He pointed at the armor controls. "Almost like you're doing this to yourself, although I'm not sure how, so don't ask me to explain."

"Don't worry about that," I retorted, looking away from him.

The thought stuck in my mind, however. Whoever was helping us had predicted my actions or at least offered me courses of action I would take. That made it even more confusing. Before, I would not have thought myself capable of doing the things I had done or going the places I had gone to. Charging into a battle, standing toe-to-toe with a Questioner, escaping a prison. Helping my new companions escape another. I had faced councils on three different shells, none my own. My hand shifted up to grab my braid, only to find it missing. Another difference, and one I'd hardly noticed. A lot had changed.

My eyes shifted to the armor controls, and I pressed my hand to the panel.

"Becoming introspective, are we?" I asked, setting my stylus down.

"Moments of realization like that are worth noting."

I smiled.

"So, did anything happen?"

"I'll say." She chuckled. "Just about scared the pee right out of me, too." Her cheeks flushed a bit, a hand covering her mouth. "I'm sorry, that was impolite."

"Don't apologize," I said. "It was funny. Part of why I enjoy this is getting to know who people really are. Moments like this are revealing."

She smiled and shook her head.

"Still, it's not the image I want to portray."

"What image is that? A woman who knows how to be self-deprecating when the moment calls for it?" I frowned at her. "If it's who you really are, why hide it?"

The grin faded.

"Because I haven't been that person for a long time."

"Since before this story began?"

"There have been moments, flashes where I felt like that person."

She tapped a finger on her chest, just below the line of her gown. "Like she's hiding, waiting for something to draw her out."

"Or that it's safe to come out?" I asked.

She sat there, her eyes moist. I waited for her to go on, to tell me more about what made her who she was. She took in a deep breath, looked away from me, then shook her head.

"She's gone."

I watched her for a moment. "But not forever."

"Maybe." She looked back at me. "But she's buried so deep I doubt she'll ever see the core light again."

Uncertain what to say, I looked over my notes. "So, you touched the panel, and the next part startled you. What was it?"

She laughed through her nose and nodded at the window. "The ship fell."

The whole panel lit up the instant I touched it. Then the central panel darkened, and a translucent display appeared at eye level. We saw the shell's underside with a flashing light at the center. A path appeared next, blinking down toward the core.

"Whoa," Quentin whispered.

His hand brushed my arm as he leaned forward on the armrest. Outside the glass, sheets of metal slid up to cover the window, the vessel trembling as each piece set in place. Then the ship went still, and the panel flashed green. An image of the vessel, now fully armored, hovered before us.

"We look like a tunneling device," Quentin said, drawing a finger along the sides of the image before pointing at the armored joints. "Cone-shaped, with grooves?"

"Looks like it," I said, nodding. "So, now what?"

Suyef pointed at the display before me.

"Are those controls different from those on the panel?"

I looked at the edges of the image.

"Maybe." I gazed at each one. "Not for flying, though. 'Status.'"

I opened a display that showed the ship alongside an overhead shot with a circle flashing out repeatedly from the ship.

"'Radar.'"

"Engines, also," Quentin said, leaning closer. "Biometrics?"

He tapped the symbol, and three body shapes appeared, outlined in yellow. A green line scanned down and then across. The bodies flashed green and stayed that way.

"I think it just declared us healthy," he said.

"A medical ship?" I asked Suyef.

"Could be a short-range rescue vessel. That armor can withstand a beating." He pointed at the bottom of the display. "What's that?"

I tapped it, and a compartment below the control panel opened. An apparatus shifted out and up, a single pylon with a handle on each side at the top.

"Manual control," Quentin said, grinning. "Fun."

"Not blind, it wouldn't be," I said, pushing one handle. "It's stuck."

Quentin shook the other handle.

"Locked. Must be a way to release it."

A chime drew our eyes to the display to see a symbol flash over the view. A simple statement with a question construct branched off of it.

"'Clear. Activate.'" I read aloud. "Clear? What's clear?"

Suyef pointed at the display. "The ships are gone, or just out of range."

Quentin snapped his fingers. "The path's clear. It was waiting for that."

"So, do I—"

"Yes," Quentin exclaimed. "Let's see what this is all about."

Suyef looked at Quentin, then at me. His head lowered. "It's your choice, but I agree with him."

"Time to see how deep the tunnel goes," I said, pushing the symbol.

A warning light flashed around the display's edges, and a countdown replaced the symbol.

"Ten seconds," I said.

My companions moved to the rear, activating the harnesses as they sat.

"Five."

I pushed a button on my chair, activating my harness.

"Two."

"Here we go!"

"One."

CHAPTER 39

CORE

When the ship launched, I expected something dramatic, exciting. Anything, really. Instead, nothing happened. The display showed the ship shooting away from the shell, accelerating. Beyond that, we felt no sign of movement.

"Why have these harnesses?" Quentin asked.

"Seriously. Very anticlimactic." I looked at him, then pointed at the armor controls. "Makes that seem unnecessary."

"We have yet to reach the core," Suyef said.

"Care to share what the Nomads know?" Quentin asked. "Or theorize?"

Suyef grunted. "As much as Colberra knows."

I tried to release the harness. A chime sounded, and a red light flashed over the display.

"Please do not remove the safety harness during descent," a familiar-sounding computer voice said. "Harnesses will automatically release once we achieve orbit."

"Such a polite ship," Quentin muttered.

Noticing a panel on the armrest, I tapped the controls and turned the chair to face the rear.

"That's better," I said, rubbing the right side of my neck. "Looking back was hurting." I nodded at Suyef. "So, what do your people know?"

"Same as you. The core is some kind of interstellar phenomenon," he said. "Most likely a singularity or a star. It produces three things in abundance: gravity, energy, and light."

"Do we know what kind of effect that much gravity is going to have on time?" I asked.

Quentin pulled out his padd and tossed it to me.

"Compare that to the ship's chronometer."

I turned to the panel to look, finding them almost identical

"The ship is just a few milliseconds behind," I said, tossing it back to him and looking at Suyef. "The shield wouldn't affect relativity, would it?"

"What we know is mostly from observation."

"Right. So, the shield absorbs and transmits energy," I went on, "emits just enough gravity to hold the shells in orbit, and lets a lot of light through. But we don't know what they did to account for relativity."

Suyef pointed at Quentin's padd.

"Clearly, the effect is still present."

"Maybe the lower shells are just at the effect's upper limit," I said. "Or they're at a different level, and we're all under its effects."

I turned and tapped a display panel. A moment later, I found the information I sought.

"The gravitational forces are increasing. So time may indeed dilate for us."

"We will not know until we go back," Suyef stated. "Assume a lot of time will pass."

I stared beyond them, thinking about what we were leaving behind. We still didn't know where this ship was taking us.

Quentin moved, drawing my attention.

"I think we're rotating. Something is putting a lot of torque on this structure."

"You can feel that?" I asked.

Suyef touched a bulkhead, eyes never leaving Quentin.

"It's vibrating. And getting stronger."

"So we're spinning really fast," Quentin said, "or something is exerting a tremendous amount of force on us."

"Possibly both," I said, turning to check the display just as a chime sounded

"Orbit achieved," the computer said. "Optimal route to destination selected."

"Optimal route?" Quentin asked.

The harnesses released, and my companions jumped up to move beside me. I tapped at a display to my left.

"Armor's holding strong but . . ." Quentin's voice trailed off.

"Look at our energy reserves," I said, nodding at the readout.

"That's an incredible amount of force," Suyef said.

"No wonder this thing is vibrating." Quentin pointed at an engine status display. "That thing's generating more energy than an engine this small should be able to do."

He whistled as he brought up a side-by-side display showing a series of bars decreasing at an alarming rate. I leaned closer to examine it.

"Look how fast the ship's burning through that energy." As I watched, they all blinked and rose back up a little. "Did you see that?"

I toggled the display to full-screen mode.

"Maybe the ship's absorbing energy from the core," Quentin said. "They built a gravity emitter that small, so making energy-absorbing armor wouldn't be that much harder."

Suyef pointed at the armor display. "Watch the force exerted on the armor. See that spike?"

I toggled a comparison view of the armor and energy readouts.

"The gauge jumps back up when we get hit hard," I said. "You're right. Energy-absorbing armor."

"Not just that," Suyef said, looking at a different display. "Look at the armor."

I stared at the display. As the pressure intensified, the vibrations rose to match.

"Oh, there's a matching increase in energy with the more intense vibrations."

"So, energy absorption combined with kinetic energy conversion," Quentin said.

"They built this ship to do this," I said, watching the surrounding displays. "The absorption/conversion rate does not look like enough to circumnavigate the entire core. So, we must have a destination."

Quentin pointed at the window.

"Can we get a visual display through this armor?"

I looked for the right controls, then opened a display showing a top-down view of the ship. Multiple sections around the sides flashed. I tapped one along the front, and the window flashed white, then turned translucent.

The expanse lay below us, dominated above by a massive sea of bright yellow light. Our world's center. Even with the ship filtering the light, it still made me squint.

"Why are we upside down?" Quentin asked.

"Angle of descent," Suyef said. "Can you do anything about it?"

"It's on automatic. I don't see how to change that."

"Would you like me to alter the ship's path?" the computer asked.

"That computer is getting uncanny at anticipating my questions," I said.

"Learning from what you were doing."

I nodded at the Nomad and addressed the computer.

"Can you rotate the ship a hundred and eighty degrees?"

"Adjusting."

The core's horizon turned sharply, threatening a wave of vertigo. I closed my eyes, taking in deep breaths. When I opened them, the core's bright light shone up from below.

"Amazing!" Quentin exclaimed. "Computer, can you scan the surface?"

"Affirmative."

"Do so, please."

A translucent displayed appeared to my right, an icon blinking on the bottom left. It never moved.

"Scan complete. Insufficient data."

"It didn't even write a column of data," I said, pointing at the display.

"Maybe something we know will work," Quentin said. "Computer, scan for breathable air."

A moment later, several columns of data flowed onto the display.

"Nitrogen, oxygen, and trace amounts of several other gases," I read off. "All correct."

"So, it works," Quentin said. "So, why not the first time?"

Suyef shifted, looking first at the display, then out the window.

"Because it did not scan the core."

"The shield," Quentin and I said together.

"It stopped the scan," I continued. "So, nothing to display."

Quentin snapped his fingers.

"Computer, can you scan beyond the shield?"

"Unable to answer."

"Worth a shot," he said, shrugging.

"Computer, what is our destination?" I asked.

"Arrival at destination imminent."

"No, where are we going?"

"That information is unavailable."

Quentin chuckled. "As useful as Nidfar's computer."

"It is the same voice, right?" I asked.

"Slight difference in pitch," Suyef said.

"You can hear that?" Quentin asked.

"It is easy," Suyef said, looking at him. "Practice listening better."

"That was a joke," Quentin said, punching me in the arm. "We're rubbing off on him."

Suyef sighed, and I smothered a smirk.

"Kind of humbling," I said. "Everything going on in the world dwarfed by whatever is in there."

"Can you imagine the Ancients' power to have built that?" Quentin asked.

"They still couldn't prevent the Shattering," Suyef said, his voice quiet. "According to the legends."

"At least you have those," Quentin said. "On Colberra, the government sanitized everything about the Shattering and the Ancients. You won't find a trace in our history archives."

"Can't really call it history, can you?" I asked, looking up at Quentin.

"Propaganda is information tailored to keep the people in line."

"Government controlling the history is bad, but you've got a pretty cynical view of the Colberran people," I said. "Are all Islers so pessimistic?"

"Just stating the facts," he answered. "Considering your experiences, I'd think you would agree."

"Didn't say I disagree. Is it normal for Islers to be so pessimistic?" I pointed at Suyef. "Or is this from living on his shell?"

Quentin shrugged.

"Both, probably. All things considered, I've had very little positive interaction with Colberrans." He glared down at me. "And let's not forget they just wiped out my home."

"Seekers," Suyef pointed out. "Not all Colberran people."

"That society bred the Seekers into existence," Quentin said. "No, Seekers helped shape Colberra into what it is today, but that's the same thing."

I pointed out the window

"We're a long way from Seekers *or* Colberrans."

"Not all of them," Suyef interjected, hand raised.

"If they could get here, don't you think Colvinra would have done so by now? Whatever is down here, the dragons know about it. All of them."

"Yes, but what is down here?" Quentin asked.

"The network."

"Yes, but the network isn't physical. It exists at the quantum level." He held up a finger. "I know. The control interfaces are physical, but not the storage and processing power. That's at a quantum level."

"We have to access it from somewhere," I pointed out. "The citadels have to connect to it somehow."

"A gateway? Yeah, there are theories on that." Quentin nodded at Suyef. "His people have a legend telling of a gate device that served as the original access point to the network."

Suyef nodded.

"Third Gate. But that's all we know."

"So, there were two others?" I asked. "Third of its kind? Third attempt?"

"Your father educated you on the network, yet he never even mentioned Third Gate? Colberra's history contains nothing about it. Nothing exists beyond legend."

I looked up at him.

"The Greens?"

"Or the Reds. They probably both kept the answers secret." He looked over at Quentin. "Some questions should remain unasked."

"That's a different discussion," Quentin muttered.

Suyef stared at him for a moment, then chuckled. "First time for everything," the Nomad said.

I grinned at Quentin just as Suyef touched my shoulder. He pointed at the display.

"That shows we've arrived."

We all leaned forward. At first, we saw nothing. Then the air ahead shimmered, and Quentin whistled and Suyef murmured something. None of us looked away from the sight before us.

There, sitting on the shield where just a moment before there was nothing, floated the largest citadel I'd ever seen.

"You first saw one in person on the Nomad shell?" I asked Micaela, who nodded.

"I'd seen images and schematics of Colberra's and knew enough to know this one was different."

"What made it so? Other than the size?"

She shrugged.

"It was just . . . I don't know . . . *somehow*."

"Somehow what?"

"No, I mean it was that." She chuckled. "Somehow. Sorry, it's something we edge dwellers used to say when something feels off, different. Or when you're not sure what something is."

"Okay." I made a note. "Somehow."

"Yeah, different yet familiar at the same time." She paused, then snapped her fingers. "Have you ever been to some place you knew you'd never been but felt like you had?"

"A lot around here feels like that. I think it's the Ancient architecture."

"Exactly. Take everything Ancient, architecture and culture, and put it all together. Then make it several magnitudes larger than you've ever seen." She pointed out the window. "I knew instantly that we'd found the network's heart."

"Yes, For'a Dal. The control citadel." I pointed at the Queen's cavern. "It's our directive for all of recorded history. Keep the location protected so no one could commandeer the network and endanger the world. Again."

Micaela cocked her head to one side. "And now?"

"Nothing's changed."

"Yes, but everyone knows where it is now, and the Greens don't control it anymore."

"True, but the network remained secure," I said. At her raised eyebrow, I added, "Well, until recently."

"Which means whoever was controlling and protecting it is losing that fight."

"Until the Queen summoned me, I didn't know someone else controlled the network."

"All the more reason for you to succeed, I would say," Micaela said.

She looked back out the window, and I watched her for a moment.

"This entire war was your doing."

Her gazed returned to me.

"All three of you. You were just the excuse Colberra needed. But this?" I asked, waving at my current notes. "You three going to For'a Dal? That was how everyone found it."

"Not everyone," she said, her voice quiet. "Just a few people."

"And they followed you. Didn't they?"

"Maybe." She shrugged. "I believe they knew all along. They just couldn't do anything about it until we got there."

"Until you got there?" I frowned at her. "Why did that matter?"

"We unlocked the citadel," she said, "and then lost the fight for it." She looked down. "Lost a lot more than that, actually."

"Lost it to whom?"

"You already know who."

I paused, pondering who might have beaten them to the citadel, known about it already. Wanted that kind of power.

"Colvinra."

She nodded.

"He was waiting for you?"

"No. He got there after us."

She fell silent. I let her sit for a moment before continuing.

"So, what did you find when you got there?"

She shifted, looking at her hands, the window; everywhere but at me. After a moment, she looked at me. "Death."

CHAPTER 40

TOMB

The sight of the mighty citadel filled me with an urge to move. Goose bumps spread across my arms as I leaned forward and stared at a sight unseen—as far as we knew then—by human eyes since the Ancients walked the world. Most have seen a citadel, if nothing else, in holos. Until the Nomad shell, that was my experience. They are awe-inspiring structures, however, they pale when compared to For'a Dal. If you haven't seen it, or at least an image or holo of it, it's hard to describe, but I will try.

The ship flew in a slow, wide arc above the tallest structure, allowing us a panoramic view of the place. Single massive structures dominated all citadels, but this one, much taller than those I'd seen, contained a unique superstructure: four enormous towers arranged around an even taller central structure. Around that central structure stood four concentric rings of tall spires, which, upon closer examination, proved identical to the central spire: four smaller ones arranged around a taller central structure.

"Eight of these spire structures form that innermost ring," Quentin said. "Doubling each ring out to sixty-four on that outermost ring."

"So, a hundred and twenty spires," Suyef said. "That is a lot of space."

"Are those bridges connecting those spires?" Quentin asked, pointing down at the citadel. "Looks like a wheel, kind of."

"Four-spoked wheel, yes," I said, nodding. "And those spire structures all follow the same pattern."

The ship moved down to fly level with the outermost ring, affording us a look at the citadel's profile.

"Interesting," I said. "From here, the height of the spires makes it look like steps down from that center structure."

"That shortest ring is easily as tall as that prison's tower," Quentin said. "What are those along the outside? Simple buildings?"

Around the concentric rings stood an unbroken circle of smaller buildings constructed from the same Ancient material as the rest. The tallest of these stood half the height of the outer ring of towers.

"Yes, they look like Colberra City's buildings, just not made from modern materials." I pointed down as we flew over a large bridge connecting the outer buildings to the rings. "See that? There are four along the base of the citadel. That's the spoke we saw above."

"There are matching bridges connecting the rings to the superstructure." Suyef said, pointing up. "Those give it the stepped look."

"It looks like those four bridges form the only connection between the rings," I said. "Well, four on the bottom, with matching ones above."

"Yeah, there's nothing in between the upper and lower bridges," Quentin said, pointing down as the ship pulled up into a higher orbit. "Look at one of those spires. It looks like small bridges set every few levels connect each of the smaller outer towers to the spire's central tower."

Suyef leaned forward, peering at the spires as we flew by them.

"The ring bridges are the same," he said. "One at the base of the spires, one at the top level." He pointed. "See how all the spires' outer towers have platforms as tops? The upper ring bridge connects to the two lined up with the circle."

"And the other two towers line up on the inside and outside of each ring bridge," I said. "Like a plus sign when you see it from here."

We descended around the citadel. The buildings glistened in the core light, which refracted off balconies surrounding each building except on levels with a bridge. After a third full orbit, we neared the outer wall where a large platform stood just beyond, near one of the major thoroughfares. Just below the platform, we saw the telltale shimmer of the core shield upon which the citadel floated.

"There's another ship there," Quentin said, pointing ahead. "No, two of them."

"Someone may already be here," Suyef said.

"Or they left those here," I said.

"Also possible," Suyef said, staring silently for a moment. "I don't like it."

The ship slowed, rotating around just above the surface before lowering to land with a slight bump. Glowing light shone up beyond the landing deck.

"That's going to make it hard to see," I said, pointing out the window.

"I'm sure they prepared for that," Quentin said.

He tapped a release panel on the storage compartment below his bench. Peering inside, he grinned. "Yep," he said, tossing me a small plastic case.

It contained a pair of light-framed glasses with clear square lenses. A small appendage jutted down from each arm.

"Comfortable," Quentin said after donning his own pair.

He tossed another case to Suyef, who pulled out the spectacles and put them on. When I put mine on, a chime sounded and a small display flashed onto the glass. Information appeared: air quality, temperature, humidity, physical readouts of my companions. Even the ship's status appeared, shifting down to one side.

"The glass is clear, though," I said. "And there's a gap around the sides."

Quentin tapped the glasses' left arm. A black inner lining extended to his face, and the lenses darkened, then lightened.

"Maybe they react to the light level."

I found the button and pushed it, feeling the lining extend to my face as I watched Suyef do the same. Then he pulled out his staff and nodded at the rear door.

"Shall we?"

"Let's go find . . . something," Quentin said, pulse guns out.

Quentin pressed the release button as I neared the hatch. A blast of air rushed in, heating my skin and causing a tingling sensation that made me shiver once. The air weighed on my lungs, and sweat beaded on my skin.

"Wow," Quentin whispered.

Quentin moved down the ramp to the deck, Suyef beside him, both looking around. When I joined them, the lenses did their job, allowing me to gain my bearings.

"That's . . . amazing," Quentin said.

He faced away from the citadel, looking beyond our ship. The platform extended another few meters, ending at a waist-high, translucent wall. Just off the edge, glistening and glowing like the Nomad sea, the world's light shone up toward the expanse. Looking over the side, I could just make out the shimmering shield surrounding the heart of our world.

"That's humbling," I said as the three of us stepped near the wall.

"The core?" Suyef asked.

"And the shield. This place. All of it." I looked up. "The sheer power and skill needed to construct all this. It makes me feel small."

"We know so little of the world," he said, turning toward the citadel. "Or of what we face."

I turned to look at the massive fortress, at each level of the soaring towers. At the uppermost structure: a glistening dagger slicing through the expanse.

"Somewhere in there is an answer. To some of this, maybe everything," I said. "And I'm feeling like I will not like it."

I've often considered what came next. Whether I might have left if I'd known what came next. How things might be different if I had. I know one thing.

I hated what we found there.

"The air stood out to you?" I asked Micaela.

She was near the window, face turned away.

"Yes, Logwyn. It was my first time in any humid air. Even when the wind isn't stealing your cloak, Colberran air is never warm or humid." She ran a hand up her bare arm to her shoulder. "I felt perpetually chilled all my life, always wanted more clothing. The urge to remove clothing was a novelty."

"It is warmer down here," I said, nodding. "I found the Nomad shell notably colder."

"This," she said, touching her dress, "is never in fashion where I grew up."

"You don't live in Colberra now?"

"With current affairs, returning to Colberra is . . . complicated," she said, never looking from the window. "Here is as good as any other place, for now."

"Are you in the same quarters as when you were here before?"

"No. I requested more privacy," she said, smiling at me. "I possess a certain notoriety here."

A smile tugged at my lips as I dipped my head slightly.

"So, what did you discover inside?"

She turned back to the window, arms folded on her stomach. Her torso rose and fell as she stood in silence for several moments. Looking at the core, I realized. I opened my mouth to speak twice, thinking of distracting her. Each time, a sense of unease shut my mouth. *She will speak when she's ready.* I looked at my notes, contemplating the information. A rustling sound drew my eyes to see Micaela looking at me.

"Answers. And none of them good ones."

We crossed the walkway to the city and approached an entrance, doors sealed tight. An interface panel stood to one side. Suyef and I both looked at Quentin.

"What?"

"You have a knack with these things," I said.

"Something tells me this one is going to prefer you, Micaela," he said, stepping close to the panel. "Standard interface." He tapped it, then slid a finger across the middle. "It's not locked; just unresponsive."

I pressed a finger to the screen. It blinked, flashing a yellow tint before green. Something mechanical uncoupled and the doors slid open.

"Something you want to tell us?" Quentin asked, smiling at me.

"Someone wants us here."

"Well, *you*, at least."

Silence fell as we entered, but not from a lack of words. It just felt rude to speak, like talking in a funeral home. As we stepped through the doors, we entered a place last occupied by the people who built the citadels, the network, the shields. Everything that sustained our world. This, their greatest achievement, lost for centuries and forgotten by almost everyone, lay covered in history's dirty grime. Well, not counting the extra ship outside, which we still didn't know if it was a recent arrival or something left here.

Of course, I didn't know most of that then. I suspected its importance, but didn't really know. The farther we went, however, a weight grew in my chest, each step making it clear what I felt.

Dread. Dread of the place's meaning, of what had happened to it. Of what we might find. That one weighed heaviest of all.

Like all Ancient structures, the place felt very utilitarian: straight lines, sparse decor, and little imagination beyond the citadel's overall unique design. We moved toward a set of doors, pausing at that intersection partway and looking to see doors set at intervals to either side. Both walkways curved out of sight in the distance.

The doors opposite our entrance slid open onto a wide thoroughfare leading to the first ring. Warm air whipped across the bridge, light shining up from below.

"This place is massive," Quentin said, head tilted back. "I could probably save us some time and fly us up to the top of that ring."

Suyef pointed to the first ring.

"I want to see inside that first."

"I agree," I said, nodding.

That statement drew a weak chuckle from the other two. Humor, like speaking, felt out of place, and we moved on in silence.

At the far end, we entered the tower and found a hallway leading to the tower's center. Multiple hallways that ringed the tower crossed this passage, each with doors at regular intervals.

"They loved their uniformity," Quentin said, pointing at the doors.

We continued, the doors at the end of the hall opening on our approach to reveal a large open space. A pillar stood at the exact center.

"A gathering place," Quentin said, his voice echoing. "And look: businesses."

I motioned him to be quiet as we paused, looking around. Clusters of tables stood just outside windows set above a bar shelf. Benches surrounded fountains, long since dry, that alternated with enclosed spaces containing climbing apparatuses.

"Places for children to play," I whispered, pointing at them.

Above the businesses, balconies set at each level ringed the space up to a large platform several stories above. Light shone down through gaps built directly over the fountains and play structures.

We approached the pillar and found elevators facing each hallway opening into the communal space. We stopped there, looking around.

"Not what I expected. I mean, people clearly lived here. Many people."

"In Ancient times, citadels were centers of commerce, study, politics," Suyef said. "Life was here."

"Not anymore," Quentin muttered from behind me.

I turned and saw him pressing the release on the elevator. The doors slid open, and he stepped inside. "Shall we see what's at the top?" he asked.

"Before we do that, I want to peek inside." I pointed at the balconies. "See their living spaces."

Quentin followed my gaze, fingering his belt.

"I can get us up there," he said, stepping clear of the elevator.

I put my hand on his shoulder. "No. Let's do it how they did."

We returned to the rings of hallways and approached a pair of doors. Quentin stopped at a piece of bronze-colored metal melded into the wall.

"This might be a name," he said. "I think it means *weave*."

I moved closer and looked at the column. Recognition dawned the moment it came into focus.

"Weaver," I said, pointing at the top of the column. "That extra line makes it a noun."

"Right," he said, snapping his fingers. "Not just a noun, though. Like *the* weaver?"

"Yes, a professional," I said, nodding.

He smiled and stepped over to the door's control panel and opened the door. Inside stood a large room with eight beds, each enclosed with a glass cover, headboards to the wall.

"Why work this time and not before?" he asked.

I shrugged and moved inside. A screen stood above each bed, built into a mount with several retracted articulated arms splayed out on each side. Lights hung down over the enclosures.

I only barely noticed all of that. Along the opposite wall sat a ninth bed. Just visible through the glass cover lay a skeleton, a knife stabbed through its fleshless ribs.

CHAPTER 41

SHADOWS

"The enclosure remained intact?" I asked, holding up a hand to stop Micaela.

"Yes."

"So, someone left the knife." I pointed at my side. "Through here? Or more to the front?"

She pointed her left hand, index finger in, against her left breast.

"Right between the ribs. Through the heart."

"The amount of force and precision necessary for that," I said, looking at my hand. "So, they either knew what they were doing or got lucky."

"And no damage to the bones," she said. "That was all we could tell. We saw nothing to show if the victim was a patient or medical personnel. My guess is the murderer studied physiology. Either way, it's moot now."

"Begs the question: What happened and when?" I asked, to which Micaela shrugged.

"I don't know. We discussed it then and suspected the person was an Ancient. Obviously, he or she was not alone."

"Did you find others?" I asked. "Not just murder victims. Anyone else?"

"Many more."

A new sense of urgency gripped us as we left and returned to the elevators on our way to the citadel's central structure. The lift, lacking windows and allowing light in from above, moved at high speed, depositing us after maybe twelve heartbeats. We exited and faced a low wall surrounding a gap to the space below, with a wall of glass extended up from it to the ceiling.

"It's brighter inside the gaps," Quentin said, pointing up.

"Natural light?" I asked.

"I can't make it out. You?"

"It is not important," Suyef said as he circled the pillar.

We followed him to find another hallway leading out of the tower on the opposite side. As we headed to the exit, I turned down a cross passage.

"Let's look inside a living space."

"How many people do you think this place could hold?" Quentin asked as we approached a door.

"The world, once heavily populated, built citadels to match their numbers," Suyef said. "So the legends say. But they also hint that the world couldn't handle the number of people."

"So, the only answer was to break it apart?"

The Nomad pointed at the door, eyes never leaving Quentin.

"They thought it was."

The skeleton came to mind. If those capable of building such wondrous places could give in to such violence, destroying the world to fix a population problem didn't seem so far-fetched. It sent a chill down my back.

Quentin opened the door and moved inside. Inside stood a large living space, sitting area on the left with a small lavatory beyond, a dining table to the right, and a food prep station opposite the door. Quentin stepped toward a hallway just beyond the table. One door opened immediately to our right to reveal a larger lavatory. The other three doors, two on the left, led to bedrooms.

"There's an enclosed bed in here."

I followed Quentin into one room, pausing in the entryway. The room possessed little furniture, with a single light hung above and a piece of abstract art to the left. Quentin stared at a desiccated body inside the glass case.

"What happened here?" Quentin whispered.

"Let's go find out."

We went through the three inner rings, each tower exactly like the first: massive dwelling spaces surrounding a variety of public parks and venues. We entered the next ring near the upper levels of that tower, continuing on.

In the last ring, we found a market of sorts, with rows of freestanding walls forming the spokes of a wheel around the pillar. Many reforge stations—circular depressions with control panels to one side—stood in the walls. Quentin tapped at one screen, then shook his head.

"Not functioning," he said, pointing at a sign above the station. "Textile station."

"This entire row is," I said.

"Many are," Suyef called from several rows away.

"Why different stations for specific items?" I asked. "Reforgers can make everything."

"Maybe they didn't enjoy having clothing made next to someone getting some *fresh* keemcha," Quentin suggested.

"Yeah, that stuff has a strong odor," I said, moving to the elevator.

"Letting something ferment that much before serving it is bonkers," Quentin said, grimacing. "Even worse. They fermented it. Voluntarily."

I chuckled, and Quentin grinned. Suyef joined us as we entered the lift. At the top, we exited the tower, stopping outside the doors to stare at the heart of the citadel.

"Is it just me," I asked, "or does this gap feel bigger than the others?"

Suyef grunted, and Quentin remained silent as we walked on. As we neared the other side, I saw Suyef looking back.

"What is it?"

He didn't answer at first. We kept moving, the Nomad walking backward. After several moments, he shook his head. "Something is not right."

"We're standing in the most famous citadel in our recorded history, and all we've seen are dead people, one apparently murdered," Quentin retorted. "What *doesn't* feel off?"

Suyef glared at him. "This is different," he said. "And familiar. Like an itch you already scratched."

"An itch is just annoying," I said, looking back. "This sounds worse."

He nodded. "Much worse."

"What did he mean?"

Micaela frowned.

"You interrupt me to ask that?"

"There's no telling when I'll get an explanation." I leveled a finger at her. "You're like an author, being cryptic. Dropping bits of melodrama here and there, dragging things out for tension, keeping me hanging on your every word." The side of her mouth twitched, but I went on. "I usually avoid books or holos that do that."

"You don't strike me as a holo consumer," she said, head tipping to the right. "A reader, yes. But holos don't seem like your thing."

"I've seen a few," I said, shrugging. "Although it's been a while. And you're changing the subject."

"No, I'm talking. Doesn't that count when getting to know your subject?"

"We are trying to solve a mystery," I said, holding up a page.

Micaela sighed quickly through her nose, looking away.

"So, what was Suyef worried about?"

She remained still for a moment, then looked at me. "Shadows."

Quentin forged ahead as we continued, Suyef still watching behind us. We made no more stops, didn't alter our course. The simple Ancient design gave us a straight path to follow: a direct line from our ship to the center. Even in one of the four towers forming the central cluster's outer ring, which employed a different layout, we still didn't turn or change directions, just walked in a straight line.

A shorter hallway, about five meters, stood inside the double doors. No passages crossed it, no art adorned the walls, and no doors opened onto it save those across from us. Beyond those, the tower proved almost entirely hollow.

We stood on a balcony that ringed the open space. To either side, we saw doors that opened onto the balcony. Wide rectangular windows separated these. On the far side, we saw matching balconies, doors, and windows at every level.

"Look at the size of those gaps," Quentin said, pointing down.

Twenty levels down stood a platform of sorts. Gaps shaped like pie slices cut through it, leaving very little surface space to use.

"Four bridges crossing in the middle," Suyef said, pointing to the far side as he looked behind us. "Keep moving. It's quite a walk to that exit."

His discomfort remained hard to ignore. His instincts had served him well his entire life. Knowing this, I felt very uneasy by the time we entered the short hallway leading to the doors opening onto the bridge and the inner tower. As we stepped outside, Suyef paused in the doorway.

"Something is there," he whispered. "Just out of sight."

The core light cast long shadows that reached down the hall where the balcony doors remained open. Suyef moved closer, eyes never leaving the hall.

"Why didn't those close?" I asked, to which he shook his head. "Something in our shadows?"

He shrugged. "Something is there."

"Are you guys coming?" Quentin asked, his voice quiet in the howling wind.

I looked at him, partway across the bridge, and our destination beyond.

"Maybe our benefactor is watching," I said. "Using the panels."

"No, the air is moving," Suyef said, waving a hand at the bridge. "Before we came out here, I felt it."

"*You* can feel that. Not us."

Suyef frowned and moved toward Quentin. "It's a skill anyone with patience can learn."

"Maybe later," I said, following him.

Halfway across this bridge, the straight lines of Ancient form ended in a convoluted tumble of metal that burst out from around the far doors. The metal flowed into an overhang that swept down to the bridge's sides, breaking into tendrils that twisted around each other until they merged with the half-walls. A mix of black-and-white tiles mirrored the tendrils, covering the edges of the surface out to the middle. A single path made from Ancient metal led to the doors.

We walked on, feeling as out of place as the convoluted bridge. When we reached the doors, Quentin tapped on the access panel, but they didn't move. He leaned closer to look.

"Locked, maybe," he muttered.

"Does it have a full interface?" I asked, joining him.

"No, just the door control mechanism." He pointed at the bottom of the screen. "That's a shell program for maintenance, I think."

"Maybe if you—"

The screen flashed orange, then changed to green, and the doors slid open.

"Keyed to your voice," Quentin said. "Somebody really is eager to meet you."

"Yes," I said, watching the doors as I straightened. "I noticed."

Suyef motioned us through the door, still looking behind us. He shrugged at my glance.

"We are not alone," he whispered.

"Obviously," I said. "In more ways than one." At his quizzical look, I added, "The dead people. Celandine, potentially." I waved my hand around. "Whatever else you're sensing, as well."

"I don't like this."

"None of us do, Suyef."

"No, something more," he said, looking across the bridge. "Something about the people."

"Because they're dead?" I asked.

"No," he said, shaking his head. "And yes."

"Conflicted, are we?" Quentin asked.

"Very much so."

"Coming here is unsettling. Being this close to that." He pointed at the core and then looked over at the tower. "Being here."

"This is a trap," Suyef said. "Why else let us come here?"

"To help us?" I asked.

"Maybe. But this place. It's dangerous. The Greens would not have hidden it if it weren't."

"The Ancients hid this place because it was dangerous."

"The odds of successfully keeping a secret are inversely proportionate to the number of people who know it," Suyef muttered. "So, why let us find it?"

"You think the Greens let us come here?" Quentin asked.

"Maybe not the Greens," the Nomad said.

"Someone else," I said. "Someone that looks like me."

Suyef nodded.

"But whose side is she on?"

"You're assuming she's on a side," Quentin pointed out. "She may not have a speeder in this race."

"If so, then someone else led us here," I said. "Maybe she's just another pawn."

"Colvinra?" Quentin suggested. "Or the Reds?"

"I think we'll find out soon," Suyef said, starting toward the doors. "And none of us will like it."

Quentin and I exchanged glances.

"Didn't you just say that?" he asked, smiling.

I frowned, shook my head, and followed Suyef into the tower. The hall ended at an intersection, two halls curving out

of sight to each side. A metal sign with etched column structures lay embedded in the wall before us.

"That's a list of jobs with"—I paused, tracing the columns—"locations. Offices or workspaces, I'd guess."

"Which way?" Quentin asked.

Suyef moved off to the right, and Quentin followed. I
remained staring at one column.

"Look at this one here," I said, waving them back.

Quentin came back as Suyef stopped just where the hall
bent out of sight to look at something on the wall.

"What do you make of it?"

Quentin's blue eyes climbed up the structure. "Central
engineers?"

"Maybe core engineers?" I offered.

"Core," Suyef called, waving us to join him.

The Nomad stood facing a hallway leading to a pair of
glass doors. Beyond, we could see another platform and a beam
crossing another open space. Over the door lay a single column, carved perpendicular to the ceiling.

"'Core,'" Quentin read aloud. "Odd."

We paused a few paces from the doors. The open space
beyond made the other interior spaces we'd seen seem small. I
could just make out the far side of the tower.

"This entire structure is hollow," Quentin said.

"Just like the Sunken Citadel," I said, nodding.

Quentin stepped toward the glass. "Was it as large as this?"

"Not by half."

"What would need this kind of space?" he asked.

"Time to find out," I said.

The doors slid open, and we stepped out onto the platform. A long whistle escaped Quentin's lips as Suyef joined us.

We stood about a third of the way up the superstructure.
Platforms set at evenly spaced intervals along the interior broke

up the smooth surface. At multiple points, bridges formed an X across the middle of the tower. Most platforms lacked bridges, including the one we stood on. Around the bridges lay an intricate web of cylindrical beams, each extending out from small, disc-shaped objects on the wall, the edges of which overlapped each beam. These pointed like fingers to the exact center of the superstructure.

At the focal point of those fingers floated a giant ring of Ancient metal, precisely the same width as each of the beams, with smooth, rounded edges and a series of intricate symbols carved along every visible section.

"That looks like a travel ring like we used," I said. "Right, Suyef?"

"That's not a travel ring. It's a reforger." He looked at me. "*The* reforger."

My skin tingled as I looked back up at the ring, at the device that legend told us had ripped the world apart.

"The heart of the network," Quentin whispered. "Third Gate."

CHAPTER 42

LOCK

"So, you've actually seen the legendary device," I said, drawing Micaela's eyes and her frown.

"You find that odd, Logwyn?"

"I've never met someone who has seen it," I said. "What better way to protect something than hide its existence, even from those protecting it?"

"It's moot now, considering how the Intershell War ended."

"That war changed a lot of things, but not access to For'a Dal."

"Yes. We revealed its location. And that something controlled it." She chuckled. "At least something did when we left."

"What do you mean?"

Her shoulders barely lifted in a shrug.

"That place remained locked down, still operating the network and all that. Beyond that, it couldn't take control of the other citadels, because something blocked it from doing so."

"And you three changed that? Unlocking it, I mean."

"No," she said, face twisting in a grimace. "Only one of us made that choice."

"Quentin?"

"He wouldn't listen to reason." She took in a long breath and let it out. "To me." She stared at the window for a moment. "His blasted curiosity always got the better of him."

"Wouldn't he listen to Suyef?"

Micaela's entire frame sagged at the name, head listing to one side, eyes closed.

"No, he wouldn't listen to him, either." A tear slipped down her cheek. "*Couldn't*, I mean."

"What does that mean?"

"Suyef was gone," she said, her eyes still closed.

"Where?" I asked, watching her.

"Gahana."

I froze at the word. Her eyes opened and locked with mine.

"The After."

We ascended the tower using randomly placed elevators, returning to the central space to check our progress. This slowed our pace, heightening Suyef's uneasiness.

On one return to the central shaft, we looked down at the control device. I saw something shift on a platform below.

"Something moved," I whispered, pointing.

My companions leaned over the edge.

"I see nothing," Quentin muttered, craning his neck.

"In the shadows of those beams," I said. "Two platforms down, opposite side."

"I saw it before but not clearly." Suyef moved away from the railing, Quentin following. "We should hurry."

"It's the shadow assassins again," I said, moving alongside Quentin.

"Maybe the same bunch, maybe not. Either way, it's bad."

A shiver ran up my spine, and I looked back. "If assassins are following us, do you think that monster that attacked us in the prison is, too?"

"Maybe," Quentin said. "If it is, we're ready this time."

I wondered if a shield construct would stop a shadow assassin or the strange bolts they shot, that monster that attacked me.

"Suyef."

The Nomad looked at Quentin, eyebrow raised.

"I'm using fire this time."

"That secret turned to wind," Suyef said. "No sense trying to catch it."

"Fire?" I asked.

"You'll see," he said, a slight grin on his face.

We continued, Quentin taking the lead, Suyef keeping a wary eye behind. We approached any shadow with caution, but they remained still. *Had it been a trick of light?* When I mentioned that to Suyef, he shook his head.

"They are there."

In the upper levels, the hallways no longer opened onto the central space. The halls remained well-lit, preventing our suspected tail from approaching. Despite this, the normally stoic Nomad's unease fed a sense of trepidation in my stomach.

We exited another elevator at its highest level and found a massive room similar to Mortac's prison office. A large window formed the far wall, revealing a magnificent view.

"Whoa," Quentin whispered.

A spectacular view of the citadel lay before us. Beyond the citadel's edge, the sea of light shifted and swirled in a dizzying dance. Closing my eyes, I turned away and took a deep breath.

"You all right?" Quentin asked.

"Dizzy," I said and nodded. "Oh! Nope. Can't do that."

I placed a hand to my head, the other against the window to steady myself.

"Yeah," he said, the sound of his voice quiet.

When I opened my eyes, my companions stood nearby, watching me. I nodded and looked around.

"An observation deck, maybe?" Quentin called back. "The glass continues all the way around."

"This could be that overhang we saw," I pointed out.

"Likely," Suyef said, looking at the ceiling. "How do we get up from here?"

"Check this out."

We joined Quentin as he approached the pillar directly opposite the elevator.

"Along here," he said, pointing up.

The wall—as smooth, pristine, and gray as the rest—contained a unique feature. A faint line started near the ceiling and swept down to the right and left, forming a large circle that almost touched the floor. Another line split the middle from top to bottom. At the center, cut into the indestructible metal, lay an intricate etching.

"Do you recognize that?" I asked, pointing at the circular image. "It looks like something my mother showed me once."

"It's an old piece that dates back to the Nomads' ancient history." He pointed at the center. "The core. The water shield"— he traced the outer edge—"and the shells in between."

I looked closer at the shells.

"Those look like someone pushed a brush down on an art padd and dragged it to the side."

"My settlement's government building had something like this," Quentin said. "No one really talked about it, though." He waved a hand at the etching, then pointed at the center. "Since this thing looks like a door, that being here can't be a coincidence."

"I'll bite," I said, nodding at the image. "A lock?"

"I don't know." Quentin shrugged. "We've seen stranger things."

"This is the key, if there is one," Suyef said.

His hand moved along the etching's outer edge. Quentin tapped a finger on one shell, head tilted a bit, eyes darting back and forth.

"Something is off," he said. "It's not right. The image is wrong."

"A different version?" I glanced at Suyef. "An homage to the original?"

He nodded.

"I know different versions exist."

"Yes, but most are at least obviously different," Quentin said. "Different mediums, different ways of depicting the world." He moved his hand over the etching. "But this one is almost identical to the one I saw. Same etched metal work and everything."

Quentin fell silent, eyes closed. He brushed his fingertips over the etching.

"It's the shells," he said, eyes opening. "They're in the wrong place."

"Where should they be?" I asked.

He pointed at one down along the outer right edge and slid his finger in an arc up to the top.

"This one should be here."

He waved at another shell on the lower right side.

"This one should be—"

"There," Suyef interjected, nodding at the bottom.

"Look at those two," I said. "That pairing feels off."

"That one," Quentin said, pointing at the one closer to the center.

"Yes, it should be farther up here near that upper left quadrant."

We stepped back, staring at the etching.

"Anything else different?" I asked.

"That small one just next to the center piece sloping down to the left," Suyef said. "It's a trail piece that should be bottom center."

"Here."

I pointed just below the bottom edge of the core piece. Then I reached toward a larger piece along the same circuit.

"That's in the right place."

At my touch, the piece turned white, followed by the other shell pieces.

"A cypher lock using the image," Quentin said. "I've never seen one using this piece."

"So, we move the pieces," I said. "To where we think they should be."

Quentin pushed the small trail piece.

"It won't move."

"Trace it," I suggested.

He traced a line with his finger down to where the piece belonged. The image blurred and slid with his finger. Quentin jolted, his finger jumping past the correct spot. The piece flashed and fell into place.

"Fascinating," he whispered, examining the new piece.

"Do the rest," I said, tapping his shoulder.

As he reached for the next symbol, the sound of a machine echoed throughout the chamber. The bright light faded, drawing our gaze to the window where large blinds slid down.

"What did you do?" Suyef hissed, whipping his staff out and igniting it.

"Nothing," Quentin said. "You were watching."

"This feels like a security measure," I said, cutting them off. Suyef pointed at the lock.

"Let her finish."

Symbols shimmered around Quentin's hands just before balls of fire ignited in the air over his palms. He flung his hands down, and the fiery balls dropped to dangle, more symbols shimmering in the air between his hands and the fire. With a whip of his arms, he sent them into a forward rotating spin around his hands. He stepped sideways and stalled the rotation to bring the fireballs into a counter-directional spin opposite their initial orbits. The light they cast shifted and flickered, joining Suyef's staff in keeping the shadows at bay.

"That's impressive," I said, moving toward the lock.

Suyef's staff spun into a blur, and a dance of flickering light surrounded us. My shadow loomed large when I neared the lock.

"Step to my side," I called.

They obliged, backs to me as they moved. Quentin stalled the fireball behind him, left hand reaching over his shoulder to let it hang there. This gave me a steady bright light. He spun the other in a larger clockwise rotation.

"Definitely an improvement from your last encounter with fire," I said.

He chuckled, head not turning.

"I wasn't trying to impress you."

"Are you now?"

He shook his head.

"Far from it."

"The lock?" Suyef asked.

Just as I looked at the Nomad, the shadows beyond the edge of their flames surged forward.

"So, he spun the fire?"

Micaela nodded, holding an arm down off the side of the couch and rotating it in a circular motion.

"And they just floated there?"

"Sort of. He tied them to his hands using a very thin thread of scripting. That way, he could spin them without the limitations of a physical chain or rope."

"Fascinating," I said. "I've seen similar performers. And he used these as a weapon?"

"Said it was based on a weapon that predated the Ancient era. Don't recall the name."

"I'll ask him if he lets me."

"Has he been avoiding you?" she asked.

"I think he enjoys making things difficult." I shrugged and set my stylus down. "Suyef thinks I'm getting through to him, but I doubt that sometimes." I held two fingers close to each other and looked at her between them. "One moment, I'm this close to getting through. The next, he's gone, and I'm left wondering what set him off."

Micaela stared at the nearby photographs.

"It's frustrating, but give him a chance," she said, her voice soft. "Something broke, right here"—she tapped her head, then her heart—"and here."

"Like you?"

I regretted the words as they left my mouth. A deep furrow split into her forehead and her eyes widened, nostrils flaring.

"I've given him more chances than anyone else." She pointed at my notes. "Like all this."

She looked away, breath hissing through her nose, jaw clenched tight. I tried to find some words of apology, hand fidgeting with the stylus I couldn't recall picking back up.

"I'm sorry, Logwyn," she whispered. "That was unfair."

"Those were harsh words, High One. I owe you the apology."

"You did not mean to be harsh. You're doing your job. But what I said was true." She pointed at the photographs. "I've given Quentin so many chances but nothing ever changes."

She closed her eyes, taking a long breath in and holding it for a second.

"I'm tired of being hurt," she said after letting the breath out.

"Are you done giving him chances?"

She looked at me through narrowed eyes for several seconds before looking away.

"That remains to be seen. Part of me says no, I'm not done. Another part just wants this to be over."

"It sounds like you and Quentin are bad for each other," I said, looking at my notes. "Contrary to what Suyef said."

"What was that?"

I flipped through the pages, scanning for the words.

"Something like you two are an unstoppable force." I tapped the paper. "Here it is. Alone you're powerful, but together something the world has never seen before."

I looked up at her. "Paraphrased. Still, high praise."

"That man," she said, smiling. "I'm not sure what we did to earn his loyalty. Despite everything that has always remained."

Her hands began fidgeting, something she had yet to do during our interviews.

"Even when I thought it was gone forever."

"You mean him going to the After?" I asked, frowning.

"Before we get into that," she said, "there's something else I wanted to say about Quentin and what you asked me before."

"About you giving up on him?"

"I'm not giving up." Micaela held up a finger. "But you must understand, this problem with Quentin goes back a very long time." Her eyebrows rose and fell. "In terms of our friendship, he's made a lot more withdrawals than he has deposits. A person can only give so much."

"But if something truly broke inside him," I started, but she raised her hand.

"Sometimes, people don't want to be fixed. Or they aren't ready."

"So, we stop trying?"

Her jaw clenched as she looked back at me.

"I'm not quitting. Just . . ." She trailed off.

"Reassessing?" I asked. "Taking a fresh approach?"

"Maybe." Micaela shrugged. "Or just accepting this is the new norm."

She fell silent, eyes returning to the window. I scanned my notes, marking things to revisit later.

"When you're ready, what did you mean about Suyef?"

Micaela shrugged.

"It's not that cryptic. He is extremely loyal. To Quentin." She looked at the photographs. "To me. To us both."

"You implied that loyalty was all you had at one point," I said.

"At one point, it was all I had left."

"Why?"

"Because I didn't see him again for a long time after leaving that citadel." Her chest rose and fell. "So long I'd almost forgotten what it was like to have him around. And I missed it. As did Quentin."

"You left there separately?"

She held up a hand.

"How about I get back to the narrative and let you put it together?"

"By all means," I said, nodding.

She looked down at her hands, fidgeting again.

"Suyef died."

CHAPTER 43

CHOICES

When the shadow assassins attacked, Quentin and Suyef surged back and forth, fire spinning in a blur as I traced the markings to their proper location. As I reached for one shell, Quentin crashed into me, shoving me up against the wall and blocking my vision. The sound of fire whipping through the air filled my ears, and Quentin's body shifted. The next instant, something detonated with a sickening pop.

"Sorry," he hissed, moving away.

Suyef dispatched another assassin as I regained my footing. Dredging the image from deep in my memory, I resumed work, urged onward by my companions' grunts and the disturbing sounds of shadow beings dying. I looked over halfway through the sequence and froze.

Along the edge of the flickering light, the shadows boiled like water at maximum heat. Acting on instinct, I spun around and prepared a shield.

"Get close!" I yelled, tracing the air to help visualize the symbols.

Quentin turned, spinning a fireball behind him to dispatch an assassin. Another shadow materialized directly over him. I flung the half-completed construct up, and as the partial shield formed, something struck me from behind. I heard Quentin scream as I hit the ground near the wall. My vision blurred, but I just made out Quentin as he flung a fireball beyond me. Another pop filled the air.

Turning to see what had hit me, I froze, everything around me falling away from my senses.

Suyef lay crumpled up against me, a black shaft jutting out of his chest.

Suyef sat at the table, eyes closed, arms folded across his chest. Quentin's head lay on the table, and I heard a soft snore

"Welcome back," Suyef said, eyes still closed.

"Is he agreeable today?"

The Nomad shook his head. I sat down across from him.

"The shadow assassins. That must have hurt."

He nodded, opening his eyes and pointing at his chest along the left collarbone.

"It came out here," he said, then pointed over that shoulder. "Struck here first."

"That sounds excruciating."

"Actually, after a burst of pain, all feeling just drained from me. Warmth, fatigue, pain. Everything."

"Did it leave a scar?" I asked, glancing at his chest.

He looked at Quentin for a moment, eyes narrowing, body shifting.

"There should be one. You're going to have to ask Micaela and him. I can't tell you about things I didn't witness."

Quentin remained with his head still down. Then, just as a new thought came to my mind, he cut in.

"Hard to do anything," Quentin said, head still down, "when you're dead."

The shadows boiled up as fast as Suyef and I dispatched them. We fought a staying action, holding them off so Micaela could open the door. I focused on those that came too close. Having two balls of fire hanging from your hands is an effective deterrent for most creatures.

The shadows, very adept at dodging, persisted. One even knocked my fireball back at me, forcing me to use the belt to dodge the attack. I misjudged the amount of force needed and crashed into Micaela. She fell to the ground, me almost sitting on her as I tumbled back against the wall.

"Sorry!" I called, lunging forward and striking the assassin.

If she responded, I never heard it. As the assassin died, a string of shadows lunged out. The fireballs I created dimmed, so I fed power into them. They flared, streaking through the air as they spun in unison, one in front and the other behind me. The shadows to my right fell back, but one tried to slip past on my left. I stalled the spin in front of me and turned to the left, reversing the rotation by yanking the left fireball up over my head and down behind me while spinning the right ball over to the front. The assailant, focused on Micaela, never saw the streaks of fire as they went down its front and back. The shadow vanished with a resounding pop.

My momentum brought me around to face Micaela. She yelled something, but I didn't hear it. Beyond her and above, a shadow coalesced from the corner of the ceiling. Suyef spun and lunged toward her. Then everything slowed.

The shadow plunged toward Micaela as Suyef brought his staff up. Micaela lifted her hands toward me, her lips moving. The shadows beyond Suyef lunged forward to attack his exposed back.

I tightened the spin on my right hand to throw the fireball. Suyef leaped forward, crashing into Micaela just as the shadow struck, driving its dark blade into my friend.

Something hit me from behind, knocking me into a tumble. I rolled upright and spun to see an assassin melting into the telltale shimmer of a shield where I had just stood. Nearby, Micaela clutched at Suyef's head.

"Suyef!" She shook him. "Suyef!"

The boiling shadows threatened to swallow us, so I did the only thing I could think of: light the floor on fire. Spinning in place from right to left, I laid down a trail of fire in a semicircle. I fed the flames more power, and the fiery wall flared and blinded me as I turned away. Fighting a wave of dizziness, I focused on the etched image. On the unfinished symbols, the unopened lock. Now our only escape.

Stumbling, I leaned over my friends and traced the last few symbols to their correct places. The entire image flared white, a sliver of light running down along the middle line. The glowing section detached inward, then split and slid to either side, allowing bright light to pour out. I lifted Suyef's prone form with my belt, easing him into what I hoped was an empty room. Micaela followed, the doors sliding shut the moment we cleared the threshold. The sounds of flickering fire and hissing shadows vanished, leaving us in silence.

I set Suyef down, and Micaela wrapped her arms around his torso and supported him.

"Suyef, can you hear me?"

My friend gasped for air as the dark blade evaporated, leaving a smoking hole surrounded by black dead flesh in his chest.

Black flesh that expanded with each of Suyef's desperate gasps. He became hoarse, one hand clutching Micaela's arm, the other reaching up toward me. I grasped his hand, marveling at the strength in his grip.

"Don't . . ." He coughed. "Don't . . . let her give up."

I frowned, but nodded.

"Suyef, just hold on," Micaela said, voice trembling. "Save your strength."

He shook his head and clutched her hand tighter. "Don't give up. Ever." He squeezed my hand. "Don't let her."

Words failed me, so I gripped his hand instead.

"Please don't leave," Micaela whispered. "Please."

Suyef coughed, a tremendous thing that shook his whole body. His mouth opened, struggling to speak. "I . . . f-fee-feel . . . fee-feel . . . no-no-noth . . ."

He never finished, the last word fading with one last gasp.

"Nothing," I said for him, wishing I could say the same.

I stared at Suyef.

"Then what?"

He shook his head.

"Clearly, you didn't die," I said.

"Oh, I was gone," he said, voice quiet. "I remember seeing the two of them looking down at me. Then blackness gripped me like a very heavy sleep taking hold. I struggled, trying not to fall in, but could not hold it back."

"You resuscitated him," I said, looking at Quentin.

"Nope. I couldn't even heal that injury now, let alone then," he said, making a hole with his hand. "It kept growing, even after he . . ." His voice trailed off, and his hand dropped. He shook his head and sagged back in the chair.

"It kept growing, smoking," he said, voice shaky. "I might not have seen it without that smoke."

I looked at the Nomad, his eyes on me. I wondered what kind of scar remained on his torso. On him. Instead, I pointed at him.

"So, how are you here?"

Quentin fell forward on the table, burying his face in his arms. Suyef nodded at him.

"He did something stupid. Again."

Despite the seriousness of the wound, I still tried. He was my best friend, one of the few I ever had. I leaned down and held my hand near the black wound on his chest. A searing cold shot through my arm, pain exploding in every joint up to my shoulder.

"What is it?" Micaela asked, grabbing at my hand.

"This wound. It's so different," I said, staring at it. "Cold. I felt it up through my arm."

"The weapon felt like ice against my shoulder."

She held her hand near the wound on Suyef's back, where the shadow assassin's blade had entered, but she jerked back the instant the cold hit her.

"Ow," she moaned, shaking her arm. "It's the same on his back."

"It's festering. The weapon must leave traces behind, probably on purpose. If we can't stop it . . ." My voice trailed off as

I looked at her. She stared at the wound, a frown twisting her features.

"Neither of you can stop that wound or save his life," a voice said from behind me.

I spun to face a figure, a woman. If I hadn't been sitting next to Micaela, I might have mistaken the woman for my friend. She stood the same height and build as Micaela, her skin an identical tone, her face bearing the same structure. Her hair, a matching red, mirrored my friend's. She stood there, looking down at Suyef.

"Where did you come from?" I asked.

The woman's eyes—almost the same color—lingered on the Nomad a moment, then looked at me. Micaela continued to examine Suyef's wound as if no one else was there. The woman chuckled, an eerie echo of Micaela's laugh.

"She can't see me," the woman said. "Or hear me. She won't even notice you talking to me. You aren't, really."

"Excuse me?"

"I'm not here." She looked around the room. "Well, not physically here. I am present."

"A projection? A hologram?"

"More like a figment of your imagination," she said, smiling.

"Are you seeing this?" I asked Micaela.

She didn't move, nor seem to breathe. Beyond her face, the smoke from Suyef's wound hung suspended in the air.

"What did you do to them?" I asked, waving a hand in front of my friend's face. "And who are you?"

She chuckled. "You know the answer to that last question, I think."

"We saw you in the viewscreen." I pointed at Micaela. "We thought it was her."

Her head bowed. "Maybe I won't have to explain everything."

"Would you?" I asked, then held up a hand. "No. Can you help him?"

"No," she said, looking at my fallen friend. "I can't."

"Can't or won't?"

"I would gladly do it if I could," she said, shrugging. "Right now, other things bind my hands."

I glanced at her hands, and she smiled at me, wiggling her fingers.

"Not physically."

I frowned but said nothing.

"Let's just say something locked my ability to help."

"Is it this room?" I asked, pointing at the door. "My fireballs extinguished the instant we crossed." I paused, staring at her. "Are you a prisoner? Is that why someone locked this room?"

"This room is not a cell." Her head tilted to one side. "Nor am I imprisoned here."

"Trapped?" I asked, and she nodded. "So, let's leave this room."

"The door locked when it closed." She tapped her forehead. "And this room is not the prison I am locked in."

I looked down at my fallen companion.

"You can't help him because you're in my head? Some manifestation of my inability to save him?"

She chuckled, shaking her head. "Oh, a very insightful thought. But no. We talk at a subconscious level."

"The pain is gone," I said, holding up my hand.

"Yes, from the cold."

"So, you were listening."

"In this place," she said, head dipping forward, "I see and hear everything."

"Just in this room?"

"No."

"That's not creepy at all," I said, flexing my fingers. "Weird. My entire arm hurt. Now nothing."

"You simply aren't noticing it right this second." She tapped her head. "At this level of consciousness."

"Is time passing here?"

"Why would it?"

I shrugged.

"Dreams take time. Maybe not as much, but still."

"If it helps you conceptualize it, think of this as your dreams near the end of a REM cycle."

"So, a dream," I said, looking down at my companions. "Which is why they seem frozen." I nodded at her. "Neat trick."

"You'll find time is a very liquid and malleable substance where I am concerned."

"And who exactly are you?" I asked. "Beyond Micaela's *benefactor*."

She arched an eyebrow at me.

"Stop it," I hissed.

"Excuse me?"

"The thing with the eyebrow." I waved at her face. "Stop doing stuff like that."

"Why?"

"Because it's freaky enough how much you look like her," I said, pointing at Micaela. "When you do things like that, it's really weird."

I looked around the room.

"More weird."

"I can't help the similarities she and I share."

"Wait, your choice of appearance wasn't intentional?"

"This is what I look like," she said, glaring at me as she pointed at Micaela. "Trust me when I say our physical similarity has caused me an immeasurable amount of grief and annoyance."

"But this is my subconscious. So, did I make you look like her?" I shook my head. "No, you looked like her before. But that could have influenced my mind. Us talking about you influenced my subconscious mind."

"And I thought you had this figured out. I am not her, nor a random creation of your imagination." She held a hand to her chest. "This is what I actually look like."

Her hand fell to her side. She took in a deep breath and let it out slowly.

"Well," she whispered, "how I once looked."

"Are you dead?"

"No." She shook her head. "In one sense of the word, I am very much alive."

"Are you or aren't you alive?"

"Yes, and no."

I frowned. "You can't be both."

"Philosophers have debated that topic for centuries," she said, smiling slightly. "So many centuries."

She fell silent, eyes moving to my friends.

"I think we started off on the wrong foot," I said. "We skipped introductions. My name is—"

"Quentin," she whispered. "Suyef. Micaela." She pointed at each of us as she said our names.

"Right. And what's yours?"

"Unimportant."

"Hardly," I countered.

She shook her head. "It's better if you don't know it for now."

"Celandine," I guessed.

Her mouth snapped shut, and she glared at me.

"So, you're the one who helped her father." When she looked at Micaela, I continued. "And you've been helping her. The question is *why*."

"Why what?"

"Why help her family? Help her?"

"You assume I'm only helping her?"

She moved to the room's center.

"Oh, I'm sure you'll benefit, too," I said. "But you avoided my question."

"No, I didn't answer it."

She folded her hands in front of her torso and smiled.

"It's the same thing."

"Slight difference in interpretation."

I took a deep breath and let it out.

"Why are you helping her?"

Celandine looked at Micaela, as still as my companions. Then she took a deep breath.

"Because she's going to need my help soon. And she won't just accept it from a stranger." She pointed at Suyef. "Especially after this."

I glanced at the pair.

"She may not agree that what you have been doing was help."

"She won't," Celandine said. "But someday she will. And when that happens, she and you and everyone else will be glad I did."

"You get points for being cryptic."

"I know things you do not," she said, glaring at me. "And I have good reasons to not share what I know. That does not mean I'm being cryptic."

"Maybe not to you. But it does for the 'less-informed' to paraphrase you."

"I'm sorry." She dipped her head. "I didn't mean to act like that."

"But you did."

"Maybe a little," she said, nodding. "I get little interaction with people."

"According to her father," I said, pointing at Micaela, "that's not true."

"I'd hardly call that interaction."

"It's something."

"Granted."

She fell silent. I nodded at Micaela.

"So, why her?"

"To call it a choice is to give me too much credit," she said. "Let's just say forces beyond my control have forced me to ally myself with her." She shrugged, a slight motion, then favored me with a smile. "That's something you understand, right? Circumstances leading you to help her?"

"I'm a helping person by nature," I said.

"It's more than that, and you know it."

"We're not discussing me."

"You three are precisely why I am here," she said, waving at all of us. "Such rough times you've been through. People usually try to avoid difficulty, challenges."

I chuckled, nodding. She smiled, eyes on my friends.

"I see you agree. But it's necessary for growth. For friendship." She looked at me. "For love."

The skin in my armpits itched, and I looked back at my companions, Micaela clutching Suyef. At his still form.

"This bothers you, doesn't it?" Celandine asked.

"My friend suffering like this?" I glared at her. "Of course it does."

"But which friend?" She pointed at Suyef. "Him because of his wound or her"—her finger moved to Micaela—"because of her pain?"

"Does it matter? Both are hurting."

"And you?"

I looked down at my hands, longing for the skill to save Suyef.

"Yes, and not being able to help makes it worse," Celandine continued. "But are you really out of options?"

I lowered my hands and looked at her. "Why are you messing with my head instead of helping him?" I asked.

She held up her hands, brows furrowed.

"I am bound. You are not." She pointed at my friends. "The question is both simple and difficult: Who will you help?"

I looked at my friends, then back at her.

"What kind of question is that?"

"Not between the two of them," she said, stepping closer to me, eyes cast down at the pair. "Will you help them or yourself?"

Celandine stopped, still looking at my companions.

"Now you're just doing it on purpose."

She looked up at me. "No, you're not thinking clearly. That's why I'm here," she said, pointing at her chest. "To make sure you are."

"Thinking clearly? About what?"

"About your feelings for them. For her."

I frowned at her.

"What do you mean?"

"Look at her."

Celandine leaned toward me when I refused to move. She pointed at Micaela.

"Please."

Gritting my teeth, I looked at my friend. Micaela remained still, one arm around Suyef.

"That hurts, doesn't it?"

I glanced at Celandine, who nodded at the pair.

"To see her like that. Holding him."

"What's your point?"

"Self-awareness is a powerful tool. Especially when facing our own worst enemy."

When she didn't continue, I looked over at her. She pointed at her heart.

"Ourselves."

"I bet you practiced that line," I said, smiling.

"I do not lack time," she said, laughing a bit.

The amusement faded, and we looked back at my friends.

"You're not wrong," I said. "Self-awareness is not a strength."

Celandine laughed. I looked up at her.

"Trust me, I know," she said.

"You're not the first person we've encountered claiming to know us."

"Yes, your other . . . pursuers." Her face darkened. "I am involved in part because of them." She held up a finger. "They are tomorrow's problem. Right now, we're discussing you."

"Why am I so important?" I asked, pointing at Suyef. "He needs help."

"Because you can save him."

She locked gazes with me. I shook my head, holding up my hands.

"My ability to script is amateur, especially in healing."

Her head tilted to one side. "You won't heal him by scripting."

"How then?"

"By choosing."

"Choosing what?"

"Him," she said, pointing at Suyef, "or you."

"Excuse me?"

She repeated herself.

"I don't understand."

She folded her hands across her belly.

"You are facing a unique choice few people get: to affect the outcome of an important event. This could all still go off the shell. But I'm fairly sure everything rests on this decision."

"It sounds to me like my choice doesn't matter."

She dipped her head. "It's not my choice to make. It's yours."

"Why?"

"Reasons," she said, shrugging.

I glanced at my friends.

"My choice has to do with them, doesn't it?" I asked.

She nodded.

"With him specifically."

She didn't move.

"About saving him. But how can I choose to save him if I can't do it?"

"Would you?" she asked.

I frowned.

"Of course I would."

"Would you really?" she asked, nodding at them. "Look again."

I grumbled but looked anyway.

"So what? I see my friends in pain. I would help them if I could."

"Even seeing them as they are now?" she asked, moving up beside me. "Knowing what this could mean?"

"If you mean it looks like the two of them care for each other, I know that already."

"And that doesn't bother you?"

I rounded on her.

"So what if it does?" I asked. "He's my friend. I wouldn't let him die just because I like her. What kind of person do you think I am?"

Celandine watched me for several heartbeats.

"The kind I wish someone else had been long ago," she said, looking at my friends. "One that would choose a different path. A better path."

Silence filled the room as she stood there, staring at Micaela. After a few moments, I broke the silence.

"I'm sorry that happened to you. I really am. But that's done." I pointed at my friend. "He's dying right now."

Celandine stood still a moment longer, then looked up at me.

"He's lucky you are his friend." She sniffed, then wiped at her nose. "Very lucky."

"Why?"

Her eyebrows furrowed, jaw clenched.

"The world would have avoided the Shattering."

CHAPTER 44

HEART

"Wait, she said that?" I interjected.

Quentin's nostrils flared, and he dropped his forehead to the table. He bounced his head a few times, then pointed at me.

"Why are we doing this? She's questioning every little detail."

"Don't be rude to Logwyn," Suyef growled at him. "Answer the question."

"I'm not saying I don't believe you," I went on. "But really? If you had been there, the Shattering might not have happened."

Quentin thumped his head against the table a few more times.

"No, she said if someone *like* me had been there."

"Because you would save a friend despite potential consequences," I said, echoing Celandine's words.

"That." Quentin sat up, pointing at me and nodding. "I think. I didn't have time to ask."

"Why?" I asked.

"Someone sprang the trap."

"You only have one shot at saving him," Celandine continued, moving back to the room's center. "And you will not like the accompanying risk."

"How so?"

"You're going to have to free me."

"What's the catch?"

"Freeing me unlocks this fortress. Anyone could take control of it."

"Including those who would abuse that power," I said, rubbing a hand across my face. "Like Colvinra."

She pointed at Suyef.

"I can't help him unless you do it. If you do it, you risk something that could threaten this entire world."

"Do you know for a fact that will happen?"

She shook her head.

"All I can say is that the lock stopped others from controlling the citadel in the past. What path you choose, and the consequences, is up to you."

I looked at Suyef, at Micaela holding him. I felt that tug, that twist in my gut.

"This is not fair."

"Nothing ever is."

"How do I justify this? Save him, and put the entire world at risk. Or let him die, and she hates me."

I sat down on my foot, arms wrapping around my upright knee, face partially buried in my elbow as I looked at her. I pushed my face down, shutting out the light.

"She will never forgive me either way."

"Maybe," Celandine said. "Maybe you aren't giving her enough credit."

"You clearly think she would make this choice harder, seeing as you excluded her."

"All I can say is it must be your choice."

I blew out a deep breath, then looked up.

"Do it."

She watched me for a moment. "You sound uncertain."

"I don't like either choice, but I won't let my friend die. And, I really don't like that I considered letting him. So, just do it."

Her head tilted to one side.

"You really care for them both?"

"He's my friend."

"But," she said as she pointed at Micaela, "there is something more with her."

"Maybe." I looked at Micaela. "Right now, we're saving his life. We'll tackle the next part when we get to that pipe."

She watched me a moment longer, then nodded. She raised her hands up next to her head.

"So be it."

A massive hiss cut through the silence, followed by a cloud of mist from above. The ceiling separated into pie-shaped sections, each slice pulling out of sight.

"What's happening?" Micaela called out.

I turned to look at her but stumbled. Something tugged at me, pulling me across the room. My vision blurred, and I leaned over on my arm. I was sitting next to Micaela, my head spinning. I blinked and focused on Celandine.

"Can she see you?"

"No, but she can see and hear you." She placed a finger to her lips. "For now, just listen."

She kneeled on Micaela's far side. At that angle, the resemblance was uncanny.

"You will want to tell her about me," Celandine said as the ceiling retracted. "To tell her about this conversation, explain your choice."

She leveled a finger at me. "Do not tell her anything, about any of this."

I frowned and opened my mouth, but she cut me off.

"She will meet me soon. It's best if she knows nothing of me before that happens."

Micaela looked away from the ceiling.

"What's going on, Quentin?" she asked.

Celandine smiled, nodding at her.

"You can't tell her. Actually, you can, but I'm asking you not to."

My eyes darted between the two women, and I settled on the simplest answer. "I don't know."

Micaela looked back up, squinting as bright light filled the room.

"Maybe whoever has been helping us is up there." She clutched at Suyef. "Maybe she can help."

"She?" I asked, looking at Celandine.

"She has to," she went on. "You remember, right? Celandine. She must be here."

I stood up, my gaze never straying from the woman.

"We'll find out soon."

Celandine stood and moved between Micaela and me.

"Trust me," she whispered. "Almost time."

Once the ceiling retracted, a crescent-shaped section of floor lifted us into another hollow shaft. Micaela shielded her eyes as she looked up.

"Can you see anything up there?"

I turned to ask Celandine a question, but the woman had vanished. When I looked at Micaela, her head tipped to one side.

"Are you okay?"

I looked back and forth before shaking my head.

"Thought I heard something," I muttered.

The light brightened as we rose, forcing my gaze down. Micaela, hand shielding her eyes, looked at me when I kneeled next to her. She took her arm from around Suyef and touched my shoulder

"Something is wrong. What is it?"

A torrent of sensations flooded me. A throbbing ache in my jaw, a sharp pain in my head, my heartbeat echoing in my ears. Heat burned in my gut, and my extremities trembled. Emotions, ignored for a time, grappled like Nomads in their tribal competitions, each seeking purchase, pushing against the other, looking for a flaw before all strength gave out. I felt so much, so quickly, felt overwhelmed and swept away like a cloak caught up in the wind.

"Hey."

Something cool touched my face, a welcome counterpoint to my inner turmoil.

"Stay here," Micaela whispered.

I took a deep breath, letting it out slowly. I opened my eyes to see Micaela leaning close, hand held to my face, eyes locked on mine.

"Are you here?" she asked.

I nodded, trying to speak, but my voice caught in my throat. She held my gaze, her eyes pools of color I could get lost in.

"Is this about him?" she asked.

Unsure what else to say, I simply nodded.

"Whatever you're feeling, it's okay to do so," she said. "Just don't get lost."

I nodded again, confused over what I felt. Anger? But what did I have to be angry about? Because my friends were close? Because of the choice I faced? It wasn't their fault.

Still, there it was. A boiling, seething rage tearing at me like that wind. I closed my eyes and leaned into Micaela's hand, taking several long breaths in a row. After the fifth exhale, a slight bump jolted the floor and brought me back.

We kneeled in a large room, a series of touch screen control interfaces standing at waist height along the curved outer wall. Stools sat at each station, a wall of windows above. Outside, the core's bright light reflected off the top of a single tower.

Several paces behind us stood a circular wall of glass that surrounded a large open space. On the far side, I saw a room identical to the one we just entered; to the right and left, two more. Four circles overlapped in the middle by a fifth.

Micaela lay Suyef's limp form down, then stood and moved toward the glass wall. I followed her.

"It's the large open space in the tower," she said. "I can see Third Gate down there."

I turned back to the control panels, noticing one station that looked different.

"What do you make of this?" I asked, moving toward it.

The station, covered by a smooth metal surface, lacked a touch screen. In the exact middle lay a small circular slot with a lever jutting out. I leaned closer to examine the odd interface.

"It looks like wood."

"It looks like that old man's stick," Micaela said. "But what does it do?"

"It's the key."

Celandine's voice echoed in the room, drawing my gaze to the glass wall. Micaela didn't move.

"Pull it out or leave it," Celandine went on. "The choice is yours."

I looked at Suyef, at Celandine. Then I reached for the lever.

"What are you doing?" Micaela hissed, smacking my hand away.

"We need this computer to help him."

I reached out again, but she grabbed my hand.

"You don't know what that will do. The last person we saw with something like that talked to it."

I stared at the lever, arm trembling. Then I looked at Micaela.

"I have to," I whispered. "I don't have a choice."

"We always have a choice."

Micaela held my gaze and my hand. At the edge of my vision, I saw Celandine moving near Suyef, one hand held out, eyes locked on me. She paused, hand near his still form, and nodded at me.

"Not this time."

I pushed through her grasp and took hold of the smooth lever. Every panel in the room lit up. Sounds filled the room as computers came to life. Displays of information rolled across every screen. When I turned to look at one, the lever came free. I held it up to examine it closer. It bore a remarkable resemblance to that old man's stick.

"Suyef!"

Micaela rushed toward him. The Nomad's body, still parallel to the floor, hung suspended in the air before Celandine, her hands hovering above him, lips parted, brow furrowed. His body shifted, moving upright before us. The blackness around his wound receded, collapsing inward.

"What's happening?"

I pointed at his chest. "He's being healed."

"By whom? Celandine?" She moved closer. "Where is she?"

Micaela stopped in front of the Nomad, directly opposite Celandine. The woman remained still, arms outstretched, but her head shifted from side to side, begging me to remain silent.

Before I could do anything, Celandine lowered her arms, and Suyef came down to the floor. When his feet touched, he gasped for air and fell to his knees. Micaela and I rushed closer and kneeled next to him. She grabbed his hand while I reached for his chest.

"What happened?" he asked between gasps.

A cold, familiar voice answered the Nomad's question.

"You had a nasty encounter with a foul blade, my friend."

Micaela and I looked over at the last person we wanted to see, but the one we knew would come.

Colvinra.

"So she healed your wound?" I asked. "Completely?"

Quentin jumped up.

"Logwyn. The Questioner arrives, and you're asking about his wound?"

"I'm curious about the extent of the injury."

"I've felt nothing from the wound," Suyef said, waving Quentin down.

"So, she knew what she was doing," I said.

Quentin snorted, grimacing. Still standing, I noticed.

"That's putting it mildly."

"She once was a very skilled doctor." Suyef pointed at Quentin. "Or so he tells me."

"You know her?" I asked. "Or did you research her?"

"Neither," Quentin said, voice tight. "I met her husband."

He shifted around, hands in his hair, head turned to his room. Suddenly, he bolted down the hall. I stood, but Suyef shook his head.

"Give him time," the Nomad said. "This is hard."

I sat, nodding at his empty chair.

"He met Celandine's husband?" I asked.

Suyef nodded but said nothing. A few minutes passed as I looked over my notes. Then Quentin walked back in and sat down.

"Where were we?" he asked.

"You met Celandine's husband," I answered.

"Right," Quentin said, nodding. "He was the next man to enter that room."

"*Friend* is an odd choice of words."

I moved between the Questioner and my two companions. Celandine, I noted, was gone.

"Watch your mouth," Colvinra growled, eyes narrowing after glancing at my hand. "So, you spoke truth, girl. You didn't have it. He did. Did you give it to him?"

He looked between us, then his eyebrows rose, and he snapped his fingers.

"No, you just got it. Yes, it all makes sense now."

I held up the lever.

"This is what you were after?"

He shook his head.

"No. Well, yes, but now it doesn't matter." He looked around the room. "Now that you unlocked this place, it's immaterial."

I tucked the lever away and stepped back next to Suyef.

"That doesn't mean you get to keep it." Colvinra held out his hand. "That device has caused me no end of trouble."

"I'm not giving it to you."

He nodded at my friends.

"You will if you want them to live."

"Stop pretending like you will not kill us," I said. "We're a liability, and not just because we know about this place."

"Everyone will know of this place soon enough," he said, shaking his head. "Or, should I say they will remember it? And the power it has over them. Power I now control."

"You're not in control yet," Micaela said.

The Questioner ignored her, holding his hand up higher. "Give me the ke—"

"And you'll let us live?" I asked, cutting him off. "Stop insulting our intelligence."

A smile split Colvinra's face. "Not as thick as usual."

My back itched, and my face grew warm. Micaela moved next to me.

"What are you going to do with it?"

"Finish what I started," he said, gaze still on me. "Last chance."

"You won't let us leave either way," I said. "You could have killed us before we knew you were here. So why do you need us alive?"

"He needs an ace in the hole," another familiar voice said from behind me.

Mortac, standing astride another platform, rose into view.

CHAPTER 45

BEGINNING

Micaela stood near the window when I entered the Queen's chamber.

"High One."

"Still calling me that, Logwyn?"

"Apologies." I bowed my head. "Did you rest well?"

"Colvinra. For a Dal," she said, not turning around.

I stared at her, then moved to my desk. If she wanted to start, who was I to argue? I pulled my notes out, my hand brushing the box. I thought about mentioning it, but Suyef's words tickled my memory like the box's smooth surface brushing against my skin.

"And Mortac," I added.

"That man and his self-delusions." She shook her head. "My life would have had a lot less anguish in it had I never crossed his path."

"And is this where you figured out why he and Colvinra acted like they knew you?"

She leaned against the glass, arms folded across her torso.

"Because they *did*. For a long time."

"You mean they thought they did, right? Confused you with Celandine?"

"No, they'd known *me*." She turned from the window. "For centuries."

"Ah, my old friend," Colvinra exclaimed. "Good of you to join us. Very appropriate. Everyone who should be here finally is." He looked around the room. "Now that the room is unlocked and the shielding around this space removed." He looked at Micaela. "Thanks for that. However, you took long enough. I'd been waiting below for quite a while."

"Is that your ship we saw when we landed?" Micaela asked.

Colvinra nodded, and Micaela looked at Mortac.

"How'd you get here?" she asked.

"I have my ways," he answered, then looked at Colvinra. "Stop calling me your friend. I doubt you ever were."

The Questioner frowned at him.

"After everything we've been through, that's how you're going to be? Look"—he pointed at me—"she's here. Shouldn't that count for something?"

"And I should just ignore your actions?" Mortac closed on the Seeker. "With you, everything ends the same way. You take her away from me."

"Can I ask something?" Both heads turned to me. "What are you two talking about?"

Colvinra chuckled, pointing at me while looking at Mortac.

"You see," the Questioner said. "Nothing has changed."

"Because she doesn't remember."

Mortac's face twisted with emotions, and my heart twinged at seeing his struggle. Colvinra shook his head and snickered.

"You still think she just forgot?" He pointed at me. "It's been long enough for even you to see the truth."

I looked between them. "What did I forget?"

Mortac pointed at the tower's center, eyes still on Colvinra. "You don't know what that thing did to her. No one does."

"Wrong." Colvinra pointed at Quentin. "He knows as much as her."

"What did I forget?" I asked again.

Mortac looked at me, shifted back and forth, eyes darting around.

"Oh, for core's sake," Colvinra hissed, then tapped his head. "He thinks you have amnesia. That this"—he waved a hand at the three of us—"isn't who you are."

Suyef moved next to me, eyes on Mortac.

"Who do you think she is?"

Colvinra opened his mouth.

"Don't you dare," the warden blurted out. "This isn't the time or place for this."

"But it is, Mortac." Colvinra looked at me. "All things considered, you won't find a better opportunity."

"Neither of you is saying much at all," Quentin said.

Colvinra pointed at me.

"He thinks she's his wi—"

Mortac punched him right in the face, knocking the Seeker down. Suyef's staff and Quentin's pulse gun appeared on either side of me. Mortac stood over the Questioner, who started laughing.

"Haven't lost your dramatic flair." Colvinra rubbed at his jaw. "You have learned how to punch."

Mortac pointed at the fallen man. "Stay out of my business or you'll get another."

"Must all men settle differences like this?" I asked, glancing around.

The Nomad shrugged.

"I'd rather they explain why they are fighting."

"He said it," Quentin said. "They think she's Mortac's wife."

"But why?"

I looked at Mortac, who refused to look at me.

"It's a long story," Colvinra said. "One he clearly wants to tell you himself."

The Seeker stood, cold, dark eyes locked on Mortac, oily long hair framing his face.

"I don't have the time or the desire to wait for that," the Questioner went on. "You know why I'm here, Mortac. Are you here to help me, or shall we continue this fight?"

Silence fell as the two men faced each other. Mortac looked at me, shoulders sagging. Then he faced Colvinra, hands balling into fists.

"Not again," he growled. "I helped before, and it cost everything."

"Then watch her die." A smile split Colvinra's face as he looked at me. "Again."

"Again?" I asked, interrupting Micaela.

"Yes, Logwyn, that's exactly what he said." She shook her head. "We felt just as confused as you."

"So, you've died in this story as well."

She held my gaze as she said her next words. "Sometimes I've wished I had."

"So, more people confusing you with someone else," I said, jotting some more notes.

"Confusion implies lack of knowledge or understanding," Micaela said. "Mortac? He made a willful choice to believe something. Colvinra just acted confused. I'm not sure what he really knew or when he did, but he played with Mortac's genuine confusion for his own ends."

"Those being?"

"To destroy all that."

She nodded at the window, and I looked out the glass for a moment.

"And he used you to achieve that?"

"He used everyone." She pointed at the pictures. "Them. Me. Mortac. Everyone." She waved at my notes. "And this is where it started. From a certain point of view."

Experience told me not to press her for more information. Instead, I looked over my notes.

"So, how did it start?"

"Colvinra tried to kill me."

The Questioner struck the next instant, flinging his hand toward me. Something hit me hard, dropping me to the floor in a heap. Without thinking, I erected a protective shield around myself.

Mortac attacked Colvinra as Quentin and Suyef moved up on either side. The Questioner blocked a head strike, then flung his hand at Quentin. A ripple rolled past my friend, clipping him as he dodged to the right. He fell in a spin as Suyef charged, staff held overhead. Colvinra knocked Mortac's legs out with a spin kick and caught Suyef's staff in an upheld hand.

The impact resounded as a flash of symbols shimmered from reinforcing his arm.

Quentin fired at the Questioner as he got up, but the shot ricocheted off Colvinra's back. It struck the glass wall, sending cracks darting across the surface.

Suyef slid across the floor with a grunt, shoved by Colvinra as the Seeker climbed to his feet. Mortac rose behind Colvinra, and Quentin darted past me. He slid around Suyef, firing several pulses at the Questioner.

I tried to attach a shield directly to Quentin's chest, but missed. It appeared about a pace in front of him, knocking his arm to the side. He held his hand to one side to get around the shield and fired at Colvinra, each bolt dissipating against the man's shield. He shifted back in my direction, allowing me to narrow my shield and properly attach it to his torso.

Mortac lunged at the Seeker as Suyef swung a strike at the man's back. Colvinra grabbed Mortac and fell away into a roll, flipping him over to crash into the attacking Nomad. The two men fell back behind him as Colvinra came to his feet. He looked at me and smiled.

Quentin lunged toward the Seeker. Colvinra leaned forward, his arm vibrating in front of him. He slid back across the smooth, white floor as Quentin closed on him.

The Seeker slid near Suyef, who grabbed his foot. The Nomad yanked, and Colvinra fell flat on his face. Mortac leaped on top of him, fists striking the man's head. Suyef, now on his feet, moved around toward me.

He took three steps, then Colvinra struck back. Light flashed to my right, and a blast of wind shoved me back against a panel. My vision blurred with tears. I saw a few white spots, and I heard bodies tumble down on the floor. Something lifted me up, and the room shifted around me.

With a jolt, I fell to the floor, striking my back and knocking the wind from my lungs. Blinking, gasping for air, I saw cracked glass to my right. My body twitched in the invisible grasp. Colvinra stood, hand out toward me, facing Mortac, his hand also reaching toward me. The air shimmered around their hands.

"It's the only way, Mortac! Until she's gone . . ."

"You already took her from me once," the warden growled. Then he dove forward.

I flew sideways into Quentin's legs, and he fell on top of me. Colvinra dropped his hand and spun into another kick. The warden hopped over it as Suyef jumped into the fray. The Seeker caught the Nomad's fist and threw him into Mortac.

"Move!"

Quentin pulled me up. Colvinra aimed a pulse gun at him, so I threw another shield at the Seeker. It hit him square in the torso, knocking him into Suyef just as the Nomad stood up.

"Nice!"

Quentin charged the struggling pair. They fell past Mortac, who tried to kick Colvinra. Then Suyef used his leg to slow his rotation, one hand pinning the Questioner down at the neck. Colvinra blasted my friend square in the chest with another pulse gun. The impact knocked Suyef up and back onto the panels. He landed hard, gasping for air.

Quentin lunged at the Seeker, who rolled to his right. Quentin slid past him, coming to a halt next to Suyef, his own pulse gun leveled at the Questioner. I shielded them from any attack. Mortac groaned and stood facing the Seeker, who grimaced.

"Why can't you just stop, Morris? It's over. It was over when we started this." Colvinra pointed at Quentin, then me. "When they stopped us."

"Don't call me Morris. And they didn't stop us. We tried to do the impossible." Mortac waved a hand around the room. "Even with all this technology, what we did was wrong. It threatened the entire world, all so you could prove your theory, get revenge."

"It was more than that, and you know it."

"Maybe when you first approached me. By the end, you only cared about power." Mortac's hand twitched toward me. "And you sacrificed the one thing dearest to me to get it."

"You never would have finished building the gate if she had been there." Colvinra pointed toward the device, currently out of sight. "And without that, she could never come back. You know it saved her life."

"And I lost her," Mortac whispered. "Lost myself."

"Exposition aside, you still aren't making any sense," I said.

Both heads turned toward me. Colvinra chuckled.

"Her mind remains broken. She never came out of that thing the same."

A cough from the far side of the room drew all our gazes. There, clothed in his multicolored cloak, stood Nidfar, looking between the warden and the Questioner.

"Am I interrupting anything?"

"Finally left your tower, old geezer?" Colvinra asked, chuckling.

Nidfar looked around the room and stopped when his glance settled on me. A smile danced across his face.

"Ah, so good to see you again. Which one are you now?"

His head cocked to one side, eyes darting up and down.

"Ah, yes, the hair. You haven't worn that style in a long, long time." He shook his head, a small smile twisting his lips. "I hardly remember."

"What are you doing here?" I asked him.

He moved around the glass wall, tapping his head with his hand.

"I'm not sure. I lost something." He patted his cloak. "And I remember being here. Well, seeing me here, so I had to be here if I remembered seeing me here, right?" He looked around. "And I know I lost something."

"Your stick?" I asked.

He snapped his fingers and looked about.

"Yes, it wandered off. Again."

I glanced at Quentin, the lever still out of sight. He shrugged at my look. I stepped closer to the old man.

"Where did you last see it?"

Colvinra cleared his throat.

"Why are we wasting time with this senile old man? If he's lost his toy, too bad." His arm rose. "Makes this even easier."

The air around his hand shimmered. I jumped in front of the old man, erecting a shield. Colvinra's attack struck my shield hard, rattling my bones and knocking me up into the air. The room spun as the glass wall rushed closer. I curled into a ball just before smashing through the already cracked surface and down into the core.

CHAPTER 46

ENDING

"Quite an odd time for Nidfar to show up."

I jotted a note and heard Suyef chuckle.

"So true, Logwyn."

"He's a nuisance." Quentin stood in the doorway, hair disheveled and face red. "Last time he visited, I couldn't find my paper for a week."

"So, he does come here?" I asked.

Suyef glanced at Quentin, who shrugged.

"Occasionally."

"You know his name, now," I pointed out.

"Of course I do." He looked at Suyef. "Does she think I'm nuts or something?"

Suyef glanced at me. "Or something."

An awkward silence followed. Quentin shifted but didn't sit down. He stepped toward me, then back.

"Why wouldn't I remember his name?"

"Didn't you have a question for Quentin?" Suyef asked.

Taking his cue, I picked up my notes, trying to think of a question. Something at the bottom caught my eye.

"Um, Micaela protected Nidfar when Colvinra attacked," I said.

"What?" Quentin asked.

"Colvinra attacked the old man, and she stopped him."

I looked up at him. He stared at me and remained quiet.

"And then she fell through the glass."

He frowned at me.

"Is there a question I'm missing?"

My jaw tightened. I closed my eyes and took a breath. "What did you do?"

I looked up at him and saw his face go slack and his shoulders hunch over. He clutched something in his fist: a crumpled piece of paper. When he spoke, I had to strain to hear him.

"I jumped after her."

Micaela soaring toward the glass sent a jolt through me, every inch of skin tingling.

"Go!"

Suyef shoved me as I stood. Grabbing the ceiling, I jumped, trying to catch her before she hit the glass. The beams refused to focus, defusing against her shield. Then she smashed into the glass.

Ancients made their structures to last, including the glass. Their constructs survived the Shattering and massive shell collisions later. I expected the glass wall to hold, not to shatter into a shimmering cloud of dust around Micaela as she fell into the shaft.

"Cel!"

Mortac's cry followed me as I flipped over the railing and down after her. I saw Mortac rushing forward and Colvinra throwing out his leg to trip him. Then I was falling into the shaft. Below, Micaela bounced off one wall and flipped the other direction. I tried to grab her shields, but she slipped free like water in your bare hand.

"Micaela! Drop your shield!"

She hit the other wall, bouncing back into the open shaft and toward the large beams. I wrapped my arms around my body, shoving at the walls for speed. Then I shot free of the tunnel and after Micaela. She flipped upside down, and we locked gazes.

"Drop your shield!"

She held a hand to her ear. I cupped my hands around my mouth and tried again. She shook her head. I made fists, then flung my fingers wide. Her momentum carried her over again, but the shimmer surrounding her vanished. Quickly, I locked several beams across the length of her body, slowing her spin.

The enormous, ring-shaped object known as Third Gate loomed ever larger as we fell. I grabbed at the passing beams to slow our descent, to pull us to one side. The blue beams warped, bending down toward the ring object. My grip on Micaela wavered, and those slowing our descent shook, losing their grasp.

We fell toward another of the metal arms, and I tried to guide Micaela at it. My entire body trembled with a violent shake as the belt lost its grip on a beam above us. Micaela slammed onto the beam, and I fell past her, crashing into a beam that sloped down.

Gasping, I rolled over, wrapping my arms and legs around the structure. The friction heated my face and hands, but I had to slow myself. After a few terrifying heartbeats, I came to a halt, my entire body trembling.

"I've got to stop doing this."

"Quentin!" Micaela called from above. "Quentin?"

"I'm fine!" Another shiver ripped through my torso. "You?"

"I-I'm not sure." She coughed and gasped. "I can't move."

"What?"

"I can't move my legs!"

I looked up from my notes.

"Paralyzed?"

"No feeling at all from here down."

She pointed at her waist, then waved at her legs. I stared at her for a moment while tapping the stylus to my cheek.

"Does anything that happens to you three ever stick?"

"Really?" she asked, glaring at me.

"I'm serious." I held up fingers, ticking them off as I went on. "Quentin died. Suyef died. You got paralyzed." I arched an eyebrow in my best imitation of her. "They're not dead, and you're not a paraplegic."

Micaela scrunched her nose and looked away.

"Enough stuck. Trust me."

I looked up at the beam.

"But your arms are fine?"

"Yeah." She waved her arms, just visible on either side. "But I can't feel anything below my waist."

I sat up and looked around.

"Can you get up to me?"

"That ring is messing with my belt."

"We need to move." She started pushing herself away from the end of the beam. "It's not safe this close."

"None of this seems safe," I muttered.

"What?"

"Nothing." I waved at her. "Your beam is almost horizontal. Keep moving back toward the wall."

She moved some more, then looked over the side at me.

"What about you?"

I glanced toward the nearby wall.

"Pretty sure I can just slide the rest of the way down. Keep moving, and I'll see if my belt works better near the wall."

Ignoring the pounding of my heart, I slid toward the wall. Suddenly, crackling energy tore through the air. Bursts of light cast shadows across the walls. About a hundred paces behind me, tendrils of energy arced along the ring's inner edge, some reaching out to touch in the device's open center. With a near-deafening bang, the tendrils formed into a wall of white light inside the ring.

Micaela yelled in frustration and gripped the beam as she slid back toward the device. Something tugged at my body, pulling me up the sloped beam. Gripping the surface with my belt, I rolled over and rose to my knees. Focusing on her beam halfway between Micaela and Third Gate, I took a breath and leaped, using the belt to augment my jump. The ring's power bent my jump in an arc toward the device. My momentum, however, carried me up level with Micaela.

Flipping over, I locked the belt onto the device, suspending myself in midair between her and the crackling wall of light behind me. I pushed back against the gate's magnetic power and held a hand out toward Micaela. I tried to script, tried to fuse molecules into something that might slow her momentum. My body trembled, sweat pouring from every pore as the air warmed around me. Then the air between us blurred, and an enormous chunk of ice enveloped the end of the metal beam.

The crackling energy grew louder, and the light flared at an ever-increasing pace. Every pulse sent a tremor through my body. Blackness crept into my vision. I shook my head and heard the ice crack. Drips of water hit my face.

Somewhere nearby, I heard a voice call something, call my name. Her name. Someone was coming.

Every joint in my body cracked with another tremor, and the darkness swarmed around me. I tried to say her name, to apologize. I never got the chance.

A powerful energy wave struck, and I felt my belt shut down. The ice cracked, large pieces smashing into me as I fell toward the pulsing light. I just made out Micaela, arms outstretched behind her. Reaching for something. For someone. Someone running at her along the platform.

I tried to push a chunk of ice back against her, tried to slow her down. To help that dark blur racing closer. Nothing worked.

Micaela soared toward me. The light burned my eyes as I fell into it, pain ripping through me at its touch.

Only then did the blackness swallow me.

Quentin fell silent and stared at the floor, hand still gripping the crumpled paper. His torso shuddered, and his mouth opened and closed several times.

"Quentin, it's okay," Suyef said. "I know you don't like to talk about it."

I nodded at the Nomad.

"So, where were you during all this?"

"At first, protecting that old man." He chuckled. "Or so I thought. That old man is more resourceful than he appears."

"How so?"

"He knew Mortac and Colvinra better than they knew themselves."

"What happened next?"

The Nomad pointed at Quentin, who shuddered. "Just after he dove into the shaft, Mortac ran forward, screaming a familiar name."

"Cel. Short for *Celandine*."

He nodded.

"Colvinra tripped him," he went on, "but that only slowed him on his way to jump in after them. But the old man screamed at him to stop Colvinra."

Quentin gasped, and he wrapped his arms around his torso. He started shaking. Suyef, eyes on his friend, didn't move as he continued.

"The look on Mortac's face. Pure agony." He looked at me. "You know by now who he believed Micaela was."

"Celandine," I said, then looked up. "That's his wife. She's inside the network."

"*Was* his wife. Now?" He shrugged. "I moved closer to Nidfar, but he shoved me toward the shaft, yelling for me to go after them. I protested, but he touched my belt and said it still worked."

"He knew you broke it?"

"I stopped trying to understand how that man knows things. But I know he has an affinity for technology, particularly grav-belts and boards."

The Nomad glanced at Quentin and frowned. After a moment, he shook his head and looked at me.

"So, Nidfar pushed you to follow him?" I asked.

Quentin answered for him.

"No. Something threw him after us."

Before I could object or ask how I was supposed to help, the old man shoved me over the railing. I tried the belt, but the thing wouldn't function right. My momentum flipped me upside down, and I saw the old man leaning over above and pointing to one side. I cleared the shaft and saw a ledge in that direction. The old man made a throwing motion, and something grabbed me and sent me into the railing. I grabbed on as his grip vanished, climbed over the railing, and fell to my knees, breathing hard.

The old man, colorful cloak billowing around him, fell down into view, his stick pointing toward me. Some gray material shot out of it and stuck to the railing, forming a rope. The old man swung down to a platform below me, cackling the entire way.

"Jump!" He waved me down. "I'll catch you."

I hesitated, but he just kept waving and flashing his toothy grin at me. He had just caught me, so I braced and vaulted over the railing.

He missed, and ice gripped my heart. Then I saw his rope and grabbed it. The rope ripped free from the railing but not his stick.

"Leave off!" he screamed, shaking the stick. "Leave off!"

The material grew taut in my grip and vibrated as I fell past him. The old man, still shaking his stick, didn't notice until my momentum yanked him into the railing. Still, he held his stick with a white-knuckled death grip.

"Let go!"

Before I could do anything, the rope ripped, and I fell toward the core.

"It just broke?" I asked, looking up from my notes. "Was it damaged?"

Suyef shrugged.

"Or he tried to make it vanish, and it lost its cohesion."

"Inconvenient," I said, shaking my head.

"Very."

"So, what happened?"

"The Dragon Queen caught me."

I stopped and looked up from my notes. "Wait, what?"

"This is a waste of time!" Quentin smacked the doorframe, then rushed down the hall.

I ran to his room and found him grabbing his sketches of Micaela's eyes, pulling them down in clumps.

"This is all wrong. She's mad at me." He rifled through the sketches. "I messed up. It's in her eyes."

He held one close, staring at it before flinging it across the floor.

"I broke this," he whispered, looking at the surrounding images. "I did this."

He fell to his knees, a sketch gripped in each hand. His head sagged, and his torso shuddered. I moved closer, mindful of stepping on the images, and squatted in front of him. I pointed at the sketches he held.

"What's wrong, Quentin?"

He jolted, head coming up, blue eyes locking with mine. He waved one sketch at me.

"I am," he whispered, tears falling. "It's me. I did this. Her eyes are so sad."

He looked at the other sketches, then pointed at one near his bed.

"There. She's mad. There, too." He pointed at another. "And look."

He grabbed one and held it out to me.

"Sad. Because of me. I did this. It was me. It was all me."

I took the proffered image, looking into the now-familiar eyes. Eyes filled with raw emotion; sadness. I held up the image.

"Quentin, is this how you see her eyes?"

His head jerked in a nod, and his jaw clenched. A sob shook his entire body, and he rocked back and forth. I tried to take his hand, but he jerked away.

"Don't touch me!" He shuffled across the floor, heedless of his sketches. "Leave me alone. I can't think." He gripped at his blanket, pulling it up to his face. "Why did you do this? Why did you ask me all this?"

He screamed something unintelligible into the fabric, then glared at me. "Go away!"

I found Suyef in the hall, my recording device in hand.

"What's wrong?" I looked at Quentin. "He's . . . different."

"He always has been," Suyef said, his voice soft. "Ever since it happened."

He handed me my device and pointed at the sketch in my other hand.

"She looks sad," he said. "But is he drawing her how he saw her, or is he drawing how he feels and thinks she sees him?"

"I don't know." I nodded at the now-weeping man. "Neither does he, I think."

The Nomad shrugged. "I think it's both."

I watched Quentin a moment longer, then looked at the sketch. Finally, I shook my head and looked at Suyef.

"The Dragon Queen helped you?"

He glanced at Quentin, now on the floor, hand still gripping a sketch. Then Suyef moved down the hall, away from the main room and toward the outer platform. I followed him until I stopped at the edge and looked down.

"She helped me escape. The old man helped me get to them."

"To what end?"

"To help them. The man is meddlesome but never wavers in his loyalty to Micaela."

I nodded, making a mental note to ask Micaela later.

"So, what happened?"

He shook his head.

"I failed them."

I landed on a platform just above Micaela, then fell over into the railing as something pulled at me. Then I heard Micaela yell as she slid toward the ring, arms spread to slow down. Quentin jumped up toward her and flew in an arc toward the device because of the force it exerted. He flew up between her and the device, one hand outstretched toward her. A cracking noise filled the air as a massive ice block engulfed the platform. Micaela slid up against the ice, but the block began to crack and melt.

I vaulted and landed much farther down than expected. The device had altered my momentum, an aid and a hindrance all in one.

Warily, I ran toward her, calling her name. She turned mid-slide and reached back at me just as the ice cracked. Quentin lost the fight against the device. The ice fell away, and I saw him dissolve into the swirling light, screaming until he vanished.

"He dissolved?"

"Like fabric dropped into acid."

I paused, imagining the agony. Trying to, at least.

"He screamed until the end?"

Suyef nodded. "I still hear it in my dreams."

"So, he went into Third Gate."

When he didn't respond, I looked at him. His torso trembled, then he shook his head, clearing his throat.

"Yes."

"Did that break him?"

Suyef shook his head.

"No, that was his own doing later. This just set him and her on the path to that event."

I looked out into the expanse with him.

"So, then what?"

"When Quentin vanished, the last chunk of ice holding her crumbled. But he did enough for me to reach her." Suyef fell silent, his shoulders sagging. He looked down at his hands. "But I still couldn't save her."

I lunged for Micaela, grabbing for her hand. Our fingers touched, and for a moment, I believed I had her. Then her touch vanished, and I landed hard. As I slid toward the ring, her scream ripped through me like a knife. Then she was gone.

The flashing lights pulsed, and the ring's pull vanished. I slid a few paces and looked up, but I saw nothing. Both of them were gone, the light with them. Only their screams remained, the look on her face as she flew away. Quentin's face as he tried to save her.

A scream yanked me back to the moment. Far above, Mortac leaned over the edge, his mouth open in a guttural cry. Then he slipped against the railing, cutting off his scream. He looked at me and waved me back, yelling something unintelligible.

Then the device crackled with energy, arcs of light jumping out to the beams. I turned to run, but a new sound echoed from above. A voice calling my name. I looked up to see the most majestic green dragon I'd ever laid eyes on soaring down inside the giant citadel, heading right at me.

The Queen.

"Wait, she fit in that chamber?" I asked. "The Queen is much too large to fit inside a citadel, even For'a Dal."

"Dragons can't adjust their size?" he asked, leaning on the platform wall.

"It's difficult to do."

"Even for the Queen?"

I shook my head.

"No, I just thought you might have been mistaken." I shrugged. "It's a complicated process, almost as much as gaining the initial blessing that allows it."

I looked down, the memory of my test coming to mind. Suyef sat in silence until I nodded at him.

"So, I'd recognize her anywhere," he continued. "I had never seen her prior to that moment, but I knew it was her."

"Okay, so what happened?"

"I took a leap of faith."

An arc of light struck the platform as the Green dove past. I didn't hesitate, leaping into its spinal column. The Green spun, forcing me to hug the bone structure. Then she bellowed out a warning before turning left in a sharp spiral. I nearly blacked out from the inertia and grabbed the bone in my hand. I blinked at the spinal structure, realizing it had shrunk. Then she cried out another warning.

Ahead, a single large window lay in our path. I ducked against the dragon as she smashed through the glass. Shards fell along her spine, filling the air with an eerie refrain. Another sharp turn followed, this time up and straight away from the citadel. As we climbed, she returned to her normal size.

Behind us, the Greens swarmed around the citadel. Then she roared, her cry echoing across the skies. The Greens turned as one and spiraled away toward their shell.

A wave of blackness shot out from For'a Dal, enveloping the core and dimming its light. The citadel began visibly vibrating as the light dimmed.

A flash of bright light filled the expanse, and the citadel rose from the surface. The core light returned, illuminating the massive fortress as it soared past us and into the expanse above.

The Dragon Queen followed, and soon I could make out two large fleets—one Nomad, the other Colberran—locked in combat between the shells. The citadel ascended with astonishing speed, plunging straight into the middle of the battle.

Caught unaware, the fleets fell away in a jumbled mess. As they flew around this new foe, some still battling, the citadel opened fire.

I sat astride the Dragon Queen, helpless, as the citadel completely obliterated every ship.

EPILOGUE

I returned to the Queen's chambers but found no sign of Micaela, not even her morning repast.

"Of course, when I finally have something good to ask you, you're not here."

The Queen's antechamber also stood empty. I crossed it and went through my original entrance of so many weeks ago. As before, darkness greeted me, as did the oppressive silence, the urge to kneel.

"Your Highness?"

Only my echo answered. I took a few tentative steps, wishing desperately for a portable light. After a moment, I turned back, but a chime sounded from my travel sack. Frowning, I pulled out the padd. A flashing light marked receipt of a new file. Three files. I opened the first, and a translucent image of a man appeared above the screen. Nothing happened, so I peered closer, trying to see more detail.

Then the person spoke.

"First Officer's log, Colberran sky-cruiser *Dominance*. Battle has proceeded as predicted. The Nomad scum hold close to their shell, forcing our use of more floating islands. The fools don't know they have already lost, as we've yet to deploy our full force. No reinforcements have come since the invasion began. Even with our previous losses, we outnumber them two to one." He smirked. "This war will be short."

Something moved off the screen, drawing his attention.

"What's going on back there?"

He turned away from the camera, revealing a command center. People ran about as someone barked orders. Rows of computer terminals lay to either side of a walkway, all facing the large window opposite the camera. Ships locked in aerial combat filled the expanse beyond. A tall figure dominated the floor, her voice booming as she pointed first to one side and then the other. She turned to look at the first officer. As she did, a citadel rose into the battle.

"Commander Flynn. Send a message. Tell them we're under attack from something new. The battle has changed."

The ship trembled, the captain stumbling to one knee. Commander Flynn spun back to the camera.

"Mayday! Mayday! They are attacking with an airborne citadel."

The captain cut him off.

"It's not the Nomads! The blasted thing is attacking them!"

"Repeat, the citadel is attacking all of us. Send hel—"

An explosion ripped through the bridge. For an instant, a look of terror gripped his face Then, the flames enveloped him and static filled the feed.

The file ended, and a second started, followed by a third.

A giant ring filled the screen, beams of metal reaching toward it from off camera. Energy crackled around the ring, arcing out toward the metal beams.

A man that looked like Mortac sat on one of those beams, hardly moving, staring into the device, at the energy. Staring at the only thing he cared about.

The device held the person he thought to be his wife, body likely turned to energy, mind trapped inside the powerful machine. He looked down and closed his eyes for several heartbeats.

Looking back up into the gate, Mortac sat there.

Staring.

Crying.

Blue energy crackled across the screen, whorls and swirls of light merging and spinning at a dizzying rate. Micaela fell into view, head turning back and forth.

"Quentin!"

She fell in a fast spin, one hand near her face, the other arm waving against the rotation. Her face twisted and reddened as she looked for something.

Suddenly, her outstretched hand grasped at something. Just beyond her, Quentin fell head over heels toward her. He spun upright relative to her, one arm reaching out. Micaela struggled to grab his hand.

Their hands collided but failed to grasp. She called out and lunged at his other hand as his torso spun away, grabbing his sleeve and gripping tight. He twisted over and locked his hand around hers.

Micaela pointed behind him, at his legs dissolving into the energy.

"Quentin!"

He just pointed as her body melted away. Only their head and arms remained. Blue light poured into their eyes, heads vanishing. Only their hands, still holding tight, remained.

Then everything dissolved into light.

The translucent video vanished.

I lowered the device, mind still pondering that last image. Did they let go? Had they held on? Were they ripped apart?

I looked into the still-empty cave, then through the door at the Queen's empty chambers. Micaela and the Queen, both gone. I slumped, feeling the weight of all I'd been told, the mystery. All the unanswered questions. I looked into the darkness and asked the only question I felt mattered just then.

"Where are you?"

Silence was my only answer. Pondering my options, a thought occurred to me, an idea. A name not on the Queen's list but an important one. I spun on my heel, leaving the Queen's chambers and cave to find a ride to the only place I knew he might be: a prison in Colberra.

"I hope you have some answers, Mortac."

THE END

APPENDIX I

SHATTER

Scribe's Note: The following event occurs during a sequence of events that predate Rise and Fall. Mortac, finally found by myself, agreed to share what he knew of past events. This scene was recounted to me during that interview.

She lay on her back, a white cloth pulled up over her chest and tucked under her arms. The table upon which she lay stood in the center of an empty room. Off to one side stood a chair, and in it I sat. I couldn't bear to look, instead hiding my head in my hands, elbows on my knees, as I rocked back and forth. A single repeating beep echoed in the silence, emanating from a screen opposite where the man sat.

The still form of my wife moved, taking in a deep breath. I looked up at the sound, standing up just a bit, eyes locked on the woman. When she remained still, I flopped back down, leaning back and knocking my head against the wall over and over.

"What is it going to take? What do I have to do?"

I closed my eyes, letting out a long breath, and remained there motionless for several moments. She murmured, a small sound that barely escaped her lips. I looked over at her, stood up, and moved to stand next to the bed. I stared down at her face, my soul twisted in pain.

"My sweet Cel, I don't know what to do anymore." I leaned over her face. "I've tried everything. We all have. This thing, this disease, it's just too fast. It adapts faster than we can work." I looked toward the only door into the room. "I don't see any other way to help you."

The door hissed open and Vincent, my best friend and counterpart in this search, entered.

"Morris," he said by way of greeting.

"Vincent."

"How is Cel?"

I looked back at her.

"Unchanged. And the machine?"

Vincent nodded. "It's ready. As ready as we can make it. We've run every test we can think of but there is still so much we don't know about it."

"Have you tested the connectivity?"

"Yes, we connected to every citadel node across the globe. No delays that we can connect."

"And the library?" Morris asked.

"Uploading now. We'll keep the back-ups in place just in case, but I doubt we'll need them." Vincent stepped closer. "You'll never believe this, but we aren't even using an infinitesimal of a fraction of the capacity. The storage space is so large we can't calculate it."

I nodded, taking my wife's hand in my own.

"All that and we still don't know if it can do what we need it to."

My friend stepped close to the bed opposite me.

"Power is our primary setback, you know that. As amazing as the Gate device is, it still doesn't have a stable enough power source."

I felt my torso sag. Vincent, seeing the effect his words had, waved a hand at me.

"We'll find one. You know we will. To start, we can use it in spurts. Right now, for the data upload. Later-" he looked down at the still form of my wife "-later, we can do more."

I looked up. "How long until the upload is complete?"

Vincent shook his head.

"If we push the upload window to the maximum…" He frowned, pursing his lips. "I don't know. I'll go look."

He looked down at Cel.

"I know how much she means to you, but you need a break."

"I'm not doing anything. Just sitting here."

"Exactly. You need exercise. A decent meal. Some sunlight."

I shook my head.

"I'm staying here."

Vincent nodded and stepped near the door.

"Just think about it, okay Morris?"

I glared at him.

"I'm not leaving my wife. I've lost too much time already."

At that moment, she stirred, drawing my attention. I hovered over my wife, one hand still holding hers.

"Come on, Cel," I whispered. "Just hold on. We're almost there."

My voice seemed to stir her from the grip of slumber. Her head rolled to one side, her mouth falling open as a quiet murmur escaped past her lips. I released her hand and cupped the side of her face, shifting it back upright. As I did, her eyes fluttered open.

"Mor-"

She broke into a fit of coughing, struggling to speak between gasps for air.

"Mor-, Morris. Are yo-, you there?"

"I'm here, sweetheart. I'm here."

I leaned farther over her, my head casting a shadow onto her face. She blinked, eyes focusing on my face. A small smile tugged at her lip.

"I had the most pleasant dream," she whispered. "We were far from here. In the mountains. You remember our last time there?"

I nodded, touching a hand to her cheek and looking up at Vincent. He was gone.

"It was a good trip, but I seem to recall someone complaining about the cold the whole time."

She frowned at me.

"It was winter, of course it was cold. And you know I'm practically cold-blooded."

I chuckled. "It did make you more snugly."

She laughed, then broke into a fit of coughing. I moved up beside her, wrapping one arm under her as she coughed off to the side. After a moment, the fit passed and she lay there, head resting on my arm, one hand clinging to mine.

"I'm not getting any better."

"Don't say that," I whispered, holding her close. "We'll find a way."

"You've said that before."

"We're so close. The machine is almost finished."

She shook her head.

"And what will that do? What will that change?"

"It could change everything," I whispered.

"Or destroy it."

The pair fell silent. I reached a hand up to brush her hair and Cel moved to push up against my touch.

"I miss this," she said. "I miss you."

A tear slipped down my cheek.

"Can we please leave this place?" she asked. "Away from all this. I just want to be alone with you."

I clutched her shoulders.

"You wouldn't survive a trip."

"I'm not going to survive anything," she said. "At least let me pass somewhere I'll be happy."

Another fit of coughs ripped through her body. I held her cradled in my arms as she gasped for air. A soft beep emitted into the air, a sharp sound that cut into the room like an intruder.

"What's that?" she sputtered.

My eyes were locked on the screen. I didn't move, didn't respond. I simply closed my eyes and lowered my head.

"Why didn't you tell me?"

Cel shifted and her hand touched my face. I opened my eyes to look at her.

"I knew it was wrong. I knew your body couldn't handle such things," I went on.

Cel craned her neck to look at the screen and her mouth fell open.

"Computer, blank the screen!" she cried out.

Cel turned back to look up at me.

"I was just as surprised as you," she whispered, taking my hand and placing it on her belly.

Another tear rolled down my face.

"You...you," I began, then paused, closing my eyes. "You won't survive that."

She reached a hand up to touch my face once more.

"Morris, I don't care. I can give you this much. A ray of hope in this stark, gloomy prison you've locked yourself in."

She pulled my face closer to hers and place a small kiss on his lips. "They can save her. I know they can."

I looked down and shook my head.

"I can't do it. I can't do that without you."

Cel coughed once, pulling me down and pressing her face against mine.

"Yes, you can."

Her voice became faint.

"Promise me, Morris," she whispered. "Promise me you'll live. You'll go on."

I shook my head.

"I can't make promises I can't keep."

"Promise me," she said, her eyes opening and locking on mine.

I stared back and a small smile tugged at one lip.

"I promise."

She smiled.

"And promise you will get her out. Get her into an artificial womb."

I nodded at her.

"I promise that as well."

Her eyes closed as another, more insistent beep began to fill the room.

"And don't put me...in..."

She broke into another fit of coughs.

"Into that..."

She fell back down, her eyes fluttering. Her face glistened with sweat as she collapsed down onto his arm. A trickle of blood seeped out of one side of her mouth.

"Cel?"

I shifted, laying her down and looking up at the screen. I brushed a hand across her bright, red hair and a piece came loose, falling to the floor at my feet.

"No, no, not yet." I looked at her belly. "It's too soon!"

I ran a hand through my hair. Cel remained still as the beeping accelerated. I looked at the screen, then at her, then the screen again. The next moment, I made my choice and began to move.

Scooping her up, I fled the room.

APPENDIX II

THE MAN WHO WILL CURE

A young man's face appears on the screen. Soft gray eyes surrounded by sharp features stare out. A sweeping nose juts down between his eyes and long black hair frames his face.

"Is this thing on?" he says. "This is log number 425, recorded on the 15th of April. My name is Morris Tackett and I'm the man who will cure the plague.

"That always sounds good, doesn't it? You're probably tired of hearing it, but mantras don't work if you avoid saying them all the time." The sound of paper shuffling fills the recording. "So, as usual, here's a progress report. Tests are moving along. We've managed to get the cells to recode after infected, but then the disease moves on to other cells we haven't touched yet." He shakes a piece of paper at the screen. "This set today looks promising. The lab tests proved successful last week. We'll be moving to this series of treatment today."

Morris sets the paper aside and pauses, his eyes looking somewhere off-screen. His head shakes suddenly and he refocuses on the camera.

"These tests need to make some progress. We're running out of time." He holds up a finger and points at himself. "No, I'm running out of time. This disease is spreading and our funders are growing impatient for some proof of concept, something to hang their hats on."

A chiming chirp fills the air and the man frowns and picks up a small silver device. "Pardon me," he says to the screen, holding the device to his ear. "Hello? Yes, I'm just starting." His lips compress, a glare crossing his eyes. "What? You know I can't. I'm needed here. These tests are important."

He goes silent, listening. His jaw clenches and the sound of teeth grinding comes faintly through the monitor.

"I told you already," he finally says, shaking his head as he speaks. "I can't leave yet. These experiments are delicate. You know I'm needed here." He pauses, then cries out as his hand runs through his hair. "No, I can't leave them to Cole," he says, his voice strained. "The man is barely competent. He's got more dream in him than actual science and I can't leave such delicate work in his hands."

Another pause and his eyes close. "I told you already why." His voice drops to a whisper. "I'll be home as soon as I can, Cel. Goodbye."

He taps the screen on the device and tosses it aside. The recording is filled by the sound of its clattering. Morris stares down at the desk for several moments. Finally, he looks back up at the monitor and shrugs.

"I'm sorry but I have to go," he says, a pained look crossing his face. "Something's wrong, I know it. I know what I said, but she wouldn't call if it wasn't. We're not exactly on good terms right now, but she still wouldn't call if it wasn't important."

He stands up and reaches for the monitor. "I'll post another update tomorrow."

The recording ends.

The screen turns on as Morris's face appears again. He looks gaunt, eyes sunken, hair hanging limp around his face. His skin seems stretched tight around the bones of his face and his eyes, upon closer inspection, are very red. He sniffs once, his mouth moving though no words come out.

"Log number four hundred and...and"—he pauses, closing his eyes and taking in a deep breath—"twenty-six? No, 427. It should be 426 but the fraggin' computer won't let me use that one." He opens his bloodshot eyes to stare at the monitor. "Today's date, October 30th." He pauses again, his eyes wandering. "I'm supposed to give you a report...a progress report, yes?"

He stops talking again, eyes closing, a tear creeping down his cheek. He doesn't speak for several moments. Eventually, he opens his eyes, sniffs once, takes a deep breath, and begins to speak.

"Our progress has been...rampant of late. The experiments." He shrugs. "Let's just say the experiments are over. Not that we succeeded, mind you. No, we did *not* succeed."

His eyes wander off to his right. He breathes through his nose, short soft whistles filling the recording. He blinks and looks back at the monitor.

"Our work is over. They pulled our funding." He shakes his head. "No, they pulled everything. Our accesses, our research. It's all gone. After I finish this log, I'm leaving this lab forever." He closes his eyes. "I've been... banished."

He stops talking, eyes still closed. His entire frame visibly shrinks down, shoulders bowing, head leaning forward and to one side. His mouth opens, moving but not speaking. A silent cry wracks his body.

"I . . . I lost her," he whispers. Tears begin to stream down his face. "She's gone. Taken." He looks up into the monitor, eyes wide, his words accelerating. "I tried so hard, spent my entire life fighting against this disease. And...and—" He leans back, head looking up to the ceiling, hands reaching up to grab his head. "It wasn't enough. I couldn't stop it."

He looks back down, hands dropping, one pointing at the monitor. "I told her. You heard me tell her it was important. These experiments"—he grabs a piece of paper and holds it up to the monitor—"this could have been the answer. It might have been right here." He crumbles the paper and flings to the side. His eyes follow the ruined sheet, wherever it fell. "That could have been the answer."

His head bows again and he sighs. "Then again, who knows anymore? I sure don't." He glances back up at the monitor, his eyes empty and bloodshot. "I couldn't save her. I worked so hard, put in so many hours. Wasted so much time." He shrugs, shaking his head. "I couldn't stop it from taking her."

A gaunt look fills his face, eyebrows furrowing slightly. "And it's so much worse than anyone knows." He buries his face in his hands. "So much worse," he whispers. "They think it was just her. They think they know it all."

His hands lower, and a cold dead face stares back out of the monitor. "They know nothing."

He looks around the room and leans near the monitor. "You see, they think it was just her. Just my precious Cel. They think I only sacrificed her to save her." The cold hard look wavers, a twinge of some emotion struggling to wrest control of his face away. It loses. "They think they know what happened." He shakes his head slowly. "But they don't." He leans even closer to the monitor. "They have no clue. Only I do." He points a finger at the monitor. "And now you will too."

He leans back, pursing his lips, eyes squinting slightly. "I'll make sure this is buried in the database. Before you find this, so much will have happened. I'm certain whenever this is finally found it will be too late. They won't be able to stop it now."

He takes in a deep breath and lets it out slowly. "I don't really want to do this, mind you. But what choice do I have? She's lost to me. So much is lost to me." He stumbles to a halt, eyes closing. More tears begin to fall. "It wasn't just her. I was trying to save more than her. I was trying to save all of them." He looks up to the ceiling. "Why couldn't I figure it out?"

He rests there a moment, head tilted back, before shaking himself and looking back at the monitor. "My wife is dead. And it's my fault."

His head slumps down, shoulders bowing with it. "There, I said it. I've been avoiding that for days now. I, Morris Tackett, killed my wife."

His head looks up and the cold steely face is back. "I killed her because I didn't find the answer. I killed her because it was the only way to stop the suffering. I don't care what they say in their history books or their official records. It's all a lie. I killed her, you hear me?" His voice climbs, his eyes widen and he leans closer to the monitor. "It's my fault! I did it. Not them, not Cole, no one else. Me!"

He jabs a finger at the monitor. "Don't you let them trick you, either. They'll cover this up. They can't let this get out. They've worked too hard on their image to let this ruin it. That's what matters most. Their image. We can't have the public figuring out what we are and that what we have to offer is as dangerous as everything else." He shakes his head, laughing slightly as he looks away. "The arrogance. It galls me. To think we're better somehow." He looks back into the monitor. "We're just as mortal as the rest of you."

He closes his eyes momentarily before saying, "Ask my wife."

He leans back in his chair, crossing his arms over his chest. "My wife. I loved her so much." He shakes his head. "We weren't close recently. I know that much. We were fighting a lot." He looks around the room. "My work. That's what we fought over. I was here too much. That's what she would say." He nods once. "She was right. All that time here and it did me no good in the end. Did her no good."

He closes his eyes, head slumping down toward his chest. "Did us no good." He moves forward, resting his head on his hands and looking down as he leans on the desk. "We tried for so long. She just wanted to be a mother. We couldn't figure out what was wrong. We went to all the doctors and they couldn't find a problem with either of us." He drops his right hand, looking up at the monitor. "There wasn't a reason for it not to happen. Or so we thought."

He looks off to his right and waves that hand around the room. "Turns out this was the answer. Not me being here. But why I was here." His eyes lock on something off-screen. "It was the disease. Infertility was a possible early indicator for some."

He closes his eyes and a large sigh moves through him like a wave. "Well, we thought it was, in this case." A small smile crept onto his lips. "I still remember that call. I was recording one of these, I think. About seven months ago. She was so excited and made me come home." He drops his hand and the smile spreads on his lips. It does not touch his eyes. "We'd done it. She was pregnant." The smile fades. "We were pregnant." His eyes close. "Oh, what have I done?"

His head lowers as another sob silently wracks his body. He weeps quietly for several moments before wiping his face and looking back at the monitor.

"She was so happy," he whispers. "Every day, I came home to something new added to our home. A bed, a blanket, a doll." He shrugs. "She just wanted to be a mother. She couldn't wait. We didn't tell anyone. It was so early, and the doctor warned us to be patient." He laughs slightly. "Be patient. How true those words are."

He looks back up at the monitor. "Yes, she was pregnant when the disease took hold of her. It was already there, most likely. All this time and we're still not sure how it starts. Well, that's not true. We know it begins with cells dying. We're just not sure how to stop the cells from dying. We tried recoding the cells. Tried making them new again." He sniffs once, wiping at his nose with his sleeved arm. "That's what I was working on." He waves a hand off to his left. "Those experiments. Trying to recode the cells faster than the disease. We might have stopped this." He closes his eyes. "The disease, it took the baby from us." He shakes his head, shrugging slightly. "I couldn't stop it. I couldn't save the baby."

He pauses, hand tapping on his head as he stares out of the monitor. "And I couldn't save her either. I didn't have a choice, you see." He leans close. "It was the only way. I had to do something. I couldn't just let her die!"

He points wildly off to one side. "My work. My research. It's the answer. Complete remapping of the cells leading to regeneration. Think of the possibilities. I just needed more time, more practice." He lowers his arm. "But I didn't have that. She was dying. I had no choice. She fought me—she didn't want it." He shrugs, shaking his head as he holds his hands up to look at them. "I couldn't let her die in my arms. Maybe if I'd had more time. She might still be here. My baby might still be."

He shrugs and shakes his head. "But they aren't. It's over. And my wife is all that's left. Well, what's left of her." He looks over at the monitor. "I did it to save her. I didn't know I would lose her doing that. I thought I had it figured out. I believed I knew. I still do. So I tried the next phase on her. I recoded every cell at once." He holds out a hand. "What would you have done? The research could make her body new again."

He glances over his shoulder. "Someone's coming. I have to end this." He leans close. "I'm sorry. I didn't mean for any of this to happen. Don't let them trick you. Remember this face. Remember my name when it all happens.

"I am Morris Tackett. I'm the man who they will claim murdered his wife. And they're right. I experimented on her and I killed her."

His voice drops to near a whisper, his face as cold as smooth metal.

"I also murdered my child by not figuring this out. And I won't do that again. So, remember my name. Morris Tackett, the man who murdered his wife and child."

Cold, dead eyes stare out of the monitor.

"The man who will cure death."

The recording ends.

GRAND PATRONS

Melissa L. Barnes
Gretchen Collins
Jean-Francois Dubeau
Katherine Dunley
Daniel Goldberg
Debbie Guthrie
Michelle Guthrie
Sierra Guthrie
Jesse High
Michael James
Tim Kaso
Jon D. Lockhart
David R. Nelson
George Robinson
Kathy Scarbro
Cyrstal Turney

INKSHARES

INKSHARES is a community, publisher, and producer for debut writers. Our books are selected not just by a group of editors, but also by readers worldwide. Our aim is to find and develop the most captivating and intelligent new voices in fiction. We have no genre—our genre is debut.

Previously unknown Inkshares authors have received starred reviews in every trade publication. They have been featured in every major review, including on the front page of the *New York Times*. Their books are on the front tables of booksellers worldwide, topping bestseller lists. They have been translated in major markets by the world's biggest publishers. And they are being adapted at the biggest studios and networks.

Interested in making your own story a reality? Visit Inkshares.com to start your own project, connect with other writers, and find other great books.